# ADIEU, SWEET AMARILLIS

## Philippa Pigache

ADIEU, SWEET AMARILLIS
First published in Great Britain in 2017
Copyright © 2017 Philippa Pigache

A CIP catalogue record for this book is available from the British Library.

Published by Cross-in-Hand Press
Printed and bound in Great Britain by Clays Ltd, St Ives plc
Typeset using Atomik ePublisher from Easypress Technologies

ISBN 978-1-9998674-0-9

# ADIEU, SWEET AMARILLIS

To Rupert, Grace and all those who made music at Springwater.

Facsimile from The First set of English Madrigals by John Wilbye,
printed 1598

# ADIEU, SWEET AMARILLIS

## Part 1 "... all ye need to know"

# CHAPTER 1

*At Millwater, the sound of water was always in our ears; the sound of water and the sound of music. Sometimes I thought I heard the water in the music: the scoring of strings and woodwind that Roland loved reminded me of the rush and splutter of the mill race. One pupil, less fond of the charms of nature, was heard to grumble that it was rather like trying to play music when afflicted with tinnitus, but most of us learned to love the noise, as we loved Millwater and everything it stood for.*

*It must have been spring when I first came there – March probably – because my sound-track of rushing water is superimposed with an image of daffodils; not the vulgar, buttery battalions that stand, eyes-front and erect, along the municipal verge, but the splayed, slender-stemmed clumps of small, cream blooms that grew wild along the banks of the mill stream and beneath the woodland that stretched beyond the garden. There were primroses and bluebells too: like a carpet of blue mist before the trees put out their leaves. You were allowed to pick wild flowers in those days. Ecological crime had not been invented. We would go into the woods with a length of garden twine and return with a long chain of fist-sized bunches of primroses; their furry, flesh-coloured, stems bound gently not to crush them, and the occasional short-stemmed violet breaking from its bonds. And we would fill the house with tight-packed bowls of flowers that glowed against the dark oak tables and chests. Whatever became of dark oak? These days it's all a bland blondness of stripped pine or 'natural' veneer. It doesn't set off flowers like the deep reflection of old, polished oak.*

* * *

*Have I really got the energy to remember it all, when now it is psychologically light–years ago? Can I be sure that what I recall bears a significant relationship to what really happened? I was so young. Perhaps I didn't understand what was going on; between Roland, Paola and his family; between Roland, Stefan and me; between Roland and all the music makers and music lovers that made up the magical world of Millwater.*

*And yet those events are as clear to me now as if it were yesterday. Clear, though less intense and painful. And since no one living will reveal it, perhaps I have an obligation to recall and record.*

It had started with a sore throat: nothing exceptional about that. When she had been younger she had, like most singers, regarded sore throats as an occupational hazard. It had hung around for ages: a phlegmy, streptococcal throat that consumed boxes of tissues and left her weary and irritable weeks after. The next symptom had been the puffy ankles; sometimes puffiness around the knees if she were on her feet a long time. She even wondered if she were becoming puffy in the face. She hadn't had oedema that badly since she had been pregnant with Kate. Still, 70-something she supposed it wasn't so remarkable.

It was the blood in her urine that alerted her to a condition more serious than old age. Faint spots on the lavatory paper when she dried herself, at first reminded her of the warning signs of a period when she had been fertile. She paid attention to the source of the blood. Blood in the urine or stools was supposed to prompt medical consultation. She, who had suffered little worse than a hangover all her adult life – although these, she noted, followed less and lasted longer of late – finally decided to see the quack.

She didn't tell the family. She called her usual minicab firm and made her way to the smart new Health Centre where she saw a young GP who was a stranger to her. The children had suggested several times that she take out private health insurance since she could afford it, but it was against her principles. And besides, she didn't get ill. She didn't *feel ill* now; only tired. Slightly to her surprise there had been no quick fix prescription which

4

she would almost certainly have chucked in the waste bin, but a referral to a London teaching hospital for an ultra-sound scan. She had asked the technician intelligent questions as to how the device worked, but inside her, the realisation grew that her condition was prompting an immoderate amount of medical attention, and that this one, unlike previous minor illnesses, would not be self-limiting.

"So, what's wrong with my kidneys?" she inquired. She had gathered that these were the offending organs. "Years of hitting the grape and the grain finally coming back to haunt me?"

"Not necessarily. You can get nephritis at any age," the young houseman writing up her notes had replied evasively.

"I can't tolerate antibiotics," she countered belligerently at mention of an 'itis'. She always refused penicillin for sore throats or flu having understood that these were invariably viral, and not susceptible to antibiotics.

"I don't think they will be necessary," the houseman had replied. Somehow this didn't reassure her.

By the time they wanted her to come into hospital for a renal biopsy they insisted her family be told. Mercifully Hugo, her son, was in New York and Kate, her daughter, could be persuaded to leave her in peace, but she dreaded the descent of Hugo's wife, Carole, replete with flowers and fruit, oozing concern. The one relation she was glad to see was Rosamund, her granddaughter, who was studying at a nearby London college.

"Granna; this is definitely not you," Ros affirmed, standing in the doorway of the small room off the main ward that had been allocated her grandmother. The name was an elision of the relationship and her grandmother's name – Anna.

"It's unfitting and embarrassing. For Heaven's sake keep your mother away," Anna replied.

"You ungracious old trout," said her granddaughter affectionately, "I see you have not started to respect the medical profession just because they have you in their power for once." And Ros laughed and gave her a hearty hug. She laid a bag with compact discs and paperback novels on the porridge-coloured counterpane and sat on the bed swinging her legs. They were long and slim, clad in horizontally striped black and white leggings and the lace-up boots on her feet looked heavy enough to snap her ankles.

"They wanted to dress me in some ridiculous night garment, and take my clothes away, but I wouldn't have it. I see no reason why I should not be fully dressed, from the waist up." Anna was indeed, wearing a bra, crisp white shirt, and full war paint. Her tinted hair bore evidence of recent attention. "They seem unable to appreciate that I am not ill; only undergoing tests."

"Of course, Granna," Ros replied, but her eyes were unhappy. Her grandmother certainly didn't look ill. Small and slight, she had always looked young for her years. But now she had that sharp, birdlike alertness she adopted when she was keeping her intellect firmly in charge of her emotions. Ros knew from experience that sympathy would be unwelcome. Her grandmother maintained an aura of vitality and resourcefulness. She hated to be pitied. Ros indicated the things she had brought;

"Look; they've released some new recordings of Roland Fredricks' work, ahead of the centenary of his birth, I think. I brought you the new recording of *Pippa Passes,* the opera based on the Browning dramatic poem – that's the one you worked on isn't it? It's got Haitink conducting and Te Kanawa;"

Her grandmother's face took on a more relaxed expression.

"As Ottima? Interesting. It used to be considered a mezzo role. Not Pippa, surely. Who have they got singing Pippa?"

"I don't know her. Someone new. She's quite dishy from the picture on the cover."

"I'm not sure Haitink's ideal. No one will match Beecham's recording. But Kiri Te Kanawa as Ottima: that should be good."

"And I gather they are going to revive it down at Glyndebourne after all these years. They'll certainly send you tickets."

Anna had to wait two weeks for the results of the biopsy. The consultant nephrologist invited her to see him privately in Harley Street, to save her the wait in Out Patients, and, principles notwithstanding, she accepted. She was feeling so tired.

It was a large, comfortable room with a rather a good reproduction of *The Anatomy Lesson* above the fireplace. Anna let her gaze wander over the serious, medical faces assembled around the startlingly personal corpse. They looked like faded flowers, isolated above their off-white ruffs. The consultant spoke to her in the mixture of incomprehensible jargon and schoolboy euphemisms his profession often adopted when embarrassed by the need for detailed communication with a patient. Apparently she had something called glomerulonephritis – basically the filters that sifted out the rubbish in her kidneys, were played out. She was leaking blood and protein into her urine. They could give drugs to minimise the damage. There was the option of dialysis if things didn't improve. But, at her age, a transplant was impractical.

With a sense of effort that was almost physical, she dragged her attention back to the doctor. He was fiddling with a gold pen; sliding it back and forth between his first finger and thumb and looking to some point beyond her left arm.

"This thing is incurable?"

"People can carry on with nephritis for years…" he said, not looking at her. "We'll do regular checks on your filtration rate…"

"But eventually it will kill me?"

He drew a breath between compressed lips and sat back in his chair. For the first time his eyes met hers. He raised his eyebrows in an expression of helplessness.

"We're all going to die Mrs Cummins, of one cause or another."

"How long have I got?"

"With some modification of life-style, diet… you could live for, um, years."

"And trying to live some kind of normal life?"

"Could be years; could be months," he demurred. "Infection; acute kidney failure is always a possibility. Of course there is always dialysis…"

The minicab driver had waited. She got in and slid down on the back seat.

"Home, Mrs Cummins?"

She agreed without thinking. It was warm and comfortable in the big car. She had brought a travelling rug for her knees and for a moment she thought the most sensible thing might be to go to sleep. The driver turned North up Wimpole Street and waited at the lights onto Marylebone Road. On the far side of the street her attention was caught by the familiar building of the Royal Academy of Music. Amid so much that had changed this still looked the same. Groups of students huddled on the steps or pushed in and out of the glass doors. A young man with floppy fair hair, fiddle case tucked under his arm, came out and ran down the steps. At the foot, a girl in a garish wind-cheater opened her arms and caught him, and they whirled round and round. Anna's heart leapt to her mouth, she leaned forward and spoke half aloud, "Stefan – Stefan?"

It wasn't, of course. Stefan, *her* Stefan, had last come down those steps more than 50 years ago, when they had been students there, before the war. That Stefan had lost the quiff of blond hair that fell romantically over one eye when he played *appassionato*, before he was 30. "Strange, how the image of someone as you first knew them stays imprinted on the mind's eye," she thought. "I always visualise Stefan at 19; all gangling legs and arms, falling over himself with eagerness and unfulfilled longing: dark blue eyes, dilated with desire…" (The memory made her stomach contract.) "As they were before pain and disappointment clouded them. Poor Stefan." The old memory tape was running again. These days it often took over. Not surprising, she thought. Your whole life is little more than a memory when you approach death.

She must have spoken something out loud and the driver thought she had spoken to him.

"You all right back there, Mrs C?" he said, "Docs give you a clean bill of health then?"

She leaned back in the seat again as the car pulled away, closing her eyes. She spoke softly to herself, so that he couldn't hear her this time, "No, they didn't. I'm dying, dying, dying."

# CHAPTER 2

Jonathan surfaced as dawn broke and the alcohol began to wear off. He lay still, eyes closed, getting his bearings: where was he, was he alone and had he got a hangover? It was important to take account of such variables before committing oneself to consciousness. The awareness that someone's hand was cupping his balls confirmed the prudence of this waking instinct. The hand was – whose? Helena's? No – Fiona's of course. The hand came from behind him which meant it was safe to check his whereabouts by opening an eye. No one would know he was awake or make demands he was not anxious to meet.

Six inches from his head a battered, one-eyed teddy looked forlornly back at him. Beyond it, a Laura Ashley clad rag doll lolled limply against the brass bedhead; confirmation that he was in Fiona's bedroom. They had come back here last night after the launch party and a rather drunken dinner at Langan's. *Had he* or *hadn't he*? He was pretty sure he hadn't. He was still wearing his watch. Cautiously he attempted to raise his left hand and see what time it was. If Fiona had drunk as much as he had, she would sleep on for hours and he might be able to get away unnoticed.

"You awake, darling?" The hand on his balls moved up and ringed his supine penis, drawing it against his stomach in a hug. "How do you feel?" her voice inquired sleepily. He considered silence, but then groaned;

"Terrible." That might hold her off. It didn't.

"Poor darling;" she raised herself on one arm and murmured close to his ear, "Shall I give you a lovely, sexy massage?"

He groaned again and dug his face into the pillow. The hand continued to roam his body; up over his shoulder; down into his waist and forward over his spare tyre (he resisted the instinct to pull it in). The hand returned to its previous preoccupation. In spite of himself, Jonathan felt his member stir in response to the insidious touch. He turned onto his stomach dislodging her hand.

"God Fiona, can't you ever let a guy sleep?"

"What do you mean? I don't seem to remember you being a symbol of rampant virility last night when you hit the sack!" The sexy coo had vanished. Fiona's voice had an edge like the east wind.

"It was late," he answered lamely.

"Never mind the hour. It's you who are past it. Bloody washed-up old has-been. Prostate playing you up, is it Grandad? Don't forget your Zimmer frame when you leave." And she flounced onto the other side of the bed dragging most of the duvet with her.

Engineered rows were a good escape key. Jonathan got up and looked around for his clothes. Last night's nymph turned harpy pretended to sleep, only a long tail of Titian hair showing above the duvet. He steeled his arse to yesterday's underpants and shook the worst of the creases out of his trousers. The shirt might make a second wearing, or he could pick up a new one in The Strand. To his annoyance he could only find one sock; jacket and shoes were in the sitting room. He finally located the second sock, rolled up in a suggestive ball in the crotch of his trousers. He found his jacket – the Fiona's neurotic tortoiseshell cat had been sleeping on it – and began to go through his pockets for the dread evidence of his night on the town. Screwed up credit card slips scattered to the floor like autumn leaves; his keys – thank God he hadn't been driving; some small change; no notes. Several business cards with home numbers scrawled on the back; the personalised matches of a couple of wine bars and clubs they had visited; one of Fiona's earrings that had been painful. Such dross; such a drossy existence! Not unlike the meaningless ephemera punted by the publishing house he worked for. He hunted for his cigarettes; found an empty box, then remembered he was trying to give it up.

"Shall I get you some breakfast?" The seductive coo had returned.

"Thanks no; I'll get back and hook up my drip." No reason to let her opt out of the row easily.

She was not easily rebuffed.

"Fresh coffee; crisp, crunchy bacon? A croissant with Oxford marmalade?"

"Only add to the middle-aged spread."

He had his tie on now. Fiona leaned against the doorway, some kind of exotic kimono wrapped round her nubile body, Titian hair draped over one shoulder. She was luscious enough. A month ago she had made him feel quite inspired. Why didn't his recalcitrant penis stand up and beg anymore? Was it the Baked Alaska of her mood swings: one minute sultry siren, the next ice-tongued fishwife? No, it was more that she made him feel used. Even arousing her delectable body had begun to feel like hard work. He suspected her ulterior motives. Every come-on, every sweet, wee-wifey gesture of concern, felt like bait and prompted the ominous thought "What does she want now?" Did she think he was going to supply the great career break? Her current job earned her a pittance. Or did she – God forbid – see him as husband material? Perhaps he should introduce her to Helena, and disabuse her. Except that that would make Helena despise him even more.

"I suppose you don't have a cigarette?" he asked in desperation.

"I thought you were trying to give up," she replied with undisguised scorn.

"I can't think why you waste your energy on me if you find me so despicable," he answered with some logic, then swung his jacket over his shoulder and left the flat.

He ran down the stairs with accelerating step. It was a raw, March morning outside, the wind in the east, but he felt instantly invigorated with relief. Walking away from things was therapeutic. People (women anyway) were always telling you to talk problems through: face up to LIFE. Bollocks! Nothing was as effective as turning your back on tiresome situations and doing something else.

11

He would walk over the bridge to The Embankment: the walk would do him good. There was a bank with a magic-money machine in The Strand. Then he could pick up a paper and some breakfast; shave once he got to his office in Covent Garden. He always kept a razor there for the frequent eventuality of the over-night away match. Early commuters hurried past him, their heads down against the wind, but Jonathan kept his jacket slung over his shoulder relishing the bite of the wind through his thin, cotton shirt. There were all too few moments in his life when he was unpressured and at peace. Right now there were two hours ahead of him before the daily grind started up.

He looked over the parapet to the swirling grey waters of the Thames below. The tide was low, and along the margin of the river the non-biodegradable detritus of late 20th century life jostled in oily, yellow scum: a coke tin, plastic bags, a child's broken toy and some indecipherable item of clothing. He raised his eyes to the skyline, to the blue-grey domes and spires of The City, not to mention the stacked tower blocks and cantilevered cranes, and thought of Wordsworth. He could think of a few things the earth could 'show more fair' these days, (Fiona's tits, for two) and yet the poet's image of a mighty giant asleep, tranquil before the heartbeat of human activity and commerce churned into life again, still held true. It was a long time since he had read any poetry. Modern publishers didn't get much call for verse – out of copyright or otherwise. 'Dreaming spires'; he thought of Oxford, light years away. Boyhood and dreams; the Great Writer prepares. Some writer he'd turned out, with his occasional book reviews, and his sordid cunt and gun contributions to *Knave, Hustler* or some other lads' magazine (under a pseudonym of course.)

Near Embankment tube he found a stall selling coffee and rolls. He spent some of his remaining change on a plastic cup of steaming, treacle-coloured beverage of dubious provenance. The dossers, who slept under the arches of the bridge and in sheltered doorways in their makeshift constructions of cardboard and plastic, were beginning to rouse themselves from the alcoholic stupor that had keep cold and despair briefly at bay.

Among them he recognised a man with a little black and white dog on a string. He was so worn and grimy it was difficult to guess what age he was, but he still wore one of the red and white Santa Claus caps everyone sported last Christmas.

"Want a cup of coffee, Punch?" Jonathan asked the man. He imagined the nickname had originated with the man's large, hooked red nose, or perhaps with his little dog's particoloured face.

"You're a gentleman, sir; I don't mind if I do," said the man in the hat. He had a cultured, booze-sodden voice, reminiscent of an actor like Vincent Crummles in *Nicholas Nickleby*.

"How's Judy this morning?"

In response to Jonathan's inquiry, the little dog sat up on her haunches and put her head winsomely on one side. Jonathan spent his last pieces of silver on a ham roll which Punch divided evenly between himself and the dog.

"You haven't managed to find a hostel that will take you both then?" said Jonathan. They had told him that most hostels barred pets but that, nevertheless, most of them elected to keep their companions and sleep rough. When they first met, Jonathan had asked Punch about his work prospects, and learned that he had been a musician, and played in one of the BBC light orchestras some years ago. Not all the cardboard campers were inadequates, discharged mental patients or petty criminals. Many were educated or skilled, caught by chance in the downward spiral of rising housing costs and diminishing job opportunities in the Capital.

Who knows, but that he too might soon join the ranks of the unemployed, thought Jonathan gloomily as he climbed the hill towards The Strand? As a small independent publisher with a short arts and education list, Simmonds and Sayle had survived the recent spate of amalgamations only because they were not juicy enough to attract the attention of hungry predators. They had no star authors with a guaranteed following. Their books usually started with an idea, or some new reference material, and it was up to the editors to find a writer that could help sell the work. They badly needed a hit: nothing as grand as a Best Seller, but a work that gathered acclaim in

13

the review pages and hopefully entered the reading lists for degree courses. Not that students could afford to buy books these days. Not that anyone bought books these days. The word had been superseded by the image. More than a few of Jonathan's friends and colleagues had faced the grim jolt of redundancy. With two boys at private schools and regular maintenance payments to meet, the prospect sat on his horizon like a storm cloud.

He climbed some steps and came through an alleyway into The Strand. On the corner he bought a paper and began unfolding it as he walked towards the nearest cash dispenser. It was all election guff: empty promises, engineered picture opportunities, pusillanimous party political jibes and jeers. Thatcher was gone, but the new PM wanted his mandate. Jonathan could already visualise the front page sodden among the discarded flotsam at the river's edge. "A plague on both your houses," he thought. He was not without political awareness, but this time the choice seemed to be between one bunch of bumbling rogues and incompetents or another. The cash machine was empty. He swore; debated treating himself to a slap-up breakfast on plastic at The Savoy, then, reflecting upon his unshaven state, elected to walk another hundred yards to the next machine.

In the days before Covent Garden had become a tarted up dispensary of trendy tat, they had sometimes walked through the old flower and vegetable market on their way home after a night on the town. If he looked up and fixed his eyes on the glazed roofs, he could still recall the pungent, earthy smells, the cries, the catcalls and the cockney humour that had greeted them as they wandered, he with his dinner jacket over his shoulder, Helena, high-heeled sandals in hand, between the stacked banks of produce, and fresh flowers. Once he had bargained a fiver for as many carnations as Helena could carry, with a costermonger anxious to clear his stall, and then loaded up her arms till her laughing face became invisible behind the mountain of blooms, and he had had to guide her blind to find a taxi. "Where have all the flowers gone?" he thought sentimentally. Then cynicism came close on the heels of sentiment as usual, "To the lawyers, every one."

Self-pity dominated his view of his ex-marriage these days. For years, reckless fatalism had inured him to the gradual tear opening between them: his petty infidelities and betrayals; Helena's compensating separateness and scar tissue. He had trusted domestic inertia to preserve the threads that bound them. But when, three years ago, Helena's greater optimism about change cut the final knot, his admiration for her and despair at his own profligacy, made his loss the more bitter. He sought solace in self-castigation.

There was a message from his late-lamented ex-wife when he reached the office. She had phoned last night, after they had left for the party launching their Spring List. He called her back, receiver tucked under one ear, as he went through his post. Her voice was brisk and early-morningish. He could imagine her wearing something smart, with important shoulders, crisp-collared shirt and shiny, black shoes.

"What are you planning to do with them this weekend?"

"A casserole with baby carrots and peas?" he joked lamely. Helena rarely appreciated his attempts at humour these days. She continued, ignoring the remark, "Only Jeremy has been picked for the First Fifteen and will be playing away this Saturday. Will you collect him from the school before lunch? Or would it be too much for you to take Simon, and go and watch the match on Saturday morning?"

"Are you still being a neglectful father?' he translated.

She knew he hated giving up Saturday lunchtime at the pub. But the memory of the mountain of carnations was still at the back of his mind. He spoke wearily, "Where is this match, and what time should I collect Simon to get there for kick-off?"

"He'll be ready at 09.30. I'll give you instructions when you arrive." She sounded pleased.

"Stay for a drink Sunday evening when you bring him back; Jim and Gaynor are over." She dispensed these little rewards like chocolates for good behaviour.

He put down the phone and returned to his post, in two minds about the prospect of the weekend. He had acquired Brownie points: a glass or two of

Helena's wishy-washy, white wine, and a seat in his own ex-living room were to be his on Sunday night, but at the price of weathering single-parenthood on the touchline, stone-cold sober. Ironic that, divorced, he found himself coerced into behaviour he had sidestepped so painlessly when married.

A massive document slithered from its tattered postal wrappings and spilled across his desk. His heart sunk, "God, not an unsolicited manuscript, and *handwritten* forsooth!" He began to gather up the scattered pages that had slid onto the floor: neatly penned footnotes in green ink caught his eye. While he was in this disadvantaged posture, the door of the managing director's office opened and a tetchy voice spoke behind him.

"Jonathan, can I have a word about the Fredricks biography?"

He straightened up. Pinpoints of light scattered before his eyes. He put on his jacket and went into the managing director's office. He sat at a Partner's desk as broad as the Steppes of Central Asia, surrounded by leather-bound volumes that breathed gravitas, high moral purpose, and dust. The managing director had met J K Galbraith and come within a hair's breadth of publishing the UK edition of *The Affluent Society* in the '50s. He took senior academics to lunch at the Savoy Grill, or Simpson's in the Strand, from about half past 12 until nearly four, and came back having consumed several bottles of good claret after which he retired behind closed doors until it was time to call his driver and go home. The managing director held his staff to blame for the parlous state of academic publishing in the '90s, and first thing in the morning – or to be more precise, after he had had coffee at about half past 10 – was his time for expressing it.

"Jonathan, who is this Briggs you've lined up for the Roland Fredricks centenary biography? This synopsis is deplorable. Does he know anything about serious music?"

"He's very highly thought of, Sir. Does music reviews for the serious Sundays. You met him at *The Times* literary luncheon last year."

"I can't remember him. Writes like a computer: elliptical phrases; split infinitives; verb-less sentences; exclamation marks! Is he American?"

"No; British through and through. Balliol I think; Oxford anyway."

"What are our older universities coming to? Look at his sources. No original material. He doesn't address the political dimension – all those Marxists types at Cambridge in the '30s… The Managing Director threw the despised synopsis onto the great desk and it skidded several metres. "He hasn't found any of the Millwater set; Fredricks' daughter, or Paola Pignatelli, the opera singer – she hasn't died has she? What about Anna Cummins? She was at Millwater and she's certainly still around. I heard her on Radio 3 a couple of weeks ago. Dash it: *there must be letters!*" He was still chuntering in disgruntlement as Jonathan closed the door.

Jonathan returned to his desk, snowed over with the handwritten document with the green ink footnotes. He grabbed a cardboard stationery box and shovelled it in, higgledy-piggledy, without regard to page order. He stuck the title page – something to do with the history of the British Communist Party by some obscure old don – on the lid of the box, promising to sort the whole thing out later. Then he got out the Briggs proposal and began to leaf through the pages that had incurred such ire. As it happened, Jonathan had done his doctorate on *The Interaction of Art and Politics in the 1930s*: The Left Book Club, The Unity Theatre; and several of the intellectuals and thespians who had belonged to the circle at the Fredricks' country house, Millwater, just before the war, had featured in his research. The biographer appeared to have left a number of obvious avenues unexplored. He soon became completely absorbed and began jotting down notes on the nearest envelope as he read.

# CHAPTER 3

"Mother, are you free for Sunday lunch?" Carole's penetrating nasal tones – purest Hazelmere – shrilled down the telephone not long after Anna's visit to Harley Street. She hated being called 'Mother' by her daughter-in-law, and she had small enthusiasm for her Sunday lunches either. She could have declined for health reasons; but letting Carole know that there was anything amiss, would almost certainly have brought her round at the double, in Florence Nightingale mode, which was marginally worse than her Madame de Stael, literary luncheon or soirée persona.

"I'll have to look at the diary," she hedged. She still affected the working woman's desk diary: a mammoth volume in gold-tooled leather that carried a small encyclopaedia of finely printed, useless financial and geographical information before descending to blank pages with dates. If she were honest, an A4 page-a-day was difficult enough to fill with her shrinking number of professional engagements, or social invitations that mattered sufficiently to log in advance. Nevertheless, old habits die hard: as long as they continued to send her the diaries, she would continue to chart her life by them.

The following Sunday was virgin white. She debated thinking up excuses; then decided her creativity would be better exercised in going, and in destructuring her daughter-in-law's lunch party.

"I think it may be Bill's weekend," she said, in a tone that left her room to change the story should she think of something better to annoy her daughter-in-law.

"Bill?" Carole's voice told her that she had calculated accurately, "Is that the New Zealander who was painting the house for you last year?"

Anna allowed a few moments silence to imply hurt and rebuke.

"Carole; Bill is my current lover; my 'Special Other', as the Americans say. You mustn't be snobbish about antipodeans who work with their hands." She knew it caused her daughter-in-law acute embarrassment to acknowledge that any pensioner had a sex life, let alone her husband's mother, who should properly be sitting in a rocking chair cultivating her crochet. Carole was of the genus who say 'shush' or raise rebuking eyebrows at any suggestion of sexual interest, even between consenting, married couples of childbearing age. *"Pas devant les enfants!"* she was wont to hiss.

"But mother, it's nice to keep it to family on Sundays. And besides, Browning is over from the 'States at the moment, and dying to see you again," Carole prevaricated, apparently unaware that her two excuses cancelled each other out. Browning James – a classic example of the North American penchant for wearing names back to front – was some kind of retired theological historian from Cambridge, Mass. who made periodic visits to coincide with the UK publication of his limited, library readership books. Carole had introduced him to Anna with thinly disguised, matchmaking intentions, on a previous occasion, steadfastly ignoring Anna's view that what she needed was not a rich, old husband substitute, so much as a healthy hump with a man who made her feel young by association, not by contrast.

"Browning," Anna invested it with a performer's subtle innuendo. "Is *he* still alive? Where do you dig them up Carole? Burke and Hare could have used your contacts."

To be fair to her daughter-in-law, she herself hadn't felt so alive since receiving her death sentence. She now began to worry that, foot faulted to 40/love down, Carole might withdraw the invitation and deprive her of continuing the skirmish at the weekend.

"But of course darling, if *you* want me, I'll come. Will Ros be there?" She had carefully not withdrawn the threat of Bill, keeping the card up her sleeve.

"I spoke to her; I think she's lobbying for a lift, if you decide to come down in a car."

"In that case, it's decided; tell her to ring me and arrange a rendezvous."

When she had arrived home after learning her diagnosis, she had marched purposefully to the booze cabinet and taken out a near full bottle of Scotch. She had then gone to the bathroom, collected a selection of pills, and taken them into the bedroom. Lying on her bed, consuming the Scotch steadily, she had analysed the tools available to her for a self-determined quietus.

She had no desire for the dramatic: gas ovens were no longer available thanks to North Sea gas, and carbon-monoxide exhaust was out, since she no longer owned a car. "…and, since I have no access to, or knowledge of, firearms, and anything involving knives or razors gives me the shivers thinking about the blood, it looks as though it'll have to be pills and booze, cliché that it is," she thought. "The important thing is to be efficient: no botched attempts to be interpreted as the proverbial cry for help or similar psychological claptrap, bringing down the concerted interference of well-meaning relatives and the medical profession on my head. I don't need help. The only useful thing anyone could offer me is a kidney or two. Even then, I'm not sure I value life sufficiently to undertake the palaver of a transplant."

Her impulse to kill herself was personal and private. People said suicide was an act of vengeance: a desire to punish an uncaring world. In her case it was more a question of standards: the life on offer didn't measure up to what she considered the bare minimum. Once or twice in the past she had felt similarly, when the quality of life – combined with the opportunity to modify it – had seemed too limited to be worth the effort. "Life is not so fantastic that you are obliged to carry on regardless, for purely doctrinal reasons, especially when you've already spent the lion's share of it. Beside, I've been an initiator all my life: better to initiate the end of it now, rather than having an unappealing death thrust upon me.

"It's not worth the candle," she said quietly to herself, eyes wide in the gathering darkness of the March evening. The Scotch was beginning to

20

get to her; perhaps she would sleep soon and wake with a clearer idea of what action to take.

There had always been candles at Millwater: waxy, non-drip, cream candles, made in Belgium by candle makers to the professional candle users: the church, Roland had explained. It was pure affectation of course. The house had been wired for electricity for 10 years or more, but Roland preferred the light of candles. They were stuck into ornate brass candlesticks or frosted, earthenware Calvados pitchers, their rather cold, white light reflected in the oak surfaces of chest and table that furnished the old house. Parts of it – the inglenook fireplace, with niches for smoking hams, the heavy wrought iron basket and dogs where they warmed hot punch in winter, and a fireback of the oak tree that had sheltered Charles II in flight from the Roundheads – dated from the 17th century.

When Roland and Helga had discovered it, sometime in the late '20s, the oak beams had been lath-and-plastered over and mean little grates had been fitted into the filled in fireplaces. Tacky lino covered old floorboards and anachronistic metal frame Crittall windows had replaced rotted wood. It had taken them years to strip back the layered residue of two centuries, and restore the basic fabric of the house. Some compromise between convenience and antiquarian purity had been permitted: electric light was disguised in wrought iron lanterns; a modern Aga replaced the old kitchen range and there were a couple of radiators to take the chill off the main bedrooms.

"Why waste money on central heating? The house is incurably draughty anyway. Put another sweater on," said Roland.

The furnishings were mostly rustic oak, antique or second-hand. As a concession to comfort, there were some shapeless armchairs and several large, collapsed settees and divans covered in folkweave cushions. Turkish rugs slid about treacherously upon the polished floorboards. The woodworm had feasted upon the outer layers of the boards so that chair legs not infrequently disappeared into unexpected holes. In the upper stories the floors sloped so steeply that the furniture stood at drunken angles and if you dropped a coin it rolled straight to the far corners of the room and was lost down a crack. On one occasion a large German contralto called Traudel had thrown herself upon her bed overcome by a fit of uncontrollable homesickness, and the leg of the bed had come right through the dining room ceiling.

Half asleep, Anna chuckled to herself. "Poor Traudel: so grief-stricken and lumpen; ankle strap shoes over wrinkled stockings, and madly in love with Roland of course – as were most of his pupils at Millwater. Still it was a fine voice," she recalled.

"No volume without a good sounding board; grow yourself a bosom like our Traudel and you will reach the back of the Albert Hall," Roland had said, beating upon his chest like Tarzan. Anna's size – never more than 5ft 3 and a bit at her tallest – was reckoned a disadvantage for a singer.

"You'll never do Verdi or Wagner," Paola had told her. But fortunately she had preferred Mozart and Puccini, and she'd looked a lot better in boys' clothes as Cherubino in *Figaro*, or dying of consumption in *La Boheme* than massive singers like Paola, with their great, resonant voices.

She dreamed that she was on the stage of a ruined amphitheatre: behind her, columns with a broken cornice overhung with creeper; beneath her feet, huge paving slabs with grass sprouting up in the cracks. In the darkness behind the footlights, the curved ranks of stone seats rose and receded from her. She could make out the shape of the conductor's shoulders, but the sound of the orchestra was distant and inaudible, and in a panic she realised she didn't know what she was meant to sing. She looked down to see what her costume was, and saw that her feet were bare and she was wearing a white nightgown. Was it *Lucia di Lamamoor*? Or *La Traviata*? She didn't know either role. The tip of the conductor's baton was poised above his head. Helplessly she opened her mouth – and no sound came. She was rooted to the spot. As she looked down again she saw creepers were clambering up her legs, as on the statue of Daphne turned into a tree as she fled from Apollo. And then suddenly Roland was next to her, bending to lift her onto his powerful shoulders like a child, and at once she realised what she was meant to sing: Pippa in the first act of *Pippa Passes*. Browning's well-known words came back to her:

"The lark's on the wing;

"The snail's on the thorn;

"God's in his heaven –

"All's right with the world." The notes and words were in her head and she heard them but she made no sound, like a singer miming for film. He carried her down from the stage and they were walking through the garden at Millwater, along the path fringed with lavender bushes, towards the millpond and the landing stage built by Roland and Helga and always falling to pieces. He set her down and she stepped into the flat-bottomed punt that was moored there. As the boat pulled away she saw Roland was playing his beloved Stradivarius violin. He reached out, as though urging her to take the violin, and the white silk handkerchief he kept between his neck and chinrest, fluttered to the ground like a wounded bird. The distance between them was increasing as she was carried passively away like a camera panning slowly backwards. His lips moved but she couldn't hear his words. She fixed on his eyes; tired eyes under rumpled brows, that could sparkle with devilment or fade into a bleak admission of defeat. He was asking her something, asking her to do something.

And suddenly the pain of separation and loss, of not being able to hear his voice, was so arousing that she awoke sweating, her mouth dry and her heart beating furiously. A cry rose in her throat and she called his name aloud, "Roland, I can't hear you; I can't *hear* you." Her need to receive the communication was so urgent that she sat up in bed, frustrated and bereft to find darkness all around her and the dream vanished. She played it back, trying to fathom the sequence of events and their significance, above all, to recapture his face. Perhaps if she were to lie down again and shut her eyes it would come back to her, and this time she would know what he wanted.

Old though she undoubtedly was now, Anna did not live in the past. Memories, images, feelings or sounds from earlier years, were mere grace notes to her present. Nevertheless, those who were gone were still important to her. Their latent value was occasionally reaffirmed by the prompting of external cues: a song, a quotation, a smell even. But in this instance the recollection had been provoked from elsewhere, she was sure. She had been passive, and Roland had come into her dream. Was this what made people believe in ghosts – this feeling that the initiator of an experience was external? Was Roland talking to her from beyond the grave?

She put on the light and got up, saw that it was half past 10 at night and she was fully dressed. Only then did she recall what had preceded her going to bed. She noted the array of medicine bottles beside her bed, and realised she had the beginning of a hangover. The Scotch bottle was half empty, but the feeling she had been experiencing before she went to sleep had gone. Suicide no longer seemed appealing. There were things she had to do; things as important as knowing what Roland had been trying to tell her in her dream, and which might give her a clue as to what that was.

She put on dressing gown and slippers over her clothes, and went out onto the landing, down the corridor to the back of the house. There was a door, locked, with a key on a hook nearby. Anna took it down, unlocked the door, and climbed the stairs to her almost disused studio on the top floor of the house.

# CHAPTER 4

**"FREDRICKS:** ROLAND GEORGE, (Born in Edinburgh in 1894, died in Kent in 1941 age 46) British composer. He was trained at the Royal Academy of Music where he became professor of violin in 1919 ... Fellow of King's College Cambridge, composer of chamber and vocal music ... *Latin Lyrics, The March from the North,* and opera: *Pippa Passes* (1939); first performed posthumously in 1946... His stature as a composer was perhaps overshadowed by his brilliance as a performer and teacher. See also Opera: *English."*

Thus the Oxford Companion to Music. Grove's Dictionary carried more detail, but was scarcely more generous to Fredricks' composition. "...His command of melody and delicate orchestration was ideally suited to small-scale vocal and chamber works. At the end of his relatively short life he evolved, in the opera *Pippa Passes,* an individual melodic idiom which owed much to English folk song."

Jonathan sat amid a pile of reference works and cuttings wondering if he had bitten off more than he could chew. That morning he had marched boldly into the Managing Director's office and made him an offer he couldn't refuse. He, Jonathan Burroughs, BA (Oxon), not forgetting DPhil (Eng Lit), would write the Fredricks biography: no advance; royalties only; plus expenses and two days a week for research; first draft, 18 months. He had reviewed the secondary sources, outlined the primary research leads, and now he sat at his desk both exhilarated and petrified by what he had undertaken.

"Oh shit, what have I done?" he thought. "Jumped in at the deep end, that's what; and not even sure that I can swim. If I sink, that's my job pretty well holed below the waterline too."

He had celebrated, rather inauspiciously, by going out to lunch and getting drunk. His excuse was that he had a lot of cold calls to make and it was easier to tackle total strangers when slightly pissed. He declined an invitation to 'go on somewhere' from a rather tempting advertising copywriter, whose thighs could be glimpsed above the tops of her stockings tops when she crossed her legs, and returned to his desk and his list of contact numbers.

He failed to make contact, in quick succession, with Fredricks' old school, the archivists at his Cambridge college, and with Anna Cummins at the BBC. (She had retired some years ago). A girl at BBC Sound Archives said there was nothing much before 1939 because recordings were routinely destroyed in those days. They had Gracie Fields singing *Sally in our Alley*, if that was any help? Fredricks' erstwhile record company and publishers were already planning to cash in on the centenary with reissues, re-annotations and new recordings of his better known work, but he had some difficulty in finding anyone who knew much about original recordings, scores, manuscripts or production notes left by the composer. He persisted, and finally reached an Oldest Inhabitant somewhere in the dusty bowels of the publisher's archives.

"We may have copies of early material from before the war…" said the Oldest Inhabitant sounding as though he was holding onto his perch with a shaky claw. "… though the old building was bombed in 1940."

"The *Latin Lyrics, The March to the North;* the string quartets, *Pippa Passes?*" Jonathan persisted. He'd heard that there had been an experimental production of *Pippa* down at Millwater in the Summer of 1939, before it had gone into rehearsal in London, "There must have been an annotated score and rehearsal notes for that. Didn't anyone do some kind of recording in those days… cut a disc; shoot 16mm film? What about photographs? And I'm also interested in anything unpublished. Was he working on anything when he died? Do you know anyone who might know?"

"You're welcome to come and look. But the library was severely damaged in the bombing; quite a lot if things went missing, I'm afraid." And a fit of coughing threatened to take the Oldest Inhabitant in the same direction.

Fighting the urge to fortify himself with a packet of cigarettes, Jonathan arranged to visit Abrahams, the publishers, and pressed on. The Royal Academy of Music, which had stayed put throughout the war, also invited him to inspect their records, and the Press Office at the BBC phoned back, promising to approach Anna Cummins and see if she would see him.

Emboldened by these fragile shoots of success, Jonathan decided to tackle the opera singer, Paola Pignatelli. She was reputed to have been the composer's mistress and had certainly worked closely with him in the final years of his life. She had stayed at Millwater and was to have sung Ottima in the London premiere of *Pippa Passes*, cancelled at the outbreak of war. Today she lived in luxurious solitude in her palazzo somewhere in the Tuscan Hills, the sound of her great recordings echoing through every high ceilinged room.

"She must be pushing 90 by now; she hasn't sung in public for 30 years" he calculated. Her last interview had been obtained by a keen cub reporter on *The Late Show* who had camped at her gate sending in armloads of roses in such quantities that the singer's staff had eventually prevailed upon her to relent and see him. It had been conducted in semi-darkness, the diva permitting only the sound of her voice to be recorded.

A certain amount of flannel with a secretary at the singer's one-time London agent, yielded an Italian telephone number, but Jonathan's triumph was short lived. His Italian was halting and no one at the palazzo spoke English.

"*Non può parlare con nessuno,*" said a brisk voice, in what he took to be a brush off. "*Per favore scrivi,*" an instruction to write he gathered, and the phone clicked dead. He tried again and an answering machine cut in.

His attempt to reach Fredricks' daughter, Gudrun, the only surviving relative, now in her 60s, was no more successful. Millwater, requisitioned during the war, had passed out of the family on her mother's death. He tracked down an address somewhere in Cambridge, but the telephone number

27

turned out to be ex-directory. He had had to content himself with writing a letter; something Jonathan, creature of the modern fax/phone age, regarded as tantamount to consigning all hope of a reply to fate.

This was the sum total of his first afternoon sleuthing. The next 24 hours were no more encouraging and he felt his earlier resolve slipping. Jonathan was all too aware of his own limitations. He needed external reinforcement urgently. Then, unexpectedly, chance itself intervened to offer him a break.

His unsatisfactory week's work had provided him with no reserves to face the weekend with. He had avoided contact with Fiona since the chilly morning after the launch party. He had shirked returning her calls because she would probably want to 'talk through' his unacceptable behaviour, and also because things would be even worse if she learned he planned to play dutiful parent on the touchline at the weekend. By allowing their row to continue at least he avoided further aggro.

Saturday dawned a true-to-type match day: biting east wind, leaden skies and intermittent drizzle. He drove westward to pick up his younger son at the ex-marital home. Ironic that they had chosen a house close to the hospital so that Helena wouldn't have to give up her training to become an obstetrician. Jonathan was convinced that it was her career that had made it easier for her to give up her marriage. En route he passed the hallowed portals of his Saturday local and his tongue prickled for a pint.

He lingered in the hall, casting a surreptitious glance at the post upon the table, while Helena harried his son above stairs.

"Don't be ridiculous Simon; put on something warmer. Where in heaven's name are your trainers? You mustn't keep your father waiting; you know how he is."

If his son knew how he was, he knew that he made a sight less fuss about what his offspring wore than his mother. Still there was no justice in families, let alone in divorce.

His son appeared upon the stairs; chunky trainers trailing laces glimpsed first, as his mother hauled a large sweater over his skinny ribs. His miserable face fringed with straw-coloured hair, brightened at the sight of his father, and he leapt the final steps in one bound and hurled himself at him, head to solar plexus, in a frantic embrace. For a moment they clung to each other, Jonathan ruffling the already ruffled head and making noises of inarticulate affection in an attempt to stifle the tears that sprung to his eyes.

"Burra, wurra then, Boyo; steady the buffs."

His son responded inaudibly with vigorous punches to his hips and thighs. When Jonathan bent to lift him up – it was getting a bit more difficult every time – the boy wriggled from his grasp turning his wet face away from him, and charged out into the street with a roar, to clamber into the car. Jonathan looked at his ex-wife holding a padded windcheater towards him.

"How is he?" he asked taking it from her, for want of anything else to say. It was crass making polite conversation about the health of children you had created together.

"Oh, not so bad." Her answer was equally laden with unspoken irony and pain. "The nightmares are a little less frequent."

"And school?"

"Oh you know Simon…"

They stood in silence looking at one another. From outside came the sound of Radio 1 on the car radio.

"You're looking well. You've lost weight haven't you?"

She brightened. "Yes, eight pounds. Not bad eh? And about time too."

"I rather liked your voluptuous curves," he said tenderly, an intimate note creeping into his voice. She pulled her jersey down over her hips and spoke briskly looking away.

"Well, I can do without them thank you. They don't go with shorter skirts." And she turned to go into the kitchen. "See you both tomorrow then. Drinks about six?" She spoke over her shoulder.

"OK, see you." And reluctantly he turned and left the house.

The touch line at his elder son's school had been the unlikely setting of a fortuitous encounter. Although the drizzle had eased, the line-up of team

29

supporters was thin: a few parents – dragooned chauffeurs for the most part – a few masters and boys from the home school. They stamped their feet and blew their dripping noses, pulled their collars round their ears and thrust their hands deep into pockets until it was necessary to field the next droplet. Jonathan had slipped down a swift pint at a country pub on their journey down, but was by now feeling desperate for another. He looked round covertly on the chance that there might be a good-looking mum among the parents to engage his attention. Nearby a tall, horsey woman, about his age, wearing a fur coat, was trying, without success, to light a cigarette against the wind. Suddenly the longing for a drink was overcome by the craving for nicotine, and the woman's moderate allure became enhanced by association. He groped optimistically in his pocket and against the odds found a set of book matches.

"Can I help you?" he said, approaching her, matches at the ready and his coat collar held out to make a windshield.

"How kind." It was a bright but rather superficial smile. "I don't really need it that desperately, but it's so cold isn't it? Will you have one?"

He had feared she might not ask. In the three-sided enclosure of his coat and their two faces, he succeeded in making fire with the matches and in transferring it, first to the cigarette between her lips, and then to his own. The intimacy of shared sinfulness engulfed them.

"Ghastly isn't it," the woman giggled nasally. "One tries not to indulge in front of the children."

Jonathan glanced sideways at Simon, who was momentarily engrossed in some push-button silicone chip toy in his hand. The complicity warmed him.

"I have less trouble with the young than the women in my life," he confided, instinctively not revealing his marital status. It wasn't that he particularly fancied her, though he had to admit that the thought of sharing the fraught business of lunching his offspring, who often gave him a hard ride, with another parent and child, had occurred to him instantly. It was more that, as a lifelong philanderer he instinctively played his cards close to his chest. Whether you wished them to think you available or engaged, was a decision to reserve until the lie of the land was clear.

"Son or brother playing?" he said, flattering her improbably. She rewarded him with another giggle that was half whinny.

"Oh, come on – son. Younger son actually. He's on the wing. Where does yours play?"

Jonathan was stumped; without his long-distance glasses he could barely make out Jeremy's amorphous figure on the far field, and Rugby was a game with which he was unrepentantly unfamiliar.

"Simon, what does Jeremy play?" he called. He introduced his younger son to his new companion in addiction. She responded.

"I'm Carole Cummins; that's my son Tom out there. My husband's overseas on business, so it's up to me to keep the flag flying, you know." (Another whinny.)

"Cummins?" Jonathan's mind connected with interest. "No relation to Anna Cummins – BBC music – by any chance?"

A momentary shadow, and then she smiled apologetically, "My mother-in-law. My husband Hugo is her son."

From there on, it was downhill all the way. Without effort, Carole Cummins and son were included in lunch at a local pub; the older boys eying one another with competitive suspicion and jealousy as their parents cultivated each another. Before the afternoon was over Jonathan had got himself invited to Sunday lunch *chez Cummins fils* the following weekend, with the promise that mother-in-law herself might be persuaded to attend. He had a distinct feeling that Carole would have preferred him to undertake a more intimate and clandestine rendezvous, but in view of the watchful presence of their combined sons he could scarcely be considered remiss for not arranging it on this occasion. He made his farewells aware of the familiar feeling that he might have taken on slightly more than he intended.

Despite his dislike of cheap Suave, and a lack of warmth on the part of the married couple whom Helena had invited for Sunday lunch, Jonathan lingered until they left.

"You didn't have to be so snide about Jim's do-it-yourself," said Helena sharply, as she closed the door behind them.

"I wasn't snide. But honestly – bloody Gaynor going on about his bookshelves and barbecues, when we all know everything Jim touches collapses like a house of cards."

"You're so disparaging about things you can't do," she said, collecting up the cups and glasses littered around the living room. "Do you want a black coffee for the road?"

Simon, who had until that moment been quietly watching television, began to jump up and down and fret at the mention of Jonathan's departure.

"Dad, will you play Nintendo before you go?" he whined.

"In a minute, sproglet. Right now, I need pick your mother's brains about something." He sat across the kitchen table with a mug of instant, while Helena emptied the dishwasher.

"Could you fill me in on diabetes, Doctor Helena? Type 1 I think. I mean, was the treatment and prognosis very different before the war? It wasn't fatal was it, once they'd discovered insulin in the '20s?"

Helena looked at him in surprise, "Obviously the technology has improved – disposable syringes, measuring blood sugar – but apart from the development of human insulin, the regimen hasn't changed much since the late 1930s. Why do you ask?"

"It's a biography I – we're producing. This guy died in the early '40s of a heart attack and 'the complications of diabetes'. He was only my age, and he hadn't been ill. The newspaper reports of the time implied that it could have been the booze, or even suicide."

Helena thought for a moment. "Diabetics are susceptible to all sorts of complications. It affects the circulation; increases the risk of atheroma, coronary heart disease, especially if they smoke and drink, or are overweight…"

"And can they kill themselves by not taking their insulin?" Jonathan asked.

"Unlikely. You would die, but slowly. You might feel pretty lousy. Without insulin you can't convert carbohydrates in the diet; your blood sugar goes sky high… then ketoacidosis sets in. Basically your metabolism goes haywire.

Ultimately you're dead. Before they discovered insulin the only treatment was a starvation diet. And that didn't keep you alive long. The reverse is more likely: if you take too much insulin: *that* can kill you. Excess insulin uses up all your blood sugar and you die of hypoglycaemic shock; a hypo is a constant hazard if diabetics don't match food intake and energy output to their insulin injection."

"And in the '30s suicide was illegal. They might hesitate to put it on death certificates. Would a doctor know if a diabetic had killed himself with insulin?"

"Possibly not. After death the blood sugar drops again. It makes insulin the perfect murder weapon; remember the von Bullow case? Accident, suicide, murder: no one could be sure, unless they pinpoint the site of the injection. All this is very intriguing Jonathan; whom are we talking about?"

"Roland Fredricks, the composer. We're doing a biography for the centenary in '94."

"The left-wing musician, who practised free love?"

"That, as our much maligned *ex*-biographer put it, is 'the iconography that adheres to his reputation; the ethos of the time.' Actually, untimely demise apart, he's a rather fascinating character, and I did my D Phil on the period, if you remember." Jonathan hesitated, "I – er – I've told the MD that I'll write the book myself." Helena stared at him in disbelief. "Don't look so amazed. You know I've always wanted to write."

"Yes, but…but, can you really stick at it?"

"Your faith is inspiring."

"I'm sorry, I know how much you want to write, but do you know enough about music?"

Jonathan got up and carried his empty mug to the sink. "Helena, shut up! I don't need putting down now." And he turned the tap on so sharply that water shot up from the bottom of the mug and all over the front of his shirt and face. Helena ran towards him with a tea towel and started to mop him up.

"Don't be such a defeatist all the time. I'm not trying to put you down.

I'm just worried that you are underestimating what you've taken on," she said, her hand inside the towel on his face. He looked at her, pulling down his cheeks like a bloodhound, "I think I probably have," he said lugubriously. For a moment she looked almost on the point of tears.

"Oh, Jonathan," she said, between clenched teeth, turning away and starting to swab down the counter top with vigour, "Sometimes I think there's no hope for you."

# CHAPTER 5

*How to begin?*

*In real life there are no clear beginnings, unless you count birth or death. But these are also an end, and a continuation of sorts. A marriage? A public signpost on the road of a relationship. Divorce is yet another.*

*Meetings? Yes, they are beginnings; although they can be a culmination, or the modulation of something that has gone before. Even chance meetings grow out of the events leading to the crossroads. If I begin with meeting Roland, what of Stefan who preceded, succeeded and suffused our friendship? Knowing Stefan lead to my meeting Roland and conditioned my response to him. As did Roland's reputation that also preceded our meeting. At The Academy everyone either worshipped or despised him. Everyone, without exception, wanted to be invited to Millwater.*

*In one way our meeting was genuinely virginal, because I saw him that first time without knowing who he was. I stood at the barrier clutching my ticket and waiting for Stefan who was late as usual. The prized invitation for the weekend at Millwater had come via him. Roland was his professor at the Academy and he had been several times before. He spoke of Millwater, of the parties, the performances, the lessons, the liaisons, the ambiance and the drink, (Stefan had a Pole's appreciation of extravagant drinking) like an initiate. Roland was not just cultivating his fiddle playing, he was teaching him to live. And oh, did Stefan want to live! Live life to the hilt and deeper; till it choked him, drowned him, killed him.*

In my hand I clutched a battered leather suitcase I had never used before. A Weekend Case was not something one had much call for in the circles I frequented in my teens – not that we called them 'teens' then. Teenagers hadn't been invented in the '30s. You were just young until you were grown-up; desperately trying to look 30 while you were only 18: small, respectable hat, tilted forward over one eye; white gloves, silk stockings with the seams straight, I hoped. I had found a little attaché case with old sheet music in it, cleaned it out, put in a few songs I hoped I would have an opportunity to work on, and some I was composing; a toothbrush, towel and change of underwear plus a swimsuit and cap – Stefan said everyone swam in the millpond in the nude and I wished to be protected from such a challenge.

Stefan was going to miss the train and I was miserable. I peered at my watch every 30 seconds, and checked it with the big clock over the station concourse. Stefan was always late; always in a rush, panicking because he had cut things too fine. We were going to miss the train and be late for my first weekend at Millwater. There would be no car to meet us. I hated Stefan.

And then, out of the corner of my eye, I saw someone beckoning. The train started from here, the terminus, and was already standing in the station. There were still several minutes before it was due to leave, and people were hurrying along the platform, peering through the windows and opening doors searching for a free compartment and climbing in when they found one. In one open window a large man was leaning out and beckoning, slowly and deliberately.

I didn't look up. I was acutely embarrassed.

Was he beckoning to me? Under cover of searching for a hankie in my handbag, I observed the man. He had a large, rather florid face, wild chestnut hair and a romantic beard. He wore an open-necked shirt with a red and yellow cravat at the neck. He looked rather like the sailor on the front of Players cigarettes, but more roguish and louche. He was not, thank heavens, beckoning to me, or to anyone in particular. He was beckoning to anyone – and everyone – who passed him on the platform. Not surprisingly people looked away, swerving from their determined path and studiously trying to ignore the sinister crooked finger and evil leer that enticed them to enter the compartment.

*I was fascinated and, as the minutes ticked away, my anxiety was forgotten and I watched the scene, mesmerised. Was he a lunatic, I wondered? Would someone take fright and call the guard to remove this strange character from the train? But everyone was being stalwartly British. Eccentricity was not a crime; one simply pretended the odd fellow wasn't there.*

*And then suddenly from the opposite direction, I caught sight of a flying figure. Stefan was covering the concourse in great bounds. His blond hair flew out around him, his coat and tie streamed behind. His fiddle case was tucked under one arm and a canvas rucksack swung from the other.*

*"Anna, Anna my darling. Forgive me, I'm so late. Have you got your ticket? Is the train still here?"*

*He crushed my hand to his lips in an effusive gesture then seized my elbow and, almost lifting me from the ground, swept me down the platform. To my amazement, the peculiar man opened the door to his compartment and Stefan ushered me up the step. The man said, "Come on you two; get in. I've had a devil of a time keeping the compartment empty for us."*

*Stefan made the introductions;"Anna, this is Roland Fredricks, my professor. Roland this is Anna Williams, sweet songbird; light of my life."*

*The big man's eyes, surrounded by little creases, twinkled with merriment; he bent from a great height and kissed me. A whiff of some pungent tobacco swept over me and I felt for the first time the scratch of his beard on my cheek.*

They had insisted that she was quite mad to want a piano in the roof.

"Well it isn't exactly the roof, though it does have a Mansard," she explained defensively. "It's simply the most practical place for a studio in this house. The Steinway can stay in the sitting room downstairs, but the little Broadwood I use for accompanying will be more useful in the studio. I couldn't put the synthesizer and the entire tape and music collection downstairs anyway; there isn't room."

When she had retired from the BBC about 10 years ago, she had decided she needed a studio at home, so they had converted the top floor attics of her Holland Park house. These stretched the full depth of the house and had as large a floor area as the double aspect living room on the ground floor. The piano and the synthesizer stood where the ceiling was full height, against the chimney in the centre of the side wall, and at either end they had exploited the sloping roof by fitting shelves under the dormer windows for Anna's books, music, tape and disc collections. She also had an editing deck for recording and a desk with a computer, because even though she was no longer working full time, she planned to continue broadcasting and writing articles and reviews.

"What on earth do you want a synthesizer up there for? Hugo had protested, "You don't do any arranging these days. The idea was that you were going to take things easy; do a little freelancing, teach a bit… put your feet up for a change."

"Perhaps you'd like me to take up crochet and buy a rocking chair," she had retorted. "Why do one's children, once parents, then expect a parent to morph into prototype granny? I don't have to defend the modern technology for the den. I happen to enjoy playing with my lovely Yamaha synth, and my computer," she said to herself.

It had become her favourite room. Recently, apart from a few ex pupils in need of coaching, hardly anyone but her came up here. It was her inner sanctum; her bolt-hole in the sky. She kept the door at the bottom of the attic stairs locked and it was forbidden territory to the camp, out-of-work actors delivered to her door by Char-wallahs, the cleaning company every Wednesday, who whisked round the house with vacuum, broom and spray polish, wearing frilly aprons and trilling the choruses from *Cats*. She liked the fact that she couldn't hear the door bell up there and she usually put on the answering machine unless she was expecting a call.

The dormer windows in the studio caught the early morning and the evening sun at all times of the year. In the winter and early spring it shone right across the room capturing the dancing dust and showing up the faded colours of the old Turkey carpet, the book spines and music folders. She had positioned an old chaise longue at one end and a comfortable arm chair at the other, so that she could doze with the sun on her face whenever she wanted. Once or twice recently she had fallen asleep listening to music and not bothered to go downstairs to bed. She wouldn't have admitted it to anyone, but the stairs were beginning to tire her, not just getting up there in the first place, but the need to go up and down to the loo which had lately become a frequent necessity. That winter, days or weeks had passed without her visiting the studio, but she experienced a sense of homecoming whenever she summoned the energy to climb the stairs.

The night after she had received her death sentence Anna had climbed to the studio and spent several hours so deeply absorbed that she had not even paused to put on any music, and finally she fell asleep on the chaise longue. On subsequent days she spent almost all her time up there, fortified by a few basic provisions, surrounded by files and boxes, their contents strewn around her on the floor.

Temporarily her tiredness fell away; she worked feverishly as she had 30 or 40 years ago, researching a programme. But this time, she didn't have to phone experts, rush off to libraries or play through tapes in pursuit of references. The vast bulk of the material she needed was in that room; yellow with age, covered in dust, disordered and incomplete: the records of her youth: the years with Stefan and with Roland, at Millwater.

The spring of 1992 was mild. Sunshine warmed the long room under the eaves for several hours and she kept warm with occasional use of a fan heater. In the outside world a General Election that no one really wanted, which offered little prospect of relief from the economic gloom gripping the country, encouraged her hermit-like existence. "Why go downstairs to the present when the news is full of boring little men in suits making promises they have neither the intention nor the ability to keep?" she thought. "The time I could feel enthusiasm for politics or optimism for change, has long gone."

The crumbling newspaper cuttings from the 1930s and '40s' that spilled out of her box files were like dead flowers on the grave of her political conviction. And yet when she smoothed the creases and re-read the almost forgotten words, they brought back all the fervour of her youth. The names of those old writers and journals were like a roll of honour: Bertrand Russell, George Bernard Shaw, George Orwell, J B Priestley; *Encounter*, *The New Statesman and Nation*, the *New Left Review*. There, in smudgy print they castigated and declaimed against a political system that put a million on the dole; against an iniquitous relief system – the Means Test – that broke up families, repossessed their goods and put them on the streets and drove them to march with tattered clothes and gaunt, resentful faces to the strongholds of the powerful in helpless protest. The faded photographs recorded them, the unemployed and their rulers: men in ill-fitting suits and caps, their faces hollow with hunger; men in high collars and Homburgs, getting out of cars like hearses, holding umbrellas and little bits of paper. Auden had called it 'a low, dishonest decade,' she recalled bitterly. *Plus ça change, plus c'est la même chose*. "We marched shoulder to shoulder with the unemployed; lay in front of the buses in Oxford Street, and thought our passion and polemic would produce change. But the only one who changed things was Hitler, with his battalions and his bombs."

She had fallen asleep surrounded by these relics, her head lolled sideways, creasing her neck against the arm of the chaise. With her mouth slack and half open, her hair awry, she looked older. Around her, as well as cuttings, were old photo album: tiny, grey exposures held in pasted corners on felt paper with transparent interleaves: couples clutching each other and squinting into the sun; groups posing stiffly, waving on beaches, holding instruments; solemn children in huge bassinettes, their arms rigid with encumbering clothes. And there was lined music paper too, covered with a spider scrawl spatter of notes, sheets of uneven typescript, annotated scores, postcards and letters – unfolded from envelopes stuck with unfamiliar, washed out stamps. One still rested lightly on Anna's lap where it had slipped from her open hand. The handwriting was long and sloping, moving energetically across the page.

"Anna, little Amarillis , speak to me for Christ's sake! Answer the phone. Write but a line. I was loitering with intent outside your flat again tonight;

the police finally moved me on. See me just once more. Give me a chance to apologise, excuse, explain. I need to set the record straight: make my peace with you while I can. I know I'm a prize shit. You are my muse, the 'true and onlie begetter' of *Pippa*, and of course *Adieu, Sweet Amarillis*. What is to become of our poor little Amarillis? This time it will be officially ours. I will send you the work we did on the score. Do you have the time or inclination to continue the work on it? The raddled, whisky-sodden Fredricks hulk may no longer appeal to you, but couldn't we still work together: duet for four hands? I can't write on my own. I don't even want to play. My damned fiddle reminds me of you. I think I should give it to you and Stefan, to celebrate the birth of you first child. You have a lifetime making beautiful music ahead of you.

"I made such a fool of myself with that absurd overdose fiasco. Suicide is just too easy for a diabetic: always the 'bare bodkin' – the syringe of insulin – to hand. And of course, in my hands tragedy turns to farce. I can't even make a success of a suicide attempt. It's three in the morning and the whisky bottle is empty. I can't face going down to Kent or back to Chelsea. I can't face anyone these days. But it's important to me that you know that I really love you, sweet Amarillis. How does it go on? 'For since to part your will is; O heavy tiding. Here is for me no biding. Amarillis, sweet adieu.'…"

And the racing handwriting that had grown more and more elongated across the final pages, almost straightened out, like the monitor on a life support machine when the heartbeat ceases.

The letter lay touching Anna's curled and wrinkled hand. Her breathing caused a gentle movement in the paper, like a pulse.

41

# CHAPTER 6

Ros got fed up after ringing the bell half a dozen times. She went round the side of her grandmother's house, through a rickety wooden gate and climbed onto the dustbins. There was a small window to the lavatory high in the wall with a crack always open at the top. She flicked her fingers inside the crack and dislodged the stay bar effortlessly. It was not a large opening and involved hauling yourself up on hands at shoulder level while perching on the rubber dustbin lid, but Ros was slim and quite athletic and had done it many times before. Granna had never been particularly concerned with being accessible and Ros had learned as a schoolgirl to effect entry without reliance on anyone letting her into the house. The difficult bit was coming down hands first into the wash basin under the window and dragging your legs after you without gouging a hole in your trousers or thighs on the spike that anchored the stay bar.

She gripped the basin which groaned ominously as it took her weight, then lowered her legs first to the window sill, then down to the lavatory seat and the floor. It was musty in the tiny room under the stairs. No one but the Char-wallahs used it these days. Ancient gardening coats, string bags and broken umbrellas hung on a row of hooks beside the door. Ros dusted herself down and opened the door to the hall. The house was silent and dark. She was half an hour ahead of the time they had to leave for Sunday lunch with her parents, and she would have expected some sounds of life as her grandmother prepared. She shouted, more to let Anna know she wasn't a burglar, than in anticipation of any reply.

"Granna; it's Ros. Where are you?"

She stood still, listening, but no response came. She walked to the head of a short flight of steps and looked down into the hall. The house felt disused. There was scattered post all over the doormat and the doors to the living rooms were closed.

Panic swept over Ros. "My God," she thought. "She hasn't been to the front door for days. She could be ill, unconscious, dead somewhere. She never issued an all-clear after seeing the specialist about her kidney condition."

Suppressing mounting anxiety, she began to go through her systematic search procedure. She opened doors one at a time, peering behind furniture and calling her grandmother by name. In the kitchen she was reassured to find a tray of dirty plates and glasses on top of the dishwasher, not to mention two empty whisky bottles. "So far so good: two bottles of Scotch since the Char-wallahs tidied on – when is it, Tuesday? She can't be that ill. Unless she's lying in an alcoholic stupor," thought Ros. And something like that had not been unknown in the years since she had become old enough to recognise inebriation.

Upstairs she discovered Anna's bed had been slept in, but not recently. Newspapers and several items of clothing lay across the open sheets. In passing, she noted an array of medicine bottles beside the bed and her anxiety level climbed once more. "We take her health too much for granted. Just because she's never been ill to date, doesn't make her immortal. She could of course be out, with beefy Bill the builder…" Ros had less difficulty than her mother Carole, in accommodating the idea of her grandmother having a love life.

She continued her search to the back of the house. The door to the attic, which was usually locked, stood ajar. With a flood of relief that sent the blood pulsing in her throat, Ros at last heard sounds of life. A soft rushing like air-conditioning told her the computer was switched on. It was years since she'd been in Anna's private lair and she called out to signal her arrival.

"Granna, are you up there? It's Ros. Can I come up?"

She was first rewarded by a bump, as something fell to the floor, and then her grandmother's voice, husky, as though she had just woken, but fit and fully compos mentis. "Stay where you are. I will be down shortly."

But the command came too late. Ros was as the top of the stairs and surveying the scene.

Anna, bleary-eyed and tousle-haired, sat in a heap on the floor beside the chaise from which, it was transparently obvious, she had just fallen. All around her, spilling from the desk and spreading across the floor, were boxes and files, piles of paper, magazines, books and photographs. On the desk the words on the computer screen twinkled. Ros was too intrigued to heed her grandmother's command, which lacked much authority in the circumstance.

"What are you doing Granna?" but even as she spoke, the answer suggested itself. Her grandmother was writing her memoirs.

"What shall I wear? What will your mother think totally unsuitable? A short skirt? The Cummins knees are in quite reasonable nick considering. Marlene Dietrich flaunted the legendary pins (from the front) until she was much older than I am now. It's the backs of the thighs that give you away, you know; like the backs of the arms."

Her composure quite restored, Anna bustled around the bedroom, hanging up unwanted garments and taking down things she might wear for the Sunday lunch at her daughter-in-law's.

"What about a hat?" she said, taking a white straw cartwheel out of tissue paper in a drum-shaped hat box. "Hats have always suited me, as long as I'm sitting down. Stand up, and I look like a mushroom. I wore this on camera – I can't remember what for – a Glyndebourne Gala, perhaps; Charles and Di's wedding?"

Ros looked down at her from her superior height and smiled affectionately, not really listening. Her earlier anxiety had left her in a state of post-adrenaline calm, and she watched her grandmother as one might a child, not really concentrating on what she was saying, glad that she was alive and well. "Grandma or not, she's still really pretty; and feisty," she thought. "Nothing fragile or frilly about our Granna; I can see what she had – *has* – for the procession of adoring males who stretch back 50 years." Aloud she said. "It doesn't matter what you wear. You'll probably aggravate mother anyway. You usually do."

"One has a reputation to maintain," said Anna solemnly. "In later life one is entitled to cultivate a certain eccentricity."

"One should be awarded an honorary degree in it," replied Ros, teasing. "What did the quack say about your kidneys?" she asked a few minutes later, as casually as she could.

Anna didn't reply. A calf-length split skirt, over shiny black tights, and a blazer with a gilded navel motif, worn over one of her favourite crisp white shirts, had been chosen, and she was now making up her face carefully in front of the dressing table. She was concentrating as she applied lipstick with a brush: stretching her lips over her teeth to remove the short vertical lines that broke their outline. Ros waited.

"Are you going to tell us what the specialist said? Did he recommend any treatment; an operation?" Still silence. Anna was arching her brows and lowering her lids, pulling the skin above her eyes taut enough to apply eye shadow. "They'll ask you at lunch."

A pause and then Anna said, "How rude of them. I shall tell them to mind their own business. I'm taking something for my blood pressure I believe.

"It would be frightfully useful if one had an embroidery frame for the face to achieve a smooth canvas on which to paint, don't you think?" She relaxed and the creases returned. "Do you think I should have a face lift?"

"Another one?" Ros replied, exasperated but fond.

Despite Anna's earlier unreadiness and the care devoted to her toilette, they were waiting when the minicab arrived. They sped south along the Kingston bypass towards Hugo and Carole's 1930s mansion in the Surrey rhododendron belt and, with difficulty, Ros discouraged Anna's suggestion of a 'quickie' along the way.

"The trouble with taxis, unlike boats, trains and aeroplanes, is that they are not licensed," Anna pronounced.

45

"There'll be enough booze when we get there," Ros replied.

"One needs fortifying against boring people," Anna returned, truculently. "I warn you, one becomes morose and prickly when excessively sober."

"…and exuberantly disruptive when one's had a lot of 'quickies'" Ros countered. "Do be good Granna. It's time to stop playing *enfant terrible* now you're nearing your second childhood."


"Mother, how wonderful to see you looking so well. Are you quite recovered?"

Ros felt Anna's arm stiffen in her supporting hand as Carole descended upon them, in a gaudy, Hérmés print shirt, flapping like a great bird of paradise. Long gilt earrings jiggled against her sinewy neck. One hand held a small sherry glass, the other rested caringly upon Anna's shoulder. Ros noticed that her mother was flushed and excited and smelt overpoweringly of Obsession, her 'pushing the boat out' scent. "Oh God," she thought silently, "Either she's cultivating a new social lion, or some man she fancies is among the party. Ros braced herself for Anna's reply.

"Carole, dear; you look quite *flambé*. Have you started hot flushes?" And before Carole could gasp a reply Anna had walked briskly ahead, across the hall with its professionally arranged flowers on console tables, to the double-doors leading to the prairie-sized drawing room.

Deep-pile carpet in stain-inviting cream, stretched as far as the eye could see. Plumply upholstered chairs in Powder Blue and Old Rose Dralon sat around, with spindly reproduction wine tables at their glossy elbows. Built-in, glass-fronted bookcases displayed neatly matching sets of books. The windows were richly caparisoned with swag curtains looped behind ornate gilt bosses. More vast floral displays, two or three tasteful but unobtrusive prints in gilded frames, and a plethora of china ornaments, completed the decor, which Carole changed as often as Hugo changed cars.

Around a mock-Baronial fireplace the width of the English Channel, were gathered Carole's relatives and guests. Hugo, tall and stooping, in City blue; his fine blond hair almost gone now, but his eyes still so deep blue under dark brows, they made Anna's heart stand still remembering Stefan, his father. Near him, her eldest grandson, Steven (after his grandfather); the same dominant paternal genes expressed in spare frame, dark eyes and white-blond hair. Her daughter Kate, sharp, angular and uncompromising, lay extended in one of the portly armchairs, her long, bony legs stretched sideways and her intelligent gaze above curled lips, darting restlessly back and forth in detached scorn for the assembled company. "How has Carole got *her* here?" Anna wondered. "Probably with the same bait that lured me: the prospect of a *molto fortissimo* family ruck. Kaminskis seem to thrive on it." (Anna occasionally thought of her family under Stefan's Polish name which the family had anglicised during the war.) The ancient Browning James, a desiccated but well-preserved laboratory specimen dressed by Brookes Brothers, reclined in another chair; Caribbean-tanned ankles glimpsed above elegant silk socks, carefully manicured brown hand supporting a good Havana. On a runway-sized settee sat a grey-haired woman in good tweeds and sensible shoes whom Anna recognised as Carole's mother, Joan Wooton. There was also an incongruously scruffy youth with a ponytail and torn jeans, who Anna suspected was with Kate. Kate had a penchant for oddballs.

Hugo advanced towards her and bent to kiss her cheek. Anna locked her arms round his chest and hugged him fiercely.

"*Matka*," he murmured tenderly into her hair. Their affection was so intimate and overt that everyone fell suddenly silent and Carole rushed in to fill the hush.

"Well now, what can we get you to drink? Scotch, Mother? I think you know everybody: my mother, oh, and Browning – you remember Browning? And – er – you haven't met Zak. Zak is a friend of Kate's; he's in – er – the record business, so you'll have masses to talk about. My mother-in-law worked for the music department of the BBC for absolutely ages you know Zak…"

Meanwhile Hugo had furnished his mother and daughter with drinks, Browning, who had risen when they entered the room, offered Anna his seat and brushed a kiss like the touch of a dead leaf against her cheek.

"Anna, honey," he purred in a mellifluous transatlantic baritone, "You look so elegant. What's your secret? How do you stay so young?"

"I have a picture of a raddled old hag in the attic." Anna replied deadpan. Kate snorted noisily, and Browning looked nonplussed. Ros's antennae picked up vibrations of mischief and then she realised that someone else had entered the room and was standing close behind her.

She turned and met the gaze of a tall, heavily-built man, with dark hair, greying at the temples. He adopted a solicitous stoop, somewhat undermined by the glint of mockery in his eyes.

"Ah, Jonathan, there you are," said her mother. "Jonathan Burroughs; my mother-in-law Anna Cummins. Jonathan's dying to meet you, mother. His son Jeremy's at school with Tom; amazing isn't it?" Carole explained to the company in general, "We met at a Rugby match last weekend. Absolutely freezing wasn't it, Jonathan?" And she tittered nervously.

"So this is what all the fuss is about," thought Ros. "She's got the hots for this old wrinkly."

She took her beer and sat a little apart on a window seat, where she could study the form. At this relatively sober stage the conversation was fragmented and polite: children, the weather, recent television programmes. Anna and Kate were the exception. They had launched straight in to the election campaign, a risky topic which was not lost on her mother, who considered sex, politics and religion taboo in polite society.

Carole's dreams of being a successful Surrey hostess had occasionally been threatened by her husband's bohemian family. She had learned to keep them away from her smart soirées and dinner parties, exposing only unshockable outsiders to them on Sundays. Fortunately, Hugo's work as an investment banker in the City, and his competence at fashionable leisure sports like golf and tennis, enabled him to pass muster in the smart, St George's Hill set. His Polish Christian name – Ignacy, after Paderewski, the great Polish pianist and prime minister – sheltered beneath an anonymous initial, and his outlandish Polish/Catholic/artistic ancestry was safely concealed by the anglicised family name. He and his sister had assumed a tolerant agnosticism, and neither took much interest in the arts, having been somewhat over exposed to them in childhood. The same could not be said of politics. Like Kate, Hugo had retained the family's left-wing sympathies, but unlike her he did not find it necessary to parade them. Now, to add to Carole's anxieties, it had become clear that the next generation of Cummins had adopted the same political sympathies. To someone brought up like Carole, to assume that 'people like us' naturally voted Conservative and were C of E, it was quite incomprehensible. She did her charity work; she was polite to servants and she thought the National Health Service was wonderful, though, under the private health insurance that came with Hugo's job, she rarely used it – but she was at a loss to understand why that nice Mr Major aroused such hostility, or mention of Mrs Thatcher caused foaming at the mouth.

"It's unbelievable," Kate was saying, "You'd think that the conduct of the economy was nothing to do with them! They try to put the fear of God into everyone about what a Labour government might do, as if what they have been inflicting upon us for 13 years was pure accident!"

"No one ever lost an election by underestimating the electorate," said Anna. "In times of stress, better the devil you know than the risk of change; as long as the devil wears a lounge suit and looks like a gentlemen. It was the same in the '30s."

"Surely you aren't old enough to remember the '30s, Mrs Cummins?" asked Jonathan, who had been standing beside Carole near the fireplace but had been listening with half an ear to their conversation. Anna, who hadn't fully registered him when they were first introduced, gave him a dry penetrating look. Ros braced herself for the reply.

"I'm old enough to recognise a corny compliment when I hear one. And you, my dear man, are old enough to know better."

Carole erupted in a flurry of nervousness.

"Come on everybody; time we ate. Cook will never forgive me if the beef is overdone." She ushered her guests through the hall and into the dining room. "The placements are such a nightmare at family meals, aren't they?" she whinnied through her nose in embarrassment as she planted Jonathan firmly on her left and beckoned Browning to sit on her right. "Mumsy," she

49

indicated her own mother, "Would you sit next to Hugo? Kate on his other side; do you mind, dear? Anna; I can't spare you down there, you're in such demand. Will you sit here, next to Browning? Ros, over here, and young Zak. Steve, between your grandmother and your Aunt Kate; is that OK? It's so difficult: all the ladies are relations; nobody's in a pair. What *do* you do?"

What Hugo did was to fill everyone's glass with good claret and hope that alcohol would smooth over the bumps in the conversation. Ros sat, only to find Zak's hand accidentally- on-purpose, under her bottom. Rather than give him the satisfaction of a reaction she turned to Jonathan, still pink round the ears from Anna's put-down, and said, "Does your son go to public school because you believe in it or because of family pressure?"

He frowned and took a breath and said: "…and now you mention it, I am no longer beating my wife." And they both laughed and felt at ease together.

"Anna," said Browning, unfolding his napkin with a flourish, "Tell us about the Fredricks centenary. What treasures are there in store, and will you be taking part?"

There was an imperceptible pause while Anna took slightly longer than Jonathan to think of an answer to a difficult question, and several other members of the lunch party tuned in and waited for her reply. The first to speak was Zak, casually unaware that Roland Fredricks was a sensitive subject in the Cummins family.

"Ken Russell's supposed to be doing a biopic on him – all sexy birds starkers, and heavy symbolism; that should be a gas!"

Russell's documentaries of composers were familiar to the company. There were reproving clucks from Joan Wooten. Ros, catching a dangerous look on Anna's face, cut in before her grandmother could speak.

"They're reviving *Pippa Passes* at Glyndebourne, and there's a new recording with Kiri Te Kanawa. I think they're also reissuing the song cycles, and *The March from the North*."

Interest in music that had bypassed Anna's children, had re-emerged in her grandchildren; both Ros and her brother Steve, played and enjoyed music. Steve said, "Is anyone writing a new biography?"

It was Jonathan's turn to be uncertain how to respond.

"Actually, our company has commissioned one. It – er – hasn't turned out too well so far."

"Really, how's that?" asked Browning, half his attention on proffering a vegetable tureen, but always the soul of suavity and good manners.

"There's some difficulty in – unearthing new material." Jonathan spoke haltingly. His eye was on Anna. The spoon she was holding above the tureen hesitated a second.

"Wasn't he some kind of closet Red?" asked Zak.

"I thought all those 1930s intellectuals belonged to the Communist party, and went to fight for the Republicans in the Spanish Civil War," Carole said lightly. Again Jonathan waited for Anna to speak, but it was Hugo who volunteered information.

"As I understand it, it was my grandfather who was the political activist, isn't that so *Matka*? Fredricks was something of an innocent until he met the revolutionary Kaminskis."

At last Anna spoke quietly.

"Roland was a romantic, not a political activist. Great causes, like the righting of injustice, moved him, and he turned the feeling into music. That's what it means to be a composer."

"But you did all go on those hunger marches, and lie down in Oxford Street in front of the buses?" Jonathan persisted.

"Oh yes," Anna smiled, "The noble, futile gesture. Hitler did more for mass unemployment and slum clearance than we did."

"That's obviously what we all need now: a nice little war to get all the lay-about unemployed back to work and kick-start industry," said Kate brightly, her political gloves off again. "The Falklands saved Mrs Thatcher in 1982. Where do you think this lot will send the troops? Iraq, Azerbaijan, the Balkans?"

"Kate!" Carole reproved, but the bait had brought a nibble.

"Conscription might be the answer to all those frightful young people sleeping in doorways in the West End," said Joan Wooton. "Except that nowadays they get so much in benefit, they have no incentive to work."

51

"And we all know that they have comfortable penthouses in Pimlico which they support with their begging and ill-gotten handouts," continued Kate with heavy irony.

"There's no benefit for the under18s you know Nanna," Ros broke in, "They're supposed to sponge off their parents. Even those on benefits are living six to a room."

"Well, when I was a youngster, we weren't afraid of hard work." Browning, knight errant, came to the defence of the beleaguered Joan. "We weren't too proud to roll up our sleeves and work our way through college by washing up, or cleaning windows."

"Well these days one can't get an honest workman to do a simple job of work for love nor money; hard work is beneath them," Joan continued, emboldened by the discovery that she had an ally.

"That's because you live in an area where simply keeping a roof over your head costs £50 to £60 a week," said Ros, beginning to get exasperated with her maternal grandmother. "People can only work for peanuts if they can live in trees, like monkeys?"

"Rosamund, that is no way to talk to me," said Joan, now really cross.

"My dear, what must you think of us," said Browning turning to Carole, and somewhat shaken by the rapid rise in the emotional temperature that had taken place around the table. "What a truly delicious joint of beef; done to perfection. Your English roast beef is always so exquisite." And he continued with more in the same emollient vein. Ros became aware that Jonathan was humming *La Marseillaise* very softly to her, under his breath.

The meal skated on thin ice on a couple more occasions: the question of art funding divided them and drew the accusation 'philistine yob' from Kate to Zak, after which she declared the need of 'an intercourse cigarette' and left the table. Then Joan, still smarting from her bout with Ros, weighed in with an attack on teenage standards of dress: notably T-shirts, denim jeans with holes in them, trainers or Doc Martens, instead of tie, flannels and sensible lace-ups; the order of the day in her time. This united the younger Cummins and Zak in loud condemnation of the ancients' hypocritical standards in judging people by their clothes. In this they had a surprising ally in Anna.

"In my time it was considered rather rude to comment on people's appearance. Or don't the young count as 'people' to you?"

"Mother! I'm sure Mumsy didn't mean..." Carole sprang to her own mother's defence, but Anna was not deflected.

"How would you feel if they complained about us making unpleasant eating noises because of ill-fitting dentures, falling asleep at meals, or getting gravy on our lapels?"

The barbs struck home; all three had been noted by those close to Joan during the meal. Only minutes before, she had indeed dozed off, chin falling forward onto her chest, and been gently woken by Hugo. Now she rose unsteadily to her feet, flushed with outrage.

"Carole, are you going to allow me to be insulted at your table; and, and by persons who are, are, are no better than they ought to be?" And in her fury she sent a glass flying; red wine emptied onto her pudding plate and spread across the white damask cloth.

"Oh hoity-toity; so it's in order for you to make critical remarks about others, but you yourself are immune by virtue of seniority and rank?" replied Anna, her eyes sparkling with excitement to see the enemy in rout. By now everyone except Anna and Browning, who was completely aghast at the latest turn of events, had risen to their feet. Carole rushed to the far end of the table where Hugo was already attempting to calm his mother-in-law. Steven was attempting to stem the advance of the spilt claret with his napkin, and Ros ran into the kitchen in search of a damp cloth.

By the time she returned, a tearful Joan, protesting that she was going to pack her bags and leave the house that instant, had been led into the other room and a large, calming brandy administered. Her raised voice, counterpointed with Hugo's and Carole's, could be heard in the dining room. Steven, calculating that dinner duty was over, suggested to Zak that he might like a game of table tennis and they departed. Browning rose falteringly, dabbing the corners of his mouth with his napkin, white knuckles clasping the back of his chair. He was several shades paler under his tan. He looked helplessly at Anna, who was now attacking the cheese and refilling her wine glass as though nothing had happened. His loyalty to his hostess and the woman he admired fought with his distaste for scenes. The distaste won.

"Happen I'll take a little stroll in the garden and smoke a cigar," he said faintly and moved towards the door.

"British domestic blood sports distress you Browning?" said Anna, cutting carefully into a piece of Stilton and spearing it with the forked tip of the cheese knife. The Brahman gentlemen paused and half turned.

"Maybe I've gotten a little fragile in my sunset years," he said towards her preoccupied back. "I'm not sure I can take the level of excitement you require, my dear."

Anna, Jonathan and Ros were alone in the dining room.

"Magnificently decadent piece of Stilton," said Anna with her mouth full. "What it needs to go with it is an apple: ideally a Cox's pippin. Where have all the English apples gone? We wouldn't have dreamed of serving cheese without apples when I was a girl."

Carole put her head round the dining room door.

"Coffee's in the drawing room, everyone. Mumsy has gone to have a little lie-down." Her eyes were on Jonathan. She didn't look at Anna. He hesitated, recognising the demand, and hearing the desperate attempt to recreate a sociable atmosphere in her tone. Then he sat down in his chair again.

"I thought, er, I might sample the cheese," he said aware of her disappointment, "Be with you in a minute."

Ros remained standing, staring sternly at Anna.

"I was thinking of calling your car," she said pointedly.

"Oh really?" answered her grandmother, unhurried and at ease. "I was thinking that possibly Mr Burroughs might like to drive us home; since he's so anxious to pick my brains about Millwater."

# CHAPTER 7

*I dislike the attribution of blame. Life is not a court of law where liability and retribution must be apportioned. Why does looking back so often focus on who, or what, was responsible? Why are people so desperate to make causal connections? The statisticians tell us that correlation does not imply causality. And anyway, any causal relationship between events gets muddier with time, not clearer. Why the urge to pass judgement, classify, characterise, carve epitaphs. Let others come to bury Roland, or to praise him.*

*It's not like that when you are actually living life. We influence, and are in turn influenced, but we are not always in control; and therefore not to blame.*

*They tell me I am adept at denying responsibility. To feel responsible you must feel powerful. You must believe you can cause events and control people. That kind of power we occasionally have over children, animals or the things of our creation, but over sentient adults? Surely not? I don't accept responsibility for those things others choose to lay at my door; but neither do I blame. I hold myself answerable for my own life alone.*

*They were very keen on blame at Millwater, particularly Roland's 'Monstrous Regiment of Women' as he called them. Roland blamed his Calvinistic upbringing: it was a sin to be idle, to enjoy the flesh; self-indulgence or self-congratulation the greatest sin of all. And his women: Helga, his wife; Helga, playing the martyr's role; Flora, his mother, begrudging him the praise he so craved; Paola, hungry for a physical passion that daunted him; even Gudrun, his daughter, growing up in the lee of so much discontent, blaming him as a 'bad father'.*

"He's hag-ridden," said Stefan, Roland's most loyal disciple, "He escapes into his teaching. Who can blame him?"

Plenty did: wife, mother, mistress, daughter ganged up against him; clustered in huddles churning over his failings. "I think they dance in a ring by moonlight and cast spells to damn him. It's enough to turn a man to pederasty."

Well, that was Stefan's theory. Others were less charitable. Some thought his preference for the company of young people unhealthy. He was variously alleged to be an advocate of free love, homosexuality, orgies, and illegal drug use; at the very least, Dangerous, Left-wing Ideas. Stefan put it down to envy and reactionary politics. Protest was the progressive mode of the time, and more particularly, in Stefan's Kaminski blood. "The old are jealous of his rapport with the young. The mean and narrow-minded are shaken by free thinking and the free way of life at Millwater. Charismatic teachers like Roland threaten traditional authority, not to mention powerful elites like the British ruling class, entrenched it its privilege and wealth. They either crucify the rebels or defame them after death."

Thus the Roland legend grew, embroidered by friends and foes alike. In a time of political darkness, the moths of hope gather round any bright flame.

And so I came to Millwater for the first time, in the unseasonably balmy spring of l938, in a spirit of excitement, and some apprehension. I had felt similarly, travelling to London to take up my scholarship to study singing at the Academy. As the daughter of a country schoolmaster I knew little of the ways of the world, of big cities, sophisticated artists and musicians. I was 18, an impatient virgin troubled by the first stirring of sexual attraction, and hungry for experience. It may have occurred to me, as we drove down narrow country lanes, between high hedges, in Roland's open Austin roadster, that this new encounter heralded some auspicious change in my life. I did not for a moment imagine that I might be held responsible for the dramatic events that followed.

The pilot in the geyser had gone out again. When the wind was in the east, the sash window in the bathroom let in a howling gale and the fragile blue flame that granted them hot water expired as a result. Ros stood barefoot on the worn lino wrapped in a towel, punching the red button intended to supply a spark, until her index finger was numb and bent backwards. The towel fell, and the wind that had snuffed the pilot light applied its harsh breath to her naked torso.

"Effing, bloody museum piece!" she swore, striking the chipped enamel with an ice-cold fist. The front panel of the water heater fell forward on top of her. She dumped it in the bath, retrieved her towel, and went in search of matches. She was the only person in the flat that morning and she didn't smoke. It was a question of sifting through the assorted jumble that clogged her flatmates' bedrooms, or going to college unwashed.

At times like these she had twinges of regret that she hadn't exercised her fresher's privilege of living in hall. At least there one always had electricity and hot water. But after one term of the modified boarding school regime she had scampered in search of more independence. The price of more privacy, and an un-monitored sex life, had been a daily journey to and from Brixton, intermittent main services, and communal squalor.

A sack of dirty socks hanging behind George's bedroom door swung at her like a punch-bag and winded her with the stench. Ashtrays, books, ashtrays, beer-cans and more ashtrays; no visible matches. Her stomach rebelled at a closer inspection of George's pit. George and Hamid were second year students on her economic history course. They had offered her the third room in their flat in the chauvinistic hope of 'a woman's touch' around the place. They had been disappointed. Ros was not into cooking or cleaning for others – even the men she slept with from time to time. She kept her quarters clean, cooked in her own pans, and let the others fester in their own filth.

She dug her hand down the side of the sagging settee in the sitting room, and was rewarded with a lost lighter. This time in the bathroom, she was granted a resonant explosion. The gas accumulated from the unlit pilot finally ignited. The geyser juddered into life.

Steam filled the room and Ros slid down low in the bath in an attempt to get her naked body under the waterline, out of the draft from the window.

In some sense Sunday lunch had not been a total disaster. "The barney quite invigorated Granna, considering she started out looking so peaky," she thought. "If only she hadn't whisked the old publisher Johnnie off from under mum's nose." The recollection of Carole's crest-fallen expression as they drove off in Jonathan's car, gave her twinges of guilt. "Granna makes no allowances for weaker mortals. And she hadn't the slightest intention of letting the poor man 'pick her brains' about Millwater. She spent the entire journey leading him up a succession of garden paths. Still, we had a fun evening back at her place. Primed with Granna's Islay Malt, the book-wallah turned out quite entertaining. And he finally got her to agree to talk about Fredricks, with the bribe of dinner at her favourite restaurant. I suppose some women might go for that rather stagey charm. He could be quite funny, and he's definitely got very sexy eyes. Wonder if he had any real interest in poor mum, or was he just working on her to get to Granna?"

She threw on some clothes, ran gel through her hair, grabbed her bag and was half-way out of the flat before she realised that she had forgotten her score and ran back to fetch it. The choir was rehearsing Handel's *Messiah* that night and she would have to go straight there from the library.

Ros was not a particularly conscientious student; teachers described her as 'talented but' or accused her of 'coasting'. At school she had grasped the essentials of most things easily, but found it difficult to master detail. Compared with structure and proportion, the value of quantification to three decimal places eluded her. Computers were better than people at such things anyway. Fortunately she had a retentive memory, and in the run-up to an exam, usually swotted up enough facts to get her through.

Her first two terms at university had passed in a whirl of extra-mural activity. She had joined the Union, got involved in university politics, been accepted to sing with one of the top London choirs, and been roped in to help with the college review. The Easter vac, with first-year exams two months away, caught Ros with both time and money running out. This time a last minute pre-exam spurt would not carry her through the pile of reading she had neglected. In addition, she had spent all her grant and was dependent on part-time bar-work just to continue eating. Ros feared she was on the verge of being rumbled.

The tube took her as far as Embankment and she walked from there. Now warmer weather was on the way she planned to bring her bike from home and save money by cycling. She bought an apple from a stall outside the station for breakfast, and thought about joining the queue for a cup of coffee. A funny guy in a red Santa Claus hat was putting a little black and white dog through its paces. It walked uncertainly upon its hind-legs, begging for scraps from the nearby punters. Ros felt in her pocket for loose change and came up with a 50p piece.

"What's he called?" she asked the old man.

"Sure *she's* called Judy, and she understands every word you say," he answered with great solemnity. He had a gigantic, red nose and Ros made the association instantly.

"So you must be Mr Punch?" she said laughing, and wishing she had more money to give them. "I hope you didn't beat her to make her do her tricks?"

"And wasn't I the man with the golden trumpet, pretty lady? And didn't Judy learn to dance with joy to my dulcet tones?"

"So where's your golden trumpet now?" said Ros.

"Gone to join the golden balls, lady," he replied.

She walked up the hill still smiling. As she looked back about to enter The Strand she saw them again and felt suddenly very sad. How awful to be forced to pawn the instrument needed for your own livelihood: like the craftsmen losing their tools in the Great Slump, or the Irish eating their seed potatoes in the Great Famine. It made her short-term financial stringency appear small beer.

Apart from a couple of overseas students, there were not many people about at college. The dons were at conferences or on holiday, and the majority of the UK undergraduates had gone home for Easter. She was almost alone in the library. Nearly half past 11; if she worked straight through she could get in six or seven hours before she had to leave for choir practice.

Jonathan had been almost alone in the office since eight. Two people were on holiday, his colleague, Jackie, had an appointment out of town, and their secretary had called in sick with some family problem again. Old Rathbone had come in after a late lunch and fallen into a snooze, with his head resting on his hand in simulated concentration over some proofs. Jonathan preferred the office when he was alone. It was easier to organise his thoughts, and at the moment his thoughts were increasingly full of Roland Fredricks.

He had to do something positive to shake off the frustration engendered by his encounter with Anna Cummins. He had thought himself on the threshold of a breakthrough when she suggested he drive them home, but she had been playing with him the whole journey. "So near, and yet so far," he fumed inwardly. She knew all the Millwater glitterati; she was there when Fredricks was writing his best work, yet it was as if she couldn't decide whether to confide in him or not. He wondered momentarily if she had been approached by another publisher to write her own biography of Fredricks. She had done some passable journalism and she was an experienced broadcaster, although as far as he knew she had never tackled any subject at length. And Anna Cummins – Williams, she had been at the time – was one of a handful of the composer's really close associates still alive.

Roland ran through his list of the *dramatis personae*; Fredricks' wife, Helga: dead, sometime in the '60s; his daughter, Gudrun: extant, but uncooperative; the singer, Paola Pignatelli: alive – just, but inaccessible; publisher, John Abrahams: dead. The designer Luke Gerard, who had done the controversial designs for the suspended production of *Pippa Passes*, and Ernest Grossman who was to have conducted: they must be old, but they hadn't appeared in the obit columns yet. There was a chance he could find them. He had a little on all of them. What was missing was how they fitted together, and into Fredricks' life and works. Anna Cummins must have the key to the jigsaw puzzle: the big picture which all these the pieces fitted into.

For the early stuff: Fredricks' parents, school, Academy and university background, he would have to rely on written records. He had reviewed the existing source material thoroughly. Like Grove, the *New Oxford History* and Evans' *World of Twentieth Century Music*, were pretty cursory in their assessments of Fredricks' work. Neville Cardus was more complimentary about him as a violinist and teacher. Osbert Sitwell recounted his talent for practical jokes in *Laughter in the Next Room* and there was a lip-smacking account of some racy parties at Millwater in Harold Nicolson's diaries. They added up to no more than a set of snapshots: faded, indistinct, contradictory. The real Roland Fredricks never stood up.

Somehow he had to bring clarity and coherence to the Fredricks myths by rooting them in the composer's character, and placing them in the context of recognisable musical trends and the social obsessions of the times. Perhaps he could dig up material on the composer's Calvinist childhood in Edinburgh: his pushy mother, and his childhood as an infant prodigy? There were records of him as a junior 'pot-hunter' competing at local and national music festivals.

The phone rang and the voice was so intimate it was like a touch to the genitals in public. Instinctively Jonathan looked round in case someone one had noticed. Rathbone was still snoring faintly, and no one else was in the office.

"Darling, you've been so elusive." Fiona's voice had a sinuously seductive inflection. "Where have you been all this time?"

Jonathan had to try hard to remember when he had last seen her.

"Actually I've been working." It was true. Then recollection came to his assistance, "Anyway, I thought I had been consigned to the geriatric ward."

A rich gurgle came down the line. Fiona was not to be discouraged. Her voice took on a touch of girlish pathos.

"I've missed you. The nights have been so cold." She extended the antepenultimate syllable with the equivalent of a twiddle of one of her Titian-coloured ringlets, or a flick of her forked tail. Despite himself, Jonathan found himself responding to the flattery and the blatant sexual invitation. He yanked his attention back to his professional mission.

"Right now, Fiona, I'm involved in the research for this biography."

"Roland Fredricks?"

Jonathan was taken aback. Fiona was usually only obliquely interested in his work.

"Darling, don't I always have your best interests at heart? I've found someone who knew him for you. He's very old."

"Of course he is Fiona. Fredricks would have been a hundred in December '94. Who have you found who knew him?" His first thought was that, if Fiona was offering something, she wanted to trade. He feared that the contract involved much sweat and a reliable erection.

"What would you do…", again the elasticated syllables, "To meet this fascinating source of new biographical material?"

"Fiona, stop playing around. It all depends who it is?"

"For example: how about a weekend in the country; me; a concert in a beautiful place; an accidental encounter with your source; a conjunction of events that only I can engineer?"

Jonathan found himself drawn into the game.

"A musical source? Do you mean Anna Cummins?" Fiona was not to be drawn, but she didn't say 'Yes' either.

"Daaahling, trust me. Now why don't you meet me at Peppermint Park, 6 o'clock Friday and I'll drive us to a lovely little inn I know at Box Hill, and we can take it from there?"

His mind supplied a string of useful reasons why not, not the least of which was that it sounded like no-escape entrapment for a weekend that included at least two occasions when he would be required to perform sexually for Fiona. He played for time.

"I'll ring you back. I need to check with Helena about the boys. You wouldn't, I imagine, wish me to bring them with us?"

"You're seeing a great deal of your family lately."

Jonathan detected a little gust from the ice cap, but it cut to the bone. Fiona had once proposed accompanying him on some collection/return visit to Helena in connection with the boys, and his resistance to the suggestion had earned him frostbite.

"I'm trying to make some effort to be a good absent father."

She seemed content.

As an afterthought he added, more graciously, "Thank you Fiona; it's very good of you to take an interest in my work." These skirmishes with Fiona sometimes made him forget his manners.

He put down the receiver and looked down at his desk. He had been doodling. At the top, a circle of names: Fredricks, Helga, Stefan – Kaminski, as he had been then – Abrahams, Gudrun, Anna, Pignatelli, Gerard, Grossman: the Millwater charmed circle. Beside the last five, who were still alive, he had listed numbers or addresses. Was it one of these Fiona was trailing him towards?

Beneath Anna Cummins' name he found he had written another: 'Ros' – no number, no address. He had driven her home after their evening at Anna's, so he knew only that she lived in Brixton. To the 'R' of her name his rambling hand had traced a series of curlicues that extended to embrace several other names on the page. It made it stand out more than any of them; and yet this name, of all those on the page, had theoretically nothing to tell him.

As he looked at the name he was aware of a quickening of his pulse accompanied by a surge of adrenaline. It was the unmistakable signal of amorous arousal. He had registered the sensation before, and dismissed it. After all, she was, how old: 20, *25* years, younger than he was? She was, he calculated, as much younger than him as Anna was than Roland Fredricks.

The preoccupation refused to be quashed. To the quest for the truth about Roland Fredricks was added an equally urgent one: he wanted to see more of Ros.

# CHAPTER 8

Everyone looks more beautiful across a table. Is it the ritual significance of breaking bread together; or perhaps the more modern association with the prelude to seduction? Or is it simply that soft under-lighting reflected off white table-linen flatters the downward lines of the face?

Jonathan was not a particularly handsome man, thought Anna as the waiter flicked a crisp napkin into her lap. There was a comfortable warmth about the heavy lines of his face: a disarming wrinkling of the bags under his brown eyes – especially when he smiled – and a self-deprecating humour in his manner. She liked people who didn't take themselves too seriously, but she didn't *fancy* him.

Unaware, that he had been let off one particular hook, Jonathan looked across the table at his guest and wondered if there was anything he could bribe her with to be more communicative.

"Have you kept the sylph-like figure by eating next to nothing or by sheer good fortune?" he asked, remembering an instant too late her harsh nailing of his last attempt at flattery. Sure enough the bird-bright eyes fixed him, empty of coquetry.

"Does envy or obsequiousness speak?" she replied.

Jonathan laid two broad-palmed hands upon the table.

"Esteemed Mrs Cummins, I will come clean. I admire you; I respect you. Regardless of anything else, it is a real pleasure to buy you dinner. But above all, I need your help. I have taken on writing the biography of your venerable mentor and I want to make it one worthy of his memory, and one that will do me credit, and make money for our publishing house. Now, will you please enjoy our dinner and stop trying to pin me to the wall."

She met his eye with a containment of expression that he realised was actually suppressed laughter. "She really is a remarkably attractive woman for her age," he found himself thinking, perhaps by fault of habit. "She has a reputation for being quite a raver in her time. She's supposed to have had liaisons with a number of celebrated men, quite apart from Fredricks." Despite the circumscribed nature of their encounter, Jonathan found himself evaluating her sexually. "It isn't just physical attractiveness, though she has a good skin, and great legs. It's more the aura of sophistication and experience she projects. I bet she knows a thing or two. Down boy!" Metaphorically he smacked himself upon the wrist. This was a business meeting.

Her head was bent over the menu. She ordered fresh asparagus and lamb. He said he would have the same, and a bottle of *Fleurie* to go with it. She turned her gaze upon him and said, "Well, do you ask questions or do you expect me just to talk?"

"You've never written about him, have you?" The suspicion of a shadow crossed her brow. "The only thing I could find was an article on teaching you did for *The Guardian* in which you contrasted the goal-centred teacher with the pupil-centred one? You said Fredricks was goal-centred, and that it was like fire: it burned wood but tempered steel."

He paused to taste the wine presented by the waiter. Anna's expression was distant and thoughtful. She watched the garnet-coloured liquid dance as it was poured into her glass, and he saw a look almost of pain cross her face.

"Have you seen a kind man make a child cry?" she asked. "Not only a child, a grown man, or an artist, with a world reputation? Roland could do that. His mind was so focused on the end result he didn't notice whose feelings he trod on. He drove himself just as relentlessly. I've heard him practice the same technically difficult passage over and over again for an hour or more; swearing, kicking the furniture, occasionally breaking things. He could be like that with pupils: careless of breaking things. His goal was perfection, and excuses, alternative interpretations, wounded pride, exhaustion, physical pain even, were mere flecks on a flawless surface; to be brushed aside. He never let you repeat a mistake. Repetition, he maintained, fixed things; so that as you approached the danger point you could see him waiting to pounce if it went wrong. Naturally, it made some people play worse." She paused, as if she was coming back from the past to the present. "But perhaps that's not the sort of thing you want?"

"I'm not sure. So many things I hear about Fredricks conflict: professional and personal. You say he was kind, but a bully in the cause of a good performance. His writing is opinionated; yet music critics accuse him of being imitative and having no distinct style as a composer. His pupils describe him as a powerful personality, dominant and inspirational, but the anecdotes of his contemporaries also picture him as a man ruled by powerful, manipulative women. And the stories of his drinking, the practical jokes, the sexual liaisons are equivocal. Was he a depressive, a mischief-maker, a satyr or a clown? Quite frankly it's impossible to decide from the evidence whether the man was a stud or impotent; straight, gay, bisexual or a paedophile."

She burst into laughter.

"Exactly what kind of biography are you planning?" she asked in mock horror. "Kiss and tell confessions; 'I slept with the stars,' and other saucy revelations?"

Jonathan felt sheepish. Perhaps it had been a tactless angle to put to one assumed to have been the composer's mistress. "Well, no, of course not. His music is the central interest. But there's something I've heard called the 'iconography that adheres to a reputation', if you don't find that too ponsey? I see Fredricks as more than the sum of his work. He was the genius – the *genie* of Millwater, if you like. And Millwater, in common with Cliveden, Bloomsbury, or Charleston Farmhouse, was a place that attracted people and ideas that encapsulated the spirit of a time. It would be nice to capture that in the book: life through art; the adventure of music-making. You know: the experimental productions, the blend of politics and the arts, and all the people, pupils and performers, who carried those attitudes and beliefs with them into later life. I'd like to –"

He paused because he saw that there were tears in her eyes. He felt embarrassed. "It can't have been my eloquence, surely? I thought I was beginning to sound pretentious, and that she would mock. Perhaps it was some memory I stirred up?"

The waiter arrived with delicate green spears of asparagus, displayed on black china plates. Anna waved away the bread he offered. She looked at Jonathan and he resisted a desire to pour on more words, and waited for her response. She lifted a limp green wand and manoeuvred the tip, dripping with butter, dexterously between her lips.

"A fiver both ways, you get butter on your chin," she said.

It was a strange meal.

"The fact is," Jonathan was forced to conclude, "She's a crummy interviewee. She refuses to pick up leads, darts off at a tangent at the drop of a hat – fascinating, but totally irrelevant – and nothing she mentions connects to known events. If I had a deadline I'd be up shit creek. Is she being deliberately obstructive or is she simply accustomed to dinner being the occasion for a different kind of negotiation? Harrumph; again the sexual dimension. She can't expect me to flirt with her can she? She's much too grand a lady. Anyway: is Anna Cummins seducible? I rather suspect *she* does any seducing she has a mind to."

With a twinge of guilt, he suddenly recalled Carole; the abandoned look on her flushed, unhappy face as they had driven away last weekend. "Irrational, demanding creatures, women; always expecting something that you hadn't a clue was required." Jonathan took refuge in learned helplessness, "Why fight it? With women you're condemned before you say a word. A man's place is in the wrong."

The waiter stood beside them with a trolley of cream-decked deserts. Jonathan's eye flickered uncontrollably over them. She had noticed of course. He anticipated some acerbic remark about calories, but when she spoke it was reflective.

"Roland couldn't resist cream cakes. To see him faced with a trolley like this was to see him a child again. Of course there was none of this cholesterol anxiety then. No obsession with 'empty calories'. There was this idea then that diabetics should avoid sugar, although with insulin regular carbohydrates are essential. That was his excuse anyway. Fuller's coffee and walnut cake; that was his favourite. And after eating it, he would spend several minutes picking pieces of nut out of his teeth or beard and pretending to flick them about, just to embarrass us. He wouldn't push a chocolate truffle out of bed either, or a doughnut."

She suddenly drew in a sharp breath and closed her eyes. For a moment Jonathan thought she was going to faint. Her pale hand came across the table and took his wrist. She spoke in a whisper.

"Could I have a brandy please?"

He was confused; what had distressed her in this inventory of cakes? He ordered two cognacs and sent away the trolley, then taking advantage of the hand on his, he said, "I'm not much of an amateur psychiatrist, but your memories of Roland Fredricks are obviously both potent and painful." It was the first time he had used the composer's first name; it was an acknowledgement of the fact that for Anna he was a person, not just a musical celebrity: the subject of a biography. "Perhaps organising them for our biography would be therapeutic?"

She didn't look at him. The cognac arrived and she swirled the spirit in the balloon briefly, before throwing it to the back of her throat. She lowered her chin and still not looking at him said, "It would be just." Then again a sudden change of mood, "Do you think I should write memoirs of all my lovers? We could call it *Return to Langham Place* to give it the right racy overtones."

He got no more out of her until she was about to leave. They drank a second brandy and coffee, and she seemed to have put painful memories behind her. But when she had asked the waiter to call her minicab, she gathered up her handbag and gloves and said, looking directly at him,

"I would like the truth to be known about Roland. I would like all those contradictions you speak of reconciled or dismissed for ever. But, you do realise don't you, that there are those who will be obstructive; those who

68

prefer his name… just washed out? It's one reason why I've written so little about him."

She had stood up and he panicked, fearing she was about to go with so much unanswered; nothing settled. Desperation made him bold. He caught her hand as she stood beside the table.

"Don't run out on me, Anna. You know the answers I'm looking for. Will you help?"

His words had reached her. She sat down again slowly, looking like a child rebuked. She shook her head, eyebrows raised.

"I'm sorry; that's how I am. I walk away. I accept no responsibility."

"Promise you'll think about contributing to this biography. Promise you'll tell me all you know about Roland Fredricks. You said it would be 'just' to let the truth be known."

"Young man," she said, in mock affront, "You are importunate." But she hadn't taken her hand away. He looked into her eyes and decided to treat her as though she found him attractive; many women did, and the idea gave him confidence.

"To start with, I want to know anything you know on the writing and production of *Pippa Passes*. You were in the Millwater production; you must know things. All the production notes, manuscript, annotated score, are missing. I want to know about anything else he worked on while you knew him. Then, what were the important influences upon him – other composers, collaborators, artists, friends? Can you think of any explanation for the late flowering of his musical genius: what Grove calls 'his individual melodic idiom'? Were there works *un*published? And what about letters? Do you know anyone who might still hold letters? Do you have letters? And where are the letters people wrote to him?" He charged on, aware that he was probably treading on some very sensitive issues, but, what the hell: in for a penny; in for a pound.

"Whatever happened to his beloved violin: the Stradivarius? Was it bequeathed, lost, stolen, destroyed, and why? Finally, why on earth is there such a mystery about his death? I know they were cagey about recording suicide in those days because it was still a crime, but somewhere there must be evidence for whether it was illness, accident or deliberate: death certificate, medical notes – something to add to the newspaper reports of the time."

During the final sentences she had tried to pull her hand away, but he held onto it. He held her gaze too, waiting for her reply. She was suddenly meek and compliant.

"You're very forceful. All right: I capitulate. Send me the outline of your biography and a summary of what you want, and I really will see what I can do. Perhaps not all of it... Give me a couple of weeks and then we'll talk. I can't promise at this stage – for several reasons."

And she got up and left the restaurant without looking back.

He had another coffee and a cigar before he paid the bill and strolled towards The Strand, half-heartedly looking out for a taxi. It was not an ideal time. People were pouring out of the opera, commandeering every available black cab.

It was fresh, but quite mild: the first traces of spring in the air, so he decided to walk until the theatre crowds abated. He skirted Covent Garden walking through backstreets, bright with restaurants and pubs. He paused outside one, debating whether a beer might clear his head. The frosted glass doors swung open and a crowd of kids in jeans and anoraks pushed past him, shouting to one another as they hurried away. He was momentarily engulfed in the warm, fuggy atmosphere of the pub – laughter and the smell of stale beer and nicotine; orange light on polished wood – and before the doors swung shut again, he caught a glimpse of a face that made his heart miss a beat. It wasn't a face that he associated with this part of London, his work, or pubs, and at first he couldn't place it. He was 50 yards on before he realised whom it reminded him of. The girl looked like Ros. The thought made his pulse race as it hadn't for years; not since he first got it together with Helena. He felt alive, motivated, *young*, damn it! "I've got it really bad to start imagining her face in unlikely places," he thought.

Jonathan had only short time to wait before discovering from what direction the obstruction that Anna had referred would come. A letter arrived on his desk from a firm of solicitors in Cambridge. The letterhead was black, low-key and legal; the content equally so.

"Dear Sirs, Our client, Ms Gudrun Fredricks, would like us to call to your attention the fact that all materials pertaining to the estate of the late Roland George Fredricks, her father, passed into her possession upon the death of her mother, Mrs Helga Fredricks, in January 1973, and that the copyright on all unpublished work authored by Mr Fredricks: music or written, including letters, not specifically assigned prior to Mr Fredricks' death, is retained by her, and that any publication, all or in part, is therefore contingent upon her consent. Ms Fredricks is regretfully unable to enter into any negotiation or correspondence upon this matter and wishes you to regard this communication as final."

# CHAPTER 9

"Let's take it from the top now: letter E; the soprano entry: 'He trusted in God that He would deliver him.' Give it plenty of attack, but don't squawk please ladies."

The choir master's baton came down crisply and the choir took the passage from Handel's *Messiah* again: a top G entry finishing with top A, *forte*. Ros's ears buzzed and she felt faint with physical effort. *Messiah* was as exhausting for the choir as the last movement of the Beethoven Ninth. They were on their feet and singing for most of the work, and the current fashion for singing the contrapuntal numbers staccato and fast made you feel as if you were running up a steep hill in very short hops. Once or twice during tonight's rehearsal she had feared she might pass out for lack of food. An apple, a yoghurt and a packet of crisps were all she'd eaten that day. But if they finished promptly, there would be time to get to the pub where she had a part time job and cadge a scotch-egg or some stale sandwiches. The hunger came in waves; worse when her stomach expected sustenance, but easing off between meal-times. There was some consolation in the fact that the less you ate, the less frequently you got hungry, the less potent the pangs. As long as they were actually singing it wasn't too difficult to push the pangs out of consciousness.

Ros enjoyed singing with the choir. It demanded physical energy and supplied spiritual and cultural uplift. There was something particularly satisfying about being a part of a large, richly patterned sound. Her voice was a small thing taken alone, but blended with the others, in this complex disciplined force, it thrilled the ear and raised the roof. It was like being swept along on the breast of a great wave, except that the image was too passive; it was like being part of a cavalry charge, a galleon in full sail.

"Let Him deliver him, if He delight in him!"

The harsh, derisive words of the multitude mocking the accused Christ died away. They should have been softened by the solo tenor lament which followed: "Thy rebuke hath broken his heart; he is full of heaviness." But tonight they were rehearsing only the choruses. Professional soloists appeared, with the orchestra, only at the dress rehearsal, and the choir was pitched, breathless into the next helter-skelter chorus with scarcely a break. Ros's eye lingered over the words of the tenor recitative as she prepared to turn the page. "He looked for some to have pity on him, but there was no man, neither found he any to comfort him."

Perhaps because she was so hungry she found herself thinking of the old trumpeter with his dancing dog. "I don't really know hunger. What must it be like to be cut off from food, not just temporarily, but to have no way of getting it, and to be unable to feed someone you love and are responsible for too?"

She called her mind back to the music, glancing at her watch; food was about half an hour away.

"Can those of you who are singing at Clanfield this weekend stay behind for a moment?"

Ros's salivary juices had been anticipating the comfort of stodgy pub grub. She turned back towards the chorus master reluctantly, swallowing the fluid welling up in her mouth. Eleven other singers detached themselves from the melee of those hurrying to leave the rehearsal rooms. Being selected for a special function was an honour, and they had willingly put in extra rehearsal time on the Elizabethan music to be performed at this country house concert. The choir secretary, a bossy contralto who taught in a large comprehensive, handed round a typed sheet of arrangements.

"So," continued Janos, their chorus master, when they had all absorbed the details, "You know times and pick-up points for the mini-bus. We'll have a final run-though Thursday night, with the viols and harpsichord continuo. I think you'll be surprised to find how easy it is to keep your end up against these old instruments. There's a light supper laid on for you down at Clanfield before the concert, and the mini-bus leaves half an hour after it ends to bring you back to London. In between, wander the palatial grounds, snooze on a four-poster, mingle with the illustrious guests or do what you damn well like, short of filching the Georgian silver. But whatever you do remember to save your voices. Oh, and don't drink too much of the free Champagne.

"There's just one more thing they've only just told us about: they want you in costume."

A selection of groans greeted this announcement.

"Janos, I don't have the figure for doublet and hose," moaned Ben, a bass who was 16 stone if he was an ounce.

"Neither did Henry VIII, but he wore his tights with pride," replied Janos unsympathetically.

"Do I have to white-up?" asked Kamau, a Kenyan student from Ros's college whom she had been responsible for recruiting, flashing white teeth in a broad grin. Janos was impatient.

"Look, I don't want any more objections. The Trust has booked us; the Trust will pay for the costumes; just get along to Berman's and get yourselves fitted in the next couple of days. And if Kamau wants to kit himself out as Othello, no one will mind. Off you go. And remember, before the concert: *save your voices!*"

The singers broke into groups and moved off.

"A pint at the Duke's?" said Kamau grabbing Ros's arm.

"You got any dosh?" she asked weakly, dreaming of food.

"Loaded; *Mzay* just sent me my allowance." Kamau's father was some high-up in the Kenyan government. "It will be amusing, I think, to see everyone in farthingales and ruffs, don't you?"

*I sang Cherubino from* Marriage of Figaro *for him first. His wife, Helga accompanied me. She played as though her mind were on something else, but it was competent. I could see he wasn't enjoying it. He prowled up and down the long, low-ceilinged room fiddling with things and picking at his finger-nails. So I tried an aria from* Messiah. *He interrupted me before I was half-way through, saying something like, "Don't you have anything simpler – more suited to your voice? A folk song perhaps – unaccompanied?"*

*Helga left us and I sung him* O Waly, Waly *and* Cold blows the wind o'er my true love. *He sank back into one of the deep arm chairs more relaxed, his long legs flung out in front of him, scratching his beard beneath his lower lip, as he often did when concentrating.*

*"Let the sound come straight from the heart. No artifice, no manner. Let the feeling in the words and the melody speak directly to us."*

*I hear him now: the voice, warm and flexible; deep-set, blue eyes burning under bushy brows. I was transfixed: Trilby mesmerised by Svengali. He got up and approached me, and as he towered above, the pungent smell of the exotic tobacco swept over me, as it had on the train. He extended a large, hairy hand with short, well-trimmed, musician's fingernails, and laid it on my abdomen, just below the ribs. His eyes bored into me.*

*"It starts here – the power source in your solar plexus. It resonates throughout your chest, your throat, your head." His other hand, spread wide, described an arc around my chest and shoulders coming to rest on the nape of my neck. "Feel it rise through your head – a smooth column of unhindered sound." And he took the hair on the crown of my head and tugged gently upwards, tilting my chin down like a puppet suspended on a string. "Now sing, and feel the notes float out of you, filling your trunk and head with sound."*

*My throat and neck muscles relaxed. I was supported between his two hands. The notes vibrated in my ears. He conjured music from me.*

*"A deep breath from the diaphragm." The sound rose inside me and filled the room; he played me as he might his violin.*

*Later he got out his fiddle and we sung Holst's* Medieval Songs *for voice and violin:*

*"I sing of a maiden that matchless is.*
*King of all Kings was her son iwis.*
*He came all so still where his mother was,*
*As dew in April that falleth on grass."*

As he played, Roland bent his body over the glowing instrument – his priceless
Stradivarius, the same colour as his hair – compressing his cheek into deep folds
and gripping it against his shoulder. The broad finger-tips pressed down on the
fingerboard. His nostrils dilated and I heard the rushed intake of breath that
preceded each new phrase; the crunch of the bow heel as it bit the string close to
the bridge and was drawn in a long sweep away from him, releasing the throaty
sob of the violin. Player and instrument were one; one with the music; one with
me. I was swept up into a transcendent musical nirvana.

We sat late at dinner that night, some 10 or 12 around the great oak table,
lit by wavering candle light. The picture is so clear I can almost touch it. Logs
burned in the open fireplace and threw flickering shadows on the beamed ceiling
and walls; red reflections in polished wood, copper and brass. There was soup,
with home-made, wholemeal bread, English cheese and Cox's apples, accompanied
by huge jugs of red wine and rough cider. The conversation glanced from person
to person like the light of the fire, from topic to topic: music, films, the hunger
marches, rearmament, the war in Spain. Stefan grasped my hand under the
table and his eyes shone in the light of the flames, drunk on companionship and
ideas as well as on cider.

Later that night, hot with alcohol, we walked in the garden. Wet leaves
brushed against us and the grass was damp under our feet. Above, stars shone
in a clear sky. Roland led us to the edge of the mill pond, his arms thrown easily
round our shoulders, and I saw for the first time the source of the Millwater
sound: the foaming white water disgorging from the race, dissipating its force
in swirls and eddies among the reeds. Roland's voice, spewing forth lines of verse
and snatches of song, was drowned momentarily by the deafening roar of escaping
water. The musical tide ebbed and flowed around us. His breath, smelling of
wine and tobacco, was hot in my ear as he bent to explain.

*"The spring rains are at their height. In summer there is less passion in the water."*

And he turned us back towards the house, his arms across our shoulders, steering us. We walked back along a paved path bordered with lavender and small, white-faced jonquils. Roland bent and picked some, laying their scented heads against my cheek.

" 'As dew in April that falleth on grass'," he quoted from the Holst song. At that moment Stefan, momentarily unsupported, stumbled and fell heavily against us, and I realised that they were both drunk. Undeterred, Roland seized Stefan round the waist and flung him bodily over his shoulder. Stefan, who was tall but not heavy, protested weakly, and the curious duo progressed unsteadily towards the house, Roland's voice still raised intermittently in song.

I hung back, taking in the shadowy shapes of trees, steps and hedges around me as my eyes became accustomed to the darkness. I could smell flowers and wet earth, and began to detect the gentle rustlings of the night as the clamour of the mill race receded. I climbed a flight of steps and found myself upon a terrace like a stage, looking out across a broad lawn carpeted with fallen blossom. I stood still and some small animal scuttled to safety in the shrubbery beyond.

Music started up in the house behind me: tinkling piano, strings and a flute. I turned and looked at the lighted windows. In the long music room on the ground floor, orange light glowed through drawn curtains. On the floor above, at an uncurtained window, I saw a little girl with long hair, looking out into the garden. I supposed it must be Roland's daughter, Gudrun, whom I hadn't met. Her face was pressed against the glass, and even at this distance, I got a distinct impression she was crying.

A cold wind wrapped itself round my shoulders, and I came in. I climbed to my bedroom under the eaves. Stefan was snoring loudly from the room next door.

Clods of damp earth had been scattered on my bed as though upon a coffin in a grave.

# CHAPTER 10

Clanfield House was a fine 18th century mansion surrounded by parkland, some 40 miles from London. It had been built originally for a merchant who had made his fortune in the East India Company, no expense spared. Bonomi had been responsible for the architecture, Adam, the interiors, Repton for landscaping the grounds and Gertrude Jekyll for laying out the gardens. However in the course of time the old money had been dissipated in death duties and other lordly pursuits, and the late 20th century owners, having stripped the stately pile of paintings, antique furnishings and other disposable trappings, beaten by the dry rot, bequeathed it to a charitable trust and departed to live cheaply in Majorca.

The Trust had set about removing the accretions of Victorian and early 20th century barbarism: uprooted rhododendron and laurel forests to reveal the clean lines of Repton's landscaped conception, pulled down the pebble-dash additions to rediscover the classic simplicity of the original building. The one addition spared by the stringent restorers was an Edwardian music room 'after Wren', complete with dome, carved mahogany organ, and wooden wall panels carved with swags of greengrocery 'after Grinling Gibbons'.

After some years of convalescent obscurity, Clanfield acquired a Trust tenant richly equipped with family paintings and furniture, together with a unique collection of old musical instruments, to grace its beautifully proportioned rooms. The estate's gradual rehabilitation was now augmented during the season by a series of select musical events, featuring the old instruments and the domed music room, and embellished by an elaborate meal and special-label Champagne, at an astronomical cover price, no expense spared.

Fiona drove, manicured hands resting lightly on the leather steering wheel, a smell of Chanel's Coco filling the white BMW, and Vivaldi on the hi-fi. Her cloud of Titian curls was bound to her head with a richly patterned silk scarf, and she wore a suit in cream silk edged in black satin. At her side, Jonathan felt like an ageing Spaniel on the lap of a pouting Duchess in a Lely portrait.

She had collected him, as arranged, on Friday evening, refusing to be discouraged by his late arrival, or the discovery that he hadn't brought a dinner jacket. (They made Moss Bros in time to hire one, complete with mortifying Burgundy cummerbund.) She had consumed Margaritas with no obviously deleterious effects and driven them to a hotel on the Downs where they had dinner and he had managed the required erection on retiring. He had kept to himself the fact that he had been thinking hard of Ros all the time.

At breakfast the following morning, in acknowledgement of his creditable performance, she revealed that the goodie on offer was an introduction to Sir Ernest Grossman, close associate of Roland Fredricks before the war, erstwhile conductor at the Royal Opera, now virtually retired. The Maestro was to attend a special concert of early music at Clanfield House in honour of his 90th birthday. Fiona, by virtue of special connections, had tickets.

Saturday daytime was spent ministering to the inevitable Burroughs hangover and visiting antique shops. Jonathan acquitted himself honourably by purchasing a silver bound, petit point pin-cushion and presenting it to his paramour. Lunch was eaten in a riverside inn, Fiona's knees looking particularly appetising in fashionable boy-scout-length shorts. Jonathan's hand wandered absent-mindedly up one smooth, creamy thigh, and Fiona suggested they return to their hotel to change for the evening.

On reflection he should either have abstained from that final pint or discouraged her from returning until the business of 'changing' could have been mercifully brief. His intimations of immortal longing had been misjudged, and he performed badly. Fiona removed herself from his treacherous instrument, rolled on her back, closed her eyes and masturbated. Jonathan marvelled briefly that this erotic spectacle failed to move him, before dropping into snore-punctuated slumber shortly before she reached orgasm.

Their preparations for the Clanfield concert were conducted in arctic silence. She showered and dressed, locking the bathroom door. Forbidden to smoke in the bedroom, he resorted to the mini-bar: he was, after all, paying for this part of the occasion. Fixing collar studs in a dress shirt, bow-tie and cummerbund are tasks to convert the staunchest bachelor to the necessity of a partner. Jonathan struggled alone, cursing the lack of moral and muscular fibre that had landed him in this position. His thoughts dwelt momentarily on Ernest Grossman. At 90 he was quite possibly gaga, or at very least confused about events more than 50 years ago. However, he'd worked on the abortive premiere of *Pippa* in 1939. One could but hope he remembered something.

The BMW turned off the main road at a sign indicating that Clanfield House was *CLOSED*. They drove up a long gravelled drive behind a veteran Silver Ghost with tinted windows and a chauffeur. Cars were dropping their passengers before the porticoed main door and were then directed to a parking lot by a boy dressed as an Elizabethan groom. The Rolls Royce set down an old couple in evening dress. When Fiona pulled up she got out without a word and handed the keys to Jonathan. Obediently he came round and got into the driving seat. She handed him a ticket, printed and worded in an antique style.

"See you in five minutes in the main hall," she said, turned on an elegant heel and climbed the steps to the house.

It took him somewhat longer than that to park the car, owing to the fact that getting in and out of car seats had incited his cummerbund to come adrift. He also spent sweaty minutes re-attaching his stiff collar where it had escaped the rear stud.

He climbed the stone steps and took a flute of Champagne from a flunkey in ruff, doublet and hose, with profound gratitude.

"Thank God it isn't mead!" he muttered, draining the glass and helping himself to another instantly. Indeed it wasn't; it was the real stuff and probably vintage. He found Fiona in the marble pillared hall, beside a fair-haired youth wearing black velvet doublet, knee-breeches and a small Van Dyke beard. Fiona introduced him as Gervase Elliott, creator of the Clanfield Concert Season and curator of old instruments. "Perhaps Fiona's asking his advice about mine," thought Jonathan.

"Gervase devised the early music programme. It was his idea to do the whole thing in Elizabethan dress. Isn't it absolutely divine?" enthused Fiona in her best social manner.

"Isn't that a couple of hundred years before the house was built?" Jonathan asked unkindly. The young man blushed.

"Well, we have music, and some early keyboard instruments that date from the end of Elizabeth's reign. Madrigals, you know, and an Orlando Gibbons organ work. And everybody feels at home with Shakespearean dress, don't they?" His long bony hands supplied an explanatory gesture.

Jonathan cast a disparaging look at the youth's skinny legs and thought the feeling misguided. He looked around. He didn't know much about architecture. The Adam ceilings were extremely fine, although the vast portraits on the walls seemed to him relatively indifferent. There were spindly, gilded chairs and some smooth, artistic sculpture that reminded him of graveyards.

"The flower arrangements are nice," he said carefully.

The silk-brocaded dining room had been arranged with small tables and gilt, fashion salon chairs supplied by the caterers. Jonathan and Fiona found themselves on a table with a weather-beaten military gentleman, with clipped grey moustache and monkey jacket, accompanied by a somewhat younger wife in pink satin frills who giggled a lot. Two well-barbered gays, who introduced themselves as Simon and Alex, an old lady in black lace with a basilisk stare and a companion in steel-rimmed spectacles, who Fiona whispered were Lady Something-or-other and daughter, completed their table.

The Colonel's giggling lady turned to Jonathan and said, "I love these dos don't you? They're so elegant and select. Isn't that Richard Baker over there, and Denis Healey and his wife who plays the piano?" Jonathan murmured something inaudible with his back to her as he reached for another glass of Champagne from a waiter passing with a tray. He contrived to ignore the icicle that darted from Fiona's eyes in his direction.

"Have to confess, most of the music's a bit above my head," said the Colonel apologetically, "But they do you quite well in the mess department." Jonathan surveyed the prospect of the meal ahead like a sinful believer contemplating purgatory. The waiter filled a small glass in front of him with what he took to be an amontillado sherry. The quality of the booze was some consolation.

The meal lasted an eternity. Regardless of the prospect of meeting Grossman, the fact that he had come in Fiona's car, and the fact that all his gear was at the hotel, the thought of doing a bunk entertained him more than anything at the table.

Using the excuse of needing a slash, he left the dining room and went out into the hall and lit up a cigarette. In a small room near the entrance he could see a telephone. What if he simply called a taxi and beat a retreat? Freedom now would be well worth the trade of his clothes and toothbrush abandoned at the hotel.

Away on his right he could hear the sound of musical instruments. The musicians were preparing for the concert. He strolled across the black and white chequered floor, his shoes making a satisfying clip upon the cool marble, and peered into a room which he rightly deduced to be the Music Room.

In a pool of light at the far end of the darkened room, in front of an ornate mahogany organ, a dozen players wearing simple Elizabethan dress with starched ruffs around their necks, were tuning viols and bending over the strings of what he took to be a harpsichord. The darkened space between him and them was set out with rows of the same gilt chairs used in the dining room. At the front, facing the instrumentalists and chatting quietly among themselves, was another group of young people in costume. One wore a plumed red velvet hat and matching cloak; another, dark-skinned, wore a long embroidered robe and silk turban. As Jonathan watched, an older man, not in costume, came into the room.

"Let's have you all up here now choir, to see where you will stand. There's not much room with all these chairs, and you're going to have to sing up once the room is full of people."

The singers got up and moved into the pool of light, and suddenly Jonathan's heart missed a beat. One of the girls looked just like Ros: tall and slim, with fair hair bound close to her head, and a small diadem of pearls that nodded over her high forehead. This time, despite the alcohol clouding his brain, regardless of her unfamiliar Elizabethan dress and the unexpected location, he was sure it was her, not a delusion.

Behind him he heard the sound of guests leaving the supper room.

"Jonathan, Jonathan, where in heaven's name have you been?" Fiona's tone was imperiously displeased. The man in charge of the musicians was now shepherding them off the stage; in a few moments she would be gone.

"Ros," he called, half aloud, half to himself, "Ros, it is you, isn't it?"

The fair girl flashed an unseeing glance in his direction and he realised that the lights were in her eyes and he was in darkness. A firm hand took his arm; Fiona was beside him.

"If you want to talk to Sir Ernest you will have to come now. There is only a short interval before the concert begins," she said crisply. The pain of disappointment seized Jonathan almost physically as she drew him away, but the music room was now empty. He followed in Fiona's scented wake.

A small sitting-room had been put at Sir Ernest's disposal so that he might dine away from the hurly-burly of the other guests. He sat in a wheelchair, an old tartan rug over his bony knees: a small bent figure, velvet smoking jacket hanging limply upon his rounded shoulders. He still had the distinctive plume of white hair shooting back from his high forehead, the long aquiline nose and strong brow; his hallmark upon the podium and a hundred record sleeves. But now the deep set grey eyes were pale and watery, and flitted uncomfortably from side to side, and the expressive hands clawed helplessly at the wool cloth across his knees.

The remains of his dinner rested on a low table at his side. Not much had been eaten and Jonathan noted that it had been cut up into little pieces like a child's food and only a spoon rested upon the plate. The other people in the room made little impression. A thin, colourless young man placed two chairs close to the wheelchair and beckoned Fiona and Jonathan to approach.

"Maestro, this is Fiona Hale from the gallery. You remember? And this is her friend Jonathan Burroughs who is publishing the Fredricks biography for the centenary in '94?" he said in the hushed and reverend tones used in church or on Radio 3.

The old man's eyes wandered furtively about the room before resting upon the blazing figure of Fiona with some semblance of recognition and pleasure.

"Ah yes; you acquired the Picasso etching for us, I recall." A claw came out and fastened upon Fiona's wrist drawing her to the chair that had been placed nearest him. He raised his eyes to her face by leaning back rather than raising the chin sunk low on his collar. "Very stimulating little etching, very stimulating." And a flicker of salaciousness indented the corners of his thin lips.

"We were delighted to get it for you; quite a collector's item. I'm so glad you were pleased with it." Fiona sank into the chair, closing her other pale, enamelled hand over the claw that held her wrist. Her job in a West End gallery frequently brought her into contact with minor celebrities who were keen collectors. It was one of the perks that atoned for working for a pittance and boosted her commission. The old man's eyes wandered up and down Fiona's body and his fingers twitched under her hand.

"So what have you got for us today then?"

"Maestro, you said you might be able to give my friend your recollections of the composer Roland Fredricks."

"…A Fuseli perhaps, or something Japanese?"

Fiona smiled indulgently and patted the hand under hers. A good client was not to be discouraged.

"We have several things that might interest you at the gallery. You must call round when you have time." And she repeated her question. "Fredricks, Maestro. Can you tell us about him?"

A slight sneer lifted the blue line of the lips.

"Fredricks." His shoulders shook in the suggestion of a snort and his gaze took in Jonathan for the first time. "So you want to know about Fredricks?"

"I believe you worked on the first production of *Pippa Passes* Maestro?" said Jonathan adopting the reverential tone that seemed to be currency in the presence of the Great Old Man. For a moment he thought he hadn't heard him. The only sign of life was the slight and intermittent jerk of the trunk that indicated that Sir Ernest was still breathing. Jonathan tried again, "What is your evaluation of *Pippa Passes* and Fredricks' output generally?" The breathing was punctuated by another vestigial snort.

"Some pretty tunes," he said, damning with faint praise. "It was *said…*" there was heavy irony in the emphasis, "*…said* that they had used Venetian folk songs. Browning's words and Italian folk music: not much Fredricks in the opera."

" '*They*' Maestro?" Jonathan inquired. The old man lifted his eyes to him for a moment.

"Fredricks and that Williams girl – Anna; the little soprano he wanted to sing Pippa." A look of sly amusement crept across his face, "Not that La Pignatelli was having any such nonsense; soon saw the little nightingale off the stage, did our Paola. Composer's tantrums went unheeded."

"Fredricks wanted Anna Williams to sing Pippa – *in London*?" Jonathan queried.

"Sang at Millwater though, didn't she, our grand diva notwithstanding?" said the old man relishing the recollection of old scandals, but giving up on the tongue-twisting Italian name. "He said the girl had worked on the score with him. Claimed it was inspired by Venice and *her music*." His voice took on a stronger, steelier note, "That melodic line was not in any previous Fredricks composition. All mock-Delius or mock-Vaughan Williams, that's all we'd been offered until then. Said he'd found his 'true voice' in Italy. Maybe? If so, what became of the Amarillis opera that was supposed to show the same voice?"

"Amarillis?" Jonathan was mystified. "Who was Amarillis?"

"The opera they were working on – Fredricks and the Williams girl. Never saw daylight though, did it? Blamed it on the breakup with his beloved Anna."

"Or his intervening death, more like," said Jonathan, forgetting in his excitement to adopt the deferential tone. "So he *was* working on another opera when he died. Did you hear any of it?" For a moment he thought the old man was sulking at being touched without the customary kid gloves. But then he spoke again without the irony in his voice, not looking at Jonathan.

"She sang me one or two arias: Anna. It was a lovely voice, not feeble, as Pignatelli claimed." He paused. No one spoke, sensing that he hadn't finished. "In truth, it had promise. It could have made a good opera: *Adieu, Sweet Amarillis*."

"Sir Ernest," the pale acolyte spoke into his ear, "Sir Ernest I think we should be making our way to the Music Room; the concert is due to begin in a few minutes."

The retinue prepared the wheelchair occupant for departure.

"Do you have any idea what became of the score of *Amarillis*, Sir Ernest? It was never published, was it?" Jonathan asked in desperation at the preparations for departure.

The old man jogged back and forth like a child in his chair as it was set into motion.

"Not if Pignatelli or the widow had any say in it. Probably burned it along with everything else they could lay their hands on."

"Burned it!" Jonathan could not believe what he heard. The cortege was by now nearly out of the room. He followed, trying to hold onto the conductor's attention. "Why should anyone do that – particularly his widow?"

The old man put up a frail hand, signing his minions to halt.

"Because they loathed his guts." And the word reverberated with recollected venom. "They hated the thought that he might finally be a success, and escape them." The ironic tone crept back into his voice. "Not that Fredricks was ever likely to achieve that." He signalled to the pram-pusher that he was ready to leave. As he disappeared through the doorway he spoke once more, only the white quiff visible above the back of the chair. "Why don't you ask the Williams girl? If anyone knew about *Amarillis*, she did: his amanuensis, his inspiration, his muse."

Jonathan, as Fiona knew to her cost, was not easily aroused. These days few things – except his sons – touched him. Yet in the space of 20 minutes two new things had stirred him to unusual agitation: first, the unexpected glimpse of Ros, and now a glimpse of yet another Fredricks: a Fredricks possibly on the verge of fulfilling the promise of *Pippa* with a second opera: *Amarillis;* a man to tug at his own sympathies; overcoming setbacks to achieve success, racked by the unfathomable vagaries of strong women.

How he sat through the concert remained a mystery to Jonathan: Bach's 6th Brandenburg Concerto an organ piece by Orlando Gibbons, and a group of English madrigals, which by strange irony included Wilbye's *Adieu, Sweet Amarillis*. These last especially added to his inner turmoil. Ros's pearl-crowned head nodded enticingly like a flower out of reach as she sang: the young voices weaving in and out like threads in a piece of fine lace.

"Adieu, Adieu," the voices echo each other plaintively, "Adieu sweet Amarillis," – a strange discord like a pain in the heart. "For since to part, to part your will is," – the chords pile one upon another with the weight of bad news, "Oh, heavy tiding!" – like a death knell, comes the minor key and the realisation of separation. Had Roland Fredricks felt like that when Anna left him? Had he put that passionate loss into his last opera? "Here is for me, here is for me no biding," – the music gathers pace as the rejected lover gathers up his metaphorical baggage and prepares to leave. "Yet once again, yet once again, again 'ere that I part from you," – like a deep sigh the melody rises and sinks, as the lover looks back at Amarillis receding into his past. "Amarillis, Amarillis, sweet Adieu," – for a moment he assumes a jaunty 'see if I care' face, covering his broken heart with a smile. "Adieu,

Adieu," – the voices mock him with the repetition; not 'Au revoir' but the doomed finality of 'Adieu'.

Jonathan found himself looking at Ros but seeing Anna and identifying with Roland's anguish. With her, life had begun to take on meaning, creativity had blossomed, there had been hope, a future. Without her, all was desolation. Like dead leaves under foot in autumn or the Nazi jackboots marching over Sudetenland, his women trampled him underfoot. What was the point of living a life without dignity, a life without love?

Jonathan shook himself awake. The audience was on its feet, applauding. The musicians bowed, or curtsied in their wide, stiff skirts. Ros's head sank and rose, framed in a high, Elizabethan collar. By the time they prepared to leave the stage Jonathan had decided: this time she would not get away.

He slipped quietly from his seat and out across the hall. Behind him he heard someone making a speech: something about the guest of honour, Sir Ernest, doubtless. He ran down the steps to the drive and round to the parking area where he remembered seeing the musicians' mini-bus. The service entrance to the Clanfield kitchens backed onto the Music Room. He made his way past the stacked chairs and tables of the tearooms towards the sound of excited voices in the musicians' changing room. Several young people carrying instruments pushed past him.

He didn't slacken his pace.

A crowded room with several men in underpants and socks; in the doorway to the lighted room stood Ros, still in costume, talking to the dark-skinned boy, now carrying his turban.

Jonathan didn't hesitate; he took her hand and drew her after him. She resisted, pulling away from him, as he spoke.

"I've got something tremendously important to tell you," he said, wasting no time with explanation of his presence at Clanfield.

"Jonathan, what on earth…?" She tried to withdraw her hand. Outside in the courtyard, the musicians were loading instruments into the van, breaking open chocolate bars and cans of beer, relaxing after the performance. Jonathan looked round, saw a small gate in a wall and drew Ros through into the gardens beyond.

"Jonathan, what's all this about? Where…? "She didn't finish because he had paused to put a hand gently over her mouth.

"Patience; all will be revealed."

They were in a formal garden running along the back of the house, marked out by clipped, box-edged flower beds, gravel paths and stone urns crowded with daffodils that brushed them as they passed. Lights from the tall windows of the house cast orange patterns on the garden. Somewhere not far away the soft splashing indicated a water jet or fountain.

Jonathan became acutely aware of the beating of his own heart. He had acted precipitately because he felt emphatically certain of something inside him, but he hadn't worked out how to explain this to Ros.

"There must be a fountain somewhere; can you hear it?"

Still holding her hand he led her, at a more relaxed pace, to the further end of the parterre where a stone nymph held aloft a pitcher from which water tumbled into the scallop shell beneath her feet. The bed round the pool was planted with scented jonquils. Impulsively Jonathan bent, picked some, and offered them to Ros.

"My apologies; I'm behaving like a lunatic."

She let out a short, not unkind laugh.

"You're behaving as though you are definitely a rook short of a chess set."

The sight of her smile and the fact that she hadn't taken away her hand set his pulse racing again. He leaned against a wooden bench and pulled her gently towards him. The blood in his fingers throbbed where they touched her. Something desperate was trying to climb out of his throat, but he managed to keep his voice level.

"I know this is sudden; I probably sound absurd. Believe me I wouldn't do it if it wasn't serious. Tonight I learned two things that matter to both of us." Her face was in shadow, but the light that etched her profile told him that her eyebrows were raised inquiringly. "I learned that your grandmother –Anna – knows about a second opera written by Fredricks, which his wife and mistress tried to destroy." A sharp intake of breath confirmed that she was interested; the tension in his hands received an answering frisson from her arms. "I'm beginning to have my first coherent view of Roland Fredricks, and how my biography can reveal him. It's important to me. I hope to you."

She squeezed his hand and came closer.

"That's great; it's the lead you have been waiting for isn't it? And the second thing you learned?"

He took a deep breath and pulled her towards him. The stiff embroidered material of her skirt crushed against his thighs. She didn't pull away. He took her chin and turned her face so that he could see it.

"The other thing is that – pawns, rooks, knights and queen overboard – I discover that I love you, Ros. Do you mind?"

Her body was warm against him, her breath halting, like his own. He waited long enough to assure himself she would not punch him on the nose, then kissed her – gently, lips to lips, eyes open, looking into hers. His confidence was rewarded; she kissed back.

The rest of that eventful evening passed in a dream. He had, of course, consumed a great deal of Champagne. But he was also drunk on the excitement of discovering he was in love, and on the verge of writing, hopefully something worthwhile. And he was exhilarated with having made a decision with no advance planning; one that had not misfired in his face. Experience had taught Jonathan that only rarely was he in charge of events in his life. Mostly he reacted. Mostly he started with good intentions but copped out if the going got tough. The sins in his life were all of omission. He allowed himself few opportunities for daring disaster – or inspired success. Most was damage limitation and an evolved aptitude for escape.

This skill came in useful to him that night, at a tense moment when he came face to face with Fiona while hand in hand with Ros, and with an unconcealable erection. He didn't stop to explain; simply thanked her for the invitation and wished her good night.

There was a strange, rowdy journey back to London in the back of the mini-van sitting next to Ros, gazing into her pupils, dilated with desire, and never letting go of her hand, with the musicians singing snatches of song all round them. This Amarillis wouldn't say 'Adieu' if he had anything to do with it.

End of Part 1

# ADIEU, SWEET AMARILLIS,

# Part 2 – "This Monstrous Regiment of Women"

# CHAPTER 11

*I had known it would happen since that first night in the garden – possibly earlier – from the first moment his fingers touched my abdomen instructing me on how to sing. With the certainty of inexperience I knew Roland would be my lover.*

*I had only the vaguest idea what it meant to make love. Men had held me in their arms. I had kissed and felt the strange gripping feeling, like wanting to make water, in the pit of my stomach. I had known the fraught sense of something imminent exuded by men or boys who desired me, and I liked it. It was power – power, not in what I did, but in what I was.*

*Some of the students at college slept together. Contrary to current folklore, sex had been invented before 1963. Stefan said saving sex for marriage was a bourgeois concept; that only by separating love and domesticity could men and women be truly equal. There was much talk over the late-night cocoa, and most of us espoused an emancipated sexual creed, but when his fumbling hands took over, and he attempted to turn theory into practice, I felt uncomfortable. It was like trying to dance with someone who didn't know the steps. It excited me to be desired; it confirmed my power, as a woman, but it signposted no clear channel for fulfilment.*

*But Roland had a power all his own. To begin with there was the heightened physicality of his presence – sheer size coupled with his compelling gaze, the musky smell, and the mesmeric music of his voice. Also he came 'trailing clouds of glory' – he had the charisma of celebrity, notoriety. I had heard people talk about Roland and Millwater long before we met. But all this paled before the* impact of being his pupil. In lessons and rehearsals I found myself attracted to him by an irresistible magnetic force. The others felt the same way; it was obvious as we played or sung together. And Stefan was totally infatuated.

I found myself wondering if there was something sexual in the bond between Roland and Stefan. Stefan's attachment could have been hero worship, but there was a curiously flirtatious quality in the way Roland treated Stefan – teasing, provoking, challenging, drawing him on, then putting him down – which was both capricious and rather feminine.

"Put the bow down; let's hear you make the notes with the fingers of your left hand alone," he commanded.

Stefan brought his fingers down hard on the fingerboard of the violin, but the notes were barely audible. Roland took his own instrument and, resting it nonchalantly on his shoulder, hit the notes with attack that sounded as though he were plucking the string.

"Go to the far end of the room. Now; bring the finger down on the tip – big vibrato – give it all you've got." Stefan tried again, a dark flush crept up from beneath his jaw across his cheek. The fair hair fell across his eyes and he brushed it back with the wrist of his idle right hand. The other members of the group were hushed; they had seen this happen before.

"Play, play! I can't hear you. Can anyone?" and turning to his audience Roland began to hit out the Sailors' Hornpipe on his fiddle with his left hand, drowning his pupil's puny efforts. Suddenly, when I thought Stefan must surely break, Roland descended upon him. His left arm came up under Stefan's, his large hand covered Stefan's thin, bony one; broad, spatulate fingers came down on top of the boy's, making him wince with pain.

"Develop the power of the left hand – that's where it must be. The tips of your fingers are like a girl's." And he held out Stefan's left hand and exposed it to the company, so that the boy had to catch the unsupported violin with his righthand as it threatened to fall to the ground. The tips of the fingers were red and raw: there might have been blood. Roland's left arm was still round him and his face close to Stefan's ear. His words were inexorable. "Practice; practice; practice. 90 per cent of good fiddle playing is technique and the way to get it is 100 per cent practice and sweat."

96

"Roland delights in torturing his talented favourites," said Helga, massive arms up to the elbows in isinglass with which she was preserving eggs. "Gudrun, give Mutti a towel for her hands, Liebchen."

Helga cultivated rural, domestic crafts with Germanic thoroughness. When she wasn't baking she was bottling or preserving, and occasionally stinking the house out, boiling up soap. She had a small pen with chickens which were the focus of the local foxes' predatory attentions. She tried to keep ducks on the millpond, which more often than not flew away, and she could occasionally be glimpsed, head and shoulders swathed in protective netting, tending the white beehives which housed her swarm. She was absorbed in her country pursuits as Roland was in his music, and the intensive activity left them little time to spare for their only child, except in the role of helper or pupil.

I had heard Roland teaching Gudrun – hounding her to tears, and I wondered if Helga's verdict on cruelty to talented favourites was a mother's attempt to soothe a daughter's pain.

The Fredricks women treated me with a thinly veiled hostility which grew with the frequency of my visits to Millwater. Stefan and I had the status of 'favourite' which automatically made us the objects of their resentment. To begin with I don't recall being particularly disturbed by this. My relationship with my own mother and sister was good and, since I had done nothing to justify unfriendliness, I imagined that I would soon win Helga and Gudrun round. Later in life I learned to my cost that the flip side of my confidence in attracting and being liked by others was the hatred it earned me from those who were less secure.

But as my feeling for Roland developed so my attitude to his women became more circumspect.


The night Roland took us to see Gielgud in The Merchant of Venice he had the car in town and insisted on driving us down to Millwater after dinner at Pagnani's. The party included Roland's publisher, John Abrahams, his wife, and the theatre designer, Luke Gerard – a pretty, blond youth everyone called 'Lucy' – who was transparently in love with Roland: a weakness Roland exploited

97

shamelessly. It was the first time Stefan and I had been included with Roland's smart professional friends and we both felt rather in awe of all the talk of 'Johnny' Gielgud, 'Tommy' Beecham and 'Old Henry' Wood.

It was gone midnight and much Champagne had been consumed when John and Naomi Abrahams took their leave, declining the invitation to Millwater. Luke lingered, happy to be included, and secured himself the front seat in the Austin, next to Roland. Roland had the roof down even though the night air was sharp, and we drove twice round Trafalgar Square singing Gilbert and Sullivan at the top of our voices before heading south over Westminster Bridge. In the dickie-seat at the back, I snuggled close to Stefan, his coat over my shoulders, shivering with a combination of Champagne, cold and excitement. Roland was declaiming chunks of The Merchant in stentorian tones as I fell asleep. "'On such a night stood Dido with a willow in her hand…'"

I woke as the car pulled up at Millwater. The house was in darkness; Stefan slept beside me, his head now resting on my shoulder, but Roland was still wide awake, eyes blazing, and the stream of quotations appeared to have continued unabated the entire journey. We sat round the deal table in the kitchen, warming ourselves at the Aga while Roland brewed coffee and served it heavily laced with brandy 'to keep out the cold'. Stefan's eyes grew heavy again and his fair head slid down upon the table, but I was now into a heated argument with Roland about how much Shakespeare really understood music. Luke just listened, mute adoring eyes fixed on Roland.

About 2am we all helped Stefan up to bed in the room under the eaves next to mine, where we usually slept. Roland went to find a room for Luke. "Don't go to bed yet," he said to me under his breath, pulling a face, "I think I need a chaperone." I went with him to sort out clean sheets and towels from the airing cupboard. We made Luke comfortable, then bidding him goodnight, Roland drew me from the room and shut the door.

If I close my eyes I can still recall the sensation of being next to him in the dark on the stairs. I didn't need to see to be aware of his presence. I could hear him breathing, smell his distinctive smell, feel the warmth emanating from his body, though we did not touch. Then his hand brushed my hair lightly. The smell of tobacco got stronger, and I felt the rough touch of his clipped beard on my face. His lips met mine: warm, dry and closed: firm pressure, matched by his hand behind my head. My body was drawn into the kiss, into the intoxicating danger and commitment of the act, but my mind raced ahead to the sequel. Would he, like some dream lover, press my lips and leave me, wondering what it was I had anticipated and desired? Would he make love to me there and then, with the same dominant irresistibility that drew performances out of us in music, whirling me round and round into an apotheosis of sexual fulfilment? Would he hesitate on discovering my virgin status, find me wanting in experience and leave me like some neglected morsel on a gourmet's plate, untasted?

Strange that I can still recall my virginal, 18-year-old uncertainty and anticipation so vividly, now that sex has become a practical affair more concerned with available beds, preferred positions, adequate erections and successful orgasms; something more like a game of tennis or contract bridge: an entertainment for mixed doubles practised over years with the goal of physical satisfaction. Perhaps even now, whenever lips meet for the first time there is some echo of that first, great wonder at the prospect of blending bodies, and desires in this familiar, yet ever surprising ritual?

He led me downstairs to the drawing room where the dying embers in the hearth took the chill from the room, and stood me where the glow from the fire fell upon our faces and warmed our bodies. Very slowly he removed my clothes, never taking his eyes from my face. I shivered, willingly spellbound. His large, gentle hands were dry and slightly rough; they moved lightly over my shoulders, ribs, down to my hips and thighs, as though he were memorising my body to model it in clay. When finally he cupped my breasts I had waited for the touch so long I felt faint and closed my eyes.

I was lying on one of the cushion-covered divans, eyes still closed, feeling part virgin sacrifice, part amateur performer offered an unfamiliar instrument, and Roland was kneeling at my side kissing me all over. The sensation of his beard and soft, dry lips was unimaginably erotic: roughness and gentleness seductively combined. He didn't part my thighs or touch me where I was as yet untouched, and gradually I relaxed, less fearful of the unlearned part I was expected to play.

99

*The dying fire flared up and I opened the corner of my eye to see the massive shape of his naked torso silhouetted against the light. Something soft and caressing was pulled over me, and I slept.*

*The trees grew close to the house at Millwater. Even when the windows were closed you could hear the herald bird sing at first light. I woke just before dawn to the sound of the reveille and listened, through the silence that followed, until the word was passed on and the dawn chorus started up in earnest. My eyes became accustomed to the faint light and I made out Roland, naked beside me on the divan, covered by his great fur-lined car coat. His left arm encircled me and the vast dome of his hairy chest rose and sank beside me.*

*He stirred and I closed my eyes. He began to stroke my shoulder and his breathing became shorter. He moved and I was aware of the hard, hot pressure of something between us. He lifted his hand to his mouth, wetted his fingers, and lowered them to between my legs.*

*Was this it then? In my simulated sleep, I became pliant. His wet fingers probed me, gentle but insistent, and pleasant sensations prickled all over me but I never moved. Then he heaved himself up above me and I felt his body between my thighs, pressing them apart. I drew all sensations inside me and willed it to be painless.*

*A soft nuzzling like a puppy's nose; an invading intimacy, stretching, occupying, brief hurt and then – we melted into one another. He was in me. I was his. He played me like his violin. Involuntarily, I cried out.*

They stood alone on the pavement outside Ros's flat. The remaining musicians waved and gesticulated wildly through the rear window as the minibus pulled away. It was suddenly chill and real life after the other-worldly enchantment of the Clanfield gardens. Jonathan felt embarrassed for the undignified impulsiveness which had landed him, dinner-jacketed and car-less on Ros's doorstep at 1.00am without definite assurance that she returned his feelings. The company of her contemporaries had made him feel incongruous and now she looked even younger, dressed in the student uniform of boots, leggings and battered sweater. He started to say "Sorry", but then in a fit of resurgent candour, said, "I'm not sorry."

"Whatever for, dickhead?" she replied, bending to pick up the tote bag at her feet. Her bottom turned towards him did disturbing things to the pit of his stomach, but he refrained from touching her. She straightened up and put an arm round his waist and moved him towards the steps.

"I suppose I'd better call a taxi," he said unconvincingly.

"I'd rather bonk," she said, her eyes sparkling, "Singing always makes me frightfully randy."

She turned away and put her key in the lock. He thought he must have misheard her.

"'It is too rash, too unadvised, too sudden/ Too like the lightning, which doth cease to be/'Ere one can say it lightens,'" he babbled incoherently quoting Juliet in the balcony scene.

"Oh bollocks!" she looked back at him. "It's chemistry. You're probably as old as my dad, but sometimes it happens that way. I fancy you. I hope you've got a condom."

He climbed the stairs behind her delectable bottom, stunned and enchanted by her directness.

The flat was dark and cold. Jonathan found himself in a small room with a small bed, inhabited principally by books. A bedside lamp made from a Chianti bottle threw fitful light on disorder.

Ros dumped her bag on the floor and switched on a small fan heater. She turned towards him, put her arms round his waist and raised her nose to rub it gently against the stubble on his chin. He felt sick with desire and the dread of being a failure. Her hands reached behind him, undid the beastly cummerbund and eased the shirt from inside his trousers. Fingers crept up his back and grasped the flesh under his arms. Jonathan closed his eyes and concentrated upon the sensations inside him, particularly the throbbing pulse beating in his throat. Her head nuzzled into his throat and she grasped the hired bow tie with her teeth and pulled. The elastic stretched, and then snapped back against his neck, making him yelp in pain.

Ros collapsed in giggles and fell backwards onto the bed pulling him after her. For minutes they just lay there laughing, then he said, "I fear I can't supply good references as a lover."

She looked at him sideways; lashes shadowed her cheek and echoed the line of high cheekbones sweeping down towards the fullness of her lips.

"Didn't know I had advertised a vacancy."

She turned on her side and began to unbutton his shirt leaving the absurd bow tie around his neck. Jonathan was glad he was on his back: his stomach felt flatter. Now she had undone his fly and was insinuating her hand inside his underpants. Just looking at her made him feel so giddy he closed his eyes and concentrated on tactile sensations. His cock leapt to her touch and warmth infused him. The tension that had been gathering ever since he first glimpsed her in the Music Room at Clanfield, concentrated itself in his penis. It felt so hard he thought it would have burst. He turned, his arms surrounding her and groped blindly for her mouth. Her hand fell still as his tongue explored the cavity, running along the sharp edge of her teeth to the soft skin lining her cheek and skirmishing with the tense tip of her own tongue as it came thrusting to meet him.

She pulled away and he opened his eyes to see her dropping her clothes at her feet. There was no coquetry in her undressing, just the urgency of lust, yet the fleeting glimpse of her plain Marks and Spencer underwear had a more potent effect than all the erotic French satin and lace Fiona trailed before him: briefs cut high in the leg to reveal the hollow in her slim flanks, and a slip of vest which offered slight support where none was needed for her small, mounded breasts.

He marvelled at the vertical lines of her youthful body. Age emphasised horizontal divisions: the bulges and sagging folds of increased fat and collapsing muscle. Youth was taught and upright, strung tight across the frame of bone. The slight swelling of her breasts hardly broke the clean sweep of her torso, but long shadows ran down her trunk and marked the muscles of her groin and thighs. Even when she bent to remove her briefs, hardly a crease appeared. She stood momentarily, slim, white and unmarked save for the dark smudges of her nipples and bush, then she fell upon him, winding her limbs round him and tearing at his remaining clothes.

Jonathan put his hands over his eyes. He sank into a deep whirlpool of emotion. His last few garments were whisked away and her body clung to him like a baby Koala, the touch of her skin cool down the length of his body, her mouth nibbling the skin in the crook of his neck. Jonathan was suspended in a limbo between desire and doubt of his ability to consummate it. He reached blindly on the floor for his trousers, desperate to retrieve a condom. Their bodies were side by side, but as he struggled to unwrap and put the bloody thing on, he realised that Ros's had relaxed, and her breathing was deeper and more regular. He held his breath and gradually came down from the heights. He opened his eyes. A lock of her hair lay against his face, translucent gold as the bedside light shone through it. He extended his free arm and groped on the floor for the duvet to pull it up and over them. He reached out again and felt his way to the switch on the bedside light without disturbing her. As he slid into sleep he realised he still had an erection.

Bright light shone through an unfamiliar, uncurtained window. Ros lay curled up asleep in the foetal position, the duvet shrugged off and her arm shielding her eyes. "She's so Goddam smooth," he thought. "Like silk." He couldn't see her face but blond hair lay over her outstretched arm. Below the curve of her armpit, the soft mound of a small breast with a blunt, coffee-coloured nipple. His hand ventured forth and began to explore her beauty.

Sex is supposed to be simple, but because it usually involves another person, gets confused with expectation, power, dominance and a craving for approval. Just occasionally love, lust and acceptance come together and the act rediscovers its simplicity.

Jonathan's erection stood for his love and desire for Ros. "Actually, it's stood pretty well to attention all night long, which could account for why I'm awake so early," he thought. It had recently become an unreliable sex aid, and in its absence he had learned to conjure desire with his hands. Now, as they explored the curves, hollows and moist crevices of Ros's body, they worked their magic as accomplished transmitters of desire.

She stirred and arched her back with pleasure, murmuring something incomprehensible. Jonathan felt that the time was ripe to put his new found potency to the test. He turned the woman he loved on her back and entered her urgently in the fullness of his lust. Her legs came alive and locked round his hips. Her slim flanks rose and clung to him as he thrust into her. He held back and waited until her body became rigid, her blue eyes opened briefly, and her lips uttered a choked sigh, and then he collapsed, burying his face in her throat in the ecstasy of orgasm.

"Christ," he murmured, before sliding into unconsciousness, "There's no substitute for old fashioned love, is there?"

# CHAPTER 12

In the weeks following the Clanfield House concert the pace of life accelerated for Jonathan. Roland Fredricks occupied his working day, and Ros his leisure. He threw himself into both with an emotional and physical energy he'd thought was no longer at his bidding.

That first Sunday they had stayed in bed all day, fuelled only by tinned soup and Ryvita. Jonathan's obsession with Ros's youth, and his anxiety that he would be found inadequate or ridiculous, began to abate with the joyous discovery that, not only was he able to keep it up, but that she wanted him to! Her hunger and her responsiveness were a revelation.

Jonathan loved women's bodies. It could be a dangerous appetite; but the pleasure he felt in contemplation and caressing, was not selfish. As his hands explored Ros's muscular back, her long limbs, small breasts and narrow flanks, she came alive under his fingers. She didn't say much; compared with his urge to express love verbally, she was a wordless lover. But she was not silent. As her body writhed and clung to his hands, a succession of gasps, moans, sighs and chuckles broke from her parted lips. Once, after a disconcertingly noisy orgasm, she actually burst out singing.

"Who needs words?" he thought to himself, "Words are for reassurance; for trying to capture what is essentially elusive and non-verbal." And, taking his cue from her, he put his mind into neutral and concentrated in the tactual, bodily present.

When they put on their clothes and went back into the real world, his insecurity returned temporarily. The first 12 hours they were apart he was in agony in case, when they met again, she had changed. His relief when he heard her voice on the phone, and realised that she was expecting him, that she had adopted him as a item in her life as wordlessly as she had accepted his love-making, was so great, tears sprang to his eyes.

In addition to their hours in bed, they began to develop a social life together. He shared the problems and excitements of his work on the biography with her, and she was a keen and critical listener. Jonathan had succeeded in tracking down new material on the composer's early life. A meticulous school librarian had unearthed some ancient school magazines containing articles and verse written by Roland. The library at the Royal Academy had records of his achievements as an award winner and later professor, including some of his early work as composer and arranger. They also tracked down addresses for a couple of his successful ex-students, albeit in Germany and the US. The Kent nursing home where Roland's mother, Flora, had died in 1947 thought they might be able to trace a family doctor, although it seemed unlikely that he would still be alive. He managed to wheedle his way into the cuttings library at the *Daily Telegraph* where her traced faded old clips and pictures of Roland's connections with significant contemporaries. He had apparently collaborated with Constant Lambert on one of his later ballets (they had been photographed with Lambert's mistress, the prima ballerina Margot Fonteyn), and the composer and music journalist Peter Warlock (pseudonym for Philip Heseltine) had been his near neighbour at Millwater, and had published a profile of Roland in the magazine *The Sackbut*. Roland had joined the Artists' International Association along with painters like Duncan Grant and Augustus John, and had organised concerts to raise funds in support of the Republican side at the time of the Spanish Civil War. However, the key final years of his life, 1938-41: the time of his major musical output, the possible creation of a second, unpublished opera, and the circumstances surrounding his death, remained shrouded in mystery. For these Jonathan pinned his hopes on Anna, from whom there was still no word.

"Don't rely too much on her. Granna can be infuriatingly uncooperative," Ros warned him. "Develop your own interpretation of his final years, from what you piece together from his youth."

Her confidence and directness enchanted him, and he thought, "What can have given me the idea that young girls were all obsessed with their physical imperfections and finding a husband?"

"Where did you discover your inner certainty?" he asked.

She shrugged and smiled. "I didn't know I had it. Guys usually say that I'm bossy."

Recalling his own youth, Jonathan wondered if he had sought out women to bolster his fragile ego and been intimidated by uncompromising women. Was that the reason he had felt so threatened by Helena's successful career? Ros was equally uncompromising when it came to travelling in a car with him when he had been drinking.

"I don't care how well you drive when pissed. You drive worse than when sober. We'll walk."

"We'll take a taxi."

"I can't afford taxis."

"But I can."

"I'm not a kept woman. I pay my way or we don't do things."

And so he borrowed his elder son Jeremy's bike.

"What on earth do you want his bike for?" said Helena, twigging instantly that something exceptional was afoot. "You're too heavy; you'll bust it."

"I won't; and it'll do me good. I need to get fit."

"You can say that again."

"And anyway I paid for it. He doesn't need it in term time."

Helena's quizzical look implied that she was not deceived by his new-found enthusiasm for physical exercise. He progressed unsteadily up the street the bike creaking in protest.

"Who is she?" her voice called after him.

Jonathan swerved drunkenly, narrowly missed a parked car, and steadied himself with a hand on the roof. It was the signal for a neighbourhood terrier with an exaggerated idea of its caretaking responsibilities, to identify him as a burglar and tear out of a nearby gate yapping manically at his ankles. Jonathan fielded its bared fangs with clumsy footwork. He turned and saw Helena coming after him barely able to suppress her laughter. With the best semblance of dignity he could muster he replied;

"Whatever makes you think there's a 'she' involved?"

"Past experience, that's all," she replied, smiling at him. "Here, you'd better take these, before you catch your trousers in the chain." And she snapped a pair of cycle clips round his wrist and turned back towards the house, shaking her head.

Ros and Jonathan cycled together: west to Wandsworth Common and along the Thames to Kew; north to the South Bank and East to Greenwich and Blackheath. By sticking to the river basin they avoided hills too taxing for Jonathan's flabby thigh and heart muscles. They visited pubs, fringe theatres, historic houses and concerts and brought home the occasional take-away.

They made an incongruous pair: Ros on her sturdy mountain bike, Jonathan, large and precarious on the slender, dropped handlebars racer. To begin with he had no suitable gear, but under her guidance he bought some practical denims and a pair of trainers. At the end of their excursions she usually allowed him to buy the first round, and since she rarely drank more than half a pint, the expenditure was small and soon Jonathan felt a lush if he wanted more.

One Sunday early in May they cycled the tow path, skirting the boundary of Kew Gardens, along Syon Reach to the Isleworth ferry. It had been raining, and Ros skimmed nimbly in and out of the puddles sometimes lifting her front wheel or mounting the inside bank to avoid splashing passers-by. Green shoots dusted the hedgerows and across the Thames, Syon House looked as pink and impractically ornate as a wedding cake on the green baize of Capability Brown's landscaped lawns.

Some distance to her rear, skidding and swerving in a shaky zigzag, panted

Jonathan. He attempted no agile wheelmanship, but man and machine were no longer at cross-purposes, as they had been a few weeks ago. On one or two occasions he had to put his foot down in a hurry and failed to avoid a puddle, the evidence of which could be seen up the back of his jeans, but he had stopped falling off. The sunshine was hot on the back of his neck, and he was aware of the singing of birds and the smell of wet grass. The sight of Ros's tight, muscular rump bouncing up and down on the saddle ahead of him set his penis tingling at the recollection of recent delights. On the surface he was sweaty and flustered, but inside he was full of the joys of spring.

They made a leisurely crossing of the Thames on the foot ferry, watched by the drinkers leaning idly on the wall outside the London Apprentice pub. Sunlight glinted through liquid in glass, inspiring a powerful thirst in Jonathan, and he left Ros chaining up the bikes while he joined the crush at the bar. When he returned he found her part of a small crowd gathered round a gleaming red BMW K75 motor bike.

"Isn't it brilliant?" she said in the sort of voice usually reserved for a Caribbean sunset or the Rose window at Chartres cathedral. "It makes me damp just to look at it."

Jonathan handed her a half pint and buried his nose in his beer, unable to think of a suitable reply. The glories of the internal combustion engine left him cold.

A pair of leather-clad shoulders interposed themselves between him and Ros and a husky voice said, "Fancy a spin on the South Circular, darlin'; feel my throbbing monster between your thighs?" Ros turned to find herself cheek by jowl with the designer stubble of Zak, friend to her Aunt Kate.

"It's yours?"

"Mine and the bank's. 'Jewanna ride?"

"He has to show off his big, shiny, red phallic symbol."

Kate sat perched on the wall a few feet away, a glass in her hand. Her long, thin legs, cased in thigh length suede boots, lay along the parapet and the collar of her Aztec-patterned sweater was turned up against the breeze off the river.

"I refuse to subscribe to the 'Yobo Yoof' culture," she continued. "I bring my own wheels on these occasions. Do you want another drink?"

Jonathan drained his glass swiftly and accepted. Ros kissed her aunt, but declined. She still looked longingly at the bike. With anyone other than Zak she would have accepted a ride with alacrity. Kate put her empty glass into Zak's hand.

"*You* would be wise to pass on this round. The fuzz can't miss you on your noisy metal penis. I'll have another half of bitter, and whatever Ros's friend is drinking. We've met before, haven't we?" she said, looking at Jonathan with narrowed eyes.

"Jonathan Burroughs: Sunday lunch at your brother Hugo's last March," he introduced himself with reference to Hugo rather than Carole as his host, but his presence with their daughter was not lost on Kate. Without moving her head, her eyes swept from him to Ros dancing with malicious humour.

"So what?" thought Jonathan defensively. "Age gaps obviously don't worry Kate."

"I see you don't share my disinclination to share the young's taste in transport, Jonathan?"

The gentle mockery could have been Anna's, but the feeling was not entirely friendly.

"My mother seems to have gone into mourning since the election," Kate continued, addressing Ros. "Is it metaphorical sackcloth and ashes, or is her health keeping her out of circulation?" She turned to Jonathan, offering an explanation, "My mother had a high level investigation of her kidneys some time ago and she's told no one about the results." She turned again to her niece. "I thought perhaps you knew something. You and she are such buddies."

Jonathan picked up the dig. "Is Kate jealous of the friendship between Anna and Ros because it's warmer than between mother and daughter?" he wondered. Looking more closely at Ros, he thought he detected discomfort, or impatience. He sprang to her defence.

"Actually we have seen her a couple of times. She seemed all right. No mention of her health; nor of the election results." He blushed, hoping that Ros didn't mind his use of the joint 'we' in front of her aunt. But Ros continued to look preoccupied. "I rang her once last week; the answerphone was on. I'd meant to go round and climb in but…"

Zak returned carrying three drinks that included what appeared to be a large Bloody Mary for himself.

"Tomato juice," he said, staring at Kate unflinchingly.

"My eye! But it's your funeral if you lose your licence and have to travel by tube!"

They rode back towards Clapham in silence, Ros refusing to be drawn by Jonathan's inquiries about Kate. Just before they turned to cross Hammersmith Bridge she stopped and rested her foot on the kerb.

"What's the problem?" he asked, pulling up ahead of her.

She paused before replying.

"Do you think you could you make it as far as Holland Park?" she said, "I want to see Granna."

It was beginning to get dark by the time they reached Anna's house. No lights were visible from the street. They rang the bell, aware that such orthodox modes of contact were often ineffective with Anna. They could hear the bell ringing somewhere inside the house. Otherwise there was neither audible nor visible sign of life.

"Could she be away?" he asked, infected by her concern.

Ros gnawed her lower lip. "I wonder if I ought to climb in?" Jonathan was surprised at the suggestion. "Don't worry; it's an old family tradition."

They went round to the side of the house to where the dustbins provided Ros with her customary entry point, but as she put her foot onto a lid preparatory to hauling herself up, a light was switched on in a room upstairs and water started to flow in the waste pipes running down the side of the house.

"She's in," said Ros, standing on the ground again. She shouted, "Granna, it's me, Ros. Come down and let us in!" She waited. The water continued to run and no reply came. The water stopped, and in the silence that followed, Ros called again, her words carrying audibly. Seconds later, the lighted bathroom window, which had been open a crack at the bottom, was slammed shut. A moment later, the light went out.

"Damn, damn, damn! Why must she be so obstinate?" Ros stamped her foot. "I'm bloody going in."

Jonathan took her arm.

"Slow down a minute. Isn't there some other way? Why don't we go round to the front and leave a note. Tell her to get in touch because everyone's worried. Pile it on if you like, but let her make the first contact. She's not senile, and she's quite evidently still alive. Maybe her friend is with her: whatsisname – Bill. She must have heard you. Let it be her choice whether or not to let you in."

And that was what they did: telling Anna that if she didn't get in touch, Ros would be back and coming in to get her.

Anna sat at the top of the stairs, her head tilted back and a blood-soaked towel clamped under her nose. She heard their footsteps in the porch and the sound of the letterbox snapping shut as the note was posted through, and still she sat in the gathering darkness feeling the trickle of the blood at the back of her throat; its metallic taste on her tongue. After some minutes she lay back on the landing carpet to rest her neck. She closed her eyes and sniffed, clearing the passages between nose and throat, gently and then with increasing confidence. The nosebleed had stopped.

Her eyes opened; she could just see the top of the Grandfather clock on the landing. It was slow and struck 12 every hour. The sepulchral note of its tick reassured her. Life continued, albeit slow and inaccurate. She tried to calculate the pitch and interval of the tick: a fourth, or maybe a diminished fifth? She had never had perfect pitch. Stefan had. She remembered him swearing about some madrigal group: "How can you bear it: they are at least a semitone flat!" It had passed through Hugo to Ros. She had been able to sing the *Ode to Joy* from Beethoven's Ninth symphony, perfectly pitched, at the age of five. It was in the genes: a gift. It didn't make you a better musician.

She moved her head slightly and now she could see, very foreshortened the portraits of Stefan's grandfather and grandmother that they had brought back from Poland after the war. His father Andrzej's portrait was in the sitting room. Stefan had been proud of those family portraits: his roots, he had called them. Poor Stefan, he never really belonged anywhere. He'd wanted to put down new roots with her and the children, and it had all been spoiled.

She sat up, feeling cold. She pushed up her leggings and peered at her ankles, then pressed her thumb firmly into the flesh. The imprint levelled out gradually. If her kidneys weren't clearing the fluid from her body the indent lingered. The leggings allowed her to check her fluid retention easily. It was an aspect of kidney illness she hated: puffy ankles. She had always been so proud of her legs, and the slightest sign of swelling now prompted her to put her feet up instantly, however inconvenient or incongruous: sitting at the computer or riding in a taxi. The drugs they had prescribed were supposed to help, but it wasn't noticeable.

She stood up and went slowly downstairs to the hall. The folded white paper was just visible in the darkness. She picked it up, opening it as she climbed the stairs again. She couldn't see to read but she had a fair idea of what it said. The only thing that had surprised her was that Ros hadn't climbed in when she had refused to open the door. Perhaps she had not been alone?

Light spilt into the corridor from the studio stairs. The whoosh of the computer fan summoned her from the room above, but before she could continue the climb she had to pause and get her breath. She registered laboured breathing, tramping pulse, aching muscles and sinews. The physical systems were functioning, but under protest. This was old age; this, and the swollen ankles, the bleeding nose, was death approaching.

The sands trickling through the hourglass had a small dent in them, like the thumbprint in her flesh: an indent that would not go away.

# CHAPTER 13

*Paola Pignatelli returned to Millwater in late spring. She must have been in her 30s at the time: on the threshold of her international career. She had started her career in the smaller Italian opera houses, but she also sang well in French and English, and I had seen her do a fiery* Carmen *at Sadler's Wells in London. I believe she had also sung it in a studio production on television: but it was all very amateurish in those days and hardly anyone saw it. In 1938 her Covent Garden debut was imminent.*

*I heard Pignatelli even before I actually saw her. There was a fashion for high, platform-soled sandals at the time, and I can still recall the noise of Paola's shoes as they clopped on the Millwater floorboards like horses' hooves, accompanied by the scuffing claws of the fat spaniel that plodded at her heels. These sounds, added to the throaty exhaust of her Alfa Supersport (the same as Gary Cooper's) scattering the gravel of the drive, and her vibrant tones, limbering up in the music room every morning, announced the diva's return.*

*When Paola was in residence at Millwater, the volume was turned up, the tempo became* molto agitato. *She shouted at the dog; a neurotic bitch called* Ferrier *(after the rival British mezzo, Kathleen Ferrier) who was unceremoniously dumped on the singer's agent whenever she left England; at the girl who came in from the village to 'do'; at visiting students, and the Fredricks women, all of whom, except the dog, scurried about fetching drinks, bags, books, wraps and medicine bottles as though she were the Queen of Sheba and Millwater her court. Above all she shouted at Roland; though this verb is too colourless to convey the* full complexion of her utterance: she commanded, she cajoled, she conjured and she cooed. He, by contrast was subdued in Pignatelli's presence. In public they performed a courtly and flirtatious dance; a blend of professional flattery and implied, behind-the-scenes intimacy. Arrogant in my own sexual involvement with Roland, I found the relationship unconvincing.

"How in Heaven's name did their liaison come about?" I enquired of Stefan.

"She says he will write the great role for her; and what La Pignatelli wants, she usually gets," he replied. "She eats six like him before breakfast.

Publicly nothing of my liaison with Roland was acknowledged, and at times I thought I must have dreamed the night I slept in his arms in front of the fire. Then, in a rare moments of privacy, he would explode upon me, crushing me in a bear hug, grasping my breasts or buttocks in his huge hands and almost lifting me from the floor, devouring my mouth or burying his face in my hair and his passionate words in my ears.

I was too inexperienced to know how to respond to these onslaughts. I had no knowledge of how to dissemble with men; to tease or flirt, pretending that nothing was serious. I feared the naked adoration in my eyes would betray me, and I was disturbed by these sudden, arousing embraces that were as quickly ruptured, leaving me confused and emotionally exposed.

Despite, or maybe because of my involvement with Roland, my friendship with Stefan survived. He was like the branch you cling to when negotiating a roaring torrent: familiar and safe. Nevertheless, I feared his jealousy should he discover our affair. I knew he suspected my attachment to Roland: the common devotion of almost every student at Millwater. But now, with growing resentment, he recognised that my feelings were reciprocated, putting me apart from the others. He stuck to my side and urged me, as he had not done before, to let him stay the night. He checked the times I went to Millwater, or the occasions I might meet Roland at the Academy or in town.

In fact Roland and I had few opportunities for intimacy. Once, he took me to lunch at a small French restaurant in Soho; another time he called me into his room to sing some music he was drafting. We had no collegiate reason to meet. He was not my professor. The coaching I received at Millwater was extracurricular. Meeting on the pavement in Marylebone Road, we conversed lightly on general topics, and suddenly his hand was inside my coat and under the waistband of my skirt, his palm grasped the curve of my belly and the fingers reaching down into my groin.

"If I don't get inside you again soon Anna, I think I shall explode with longing," he said in a husky, intense voice no passer-by could hear. I felt the now familiar contraction in the pit of my stomach, the dry mouth and the tightness of the throat, and looked back at him in helpless longing. The secret, forbidden nature of my love added to its potency.

These days our affair would be regarded as a standard association between an older man in a loveless marriage and a hero worshipping girl: the routine overture to a second marriage. But in 1938 it was not the cliché it is today. The flower children of the 1960s thought that they invented free-range, guilt-free sex and open marriage. But in fact, there were quite a few unconventional relationships in artistic and intellectual circles in the years between the Wars – like the Bloomsbury Group and Charleston Farmhouse set. I soon noticed that fidelity was not highly rated among the Millwater set. Strong feelings, especially jealousy or possessiveness, were regarded as dreary and bourgeois. Married couples went out with, sometimes slept with, occasionally swapped with, other partners, and would have died sooner than object to a spouse's provocative behaviour. It was after all, the smart thing to do.

"My dear, guess whom we bumped into last night at dinner! My husband, dining with his wife! Such a scream; we nearly died."

I was not born to such louche morality. My small town upbringing staunchly upheld the Christian convention of chastity outside marriage. That I felt so little guilt about my involvement with Roland had to be attributed more to my intuitive absorption of Millwater mores, than to a predisposition to flaunt public norms.

If Paola was Roland's mistress – and there were those who suggested that the whole thing was just a charade – Helga and Gudrun showed no trace of resentment. Quite the contrary; when the singer was in residence they became noticeably more confident and less wretched. In fact, the three presented an almost sinister united front to the rest of the Millwater côterie. Subsequent events supported my intuitive perception that Paola's return had focused the power nexus of the Fredricks women. It was a triumvirate I had small reason to trust.

"Guardala – *so pretty, the little one!*"

*La Pignatelli's English was excellent; she affected the flourish of Italian, like make-up, to emphasise her essential character. She was untypically* andante tranquillo *that first time I was presented to her. Only later did I learn to mark the occasions when the acrid, herbal smell hung in the air, and the thin, handmade cigarette in a gold holder, dangled from her fingers.*

*Gold and ivory bracelets clinked as she raised her arms to greet me. She reclined with her feet upon a divan piled with cushions, her creamy shoulders – a feature of which she was justifiably proud – draped in a deep fringed, Spanish shawl, splashed with vivid orange flowers. Her auburn hair was swept up and piled forward under some exotically patterned turban, emphasising the strong line of her jaw. Bright green shadow overlaid the protuberant, dark brown eyes, and her mouth was painted scarlet, with a pair of points like quotation marks in the middle of the upper lip. She was more striking than beautiful. In the recumbent position, the proud carriage of her head and her magnificent shoulders made her appear statuesque. Standing – despite the platform soles – she was scarcely taller than me and at least three stone heavier. It was a comparison she was at pains to avoid.*

*The odalisque character of her pose and attire was emphasised by the Fredricks women in attendance. Helga, on a low stool, head bent low over Paola's hand, had been enamelling the singer's nails a vivid, ruby red at those moments when she could capture their wandering attention. The hands were variously engaged in ferrying cigarette or drink – the port and lemon so beloved of singers – to Paola's lips, or in delivering extravagant sweeps of a pearl backed brush to Gudrun's long golden tresses where she sat, leaning against the divan, on a cushion on the floor.*

*At the sight of me, Paola transferred the cigarette to a brass ashtray, and extended her arms in greeting. Her sleeves fell back, baring dimpled elbows. The diva was all generosity and heart that afternoon. "Vieni, vieni, bambina!" She beckoned me forward.*

117

I approached reluctantly, holding the small bunch of wild flowers I had brought as a tribute. Was I expected to sink myself into this invited embrace? With some resourcefulness, I took her hand, kissed it gagging momentarily on the acetone fumes, and murmured, "Signora."

Without relinquishing my hand, she drew me towards her, acknowledging the flowers with a gracious inclination of the head as Helga relieved me of them and laid them on the table.

"So this is our new source of inspiration; the voice pure as a nightingale's?" She looked at me under heavy lids. Was she teasing, or trying to placate me? I had no reason to mistrust her, but I had learned enough of my position at Millwater not to expect it to win me friends. "So, what will you sing for us, carina?" She was still holding onto my hand firmly with plump fingers, heavy with rings.

I had no wish to sing for her, especially not in that company, and made some feeble excuse. The singer raised her hand in a signal that brooked no refusal; again the bracelets jangled. Her voice was imperious.

"But yes, I insist you sing for us. Roland tells us your voice has enchantment. I must hear for myself."

Miserably I protested, to no avail. Helga was at the piano. She was a leaden accompanist and, seeing I was trapped, I elected to sing alone; one of Roland's beloved folk-songs.

Pignatelli lay back among her pillows and drew upon her cigarette, surveying me with half lowered lids. My voice was thin and breathy: the first few notes were badly placed and I stopped to clear my throat and begin again. The song sounded childish and unsophisticated. I ran out of breath before the end of a phrase and my voice trailed away. I had no confidence in the recital, wanting only to get the painful performance over and escape from this disconcerting trio. Three pairs of eyes regarded me coldly – rather like cats.

"Is that it? È finita?" said Paola in the silence that followed my last faltering note. "Buono, a good attempt. Now sing us music by a great composer. What shall it be? Schubert, Mozart, what would you like?"

What I would have liked was to sink through the floor and have done with *this cruel charade. But Helga was still at the keyboard and opened some music at one of Cherubino songs from* The Marriage of Figaro – 'Non so *più,'. She launched into it at such a furious pace I was unable to keep up. Struggling to wrap my tongue round the Italian, my eyes brimming with tears of humiliation, I prayed for deliverance: prayed that Roland would come riding, like the cavalry, to my rescue. But he didn't. Roland, I was to learn, was no knight errant when the dragons to be challenged were female.*

*My pride held back my tears. Pignatelli was damning in her praise; condescending in her encouragement. As I was about to make my escape, my glance fell upon the flowers I had brought. They lay crushed upon the floor beside the table, their petals torn from their stems.*

*I had feared Paola's return, but not for the reasons that eventually made me dread her presence at Millwater. I had thought her established position in Roland's life, her fame, her vibrant voice and personality, would put my pale Anglo-Saxon flame in the shade. As immature 18-year-olds go, I was no shrinking violet, but in matters of the heart, not to mention musical competence, honesty had to pronounce me the diva's inferior.*

*However it was not as a rival for Roland's love that Paola's ascendancy expressed itself, so much as a focus of his subjugation. Under her influence the Fredricks women became not merely coldly hostile but actively rebellious and disruptive. Helga made snide comments that cut him down to size. "What do you know about fine wine? You've destroyed your palate with those filthy cigarettes and can't tell the difference between Beaujolais and cider!"*

*Gudrun's lessons were even more stormy, the child stamping her foot in imitation of her father or throwing her violin to the floor when his teaching became harrowing.*

*I had not previously heard carping comment on Roland's inadequacies: as breadwinner, father, lover, let alone musician. I did now. I learned that he had not won an award or competition since entering the Academy at 18. I learned that his early composition had been slated by the critics, and noticed that he became touchy and ill-tempered at the mention of Vaughan Williams, Walton,*

Constant Lambert or any contemporary British composer of note. His humour and clowning, which convulsed the rest of us, earned him a stony stare or withering rebuke. Most disconcerting of all, it was as if Paola's abundant physical vitality put his in question. I saw him embrace her with the same earthy grasp of the buttocks with which he had lifted me from the ground, only to have her respond with such devouring physical hunger that he drew back discomforted. With the students, her colour, her capacity to inspire and entertain, were as great as his but her generosity and warmth made him seem cruel, dictatorial and capricious by contrast. For the first time I noticed how rarely he praised. Beside her, he appeared meaner, smaller even, less vigorous and alive.

Paola first made me aware of his diabetes and his irritation of being reminded of it. She would check that he had injected his insulin, tested his urine for sugar and nag him about eating the right food at the right time. And he hated it. If, in defiance, he failed to balance his food intake and exercise to the insulin he had injected, and if, as a consequence his blood sugar fell, his women knew the signs – they were not unlike someone being drunk – and they would urge fruit juice, bananas, or some other form of sugar upon him. In the rare event that this early stage correction did not occur, then a hypoglycaemic coma could put him beyond the reach of anything by mouth. Then it was Paola who, scorning the need for doctors, injected the life-saving glucose solution needed to bring him round.

My first experience of a diabetic's 'hypo' was a vivid and distressing experience. Roland and a small group of us had spent Sunday on the river. We'd hired boats to picnic on an island downstream. Released from the watchful eye of his women, Roland was in his element, joking and clowning and leading us in song. He drank much, ate little, and on the return journey, upstream, insisted on proving what a lad he was by taking a turn at the oars. It might not have mattered if we hadn't run out of petrol coming home.

Not many petrol stations were open on a Sunday. Roland and one of the boys set off with a can to walk to the main road while the rest of us sat on the roadside finishing up what was left of the cider

On the drive back to Millwater, Roland seemed drunker than ever, and from where I sat in the back, I noticed a huge sweat stain spreading down his shirt. He parked in the drive and the others jumped out and started unloading the car or rushing to the lavatory. Roland stayed in his seat, in the midst of one of Macheath's songs from The Beggar's Opera – a part, he often said, that suited him because the technical demands were slight and there were lots of opportunities for slapping women's bottoms. His face was running with perspiration.

"Are you all right?" I asked anxiously. He rolled his eyes and leered at me.

"How about a quick roll in the hay, wench?" His speech was slurred and the vulgarity so blatant it repulsed me.

"Press her,
Caress her,
With blisses,
Her kisses…" he sang tunelessly, "Sorry, disgusting exhibition …slightly squiffy, missy." His words trailed away and his head lolled to one side. By now he was incoherent and incapable of sitting upright. He was deadly pale – dead looking. I overcame my distaste and reached out to touch his brow. It was not only wet but ice cold.

"Roland," I said, aghast, "You're ill, not drunk. Should I call a doctor?" He shook his head unsteadily and attempted to open his eyes, but his eyeballs had turned up and I saw only the empty whites. He tried to speak, but only a choking throat noise came.

"Cho… cho…clay…" it sounded. Then, more meaningfully, I recognised the word 'sugar', and it dawned on me that this was a manifestation of his diabetes. But why sugar? I had thought diabetics had to avoid sugar. He made a superhuman effort; his eyes righted themselves momentarily – pale blue and watery – a helpless pleading in them that pierced me like a dart.

"Need sugar…" I eventually understood, "Chocolate…" His eyes closed and an arm thrashed wildly as he slid sideways across the seat.

The remains of the picnic were in a paper bag under the dashboard. I fumbled feverishly: biscuit crumbs, boiled sweets, the screwed-up salt paper from a packet of crisps. Roland was now almost unconscious.

I rushed into the house, into the kitchen hunting frantically through the cupboards for anything sweet. I returned with a packet of chocolate biscuits and a bottle of green Chartreuse. Desperately I clambered into the front of the car and tried to cram biscuits into Roland's all but lifeless mouth. His limbs moved convulsively but he seemed unable to swallow. Crumbs stuck to his face and in his beard. I struggled to get him upright, and with his head resting uncertainly upon my shoulder, tipped the bottle of liqueur into his mouth. He coughed and choked, but most of it went down. Again I tipped. In horror, I recalled that Paola said alcohol was bad for diabetics.

As if in answer to my thoughts, the sound of a throaty exhaust could be heard in the drive. Paola was returning; help was at hand. With a scrunch of gravel, the Alfa-Romeo swung into the drive. Within seconds the Chartreuse bottle was firmly removed from my hand and I was displaced at Roland's side. Between them, Helga and Paola half carried, half dragged the almost unconscious diabetic across the drive and into the house. I followed, my relief at his rescue overcoming my agony at my own inadequacy.

Roland lay moaning faintly, eyes closed, on a couch. Paola had reappeared from upstairs carrying an array of medical implements. Swiftly and efficiently she assembled a hypodermic syringe and filled it from two glass phials. She rolled up Roland's sleeve, identified a vein in the crux of his elbow, cleaned the site with something from a small bottle, then, squeezing his upper arm tightly with her left hand to emphasise the vein, she sunk the needle in and slowly emptied the contents of the syringe.

To my amazement, within seconds of the injection, Roland began to revive. His eyes opened and he sat up and spoke as if nothing had happened.

"By Jupiter I'm hungry; I could eat an ox."

His women were unamazed. They busied themselves in fetching him food and drink to supplement the glucose in the injection. In quick succession he consumed two glasses of orange juice, a huge cheese sandwich and a jam doughnut. I watched from the sidelines, convinced that, without their medical acumen, Roland would have died.

That night I beat my pillow with my fists and wept in wretchedness. Roland had been helpless, perhaps dying, and I had been useless. I was dumb, inept because I was young. The older women knew what to do. They had saved Roland.

122

*He had never come to my little room under the eaves, divided by only a thin partition from where Stefan slept, but that night there was a soft tap on the door. When I opened it, he stood there fully dressed. He didn't speak but took my hand and led me downstairs, not to the drawing room with its memories of the first, the only time, we had made love, but through the French doors to the garden; down the path lined with lavender, where daffodils had been replaced by early roses, to the millpond, gentle now with small rain in early summer. For some minutes we just stood there holding hands, while he smoked a cigarette, quiet and attentive, as though he was listening for something. I was barefoot, wearing only a thin cotton nightie and shivered. Suddenly aware of me and the night chill, he stubbed out his cigarette and picked me up in his arms.*

*"Little flower, what am I thinking of! Look how you're dressed. You must be frozen. Forgive me; I wanted to be alone with you, and away from them. I wanted you to hear the nightingale. But it appears she is not singing tonight.*

*"We have to get away, little flower; away from Millwater, away from England and this 'monstrous regiment of women'; somewhere we can be together in honesty. I want to be with you, in you. Being unable to burns me up. It can't go on."*

*I lay still against his neck, the warmth of his body soaking into me, my frustration and sense of uselessness ebbing away. He walked a few steps and sat down on a stone bench overlooking the pond, resting me on his lap like a child.*

*"What would you say to coming to Venice with me, Anna? I go and play with some friends who put on Early Music concerts there each summer. If you could get away, we could be together, alone. Who knows, I might start to write again."*

*As we sat there, at last, distant and sweet, the nightingale began to sing.*

# CHAPTER 14

Ros was occupied by first year exams. Martial law had been declared, a strict curfew imposed, and basic essentials like food, drink, sleep and sex, rationed stringently. Her horizons were filled with Halsey and Hobsbawm, with poverty and state welfare; labour organisation and protest; women, domestication and the workplace. Her personal tenet – she who swots last, recalls most – which had pulled her narrowly through her school studies was about to be tested on the high seas of adult life.

Her time of trial coincided with an intensification of Jonathan's involvement with the Roland Fredricks biography. Their work places were not distant, and whenever he had been working in his office, Jonathan would drop by the college library and try and persuade her to come out for a beer or egg and chips at the café across the road. She rarely consented to take the time for a proper meal, and he had been banished from her bed until after the exams

Nothing had been said explicitly; it was just that a large part of her had withdrawn, engaged elsewhere. And for Jonathan, who was a sociable worker and would have liked to share his day-to-day problems and preoccupations with a sympathetic ear, the development was not welcome.

"Our ways of working are 180 degrees divergent," he thought gloomily, groping in his desk drawer for the packet of Silk Cut that had staged a furtive reappearance. "She puts off getting down to it but once submerged, works with obsessive single-mindedness, cut off from the outside world, needing no encouragement or relief. Whereas I work in fits and starts and need repeated reinforcement." He sucked gratefully at the mind-clarifying nicotine. "My concentration span appears to be between 50 and 90 minutes – depending on the nearness of feeding time. That's how long I go without some distracting thought of Ros's parted lips or thighs creeping into my mind. If not sex, it's a cool beer, a juicy steak or a fag: some form of oral gratification. Failing that I have to *talk* to someone!"

And since his office was a relatively solitary place offering little by way of professional support, his friends and associates were accustomed to being pestered with incessant phone calls.

The weather made it worse.

Late May and early June lived up to the reputation of exam time and the sun shone, nights were mild and girls' knees peeped out beneath long shorts or short skirts everywhere. Jonathan found himself regarding the youthful groups that clustered around the Piazza in Covent Garden, lolled on the grass under the trees in the City squares or crowded the pavement outside pubs and winebars, with a more than usually jaded eye. They made him feel, not merely old: they made him feel deprived – deprived of Ros.

"Bloody young behave as if they owned the city," he reflected, pushing Jeremy's bike between the jostling groups and feeling completely invisible. "They're so exclusive with their slim, tanned limbs, their laughter and togetherness. While my poor little visa to this enchanted land waxes pale indoors, pouring over Class, Economy and Society since Industrialisation."

Once, after spending somewhat longer in his local Covent Garden pub than intended, he'd made the mistake of taking a cab to Ros's flat and ringing the bell unannounced. After a long delay she appeared at the front door, feet bare, hair spiky, as it was when she had been running her fingers through it, and with that blinking non-recognition in her eyes that indicated her mind was elsewhere.

"Hi there you inky swot," he said, feeling intrusive, "Carry your library books? Pull you a cork? Massage your back?"

She'd repulsed his gentle efforts to linger over an embrace, refused the offer of the wine he'd brought, drunk a brief cup of coffee with him, one eye on the book open on her desk, and then politely she'd asked him to leave. He'd been sober enough to realise he was in the way. The back-of-the-cab anticipation of delighted surprise followed by a warm, sexy reunion had been miscalculated.

To be honest, he'd gone over there principally to talk about the book. His mind was so full of it these days that Roland Fredricks' friends and relations were almost as vivid as living people he met in his work.

"I would've liked to have told Ros about those poems of Roland's in the school magazine," he thought regretfully. "I wonder what she'd think of my theory about Flora's influence? Great stuff that old quack remembered – very revealing." He'd visited a few of the surviving people and places associated with Roland's early years, and was beginning to formulate a psychological dynamic that would resolve some of the inconsistencies in the personality of the composer. "I reckon he was an applause junkie deprived of a reliable fix," he expounded to old Rathbone, one afternoon, having failed miserably to pin down a more receptive audience. Rathbone's spectacles fell to the tip of his nose and he gaped at Jonathan, "Fredricks eh? They all said that man was on drugs."

"No, no. Praise: that's what he was hung up on. He was an infant prodigy on the violin, and to please his mother he had to go on winning cups. But once he grew up his talent was no longer so outstanding. His success on the sports field was stymied by becoming a diabetic, and although women appear to have dropped into his lap like ripe plums, it's my theory that he never satisfied them sexually. Diabetes ruins your erection they say."

"Dear me," Old Rathbone looked shocked, and returned with relief to revising the new edition of The History of Theosophism.

The following evening Jonathan dialled a series of increasingly obscure telephone numbers in search of someone with whom to share a new Fredricks research discovery. He was about to leave the office when a sudden thought brought him back to the phone once more, "Could I interest you in the intriguing case of the green ink footnotes?" he said when Helena answered.

For a moment there was silence; then she said, "I know; you're in a pub and there's nobody to talk to."

The level tone of her voice made it impossible to tell whether she was amused or annoyed at his calling.

"Haven't I always told you, that's the trouble with pubs?"

"Perhaps that's why you like them."

He decided that she was amused, not bored, and continued, without giving her time to cut him off, "Actually, I'm not in the pub; I'm still at the office, working. Two months ago, a dusty old don at some crumbling Cambridge college, sent me a manuscript outlining the fortunes of intellectuals who joined the Communist Party between the Wars: a thousand pages, of crabbed copperplate with *green ink footnotes*, and what do you think I found, buried therein? The key to Roland Fredricks' political awakening."

"Jonathan," she began, but he didn't let her prevaricate. Pressing home what he hoped was his advantage, he continued,

"Helena, you of all people, know me; I must show it to someone. Please can I come over? I promise I won't stay late."

There was a silence, during which he calculated that she could find no instantly available excuse for denying him. Then she said, "So what's become of your little friend with the bike?"

"Tell you when I see you," he said, and put down the receiver before she had time to think up an excuse to say 'No'.

Two hours later, pages of the lately despised academic treatise were spread all over Helena's kitchen table. The remains of the take-away Chinese meal Jonathan had brought were standing on the draining board, and Jonathan himself, wine glass in hand, was expatiating upon his serendipity, while fending off his son Simon's clamorous demands to play Trivial Pursuit. Helena, wrapped in a large white towelling dressing gown which Jonathan recognised as once his own, sipped coffee and made encouraging noises.

"Henceforth I am reformed," he declared, "I will read conscientiously every work – including legible manuscript – that comes across my desk. Do you realise it might have languished in a drawer unseen until the

Fredricks book was in print? If I hadn't reached for something to scribble a phone number on, I might never have noticed 'Kaminski' in the green footnotes. Apparently Andrzej Kaminski – Anna's Cummins' father-in-law, who was a rabid Marxist and lectured in political science or some such somewhere – knew Fredricks and persuaded him to write *March from the North*, dedicated to the Jarrow hunger marchers. Old Green-ink gives chapter and verse of meetings in the early 30s, and in '37, shortly before the work appeared, that tie in perfectly. And it also fits with what Anna's son Hugo said: the Kaminskis were the political firebrands. Fredricks was just swept along with the romance of protest and the tragedy of the unemployed.

"It seems so much more real when I tell someone about it. It's the same when I write it down," he said happily, throwing himself down in an easy chair close to her. "Unconnected fragments draw together into cohesive narrative because you're telling a story. That's what it is. When you think about it, real lives are a ragbag of incoherent events, words and unreported feelings. Just collecting them together reveals no internal logic unless you impose a theme."

He broke off, his hands wide, fingers spread, as though in the act of grasping a theme.

They were alone for a minute while Simon was upstairs hunting for the board game he had persuaded them to play.

"Don't dreams or aspirations give our lives some purpose?" asked Helena unhappily, her mind on his last words.

"I suppose they might, if the outside world knew what they were, or if we actually achieved them. As it is, I suspect most goals are invented, post hoc, to lend a spurious logic to the shambolic course of our accidental lives."

"That sounds bitter."

He looked at her, leaving, "I am," unspoken and thinking, "Does she imagine it is by design that I find myself in middle life, working for a tinpot publisher having buggered up my marriage?" Aloud he said, "So, how come I'm lucky enough not to find you engaged in the ceaseless social whirl tonight?"

It was the first personal note in their conversation. She countered without conceding his right to inquire on this subject.

"Where's the Lady of the Bicycles?"

"Taking her first year exams. No, don't say it," he continued anticipating her reaction, "I know she's too young. It was accidental, not on purpose – like I said."

Simon came back with Trivial Pursuit and Jonathan reverted to their previous topic of discussion.

"The field work on this biography has already paid off. Talking to different people clarifies my thinking. How do you feel about coming up to Cambridge with me, Simon, to interview this old buffer? While I'm there I shall try and make contact with Fredricks' daughter. I mustn't give up just because she's hostile. She can't really want to block the publication of anything he was working on, surely? If necessary I shall get in by telling her that Anna Cummins is going to talk."

"And will you publish Green-ink's history of Communist intellectuals?" asked Helena.

"Of course we will – after a little editing. I shall never turn down a serious piece of work out of hand again."

He filled his wine glass again and the torrent of his enthusiasm flowed unabated. He prowled about the room waving his arms, pounding the table and delivering vigorous bear hugs to his son by way of emphasis, the glass never long out of his hand, while his free hand returned absent-mindedly to the biscuit barrel whenever he passed. It was a manifestation of Jonathan Working that, had he stopped to reflect, had been long absent. His ex-wife recognised it. It was the Jonathan of 15 years ago, when they had first met and he had been writing his unfinished novel.

That night he slept like a baby, surrounded by computer terminals and cricketing trophies, on the bed of Jeremy, the absent son and heir, after playing Trivial Pursuit with Helena and Simon until gone midnight. He had finally succeeded in persuading both of them to accompany him to Cambridge the following Friday.

*It was the first time I had been on a seagoing boat, and sleeping in the State Rooms of the Queen Mary, would not have been more exciting for me. A little ladder connected the upper bunk to the floor. In one corner a small washbasin opened out of a mahogany cupboard, concealing beneath it a china chamber pot, and there were brass hooks on which to hang our clothes. In the wall opposite the bunks, a circular porthole dressed with a small curtain, offered a view of grey waters heaving and shifting against a paler grey sky. Perhaps it was not the ideal location for a night of passion, but the adventure of 'going abroad' compensated for it.*

*I had not the remotest idea how Roland had justified my presence on his trip to Italy. It was not, as far as I was aware, customary for unmarried couples to travel together in the 1930s. Without consulting him, I had taken myself off to Woolworths and purchased a cheap gilt ring for my left hand with which to justify my position in his cabin and hotel room. Even if I was his mistress, there was no reason the rest of the world should take note of our sinful state.*

*We were to spend the night on the Channel ferry and transfer to the Paris train in Dunkirk next morning. Passengers were making themselves comfortable on the slatted wooden seats and padded chairs of the decks and lounge upstairs, for it was not a long voyage. Roland had booked a cabin for us because this was an occasion: our first night sleeping together since the very first. Surveying the narrow bunks, I found it hard to imagine that we would do much sleeping in so small a space.*

*I leaned toward the little round mirror, brass-framed like the porthole, and steadied my hand against my chin as I applied a cautious amount of lipstick to my widespread lips. I looked embarrassingly young: the features too soft and undefined, the nose shiny and covered with freckles and my brown hair too straight and simply dressed. I tried sweeping it high above my ears. Like that, if I lowered my eyelids and sucked in my cheeks beneath non-existent cheek-bones, I could possibly have passed for 25. But when I tried to clip my hair up, wispy bits broke loose and the clips ended up sticking out at rightangles, as if I was wearing Pierrot's triangular cap. I shook my hair free, tied the belt of my cotton frock a bit tighter and decided that, since no one would notice me in Roland's broad wake, I might as well be myself and stuff it.*

*Powerful engines throbbed in the bowels of the great ship. I stepped carefully over the deep lintel of the cabin doorway and climbed a steep gangway to find Roland on deck. He leaned upon the rail looking over the side at a great churning cauldron of water belching from the ship's underbelly as it manoeuvred to turn the prow out to sea. He had a light, belted raincoat thrown over his shoulders and a soft brimmed Trilby tilted over one eye. With the wind rippling his hair and lifting his shirt collar round his neck, he looked as dashing as a filmstar to me. As I came to his side he lifted his arm and enclosed me under the coat.*

*"This is going to be a voyage of enchantment Anna. I feel intimations of impending creativity. With you at my side, sweet muse, I shall scale new heights; play like a genius, who knows. compose again. My friend in Italy, Ezra, loves playing amanuensis to artists. He suggested the poems for* The Latin Lyrics, *and last year I started a choral work for him — some kind of Strength and Unity march of the people; he's besotted with Mussolini. You'll love him."*

*I couldn't quite see how Roland squared is deep concern for the downtrodden proletariat with this fascist friend. But I snuggled up against his warm body, and closed my mind to his political eclecticism, as well as the smell of whisky on his breath. At 18, one does not easily judge mentors and lovers. Roland's enthusiasm and his flourishes of poetic language were part of his charm and I was flattered to be the object of them, but as to the role of muse; only a giddy fool would identify with it. And even then my goals in life were practical.*

*"Have you got time to look at the material I've collected on Venetian music?" I asked him excitedly, wishing to share the research I had undertaken in the Academy library as a prelude to our trip.*

*"I hope, dear muse, you are not about to intimidate a poor fiddle player with scholarship."*

*We had dinner on board, with Roland waxing lyrical about the joys of continental food and wine and ordering a second bottle to accompany the pudding, which, I recall vividly, was something piled with bright fruit, cream and liqueurs. I drank my share, but inevitably lagged behind Roland. After* dinner we took our brandy glasses on deck to look at the stars. The sea was as still as a mill pond – except that our mill pond was not still at all, but agitated by the race. The moon unfurled a carpet of light across the sea to our feet. If I had been of Roland's fanciful disposition, I might have imagined walking hand-in-hand across the water on that glassy, moonlit path. But alcohol had awoken more earthly desires in me. Clasped against Roland's chest, warded from the night air by his coat, I thought only of the body underneath his clothes, and ached to be naked in his arms again.

It was gone midnight that we finally made our unsteady way down the steep and rolling steps to the little cabin on the waterline. If I had thought it small before, that was nothing to the reduced accommodation with Roland in it. Turning round could only be accomplished in unison. Roland's coat fell to the floor and when he bent to retrieve it his face became jammed against my waist and he could bend no further. Convulsed with giggles, we tried to sit on the lower bunk –impossible because the upper bunk didn't allow Roland to sit upright.

"This is a container for sardines," bellowed Roland, falling backwards onto the bunk and pulling me on top of him. The brandy fumes engulfed me and his soft tongue came to find my lips, It probed my throat, my hair, my ears, sending delightful shivers down my spine, and finally buried itself between my lips which drew it in hungrily. I experienced the concentration of feeling that accompanies desire. All sight, sound and sensation became focused in my body as it lay against Roland's. His arms were around me gripping my shoulder blades with hard fingers, reaching into the hair at the nape of my neck to draw me closer. It became difficult to breath and I drew away from the kiss gasping for breath. His hot breath burned my throat.

I began tearing at the buttons on the front of his clothes; burrowing with my hands to reach into the warm crevices of his body, while his right hand fumbled blindly with the fastenings down the back of my dress.

"It's no good," he said, laughing helplessly, "Lust has made thumbs of all my fingers."

Sitting up as best I could in the narrow space between the bunks, I succeeded in pulling my dress over my head and unfastening the hooks of my brassiere.

*I bent and crushed my breasts against his naked chest rubbing them against the sweet roughness of his body hair. I reached under him with my arms and struggled to pull his trousers free, but his weight was too much for me. Roland was still laughing weakly. He extemporised in doggerel.*

*"A berth on a cross-channel ferry/ Is smaller than anyone thinks ... " He broke off. "Is it just me, or is this bunk going up and down? What rhymes with 'thinks' apart from 'sphinx, minx, chinks and blinks?" In spite of myself, I collapsed laughing on top of him.*

*"How about – With wine on the ferry/ We were all feeling merry/ But there wasn't much room for high jinks," I offered, in matching metre. But Roland wasn't playing any more. His breathing had become steadier, lighter, and after a few more minutes he began to snore.*

*The air was cold on my bare back; I gathered up my clothes and climbed the little ladder to the top bunk where I slept alone.*

*Feelings are less easily recalled than events. They become distorted by the perspective of time. Logic tells me I must have been frustrated and disappointed by our abortive night of passion. Though I don't think I pitied myself. I certainly didn't cry. But that night I recognised that Roland's love was not like mine. I didn't doubt that he loved me, possibly in romantic ways I could not conceive of, but it was obvious that the physical side of our relationship was not as important to him. Maybe I wondered whether I was not sexy enough for him, or lacked the sexual skill to arouse an older, experienced man? Doubts like these probably ran through my head, as I lay on my narrow bunk on the rolling seas, excited and apprehensive about the adventure ahead.*

*Eighteen months later, stormed by Stefan's physical passion, I would realise the difference. Meanwhile something exciting on a quite different plane was about to occur.*

133

# CHAPTER 15

Ignoring her solicitors' letter, Jonathan wrote again to Gudrun Fredricks. In courteous but insistent tone, he declared his intention to call upon her that weekend, giving as his reason for her hoped-for forbearance, that Anna Cummins was about to squeal, so perhaps Gudrun might like a chance to put her side of the story.

If he hoped for a telephone response he was disappointed. However, Professor Green ink footnotes (real name, Dr Gravenstede, but Green-ink he remained), sounded over the moon at the prospect of a personal visit from a real live publisher. His humble work of scholarship had no doubt languished unregarded in a number of in trays before Jonathan's, and he hoped the anticipation of success would not kill the old buffer before he was able to interview him. He was so excited at the prospect of tracking down vital pieces missing from the jigsaw puzzle, and in the company of Helena and Simon, that he forgot to pine for Ros for several days, or to note that his trip to Cambridge coincided with the end of her exams.

Helena picked him up at the office early on Friday afternoon, Simon, released early from school, bouncing up and down with joy at an excursion *en famille*. They took the motorway, planning to spend Friday night at a pub outside Cambridge and to make a first assault upon Ms Fredricks early Saturday morning. Should their mission be accomplished in time Helena had promised Sunday lunch in the ex-marital home.

"Can I sleep with you, Mummy?" clamoured Simon as they unloaded the car in the courtyard in front of the old coaching inn.

"I thought you'd want to sleep with Daddy?" Helena replied, eyes dancing with amusement at her son's dilemma.

"Oh yes; I want to sleep with Daddy too. I'll sleep with you tomorrow Mummy, I promise."

"OK Oedipus, I'll contain myself."

"Might save a lot of trouble if we all slept together," mumbled Jonathan, heaving bags out of the back of the car. Helena ignored the remark. "Hey sprog, can I leave the skateboard, computer terminal and Trivial Pursuit in the boot? Can you manage tonight without them?"

His son didn't hear. He was running up and down hotel corridors and creaking stairs, opening doors and rushing back to report, like a dog at the start of a walk, frantic with the need to express happiness.

They allowed him to stay up to dinner, gave him watered wine with his meal and when he could keep his eyes open no longer, let him fall asleep propped against Jonathan on a settee in the lounge while they had coffee. They hadn't the heart to deprive him of one minute of their treasured joint company.

Helena looked at her ex-husband and spoke without the customary defensiveness.

"Something – writing, cycling, sex with 18-year-olds – suits you, Jono. You look happier and healthier than I've seen you for years."

He glowed contentedly in her approval.

About 11 o'clock Jonathan carried Simon upstairs, asleep over his shoulder, and between them they got him into bed in Jonathan's room. The sight of his son's thin body brought a lump to his throat. Helena's face was blurred as he stood opposite her in the doorway.

"A brandy? For old time's sake?" he ventured. She looked at him, eyebrows raised.

"Do you think it's a good idea?"

"Who said anything about 'good'?"

He pulled her gently towards him by her arms. They felt firm and smooth under his fingers and the muscles of his groin contracted. The companionable familiarity of their evening, added to the past weeks' sexual abstinence had made him excessively horny.

"Helena." He lowered his lips to hers, but she turned her face so that the kiss fell on her hair.

"Time for bed, Jonathan," she said almost inaudibly.

He put his arms round her and converted the sexual invitation into a friendly goodnight hug.

Gudrun Fredricks' house was in a northern suburb composed of detached Edwardian houses with large gardens. Most boasted names like 'The Laurels' or 'Cedar Lodge' and still retained the ponderous self-importance and guarded privacy of that era. Some now bore the mark of multi-occupation: serried ranks of bellpushes and dustbins in neglected gardens. Others had been converted to mixed professional or commercial use evidenced by brass plaques or logo-ed nameplates and gravel car parks in place of front lawns.

Gudrun's, exceptionally, appeared untouched by the late twentieth century. It was dark, gaunt and dilapidated with few signs of modernisation: no Venetian shutters, supplementary plumbing or ventilation fans, no ornamental urns, no recent paint or pointing. At some time between the wars, a householder had added a haphazard timber structure to a side wall, presumably with a view to housing a newfangled motorcar. But the door, almost off its hinges, hung drunkenly open, revealing no sign of the latter.

"Oh cats! Look, lots of cats!" said Simon, who liked things on four legs marginally more than people.

Cats indeed there were: many cats. The space in front of the house ('garden' would have been a misnomer) was inhabited by cats of assorted ages, colours and occupations. They sunned themselves on slabs of broken masonry, played in the long grass or perched, engaged in assiduous toilet rituals, on rusty ironmongery undisturbed for years.

"I think I should go in alone," said Jonathan, somewhat daunted by the appearance of the house, as Helena pulled up in front of the weed-grown drive. Only the presence of numerous milk bottles upon the door step, suggested habitation. "After all, I may not be welcome. Or she may not be in."

For the first time he felt apprehensive about the venture. No information on Ms Fredricks suggested that she was anything but coldly hostile to the idea of a biography of her father. Yet to give up, when so obvious an untapped source was within reach, would be craven. He got out of the car and walked up the drive with a determination he did not feel, watched by a hundred amber eyes.

He rattled a wrought-iron letter box (there was no bell) and after several minutes, discerned light and movement behind the stained glass door panels. The door opened and two young cats darted between his legs and scampered into the garden. Through a crack no more than a cat's width, he saw a large erect woman with a mass of grey-streaked chestnut hair piled on her head. She must have been in her early 60s but was still handsome in a remote, unsexual way. She had sad blue eyes, a high forehead and a strong nose. Jonathan was reminded of photographs of Roland Fredricks: the good looks, the carriage – this was patently his daughter – but without his flamboyance. She wore a man-sized, moth-eaten Arran sweater and grubby trousers stuffed into Wellingtons.

"Good morning, Miss Fredricks, I'm Jonathan Burroughs from Simmonds and Sayle. I wrote asking if you would be kind enough to see me..."

"I know," she replied in unemotional level tones, not opening the door any wider. "I don't want to talk about him. Go away."

Jonathan had a repertory of ploys to disarm women, but was unsure what was appropriate for this occasion. He groped mentally.

"But you'd like the truth to be told surely; so that we produce a balanced picture?" While they spoke cats pushed passed his feet and went in and others came out. Several twined themselves in and out of Gudrun Fredricks' boots and a large, smelly tom rubbed heavily against Jonathan's shins. They were talking in the cat-equivalent of Hyde Park Corner. He tried again.

"Look, at least let me tell you what I have so far. Anna Cummins has told me..."

The change was dramatic.

The blue eyes dilated and flashed steel. She seemed to grow six inches and he noticed for the first time that she was carrying a large, bloody, kitchen knife.

"That woman; that evil woman! If she dares…" she hissed on a rising inflection. "Get out of my house, or I'll call the police!"

Cats scattered in all directions. Jonathan watched transfixed, as the hand that held the knife rose, and the door slammed shut, rocking on its hinges.

Helena was supportive. With reason and reassurance, she set about rehabilitating the wounded Burroughs ego. Years of seeing him trounced by setbacks had taught her all the techniques. The most important was to supply a success to counterbalance failure.

"Tackle old Green-ink next. He's dying to be helpful. With his interview under your belt, you can make a second sortie on the cat lady. The best things are not won easily," she said, and drove him to the historian's rooms near the Fitzwilliam Museum, arranging to return in an hour's time.

Dr Gravenstede was erudite and laden with authenticated references for both Andrzej Kaminski: communist wheeler-dealer, and Roland Fredricks: politically inspired composer. Jonathan rejoined Helena noticeably re-invigorated.

"Guess what: in 1939 Roland actually met Paul Robeson – the famous American bass. The solo in *March from the North* was written with him in mind."

"Well we haven't been idle either," said Helena smugly. "We've been doing research for you. We went back to Gudrun's and who should roll up while we were outside, but that nutty actress who collects stray cats; Catacomb, Catalyst or something. You must have read about her: she breaks into warehouses and hospital stores, doctors their feral cat colonies, and finds homes for the kittens. It appears Gudrun looks after kittens for her. She was bringing baskets of them in the back of a Land Rover and Gudrun took them in. There was a boy about Simon's age with her which provided the opening, and the two were quite happy to chat. So I suggest you go back, with a cheque made out to Catacomb or whatever, and see what a little bribery can do. Your mistake was starting with blackmail."

She took him back to the house and put a large Sainsbury's carrier bag into his hand.

"What is it?" he asked suspiciously.

"Tins of cat food; a peace offering. And I suggest you take Simon along. He made quite a hit."

She watched them walk up the drive and knock on the door. In the minutes before it opened, several cats had gathered round their knees. They stood talking on the threshold for a few minutes, and then went in.

Jonathan was not about to squander his so nearly forfeited access. For 30 minutes he played it cool, allowing Simon to take the initiative in fraternising with the cats and the boy whom he had met earlier with the Catacomb lady who happened to be helping out, and asking noncommittal questions about the rescue scheme.

Inside the house the smell was overpowering, and there was a constant, disturbing, shifting sands kind of movement underfoot, as cats milled around them. Despite their number, Gudrun appeared to know each animal individually. She had, he learned, gained a veterinary qualification, and although she ran no formal practice, a large room at the back of the house was equipped as a surgery and she provided emergency care for animals in the neighbourhood. It was the one location that appeared clean.

"My mother loved animals and plants, and had an encyclopaedic knowledge of medicinal herbs. I follow her interest."

"But you have no further interest in music?" It was his first, tentative reference to her father and he saw that she had registered it. "Believe me," he added sincerely, "I have no desire to pry, let alone to cause you pain…"

She sighed. "Mr Burroughs, you could not cause me any pain or misery I have not already suffered because of my father. I spent 10 years in therapy healing the wounds, and I have put it behind me forever."

They were alone, standing in her surgery, surrounded by labelled glass bottles and boxes on shelves. Simon and his new-found buddy were busy in the kitchen putting cat food into bowls.

"And your childhood, with your mother, at Millwater, was that all misery? Did you get nothing of value from it?" he enquired tentatively. She looked at him penetratingly, undeceived by his veiled attempts to forage information on her father.

"I hated Millwater. I left at 18 and never went back," she said in a low intense voice. She bent and retrieved a small tabby cat that was trying to climb up her boots. Her large, sensitive hands dug comfortably into its fur and it began to purr. Jonathan paused, aware that he was trespassing and that the wrong question might make her clam up.

"But isn't it sometimes therapeutic to recall the past: to establish the truth – as you see it? That's all I'm asking you."

They were still standing opposite each other and for a moment she looked so large and desolate, pity rose inside him, and with quite genuine sympathy he reached out and touched her arm. "Forgive me if I'm touching a raw nerve."

She withdrew as though his touch had burned her and, startled, the little cat leapt from her arms and ran from the room. A new look came into her face: one of fierce hatred.

"I believe in the therapy of vengeance," she replied. It was so malevolent that, for a moment, Jonathan felt a chill run through him. She walked past him to the windows overlooking the wild scrubland of the back garden. Jonathan waited silently, sensing that an emotion had been aroused that motivated her to speak. Silence; then she spoke with her back to him, as though he were not there. Her voice was very low; he could scarcely hear her.

"There must have been nearly 2,000 books, cabinets of music, cuttings, photographs, articles, notes and compositions. There were three violins, a viola. Are these the 'things of value' mentioned in your letter, that interest you Mr Burroughs?"

Jonathan froze; excitement at this tantalising catalogue, coupled with a growing presentiment of disaster, dried his throat and sent prickles of adrenaline down his spine.

Gudrun paused. "Everything, except the Augustus John portrait and his drawings – Mutti said Paola should have the pictures – and his Stradivarius which that woman had stolen. We carried them out onto the courtyard. We heaped them high…" Jonathan began to feel sick. "It was damp and misty, I remember, and it took a little time to catch." Jonathan stifled the cry that rose in his throat. She paused again and her voice lowered to a whisper, "We burned it all."

She turned to face him, her back to the light. He could feel the fire in her eyes as she spoke the final words like a curse.

"We burned it down to the last fragment, scrap and splinter, and then we swept up the ashes and threw them into the millpond."

There was no sound in the room, apart from the soft shuffling of the cats. Gudrun and Jonathan stood motionless opposite each other. He was speechless. She seemed exhausted at the recollection of that ritual funeral pyre. Eventually he had to ask in a hoarse whisper, "But why?"

"Because we wanted it to be as though he had never lived. We could do nothing about the existing record, but for the rest, what we didn't hold, we bought back or… obtained by other means. At his publisher we went through the files. Some people had offered letters, notes or writing. Others, like that woman, refused.

"So, after we have kept her quiet for all those years, she intends to talk, does she?"

Jonathan registered the question, uncertain what reply would encourage the unexpected confessional. Cautiously he prompted.

"You are his heir, and of course, you hold the intellectual copyright on all his writings…" In his head he was furiously calculating the life of the copyright. "But, you say you kept Anna Cummins silent. How?"

Gudrun gave a dry, slightly hysterical laugh. Her voice became hard and cutting. She spoke without conscious theatricality, he thought, and yet she played her voice like a musical instrument.

"She hasn't told you? We told her she had caused his death. That he had killed himself because she left him. The doctors called it a heart attack. In those days suicide was illegal and invalidated life insurance, so we went along with the coroner's 'natural causes' verdict although we knew he had injected himself with an insulin overdose. He'd done it before of course, pathetic creature, and then regretted it. He became a wreck anyway after she broke it off. She cast off her husband, Stefan Kaminski too, after his crash, when his career fell apart. Ask her. We made sure she knew. She was as guilty as if she had killed him."

Once more there was silence in the room. The torrent of Gudrun's naked hatred was the more shocking in the light of her previous reticence. Jonathan wanted to escape from the fierce blade of her pent-up enmity. He wanted to mourn Roland's sad death, his fatal love for Anna and the lost record of his life and work. But the researcher inside him clung on, like a tenacious dog, despite a deluge of blows.

"What made you hate your father so much? Many people adored him."

It didn't come straight away, and as he waited he braced himself subconsciously. She swallowed hard, as though attempting to staunch the flow of feeling that had overwhelmed her, then bent to pick up a cat from those swirling round her feet, and began to stroke it with steady, calming strokes.

"He was a pervert." It was so low, he hardly heard it. It was not an unfamiliar epithet where Roland Fredricks was concerned, but coming from his daughter it had power to shock.

"A pervert?" he repeated in case he had misheard, "You mean he had relationships with men as well as women?"

Gudrun dismissed the significance of this idea with a short gesture of her hand. The hand returned to stroking the cat.

"He exposed himself to me." The 's' sounds were sibilant as the hiss of a snake. She spoke with quiet vehemence. Jonathan was taken aback. Her breathing became shorter; she had difficulty in controlling the hand that stroked the cat. "Exposed himself to me. Showed me his disgusting thing.

Waved it in my face. Polluted me! Defiled me! Blighted my life!" Her voice had risen almost to a shriek. The cat in her arms wriggled and tried to get away. She held it firmly and her voice dropped to a hiss. "Do you think I could ever bear a man to touch me after that? He was disgusting, foul, a beast! I was glad that he was dead. I would have danced on his grave."

Jonathan lay on his back beside the Cam looking at the blue sky. It had taken him time to recover his perspective following his encounter with Gudrun Fredricks. But now, after a leisurely picnic and a couple of glasses of wine, while Simon, who had stuffed himself swiftly, was zooming up and down the paths on his skateboard terrorising May Week couples wandering along the Backs, he had finally told Helena the full story. She leaned on an elbow, swirling the wine in her glass.

"Of course the story could be the diseased fantasy of a jealous and neglected child," she said reflectively. "In therapy people are known to retrieve memories of abuse, unsubstantiated by any objective evidence. It's called False Memory Syndrome. After all, skinny-dipping was supposed to have been commonplace at Millwater."

"She could have seen him naked, accidentally," said Jonathan, aware that child abuse certainly didn't fit with his theory that Roland became impotent. "But the funeral pyre – that's no fantasy, I'm sure. She and Helga burned the lot; every blessed thing they could lay their hands on."

"Except the John portrait and the Strad."

"Yes. There's a photo of Millwater in an old magazine that shows the John – full length of Fredricks playing the violin. And Anna is alleged to have the Strad. I must ask her."

# CHAPTER 16

*What was it about Roland and railway carriages that brought out the prankster in him? His techniques for emptying a railway carriage were legion. When we resumed our seats after breakfast on the train travelling through France, another couple was seated in the compartment. Roland proceeded to unfold a copy of yesterday's newspaper upside down. He then deliberately made two holes, positioned side by side in opposite pages, and stared at the interlopers through them. I cringed with embarrassment, left the compartment and stood in the corridor. Soon after, the elderly couple came out carrying their luggage and making Gallic clucking noises as they peered over their shoulders at the bearded maniac behind his English newspaper.*

*I returned to the compartment furious. "You're a clown, and a show-off. I don't know what I see in you," I said, plonking myself down crossly opposite him. It was as if I were the elder and he the adolescent.*

*Roland was unrepentant.*

*"You're right, I'm unforgivable. Nevertheless, you love me for my wit, humour, my brilliant fiddle playing and my musical genius," he replied, waving his bushy eyebrows up and down at me like flags. "And I love you because you give me hope." And he took a wax crayon from his pocket and wrote a line of music on the wall above the seat. "Go on then; what's that?" I recognised the tune at once. "'For bonnie Annie Laurie/ I'd lay me doun and dee.'"*

*I took the crayon from him, drew a stave, and a line of music, "All right; what's that?"*

*It was a great game. Before the train came into the next station we had covered all available wall space with our melody quiz and Roland had started on the roof while reclining rather precariously in the luggage rack.*

*A respectable-looking French matron with a small suitcase in one hand and a small child in the other opened the corridor door to what, to her, must have appeared to be an almost empty compartment. Lifting the suitcase to the rack, her face came to within inches of Roland's beard.*

"Voulez-vous asseyez-vous au dessous de moi, Madame?" *he said, ogling her suggestively. She left like lightning dragging a tearful child behind her.*

*We bought long, crusty French sandwiches from a stall on the platform at the next station and had an ad hoc picnic in our empty compartment. The rough bread tore at our mouths, and ham and soft cheese oozed from the sides and stuck to our cheeks. We drank a local Provençal wine straight from the bottle and wiped our lips with the backs of our hands. It was relaxed and sensual. If anyone threatened to invade our privacy despite our having pulled down the corridor blinds, Roland took up his violin, which he kept on the seat opposite, and started to play. This effectively discouraged all comers.*

*The sun and the wine made me dozy and I leaned against him, ready to sleep. He bent and gently licked my lips and cheeks with his long, warm tongue.* "Umm, jambon de Bayonne, Rosé de Provençe, fromage de chévre *and essence of Anna;* je jouis!" *he murmured. And suddenly his tongue was in my mouth and his arms enclosed me, crushing me against his chest. I felt as though he were sucking me into him, devouring me with the sensual relish he had shown tearing chunks of bread and ham with his teeth and raking in the scattered morsels with his tongue.*

"Feed me Anna, feed me. Nourish me like the bread of life," *he said almost inaudibly into my hair. He began to fumble in the front of my dress, pulling open buttons and digging under my brassiere until he could scoop my breast in his large, powerful hand. He held my breast and he held me, heart and body, in the palm of his hand. I shut my eyes and all sensation condensed in palm if his hand. Churning with desire, I felt him rising hard against my belly; I grew damp between my thighs. He reached down under my frock and hooked* the loose satin panties over my ankles. Then he grasped my leg and pulled me astride his lap, still clasping my body to him with his other arm, and my hungry mouth to his own.

He reached to release himself from his flies and broke momentarily from the long deep kiss, so that I could hear him panting and feel his breath and the texture of his beard against my throat. Then he lifted me carefully and lowered me onto him.

I gasped as he shot into me, but I could not escape. I was impaled. He held me firm, driving me down on him with a grip of steel on my waist and a hand under my bottom. He reared and sank, lifting his length into my firmly held loins and then withdrawing so that the thick tip of him distended my opening, tantalising, threatening to escape. His face sank lower on my breast and I felt his tongue and teeth searching until they gathered up my nipple, drawing most of my breast into his mouth. I felt his teeth dig into me and the pain heightened my arousal. I began to sob, and sensing my passion, he pounded faster and harder into me, the fingers of his hand reaching right round my bottom until they also were pushing up into me.

Something was building up inside me. Something like a sneeze was about to burst, overturn and shatter me. I felt on the edge, about to tumble. I arched away from him, pushing at his shoulders with my hands, struggling to escape the relentless thrusting and the frightful stirring in my belly. Then, almost unconscious with the intensity of feeling, I felt my body contract onto him. A cry wrenched from my throat. Pulse upon pulse; a rhythmic flood of release suffused me.

"I have you Anna, and I love you. You're mine, mine, mine," he said against my body. And with an almighty thrust he lifted his pelvis to reach deeper inside me until I felt surely I must be torn apart. He went rigid all over. His fingers dug in, bruising the soft flesh of my hips and bottom. I became limp, my arms and head fell backwards, supported only by his arms. He was murmuring against me through the sweat-soaked fabric of my crumpled dress.

"Oh God, God … sweet Goddess, make me immortal, so that I can do this forever."

146

*  *  *

*I slept and woke to discover that we were travelling through mountains; a succession of short tunnels then hillsides covered with flowers. Roland was gazing at one of the lines of music I had written on the ceiling of the compartment, humming the tune under his breath. He looked happy and relaxed, the breeze from the open window ruffling his hair.*

*"What's that tune Anna? It's really lovely and I don't recognise it. Is it another of those rare folksongs you love to unearth?"*

*I followed his eyes to the stave, longer than the others, I had written just before we stopped playing the game.*

*"That one, I have to admit, is pure Williams," I said. "I wrote it myself. Is it any good?"*

Ros lay down her pen 45 minutes before the end of her final exam. For 10 minutes she had tweaked and tidied her answers until she realised that if she did any more it could be no better and the paper would start looking messy. Beyond the open windows of the exam room she could see cool shade under the tall plane trees in the square. Some children were playing ball; people lay on the grass reading or sleeping. Every now and then the breeze wafted the scent of the roses growing beneath the window over the sill to taunt her with the fragrance. Her arm looked pale as it caught the sun. For two and a half weeks she had scarcely been outside.

Suddenly she made up her mind. She packed away her things, took her exam paper to the invigilator's desk and, without ceremony, left the room. Several pairs of eyes looked up at her accusingly as she crossed in front of the desks. "Show-off; swank!" they seemed to say, but she ignored them. Why stay at her desk longer just to propitiate absurd British standards of modesty? She raced down the steps to the open air, across the road and into the square gathering pace as she ran. As her feet hit the grass she kicked first one shoe, then the other, high into the air. Her knapsack followed. She ran, leapt, twirled in the air, throwing back her head, half laughing half singing.

"It's over; it's over. It's finished; it's done."

Then she threw herself on her back on the grass gazing at the clear blue expanse above her. The voices of the children trickled into her ears. She closed her eyes and slept.

She woke as the lengthening shadows creeping across the grass hid her from the sun and she realised it was evening and there was nothing she had to do. She gathered up her scattered belongings and made her way to the college local; the pub where earlier in the term she had had a part-time job. The bars and the pavements outside were crammed with students, many of them in the same euphoric state as Ros, some less so, fearful that they had not acquitted themselves well, but all at the end of their annual ordeal. If your exams *weren't* finished yet, you didn't piss it up at the pub!

She met Kamau and several others on her course, and the first pints went down swiftly. She was light-headed with relief and out of practice with booze. It would have been easy to stay late and get plastered. Suddenly, with a pang, she realised she hadn't seen Jonathan – for 'seen Jonathan,' read 'had sex', she thought – for three weeks. She broke away from the crowd and went to a phone. She tried his office first in case he was working late. The phone rang repeatedly with no reply. Then she rang the flat. The answering machine clicked in after four tones. She left a message and rang off. Frustrated, she dialled Granna: she wanted to share her triumph and liberation with the world outside. Again an infernal answering machine. Frustration was beginning to be tinged with anger. No one out there cared that she had finished her exams!

Disconsolate and deflated, she said her goodbyes, collected her bike and set off for the Embankment. As she approached Charing Cross pier, she recognised a man with a little black and white dog entertaining the passers-by.

"Hi Mr Punch, how you doing?" she called.

The old man came over and Judy dropped on all fours to run to her, her body wriggling with pleasure. Ros felt in the knapsack on her back and found half a packet of biscuits. She offered them to the dog who sat up on her hind legs the instant she saw food.

"You found anywhere to live yet?" she asked the old man. She found herself wondering how old he was. "Surely if he's a pensioner, someone must take responsibility for looking after him?" she thought.

"Well now, things aren't so bad," he replied evading her question and with the faintest touch of an Irish brogue she hadn't noticed before. "The weather's mild and the tourists are generous. I got my trumpet out." And his face brightened.

His eyes were grey and watery either side of the strawberry coloured nose, the rest of the face was brown with a mixture of sun and dirt, with paler lines in the depth of the creases. His chin wore about four days of gingery-grey beard.

"Do you want to hear me play?" he said, brandishing the cloudy gold instrument streaked with verdigris. At a nod, he put it to his lips and began to play the soulful theme of Acker Bilk's *Stranger on the Shore*. It was quavery and he kept stopping to breathe, but the phrasing and dynamics were confidently those of a professional. Ros beamed at him.

"Can I buy you a cup of tea?"

"Little lady, you're a gentleman," said Mr Punch, throwing wide his arms with delight. Judy jumped up and down in sympathy.

They walked side by side, Ros pushing her bike, towards the coffee stall under Hungerford Bridge. Cars dawdled in front of traffic lights, and leisurely summer evening crowds brushed past them on the broad pavements.

"So, what else can you play on that thing Mr Punch?" she asked. "Louis Armstrong, Mozart, Jeremiah Clarke?"

"All three, little lady, all three if so it you please." And he blew a few notes of *High Society* which made passers-by turn round with surprised smiles.

She bought two cups of tea. Punch added three sugars.

"Sandwich?" she asked, thinking he was probably hungry; and to spare his pride added, "I need something; I've been drinking."

She bought two slabby sandwiches and a sausage for Judy.

They sat on the wall of Charing Cross Gardens. Ros was too euphoric with exam liberation to consider that this vagrant was an odd person to be celebrating with. She didn't even know his name.

"What's your real name Mr Punch?"

"They called me Dominic. Dominic Martin Seamus O'Reilly."

Ros smiled, "Don't tell me; you're Irish. And where did you learn to play that golden trumpet Dominic Martin Seamus?"

"I learned it at that fine and ancient establishment, the Royal Academy of Music, Marylebone Road, London town." Ros's eyes widened.

"You're a real musician Punch, a proper pro!"

"So help me God. Didn't I win the scholarship and was taught by Mr Sydney Langston, most proper."

Delighted to find herself in the society of a real musician, she probed further; discovered that he graduated from the Academy soon after the war (making him about 60) then joined an orchestra at the BBC.

"Albert Hall, Crystall Palace, Abbey Road Studios, Ronnie Scott's, The Hundred, the Royal Festival Hall; I've played 'em all. The music's in the blood, Took after mi father I did; and uncle: Archer Street regulars, all of us. You know about Archer Street?"

"No, tell me."

Unobtrusively she put another cup of tea in front of him.

"Ah well, Archer Street, just off Shaftesbury Avenue, that's where the musicians would go looking for a gig. Of an evening the guys came round: 'I need a trumpet, sax, bass and drums up West. Ten shillings a night. Take it or leave it.' (It was 12 and six for evening dress.) We knew the music; they knew where to find us. Anyone wanted a job they just hung around Archer Street in Soho – all of us, a load of musical tarts. You'd find the top players there too you know, when they were short a bob or two. Down a few beers at the pub on the corner; have a yarn with your mates. Always find enough to pay next week's rent…" He fell silent, gazing into space over his plastic cup. She wanted to know what had gone wrong; when the work had stopped coming, but let him take his time. "Took my dad's sandwiches down to Archer Street for him, before the war, I did. Those times were bad too; pitiful little on the dole, but at least you could get a room down Victoria for 10 bob a week; and the hope of a gig. Now it's all discos and synthesizers; phones, faxes and answering machines. No one hangs round Archer Street anymore. No one books musicians on the street. And the only place to lay your head is in a cardboard box under the bridge."

To her embarrassment Ros found tears in her eyes. The strain of prolonged study; the elation of finishing exams, added to Mr Punch's poetic narration, became almost too much for her.

"I think I have to split, Dominic," she said, hiding her face. I'll see you again, promise I will. I want to tell you about my music too. I sing with a choir you know."

"And there's me rabbiting on and not asking you a thing about yourself," said Mr Punch, full of remorse.

They said their goodbyes and Ros rode towards Westminster Bridge. This time she didn't look back at them. She might have fallen off her bike unable to see where she was going.

That night she slept deeply and long. Her sleep was troubled with dreams in which Mr Punch was confused with Labour Relations and the Benefits System in her exam, and Jonathan was somehow playing a trumpet with his dick. She woke mid-morning with the sun on her face, masturbated, and went back to sleep again.

On Saturday she tried Jonathan and Granna once more without success. Finally – truly a last resort – she took the train back to the family home. Late Sunday night when she returned, one of the boys had left her a scrawled message beside the phone.

"You're Gran called. She's had a burglary; can you go over."

Anna met her on the doorstep. It was probably the first time Ros had entered her Grandmother's house by the front door since childhood. Anna looked pale and brittle.

"How did they get in and what did they take?" said Ros.

"Very little, thank God. It was a bit amateurish; I think they were disturbed. I realised something was wrong the moment I unlocked the front door. Bill was dropping me off. You can guess where they got in."

"My downstairs loo window?"

Anna nodded.

Large policemen populated the house. In the sitting room drawers and cupboards had been systematically emptied, carpets turned back and curtains pulled off their rails.

"The thing that's confusing the police is that they haven't touched the silver," said Anna.

It was true; picture frames, ornaments, cutlery had been tipped from sideboard and shelves, but lay abandoned on the floor.

"Where else have they been?" asked Ros.

"My bedroom's topsy-turvy." Anna replied, and with a slight intake of breath, "The door to the study has been forced: it's chaos."

"The study? What could they have expected to find there?"

Anna did not reply.

Ros bounded upstairs to the attic. Books, music, records and files had been pulled from the shelves. Small brown photographs, yellowed cuttings, manuscript music and yards of tangled recording tape littered the floor. The VDU of the computer had been pushed from the desk and lay face down in a pile of shattered glass.

"My God! What were they doing?" Ros looked appalled at the devastation around her and collapsed in horror onto a chair. Anna's head emerged slowly, climbing the stairs with frequent rests. Ros leapt up and ran towards her.

"Here Granna, let me help you. You're so out of breath!"

Her concern overflowed. Carefully she helped Anna up the final steps and led her to the chaise longue: at the back of her mind was the nagging remembrance of Kate's fears that Granna's medical condition was serious. Together they surveyed the scene.

"Have you any idea what they've taken? Do you know what they were after Granna?"

Anna was recovering her breath. Minutes passed before she replied.

"They were looking for the past."

"The past?" Ros was stumped.

"The records of my past, and Roland's." Anna paused. "Well, let's hope they found something and they're satisfied. But most of it they've missed."

They went down stairs again and Ros went into the downstairs lavatory and secured it with the new lock that had been fitted. She found herself wondering who else had been slim and agile enough to get through the tiny space.

They sat opposite one other in the kitchen, mugs of coffee cradled in their hands. The police had left, more flummoxed than they were. Anna said, "It's happened before you know. At that time I kept most things at the office. That's why I put everything up in the attic when I retired. I suppose it must be all this talk of Roland's centenary, and Jonathan's biography, that made them try again. Though no one knows I'm writing about him except the two of you.

"Fortunately I'd taken precautions. The tapes have been copied; the text is on a backup disc; they're with Roland's manuscripts and scores in the bank. They may have taken some photographs, books and gramophone records of sentimental value to me alone. Funny actually; it was only this weekend that I copied sections of my memoirs – the less personal bits – and sent them to Jonathan with some of the original material: registered mail. It should arrive next week."

The overhead light in the kitchen was harsh on the lines in Anna's face; the skin seemed pale, taught, and paper thin.

"Is it just this thing," thought Ros, "or is she ill? What's draining the life out of her?" Aloud she said, "Are you OK, Granna? You're not your usually feisty self."

The face blazed with the practised smile: eyes wide, cheeks lifted, teeth sparkling. The professional performer was not dead, only resting. But the mask had no sooner flashed than it fell again. Anna drew in a deep breath and held it. Ros thought she was going to say something, but she let it out, sighing and shaking her head.

"I get tired darling; just tired. I've been too long at the computer, that's what it is. There's so much to recall; so much to record. It's the first time I had been out with Bill for ages."

"Well, I'm not leaving you tonight, or tomorrow. Either you get someone to move in or I'm staying."

"I won't say no," said Anna, and she got up and reached for the Scotch bottle on the draining board. "I'm glad you're staying Ros. I haven't the stomach to tackle the muddle all on my own. Come on, let's have a wee dram and go to bed."

# CHAPTER 17

*I have never returned to Venice, except in dreams. It is a city to dream of and a city made of other people's dreams. A city haunted by the pale ghosts of her glittering past; of domino-clad ladies laughing behind painted masks; peachy breasts escaping from lace-trimmed bodices; of pennant-trimmed barges and muscular gallants in parti-coloured hose. The sighs of long-dead lovers echo in the narrow dripping alleyways, beneath slanting, hump-backed bridges, across stately piazzas and the oleaginous waters of the lagoon. There is nothing virginal in a first encounter with Venice. Her reputation has gone before. She is like some ageing courtesan in a Titian paintings, hugging the shadows that soften her faded beauty and smiling with melancholy at the remembrance of her glorious past, as she subsides, cracked and crumbling, into the polluted water of her canals.*

*Venice inspires the poet in us all, though doubtless everything I felt had been experienced, and probably recorded with more skill, before. At the end of those 10 days I folded up my Venice and laid her, interleaved with tissue paper, in a deep drawer at the back of my life never to be worn again.*

*We arrived at dusk with the setting sun behind us, bathing domes, towers and façades in flattering golden light. The platform of the railway station disgorged us without preamble upon the quay of the Grand Canal. Where the forecourts of other mainline terminuses bustle with taxis, buses and cars, Venice offered us the bobbing awnings of the motor bus and the tall, toothed prows of polished black gondolas.*

*Despite of the anticipation of the visual feast to come, what actually hit me first was the smell: a mixture of ozone, engine oil, and rotting vegetable matter. After the smell came the silence. Not absolute silence: there was a distant cacophony of clanging church bells, chugging motor boats, and a sing-song of voices shouting to one another. But compared with the deafening, motorised roar of a modern city, the place was rural. I could hear birds.*

*"Roly,* caro, *you're here, you're really here!" A small, dark woman rushed towards us as we emerged onto the quay. She wore red from top to toe with drifty things around her throat. She hurled herself at Roland like a demented poodle and he was forced to drop the suitcases he was carrying in order to catch her.*

*"Did you have a good trip? You're on time. It's so great to see you," she bubbled.*

*"Satisfactory, I think one could say," said Roland his eyes catching mine with a conspiratorial twinkle over the top of a scarlet beret.*

*"Anna," he said, when he had managed to disentangle himself from the passionate embrace and the drifty things. "Anna this is Olga; Olga Rudge, concert violinist; she and Ezra Pound – the writer and composer – organise the concerts and study sessions. Olga; this is Anna Williams, singer."*

*I found myself looking into the violet blue eyes of a woman, close to Roland's age, with dark hair peeping out under her beret and a wide carmine mouth. Her appraising glance confirmed what I suspected all along: that it was the first anyone in Venice had heard of me, and that I was an unwelcome surprise.*

*Olga hailed a small motor boat and the boatman loaded our baggage and helped us in. Without hesitation she launched into a stream of animated conversation enlivened with graceful and extravagant gestures and peals of tinkling laughter. Since this was directed exclusively at Roland I was free to look about me and absorb the grand but faded pageant of the canal bank.*

*I was enchanted, even though everything seemed to be in an advanced state of decay. Rendering peeled back to reveal eroded brickwork, cracks staggered across the grand façades and metal stays clasped desperately at crumbling masonry. Ornamental balconies tipped drunkenly sideways, towers tottered and ramshackle wooden structures propped uncertainly. Nothing was remotely straight or secure.*

*"You're going to love the villa we've rented for the musicians. It belongs to*

some crazy Venetian Marchesa who's as old as the hills but simply mad about music. It's just off the Grand Canal and she's asking only 200 lire a week because we're veri musicisti."

With a stab of disappointment I realised we were not to stay in a hotel, and under my white gloves I began to ease the cheap wedding ring from my finger. Roland's colleagues would certainly know I was not his wife, so presumably we would be allotted separate rooms.

"It's so exciting uncovering all this wonderful old Venetian music. There are amazing composers like Antonio Vivaldi that nobody hears of these days – except in Bach's transcriptions of course. Indeed, where would Bach be if it hadn't been for Mendelssohn? Buried in the dust of history; that's where. They'll say the same about Vivaldi in the future, you see. 'Where would Vivaldi have been if it hadn't been for the Ezra and me?' It's taken me months to catalogue the manuscripts of the concerti in the Turin library; and there are even more in Dresden.

"Do you think you'll be able to play from the photographs of the scores in manuscript, because honestly if it's too difficult we'll get it copied out?"

I pricked up my ears at the mention of a music library. Unearthing the unknown appealed to me greatly.

"Did they let you photograph original manuscripts?" I inquired.

For the first time she looked at me as though I existed.

"Sure. Photography is invaluable in research. We've had copies of the Vivaldi manuscripts in Dresden sent over here on miniature film, which we blow up and copy to play from. Over three years we've performed all the Vivaldi works in print at our Winter Music festival, so now we're starting on the unpublished work. Are you interested in ancient music?"

"I'm more interested in folk songs," I answered a little sheepishly. Persuading the Oldest Village Inhabitant to croak out a faltering melody, or listening to equally distorted recordings in the library of Cecil Sharpe House felt infra dig compared with researching manuscripts in the university libraries of Europe.

Her eyes widened with genuine interest.

"But that's marvellous. What sort of material do you work with? Where do you find it? You've got to tell me all about it. I really want to know."

*For the rest of the short journey I was included in Olga's rapturous account of the unknown Vivaldi violin concerti she had discovered and which Roland was to play for the first time since the 18th century. She referred to the work as 'Il Cimento'; short for the full title, which translates: 'The Contest between harmony and invention'. The first four are better known today as* The Four Seasons

*The motor boat left the broad canals with their bordering grand palazzi, and turned into a narrow waterway. For the first time I registered how claustrophobic Venice can be. Because everything is at sea level you only see into the distance when you are on the Grand Canal, up one of the many towers in the city, or out on the lagoon. The buildings closed in upon us and we had fleeting glimpses of dimly lit interiors through open windows bordered with faded shutters, or small wilderness gardens full of cats, behind rusty grills. On one rickety wrought-iron balcony a canary in a cage sang lustily. On the other bank, in a busy boatyard, the graceful shapes of half- formed gondolas rested amid piles of scented wood shavings. A broad barge stacked with metal rubbish bins slid past us; a golden dog, brandishing a tail like an ostrich feather, appeared confidently in sole command.*

*We pulled in at a small wooden jetty and our baggage was carried up a flight of wet stone steps, through an archway into the neat garden of a small villa. Olga led us into a cool hall that opened at the other end into a sunlit courtyard garden. The floor was of large black and white tiles and the high ceiling was supported by wooden beams. It was furnished with antiques, oriental carpets and fine paintings and the terracotta coloured walls were painted with a delicate foliate frieze.*

*"*Benvenuti a Venezia!*" called a voice. Silhouetted against the sunlit garden was the figure of a tall, thin man waving a cane. As he drew closer I saw he wore a pointed beard, a broad-brimmed hat and full sleeved shirt. He advanced upon Roland with steps like a dancer and made several fencing passes at him with the cane. "*En garde, Signor Fredricks; *your Stradivarius or your life! How are you then, you old reprobate?"*

*"*Ezra,*" replied Roland, embracing the wild figure, who dropped his theatrical stance to return the hug. "Wouldst spit my gizzard upon a rapier's point?"*

*This was Ezra Pound: poet, composer, impresario, critic, cosmopolitan eccentric;*

*also, as I would learn, ardent fascist. He turned his blazing eyes upon me and bent to kiss my hand. Thick, wavy auburn hair jutted back from his high forehead emphasising the patrician profile. The hands were long and nervous and his manner restless. His bearing was elegant and aristocratic and contrasted strangely with his idiosyncratic speech which was strewn with words from several European languages and frequent lapses into some broad, unidentifiable American brogue. "Mon Dieu, but y'ol' friend sure do play that instrument, estupendo,"* he opined with what I assumed was some kind of American accent, leaning towards me over the dinner table. *The shadowy candlelight made his eyes look even wilder and more cat-like. "He go* scherzando *across dem strings like some ol' polecat on a haat tin roof!"*

*I had heard them rehearsing the skittering contrapuntal music of the Vivaldi concertos in the music room before dinner, and privately I thought it a lot of effort and hot wind to small effect. But I kept my opinion to myself among this company of enthusiasts.*

*During dinner I was introduced to the rest of the company all of whom seemed to be staying in the Marchesa's palazzo. Olga was principal violinist, a glossy young Italian played second violin and a jolly Czech with an unpronounceable name, played viola. The 'cellist was another American, Harry: fat, bald-headed and bouncy. The continuo part on this occasion was to be executed upon a rare and expensively hired harpsichord from Playel in Paris. I gathered that Ezra himself occasionally played the instrument, but that for the Vivaldi Olga's celebrated friend Wanda Landowska would perform and was not arriving until just before the performance.*

*What Ezra referred to as 'th'ol' vino' flowed liberally and conversation in the lofty, marble pillared dining room continued late. The chiaroscuro, candlelit scene began to swim before my eyes and I realised that I had not slept properly for the two previous nights of our journey. I looked at Roland sitting next to Olga and discerned no signs of fatigue. On my left Ezra had launched into a diatribe on Centralism.*

*"We suffered some angst letting them go, but* en principe *we felt that the right place for our* déchiffrés *manuscripts was Rome. Rome is the centre of the*

159

*new Empire: the nucleus of the corporate state where the vitality of the race is concentrated, drawing strength from the peripheral cells, and diffusing a clarified sense of purpose down the axes to the component parts.*

"Ezra," said Harry, "You're talking a load of crap again."

But Ezra scarcely seemed to hear him. He lifted the decanter and filled the glasses within reach.

"Non capisce, amigo; *the fascist state is very liberating. No one is excluded; everyone has a role – is a component in the New Order, functioning according to his abilities, growing in response to the needs of others in the great scheme. Only by living through the state can we find* 'il vero sé'..."

"If it's so mutually fulfilling why does Mussolini need to take over the newspapers, suspend free elections and intern the opposition?" growled Harry.

"Anti-social elements in society can disrupt the smooth running of the state. There are always some degenerates not prepared to work for the common good."

By now there were bright spots of colour on Ezra's cheeks as he half rose from his seat to pursue his theme. He seemed to be on fire.

At the other end of the table, a cloud passed over Olga's brow. (She had been deep in conversation with Roland and unaware of the political storm rumbling at the other end of the table). Her eye sought mine and I sensed a plea for female solidarity.

"Ezra, caro, *not politics at this hour. You've got to hear about Roland's plans for an opera, set in Venice. And besides, our new arrivals must be exhausted; we haven't even shown them their rooms.*"

But Ezra was not so easily halted. He had heard Harry mutter something about "Sieg heil*ing masses,*" and was back to the defence of his party.

"Cieco incredulo, *you've no vision! Can't you see that the usurocracy of the capitalist West is in chaos? The slavish* cachia ai denari, *is devalued currency. Only the centralised power of the Empire has turned back the tide of industrial stagnation and depression. The Empire didn't end with Caesar,* mon vieux..."

"Ezra, You're being a bore." Olga stood up, cutting him off in full spate, and the men round the table rose in response. Surprisingly, Ezra suffered this curtailment without protest.

The musicians said their goodnights and I followed Olga and the housekeeper, who had been hovering in the background, up the broad staircase.

"Tomorrow I'd like to show you some of the photographs of manuscripts we have been working from," said Olga companionably, as she led me to a suite of rooms on the first floor, overlooking the canal. There was a mosaic floored sitting room with gilded armchairs, writing desk and bookcases, from which opened a bedroom, bathroom and dressing room. She waited until the housekeeper, who had preceded us to turn on lights and close the shutters, had left, then spoke casually.

"I thought you and Roland would rather share. It's called the Briati suite. He designed the Murano glass chandelier," and she indicated an ornate structure that filled the centre of the high painted ceiling like a giant, incandescent bridal bouquet. "There's a small bed in the dressing room as well, so you have a choice of where to sleep."

Part of me was gratified by her tacit acceptance of my relationship with Roland, but a little voice at the back of my head whispered, "Which mistress did he have with him last time he stayed?" Misinterpreting my silence, she laid a concerned hand on my arm.

"Oh dear, I haven't shocked you have I? I mean, we don't put much store by being married here. Ezra and I aren't married you know. It's who you love and who you're with that's important isn't it?"

"They're lovely rooms; I shall enjoy sharing them," I said sincerely, responding to her trust.

I went with her to the door to say goodnight, lingering briefly to see if Roland were about to come to bed. The sound of instruments and raised voices filtered up from downstairs. Olga caught my eye and flashed me a conspiratorial smile.

"If it's not Vivaldi, it'll be this new Fredricks opera, I guess. There'll be no holding Ezra if Roland's planning a new work. Of course what Ezra would really love is to compose a great opera himself. He's always trying. But, failing that, he plays midwife to the muse."

The slightly distasteful image of pregnant men giving birth to little operas, stayed with me for a minute after I had closed the door.

My cheap fibre suitcase and Roland's had been unpacked and our clothes laid in a large walnut armoire. My simple cotton nightdress lay across the turned back, monogrammed sheets of a vast canopied bed, elevated upon a dais. I washed, got undressed and climbed several feet onto the mattress. I had been asleep upright at the dinner table, but now sleep had deserted me. I was too excited, too confused to sleep. I was in an intoxicating place, with exciting people, but I didn't belong. I was an alien in this exotic bed.

I got down and tiptoed across cool tiles to the window. With some effort I pushed back the heavy brocaded curtains, unfastened the casement and wooden shutters, and leaned out into the velvet Venetian night.

It was alive.

Close by, the roses clinging to the walls of the building brushed my hand and scented the air; from below, came the sound of lapping water nibbling at the banks like someone eating noisily. Three hundred yards away, at the junction with the Grand Canal, a motoscafo passed with a soft purr and a twinkle of lights. The building on the opposite bank was so close I could see into open windows. At one, two floors up, sat a large Buddha-like cat, all corpulent repose. I made a noise at him which echoed all around. He lowered one ear, but didn't open his eyes. As the sound died away I became aware of distant singing. At first I thought it might be within the palazzo, but gradually it became clear that it came from the further reaches of the Grand Canal.

I waited, my feet growing colder and goose pimples prickling my bare arms, trying to catch the song. It had a lilting rhythm ornamented with falling cadences of triplets, followed by long, descending notes, like a sigh –

"Aman…te, aman… te. Amor…e, amor…e,"

"Beloved, my lover," I detected, even in my inadequate Italian. It was a love song, of course.

And then, between the embellished façades that bordered the opening onto the Grand Canal, appeared a troupe of stately gondolas, gliding smoothly with a rocking motion through the water. Lights glimmered between the bows and on each stern a gondolier manoeuvred his single oar deftly, singing as he rowed: something about flowers, and the light of the stars… "Beloved, beloved, my lover."

It took less than five minutes for them to pass out of sight, but the echo of the *music lingered for some moments. When it faded I found myself repeating the little triplets followed by the long, lamenting cry,* "Amante, amore," *in my head.*

*On impulse I went to the grand writing table, took a scrap of paper, and wrote the phrases down.*

# CHAPTER 18

*I want it to be clear: the first music we wrote was unquestionably based on Italian folk songs: to be precise, the* rispetto *I heard sung by the gondoliers that first night in Venice. Though at the time I didn't know what it was. It is an ancient tradition that the gondoliers sing to their passengers. These days their songs are mostly Neapolitan, or from American musicals. But during my stay in Venice Olga encouraged me to investigate the music archives for the few known examples of Venetian folk music. This was how* Pippa Passes *was born.*

*To use Olga's imagery:* Pippa Passes *had been conceived by Robert Browning nearly a 100 years before in his dramatic poem. Most people only know the title verses with the famous final couplet: "God's in his heaven;/All's right with the world". Pippa (the diminutive of Felippa: the Italian spelling of Philippa) is 'a poor child' who works all year in the silk mills of Asolo, walks through the countryside on her one day's holiday singing, and her song touches the lives of those who overhear her so that they are radically changed.*

*The Browning connection was a logical outcome of our presence in Venice giving a concert in the Ca' Rezzonico where the poet had died. Pippa came with a ready-made narrative and dialogue, if not a fully formed libretto; good roles – including, in the wicked Ottima, a gem for Paola Pignatelli – and a theme that chimed with Roland's romantic idea of me: a young girl, inspiring fruitful change in his life.*

*If Browning conceived, I suppose my folk songs fertilised, and Ezra, with his customary enthusiasm and encouragement helped with the delivery, and between* us, Roland and I nurtured and raised the opera. Pippa *was our musical child. And as such was inevitably hated by the real mother and child in Roland's life.*

*Our days and nights in Venice passed breathlessly; each new and exciting experience crowding in upon another. For the first few days we saw little of each other, Roland's being spent in rehearsal, mine, in copying out the musical parts of the Vivaldi manuscripts from Olga's fuzzy photographic enlargements, and seeking out libraries and musical historians who could add to my small collection of local folk melodies and verses.*

*The study sessions – what we would call workshops these days – were Ezra's invention. They were both educational and critical and meant to be taken in conjunction with concerts to foster a broader understanding of composer and his work. Since he was usually introducing his audiences to modern or little-known composers and he insisted in serving them in massive doses, it made sense. He encouraged them to ask questions and voice criticism, so they ended up less inclined to feel the victims of avant-garde experiment.*

*Part of my time was also spent exploring the architectural and artistic treasures of Venice. I stood rapt before richly coloured wall paintings or breathtaking trompe l'oeil ceiling paintings depicting the ascension of the virgin or other more ancient and less saintly goddesses.*

*"It's all sex and violence really, isn't?" I said when we met again in the evening. "They didn't have the cinema in those days, or the Folies Bergères, 'penny dreadful' novels, or the Sunday tabloids. They had stained glass windows, paintings of the Last Judgement, with devils doing dirty things to the damned. Those ceiling paintings of luscious angels floating about in pink clouds are nothing but a thinly disguised excuse for a leg show."*

*Roland roared with laughter. He loved it when I played the iconoclast. But Ezra was shocked and berated me sternly for Philistinism.*

*"There's not one painter among them who knew a thing about playing a musical instrument," I complained after visiting the gallery of the Accademia. "The hands are all wrong; they wouldn't be able to produce a note!"*

*But the nights were Roland's and mine.*

*Perhaps, to be honest, we made sweeter music when we composed than when we were in bed. It's hard to be sure about something so subjective and so long ago. I had nothing to compare our love-making with. Was he a good lover? Were we 'good lovers'? We undoubtedly loved each other, but in terms of sexual craftsmanship, what understanding did we have?*

*Perhaps I am asking the wrong question? Technical competence only matters in professional and artistic endeavour. We were not artists or composers of love. We just loved each other as best we could, in our own way. But before we went to that high, soft bed canopied in damask with a gilded crown crested in dust and cobwebs, we wrote* Pippa. *And in this activity I suppose, we did something more creative and long-lasting in the way of reproduction than when our bodies met.*

"You have to have a libretto. You can't possibly start writing arias and choruses, without a libretto."

*Ezra needed a system, a philosophical framework for everything he did. And so Browning's poem, with the four scenes that Pippa passes, and influences with her song, was blocked out into three acts; the story broken down into scenes: arias, ensembles, choruses and recitative.*

*I had no enthusiasm for something as artificial as recitative.*

"There's no recitative in The Beggar's Opera *or* Gilbert and Sullivan," *I protested.* "There's no recitative in folk song."

*And so we wrote it both ways; that is the significance of the italic dialogue in the first editions of* Pippa Passes. *At Millwater we spoke the connecting passages. In London they rehearsed it with recitative. I was always against it, but they weren't listening to me by then.*

*We completed Act 1 while rehearsing the concert for the Ca' Rezzonico. My carefully restructured* rispetti *were only the starting point. Roland took my melodic lines and created theatre. He understood musical form so much better than I did. He would say,* "What we need here is for it to be in fugue. This would be good as a lullaby. Here we need a quartet. This has to be the chorus finale..."

And Ezra was there with chapter and verse on how Mozart, Verdi or Puccini had done it before.

Sometimes we wrote until two in the morning. None of us felt the need for sleep. Each night almost as a matter of ritual we listened for the gondoliers rowing home their cargo of well-dined tourists, and, if it wasn't O Sole Mio or Come back to Sorrento, I faithfully took down the music and what we could hear of the words in the hope of further rispetti.

And then we went to bed and made love.

Perhaps because we were writing, the 'ol' vino' flowed less liberally. Perhaps Roland's faith in his potency was restored by composing again, or perhaps we were inspired. I only know that it was good. Even when we didn't make love, we lay in each others' arms and laughed and teased and enjoyed just being together. That is all that matters. In Venice we loved each other without reservation and we were happy.

But there were distant rumblings of less peaceful times to come. The weather had turned hot and oppressive; there was little wind and a haze of humidity masked the sun during the day. At night the sweat lingered unevaporated on the skin and it was difficult to sleep, even with the shutters open.

As the concert approached Roland became noticeably tense. He was not performing in public regularly at the time and the Vivaldi concertos, although not over-taxing, were new to him. His nervousness showed itself in ridiculous eating binges, restless nights and an increased tendency to tease. On one occasion, reported to me by Harry, Roland began jazzing up the baroque rhythms of one concerto and the rehearsal degenerated into a hilarious jam session as the other players competed to 'swing with Vivaldi'. Relations between the two men became strained, Ezra feeling less confident that Roland would be 'all right on the night'.

I had met a couple of American students in a bar near the Fenice Theatre, and since my days were my own, we spent time visiting the sights together. One of them had witnessed a couple of German tourists abusing the owner of a Jewish jeweller's shop in the Cannaregio – racism unheard of at that time in Italy – and been shocked at being unable to find anyone official to complain to.

"Everything is run by the Fascist party now; not only the judiciary, the municipality and the police, but the newspapers, the schools and even the arts!"

It was true. When I checked with Ezra, I discovered that the Fascist Institute sponsored their Winter Music festival, their study sessions and the Vivaldi season; the best tickets were reserved for party officials and members bought tickets at reduced prices.

"When in Rome..." said Olga when I quizzed her about this, shrugging and spreading her hands, but looking unhappy. "If you want funding for the arts in Italy, it's the only way to get it."

We were sitting in the shade outside Florian's, drinking iced coffee and trying to keep cool by fanning ourselves with a newspaper. Crumpled tourists blinking at their guide books, stood about St Mark's Piazza in uncomfortable clusters like an under-rehearsed opera chorus, or snapped photographs of each other with drifting tides of blazé grey pigeons swirling round their shoulders. Across on the sunny side of the square the band at Quadri's, the other Venetian café half as old as time, was playing a selection of Viennese waltzes. At the time of the Austrian occupation, I had been told, this side of the Piazza was favoured by the Austrian officers and a pro-Teutonic bias persisted to the present day.

"How can they tolerate it? How can the Italians associate themselves with what Hitler is doing in the rest of Europe; did in Spain?" I burst out, incensed by her words. "How can Venice, one of the oldest republics in the world, accept a national regime that suspends democratic elections, free speech, and equality before the law?"

Any chance to discuss politics was irresistible to me. At 18 the wrongs of the world and how to put them right are so transparently clear, you cannot understand why nobody's doing it. Passionate conviction arises from strong feeling, unhampered by any understanding of the contrary point of view. Totalitarian regimes and war, we were soon to learn, dig the channel for the torrent of blind patriotism, by stifling any accurate or inconvenient information on the beliefs and experience of the opposition. Truth – the whole truth; the fully rounded out truth – is the enemy of conviction.

But Olga had chosen Italy, blemishes and all. Olga was old enough to have experienced the chaos that had provided the fertile ground for fascism. Her family had been bankrupted by the Great Crash. And she had chosen Ezra. How could anyone love someone so eloquent about fascism, without seeing it in more shades of grey than an opinionated 18-year-old?

"It's not that simple…" she began, "The Crash, and the depression; poverty and unemployment, and Communism striking at the heart of everything we thought Western civilisation stood for. Change is very frightening, and when people are afraid they hanker after strong leadership I suppose… someone to take responsibility and be in control; someone to build roads, arms, and provide jobs and bread for the hungry."

But at that moment our discussion of politics was interrupted by a new arrival. An old man approached us from the galleria leading to the Correr Museum.

"Signorine," There was a sinuous insinuation in the way he had included Olga in my patently unmarried status. "Berreste un bicchiere di vino con me, per favore?"

He was small and slightly stooped; possibly in his early 60s; (men look older to you when you are young); dark, drooping eyes, a long hooked nose and a thin but mobile mouth. I noticed the hands instantly: well manicured, clasped firmly across the protuberant belly, with expensive rings. One hand had a way of lifting sharply and snapping back into place without reference to anything he was saying or doing, the way some people tap their feet.

"Principe, I had no idea you were in Venice!"

Olga knew him and leapt to her feet in greeting. He took her hand and bent over it in a vulture kiss. Without invitation, he took mine and I felt cold moisture as his lips met my fingers. Notwithstanding the heat, he wore a fine cashmere overcoat over his shoulders and a soft velour hat tilted over one eye. The feet were small and exquisitely clad, I observed, as he gave his hat and coat to a waiter and sat down beside us crossing his legs.

Olga introduced us: Prince Spinola, Capo dell'Istituto Fascista di Cultura somewhere in Tuscany where she and Ezra ran their music festival. Olga's eye caught mine in warning: our political discussion was terminated.

The Prince insisted that we drink Champagne.

"For beautiful ladies," he said, fixing me with half-lidded, reptilian eyes, "Only the finest wines."

In deference to me we conversed in English.

"The Prince is married to that great singer Paola Pignatelli," explained Olga. "He is a great patron of the arts and supporter of our Winter Music." She spoke respectfully, but I detected no warmth in her voice.

The sparkling liquid swirled and foamed into the tall glasses. The Prince raised his in a toast,

"Alla bellezza – to beauty, and the arts!"

Somehow he managed to convey that I was the former and Olga the latter and I don't think she liked it. His salacious attentions made me uncomfortable, but mention of Pignatelli had stirred my curiosity. In view of their relationship I thought it inadvisable to mention where I had last met the diva, so I said, "I was fortunate enough to hear Pignatelli sing in London, last season. She was a magnificent Carmen."

"Ah, Carmen," The Prince enthused, "Now there's an opera close to the heart of hot-blooded Italians: love, jealousy, revenge, death. What drama and what verity! The true Italian refuses to be thwarted in love."

I was tempted to remind him the opera had been written by a Frenchman about Spaniards.

"It's a lovely part," I said feebly, embarrassed by the romantic tone the conversation had taken on.

He motioned the waiter to refill our glasses, and under the pretext of presenting mine, which was still half full, brushed his cool, dry fingers against my hand. Olga looked on edge. She probably found this sort of behaviour as distasteful as I did, but in her world the Prince was obviously above criticism.

"And she's extremely versatile too. We were lucky enough to have her perform some unpublished music of Vivaldi's at our first Venice concert, two years ago."

I made the connection: last summer, and the summer before that, Roland had been invited to Venice to perform for Ezra. So he and Paola had been here together. I wondered if Olga was letting me know deliberately or if it was an innocent attempt to steer the Prince back to more general musical conversation.

"Indeed; it displeases me much not to have been present before," he replied turning to her, "And this summer? What delights have you found to divert us?"

*Olga began to rhapsodise about* Il cimento. *He listened courteously, head inclined, tracing the fine condensation on the side of his glass with the tip of one jewelled finger.*

*My mind wandered for a moment, seeking some contrivance by which I could take my leave. And then, suddenly alerted, I could not believe my ears: Olga was telling him about Roland. And not only about Roland as soloist in the performance of the new concerti, but about Pippa and my involvement in the work. Far from being able to slip away, I was being unwrapped and handed back to the old goat on a plate.*

*The intrusive brown eyes were turned once again in my direction. Over the rim of his wine glass, they narrowed as he surveyed me. The eyes said "Ah-ha! Mistress of the bohemian composer: how intriguing," as clearly as if he spoke. Olga continued, "... so we are hoping that our palazzo will prove to be the womb for a great new opera."*

*My toes curled at the metaphor, and my cheeks burned with embarrassment. Olga's pregnancy imagery had never sounded more sickening. I would have liked to brazen out the veiled innuendo; to have stuck out my chin and said, "We're lovers; so what?" But at that stage of my life I hadn't learned not to care what people thought. I only knew that in being exposed in an unorthodox liaison, I became wounded prey for this predatory Italian aristocrat.*

*Olga drained her glass and stood up. I noticed for the first time, that she was a little drunk.*

*"Well, I must be getting back* amici. *I've only been let out for a short break, and the concert is tomorrow. We shall have the pleasure of your company tomorrow I trust Prince?"*

*"We are guests of the Princess Polignac, I believe she intends to be there."*

*The Prince had risen as she did and inclined his head in gracious acknowledgement of the invitation. I also rose preparing to leave with Olga, my Champagne glass still full.*

*"Anna darling, you have no need to hurry. Stay and finish your wine."*

*At that moment I could have killed her.*

*"Perhaps the* Signorina *would take pity on a lonely man and have dinner with me?"*

"What an enchanting idea," Olga almost squeaked with excitement, "Roland won't be back until late my dear. Why don't you go? The Prince knows all the best restaurants in Venice."

I glared at her, knowing I was trapped by the conventions of good behaviour unless I could think of a seamless excuse instantly. But she had gone; flitting down the arched galleria, with her filmy scarves floating behind her like the tail of some exotic ornamental fish.

It flashed across my mind that Isadora Duncan had been strangled by a scarf like that. Then I felt the gentle reminder of the Prince's hand upon my arm.

# CHAPTER 19

*The encounter with Prince Spinola sparked our first row.*

*"Bloody hell! Why the blazes do you want to go back to England now, Anna? The concert takes place tomorrow; we're getting on like a house on fire with Pippa and we're about to have three whole days to ourselves. Can't we even talk about it?" Roland fumed.*

*I've never been good at expressing anger or hurt. My instinct is to draw into myself, or leave the scene. I find the admission of pain humiliating.*

*"I'm no good at this sort of argument," I said biting, my lip and keeping my head down as I continued to collect my belongings and push them into the suitcase, "I just want to go home."*

*He changed his tone from exasperation with irrational women, to sweet reassurance.*

*"Listen Anna, nothing's changed between us, now. You're upset about the past – the distant past, and it's over. It never really began. Yes, Paola and I were here together two years ago. It was a moment of summer madness; nothing more. First she wanted me; then she didn't. Paola's a determined woman. A mere man doesn't gainsay her. And you know what a letdown I am. But it's history now. Not even very exciting history. I never pretended to you it didn't happen because it's irrelevant to you and me."*

*"I don't want to hear about it."*

*"But there's nothing to be jealous about…"*

*"Jealous! I'm not jealous. I've gone cold inside. I was humiliated; treated*

like a plaything – a toy. That horrid Italian pawed me; handled me as though I were a piece of china for sale!" I said, slamming things into my suitcase and desperately trying to control the feelings welling up inside me. "He professed to admire the freethinking character of the English. For freethinking read 'free love'! Obviously I was fair game because I was a loose woman; the mistress of a philandering artist. I even believe he savoured it the more because he suspected you had rogered his wife."

As I spoke the vulgarism, I felt ashamed of it; ashamed of the notional injury that I knew, in all honestly, I was constructing to justify my resentful feelings, and most of all ashamed of those feelings that were so alien and unfamiliar.

"Anna, this is fantasy, purest fantasy. It's all in your mind," said Roland, desperately trying to make light of my outburst. But the unaccustomed alcohol I had consumed at dinner with the Prince had loosened not only my tongue, but deep emotions.

"Everyone patronises me; treats me like a grace note. But underneath your superiority you feed off me – you use me to nourish your own inadequate lives."

Roland looked at me aghast. He had sunk into one of the fragile gilt settees which looked as though it might collapse beneath his weight. His blue eyes were wide and hurt and for once he did not rush to answer.

"Do I 'feed off you'?" he asked in a quiet voice.

I banged down the lid of my suitcase and snapped it shut. I heaved it off the bed and walked to the door.

"Anna," he said gently, "It's gone 11 at night. Where are you going?"

I ignored him, and marched out of the bedroom, across the sitting room and into the corridor. I was walking blindly, thoughtlessly. It wasn't until I came to the landing at the head of the staircase that I paused to consider where I was going. Downstairs I could hear music: the others were still up.

The absurdity of my behaviour had nagged at me from the outset, and now as I lingered, a light breeze from an open casement cooling my forehead, I took stock of the situation with more clarity.

Where indeed could I go at this hour of the night without further shame-making explanations? Was I to let Olga, my courteous hostess, know of my hurt? Was I to absent myself from the concert tomorrow; to walk out without explanation and try and find a hotel, a passage home, with my limited experience and resources?

I returned slowly the way I had come. As I opened the door to the Briati suite the first notes of the gondoliers' evening serenade were filtering through the open window. In the bedroom Roland slept, slumped sideways in the tiny settee, his large hands spread on his knees, palms up. The position crunched his neck into fine wrinkles and he looked old and infinitely weary. As I looked at him love welled up inside me, and a tormenting pity. I stood motionless; the sentimental strains of the Barcarolle from The Tales of Hoffmann wafting round me, unwelcome tears pricking my eyes.

Silently I left the room and passed the night in the dressing room.


The solid Baroque mass of the Ca' Rezzonico dominated a bend in the Grand Canal not far from the Marchesa's modest palazzo. The group had rehearsed in the vast painted concert room on a couple of occasions but I had been there only once: to assist Ezra in an effort to improve the acoustics of the high domed chamber by draping broad swags of fabric from the central Murano glass chandeliers to the walls. I had not been required to climb the scaffolding erected for this purpose; only to sing a few notes at various places in the hall so that Ezra could judge any improvement.

I did not speak to Roland the morning of the concert. I woke late with the novel, as yet unfamiliar, experience of a hangover. My recollection of the meeting with Prince Spinola and the row with Roland, added to the agony of alcoholic dehydration and remorse.

Everyone was so busy that day it was not difficult to keep out of their way. Around midday, I slipped out of the empty palazzo and sought the companionship of my American students. I needed the comfortable companionship of my contemporaries. I wanted Stefan. I longed to escape, but the spectacle of Roland sleeping had alerted me to my ties. I would stay in Venice, but my external lifelines were now vital.

The study session took place that afternoon, but as Roland was only playing illustrative passages I felt I could legitimately be excused. As the hour of the concert drew nigh I began to feel anxious. I toyed with the idea of asking my new friends to accompany me; but I had told them little of the circumstances which had brought me to Venice and hesitated to reveal them now. Being with older, richer people separated you from the camaraderie of youth. So regretfully I refused their suggestion that we go and swim at the Lido, made my excuses and returned to change for the concert.

Parties, pageants and processions are the Venetians' natural habitat. Dressing up is in their blood. Where the British dress with uncomfortable correctness, Americans with a democratic unconcern for convention, and the French with casual chic, Venetians go happily over the top. The glittering company that crowded the grand staircase, foyer and antechambers of the Ca` Rezzonico that night did not wear high powdered wigs, Harlequin-patterned tights or jewelled masks. They were not accompanied by turbaned Negro slaves, peacocks or monkeys on a lead, but in every other respect they were recognisably the same troupe painted above the tromp l'oeil balustrades of the Palazzo Grassi, or the Correr Museum.

I had never seen such a quantity of rich silks and satin, sequined caps, flashing jewels and naked shoulders. I felt like Cinderella viewing her sisters dressed for the ball. I wore the only dress I had; what Roland called my 'Snow White' dress because it had a black velvet bodice and contrasting sprigged cotton skirt and sleeves; on my head a black velvet Juliet cap.

They had kept me a seat near the front and at one side. Beside me was one for Ezra who was still backstage with the musicians. In the centre, behind me, were a group of red velvet fauteuils on a raised daïs under a canopy reserved, I assumed, for Venetian aristocracy and Fascist Party high-ups. As the lights dimmed these remained unoccupied.

The concert opened with a Bach suite; something familiar, catchy and digestible, to put the audience at their ease. In the middle of the second piece I was aware of a disturbance behind me. The VIPs were making a late arrival. As I and most of the audience twisted and strained to see who it was, my heart sunk to recognise Prince Spinola among the party. I turned back instantly hoping he had not seen me.

The music was not greatly to my taste; too fussy, too lacking in tonal colour and variety; a bit like the sound of trickling water. My eye began to wander round the great painted salon. The ceiling paintings were masked by Ezra's swags of acoustic drapery, but to the right my attention was caught by one showing Orpheus, being beaten up by a troupe of bad-tempered bacchantes one of whom was belabouring him with his own violin. That would amuse Roland, I thought. I must point it out to him. It was ironic how the bitter pain of last night was already receding into the distance.

There was an interval before Vivaldi's 'Four Seasons' – the main part of the concert. The audience surged into the ballroom next door, where refreshments were being served. Although the tall casement windows overlooking the Grand Canal were open, it was hot and sticky in the brightly lit salons. I made my way towards the staircase in hope of some air. Leaning over the balustrade and fanning myself with my programme, I heard an unmistakable voice. I didn't recognise the Italian words at first, then realised I was being addressed with Romeo's words from the balcony scene of Romeo and Juliet.

"'Piano; quale luce da quella finestra spunta?

È l'oriente, e Giulietta è il sole.'

Your Shakespeare sounds well in Italian, you think?" said the Prince. "And truly, you are the incarnation of Juliet leaning over her balcony in the moonlight."

He wore an impeccable dinner jacket with a white gardenia stuck in one satin lapel. Glossy patent peeped from beneath his knife-edged trouser creases and he had two tall glasses of sparkling wine in his hand. I steeled myself to be polite.

"Dear Prince, you are most generous, but right now I feel as if I will never want to drink alcohol of any sort, even Champagne, again."

His eyes widened and his brows shot up.

"A glass of juice perhaps?"

My refusal to take a glass had left both his hands encumbered. He half turned and barked something in Italian. From nowhere a waiter appeared, relieved him of the spare glass and offered me a replacement filled with orange juice.

"It's hot tonight," I said, sipping the iced drink appreciatively

"Venice is not a good place to be in the summer. When my wife rejoins us we will go north, to the mountains. It is better for my son's health."

177

*It was the first I knew of Pignatelli having a child.*

*"How old is your son?" I asked in politeness.*

*"He has one year this April. For many years I longed for a son, and now, in the twilight of my life I have been blessed. Regrettably my wife's career keeps her away from him. We travel with a nurse of course."*

*"He's with you in Venice?" I said in some surprise. The image of the suave, lounge lizard being a fond father was incongruous.*

*"Now that I have him, I will not be parted from him," he said simply.*

*The bell rang for the end of the interval, and we returned together to the concert room. Ezra's seat was still empty.*

*"You permit that we sit together?"*

*"I think the seat is intended for Ezra Pound, but I have no idea where he is."*

*"I will take it in his absence."*

*The musicians re-appeared and took their seats: applause for Olga as leader, dressed in a clinging Burgundy red dress, and for Wanda Landowska, at the continuo harpsichord. Then Roland, the soloist, appeared; more applause. I felt a sharp contraction in the pit of my stomach. He looked so handsome with his proud, erect carriage; beard above the starched white collar and long hair brushed back from his high brow. He bowed, lifted a bow, and the orchestra launched into a scurry of brisk semiquavers.*

*It was Spring; something of a cliché spring perhaps, but recognisably vigorous with green shoots bursting, young lambs leaping and birds trilling merrily. Roland's bow skittered over the strings and his fingers blurred with speed. His fine, leonine head bent low over the instrument; hair was momentarily in his eyes, then thrown back as his chin came high. The audience around me was breathless with the sheer vitality and athleticism of the playing. All reservations were swept aside.*

*A pause. The orchestra flicked pages (the loose sheets I had myself copied); Roland took a large silk handkerchief and mopped his brow. Then, the programme told us, we were into Summer: high summer – and with more birdsong, but now the calls had taken on a more plaintive note. A sad, lyrical passage in the minor for the solo violin allowed Roland to do what he did best: to toy with*

178

the emotions of his listeners. He squeezed the tone and played with the time, extending the long notes and falling precipitately into the cadences. I felt the orchestra straining as he made his own pace. Then, when the sweetness seemed almost too much to bear, the rapid semiquavers returned and they galloped into another frantic finale.

It was during the third concerto, Autumn, that I first became aware that something was wrong. In the music a hunting horn called and horses pranced; leaping arpeggios and rapid scales rushed hither and thither. At one point I felt certain that Roland was late on entry; Landowska at the harpsichord continued to play regular chords in anticipation, and finally with a slight skip, he came in, but the sense of unease in any group of musicians when something unanticipated takes place, communicated itself to me. Then a long, long note – this time extended way beyond the limits of legitimate rubatto; a slight chittering among the orchestra as entries were fluffed and the harpsichord continuo again tried to prolong the accompaniment until the soloist was with them. As the concerto careered into yet another frenzied recapitulation Roland lowered his violin and reached for his handkerchief to wipe his brow. He looked unsteady and for a moment I wondered if he had been drinking.

The orchestra finished the concerto without him. As the audience shifted in their seats and coughed, settling down for the final concerto: Winter, I saw Olga move discretely to Roland's side. Almost simultaneously I heard Ezra's voice beside me.

"Goddarn it, the son-of-a-bitch has been on the booze!"

But I had noticed the hair clinging to Roland's forehead and the damp patch spreading through the starched cotton of his shirt. As I watched, his head rolled sideways and he caught Olga's arm to stop himself falling. Masking her alarm, she lowered him into her chair, where he leaned his head against her.

"I don't think he's drunk. When did he last eat?" I said urgently to Ezra.

"Dunnow honestly. We've been rehearsing or doing the study session all day. Most of them slipped out for *spuntini de temps en temps.*"

"But this kind of playing burns up a frantic amount of energy I think he may be in hypoglycaemic shock. Did you know he was diabetic?"

Ezra's face answered for him: he knew nothing of Roland's condition.

179

"Hurry!," I urged him, "Get him off the stage quickly. He needs something very sweet to eat or drink, fast… and get a doctor, he may need an injection."

Ezra moved swiftly between the seats towards the orchestra; I followed close behind. As I reached Roland's side I could see the sweat pouring from him; he was deathly pale, his tongue lolled out of his mouth and he could barely keep his eyes open. Olga's turned to us, her voice controlled, alarm in her eyes.

"What's the matter with him? Is he sick?"

"Speak to the audience Olga. Tell them Roland has been taken ill. Play something, anything, for them. Tell them the concert will resume as soon as the soloist has recovered." Ezra spoke swiftly as he and Harry lifted Roland and helped him from the stage.

In the ballroom I found catering staff clearing away the remains of the refreshments. I commandeered ice cream and orange juice and requested that an urgent telephone call be made for a doctor. How long did they think one would take?

An Italianate shrug did nothing to reassure me.

Roland was mumbling incoherently, but still conscious. His arms thrashed spasmodically as I spooned ice cream into his slack mouth; someone pulled off his jacket and loosened the collar of his dripping shirt. His throat was clammy and ice cold with sweat. He jerked and moaned and his blue eyes rolled. I hoped he saw me; knew that someone was there who understood –understood, but who had failed him hopelessly last time. I willed myself to concentrate on feeding him; refused to let myself recall the helpless inadequacy I had shown before. Ice cream and orange juice spilled down the side of his face and fell onto his shirt.

"Why has this happened to him?" asked Ezra, confused and alarmed. "Has it happened before?" I explained as best I could about the effect of insulin and the problems created if a diabetic ate too little or took too much exercise.

"He should have told us; if we'd known we could have made sure he had something to eat."

In my head I was saying, "No, it's my fault, I should have been there; I knew. I knew that stress made him careless about eating and I contributed to that stress with a row last night." Aloud I urged, "Swallow Roland, come on, get it down. You're hypo, you fool, and this time Paola is not here."

*There was a cool hand on my elbow.*

"Permetta, Signorina,"

*I had completely forgotten Prince Spinola. Now he stood behind me accompanied by a young woman carrying a neat leather bag.*

*"I have taken the liberty of bringing our nurse to assist you. I heard you say that your soloist was* diabetico.*"*

*The young woman took from her bag the equipment that I recognised. Swiftly and efficiently she sterilised a vein in Roland's arm, drew fluid into a syringe and pressed the needle into his arm. The plunger sunk slowly down the barrel, while from the other room came the sound of the first movement of Mozart's* Eine kleine Nachtmusik. *The orchestra was filling in.*

*We waited as the nurse slowly injected the glucose solution, then withdrew the needle and swabbed the entry point. I leaned forward and wiped Roland's face. His body relaxed as he leaned against Ezra, his mouth closed, his eyes opened and he sighed. He looked from me, to Ezra," I pooped didn't I guys? I didn't make it through to Winter."*

*He sat up and his hand sought mine. Once again the suddenness of his recovery amazed me. Ezra looked more flabbergasted than when Roland was in shock. The Prince however was impassive.*

*"If you have a* diabetico *in the family you must learn how to use the...* iniezione, *injection, for both the* insulina *and for the sugar. Their life depends on you."*

*Later as Roland slept in my arms, my mind returned to what the Prince had said about the responsibility thrust upon you when your life is entangled with a diabetic's. His words had explained the mystery of Paola's efficiency with injections. "Our son was born* diabetico; *the first six years of his life will depend totally upon our care."*

*His son? Diabetes runs in families. Was it also in the Prince's? It seemed an unlikely coincidence. And from there, it took no great leap of imagination to connect Paola's brief whirlwind affair with Roland two years ago, to the birth of a diabetic child. Did Roland know? Did the Prince? Probably not. If Paola* had contrived the pregnancy it would have been with the design of giving her aristocrat husband an heir, not to let him know himself a cuckold. Roland had served a purpose; she had had no wish to possess him. But in conceiving a child by him she had inextricably bound her life to his.

Roland stirred in my arms and murmured indistinctly into my hair. "Don't leave me Anna. Don't leave me."

"I'm here; I'm not leaving," I reassured.

"I'm so deep in love with you Anna. I can't imagine life without you. I'm a no-good drunk with a small talent, but without you I am nothing."

I held him close and spoke soothing words. My body was there next to his and answering his need with my own. With my body I loved him deeply. But my mind was fluttering at the end of a leash. My mind fought this burden of another's life. I wasn't sure I wanted someone who was 'nothing without me'.

"Anna, sweet Anna; my Pippa, my muse..." And he began covering my throat and breast with kisses.

Pippa, Juliet, Amarillis, muse; for them we are never simply ourselves. We are the form, the fantasy round which they weave their dreams, and with those insubstantial visions, frame mythical enchantresses to capture the imagination of future generations of men bewitched by an illusion.

# CHAPTER 20

There were three messages from Ros on the answering machine when Jonathan got back late on Sunday night. The first sounded friendly and a little pissed; the second distinctly peeved, and the third was just an oath and a ring-off.

Guilt engulfed him. The excitement of planning the Cambridge trip with Helena and Simon had driven the fact that Ros's exams finished that weekend completely from his mind. The mere sound of her voice on the phone was enough to set his penis athrob, yet he had gone away without even a final good luck message or an enquiry as to her plans. God, he was a shit!

Should he call? "It is a bit late," answered the coward in him. "Wait until morning."

He stood by the phone and drained the last drops of Scotch from the bottle. He had been through his flat looking for anything remotely drinkable the moment he returned. Apart from a glass of red wine left in one of the empties beside the sink, this was it.

The place was a pit: unmade bed, a sink stacked with dirty glasses and plates encrusted with take-away, three or four weeks' dust and dirty clothes littering the floor. He hadn't tidied since Ros last stayed. He peered into the fridge without much optimism: some cracked cheese, half a tin of baked beans going green round the edges and an open carton of sour milk. "In films the hero is confronted by the barren fridge as a symbol of his lone and loveless existence. Is that me?"

His oral cravings had to make do with black coffee.

He returned to the bedroom, flopped back onto the bed and winced; his shoulders ached from carrying Simon in Richmond Park that afternoon, and he seemed to have caught a touch of the sun.

"It was great, being with the sprog this weekend," he thought. "I suppose it's things going well: work, and Ros; feeling fitter, more positive about life – and myself." Then he thought about Helena. He still had the occasional twinge for her. "But if I were still married to her, would I have fallen for Ros? It didn't stop me playing silly buggers before." He acknowledged honestly. He tested himself by imagining Helena taking him back and having to give up Ros. "I couldn't do it. I want her; she's good for me. But I want my kids; and Helena, as a friend too – I think. Jesus; self-doubt and introspection: I need a drink."

Just before he fell asleep he had an intriguing fantasy of Ros and Helena meeting, reminiscent of the garden scene in *The Importance of Being Ernest*. "Won't you call me sister… ?"

The phone shrilled in his ear. It was daylight and he had fallen asleep, dressed, on his bed. It took him some minutes to re-orientate. He peered at his watch: 7.30am: damned early to call. Unsteadily he reached for the receiver and knocked half a mug of cold coffee onto the floor.

"Jonathan?"

"Ros; I was going to call…"

"Where the fucking hell have you been?"

"And hello to you too. I'm very well thank you now you ask. And how are you?"

"Where were you? I rang again and again."

"I know; you sounded cross. Look, I'm really sorry, I…"

"Sounded cross? That's because I was cross – bloody cross. I'd finished my exams. I was free for the first time in three weeks; the sun was shining and I was randy as hell, and where the fuck's sake were you?"

"I went to Cambridge, to visit a contact on the Fredricks biography. And

I saw Roland's daughter, Gudrun: several sandwiches short of a picnic and a lot less enjoyable."

The mention of picnics stabbed him with guilt. He didn't think telling Ros about picnics with Helena would improve the situation.

Ros drew in a sharp intake of breath, "My God! You saw Fredricks' daughter: the crazy old witch who slaps writs on anyone who wants to write about him? I thought she wouldn't see anyone."

"Well, she saw me – after a bit of persuasion. I told her it was her chance to put the record straight; that Anna Cummins was about to spill the beans, and if she wanted her side of things to square the record…"

"You told her what?

"…. that Anna was writing what she knew about…"

"But she's a dangerous paranoiac; maybe even homicidal. Do you know how she feels about Granna? Shit! You told her that she was writing her memoirs?" She paused momentarily and her voice sank to a whisper, "That explains it. That's who's behind it." And her tone rose in pitch and volume, "Do you know what happened this weekend, you dickhead, thanks to your crass attempts to blackmail Gudrun Fredricks?"

"No; what happened?"

"Someone broke into Granna's house and ransacked her studio. Books, tapes, discs, photos and music, everything turned topsy-turvy, plundered, wrecked. All thanks to your big mouth."

"A burglary? My God! But what makes you think Gudrun Fredricks was behind it?" But even as he spoke he heard Gudrun's voice saying, "What we didn't hold, we bought back or… obtained by other means." Aloud he said, "What did they take? Are you sure they weren't just after the television and the silver?

"I'm still here. I've seen what they did. Perhaps you'd like to see for yourself: the shattered VDU; the unravelled tape; the torn papers; and all because of your mindless blabbing. On second thoughts; don't bother. You're so obsessed with your bloody book you don't care who gets hurt in the process. Right now you're not safe within reach of my fists." And she slammed down the receiver choking with emotion.

"Were you perhaps a trifle hard on him? Does he deserve such harsh blame? It was rather 'charged, tried and condemned' without any solid evidence. And not allowed a word in his own defence."

Anna spoke quietly from the other side of the room. She had watched Ros phone last night and again as soon as she was up this morning. Something more than a desire to inform Jonathan about the burglary was behind it. Now, as she stood by the phone, Ros was digging her nails into her palms until the knuckles were white and a tension muscle flicked nervously in her jaw.

"He's a skunk; a shit, an arsehole," she said between clenched teeth. "I hate him."

"It would appear that you are definitely not indifferent to him," said Anna. Ros didn't answer but rubbed the back of her hand back and forth across her mouth. Anna judged that she was near to tears. It was no time to expect rational behaviour. She held out her arms.

"Come here." Her granddaughter looked at her, self-restraint and dignity fighting with the desire for a cuddle, "Come on," Anna commanded gently.

Ros fell into her arms and the torrent was undammed.

"He's such a bloody shit, a loathsome, foul…" Momentarily her sobs obscured the stream of abuse, "… a useless, hateful, filthy…"

".. And you love him; I know," said her Grandmother patting her head and smoothing back the damp hair. Ros looked up at her, red eyes wide and wet.

"Do I?" For a moment Ros looked genuinely surprised.

"Why not?" Anna was smiling. "Love is not reserved for heroes. Skunks can be frightfully lovable."

The sun and the blue sky mocked Jonathan.

"They are always heartlessly bright when your mood is dire," he thought.

He took a cab to the office meditating on the well-known territory of his personal shortcomings.

"The trouble is I'm used to my vices. They're like old friends." He ran through the familiar inventory, "I'm selfish. I forget to call. I get pissed; and can't get a stand. (Doesn't apply with Ros). I don't pay compliments, and even when involved, I can't stop fancying other birds. Arch crime: I'm a dead loss at discussing 'our relationship'. Can't even remember what last night's row was about! They usually decide I don't love them enough to reform.

"But I do, this time. I care one hell of a lot about Ros. I care about Helena and the boys. And I don't actually like the old friend vice any more. They're like drinking buddies: easy, undemanding, but underneath you hate them because they make you hate yourself. So, why are you letting them louse things up with Ros, just as they did with Helena? The lazy fatalism of a drunk who puts off going home, even though he knows it'll get him chucked out."

The taxi had paused at traffic lights. On the pavement a girl about Ros's age, in jeans and a T-shirt, was talking to a young man. Jonathan couldn't hear what she was saying, but she was obviously pleading. Her head was on one side, her eyebrows compressed and her lips pushed forward in a pout. As he watched, she put her arms round the boy's neck and Jonathan was sure her lips said, "Please."

As the taxi began to pull away, the young man threw out his arms in surrender and allowed her to pull his head down to her lips. Jonathan felt strangely moved.

"I wonder what she wanted," he thought as he left them behind him. And his mind returned to Simon, and to Ros. "It's good to be wanted. Why think in terms of demands? They make demands because they want you, because you matter. It's good when Ros wants me to fuck her, to be with her after her exams; good to have a book to write, children to visit; good that someone like that girl wants you to do something."

He must put things right; prove that he cared; try to reform.

"Shall I send flowers? No; looks smarmy. Go and see her? Probably get the door slammed in my face. Perhaps I'll ask Helena what to do, or Anna? Women have more insight into these things." Thinking of Anna reminded him of the burglary. His heart, which had begun to pick itself up off the floor, collapsed again. "God, what a disaster! What did she have of Roland's and can it be replaced?"

The envelope on his desk was small and padded. As academic and educational publishers. Simmonds and Sayle were more accustomed to receiving thick, paper-wrapped packages tied with string, and bursting from their bonds. Their authors were mostly learned academics eking out an existence amid the dusty tomes of obscure libraries. It would not have surprised Jonathan to have received manuscripts penned in quill and Indian ink. Only in recent years had they been able to insist on uncorrected *type*script. The receipt of a computer disk was a novelty.

The packet lay on top of his post in a patch of the infernal sunshine, and he opened it first without realising what it contained. The disk slithered out wrapped in a neatly word-processed letter. The name on the letterhead made his heart leap with excitement. It was from Anna Cummins.

"Dear Jonathan," she wrote, "I have sorted through my mementos of Roland and am putting my recollections on disk. They are unfinished, but I aim to complete them soon. Once I had started I decided to put down everything – even some material unsuitable for your biography, or for publication. I only knew Roland personally for little more than three years: from early 1938 until his death in 1941. To begin with I was just an observer. Later, when I became involved in his music, I still had only partial insight. For the last year of his life, soon after the outbreak of war, when the London production of *Pippa Passes* was cancelled, we saw little of each other.

"So this is a personal partial view of the last few years of his life. But I know you want to know about *Pippa*, and the other things he wrote at the end, so I will try to get it all down.

"As I think you appreciate, there are copyright restrictions on some of the things I hold, like his letters, though I can report on their content. I will send you everything I own and hold copyright on: notes, scores, photographs registered mail, separately. I am enclosing one of my favourite snaps of Roland taken when we were in Venice.

"Yours sincerely, Anna Cummins."

Jonathan glanced at the old black and white photograph, faded brown, and cracked at the edges. It showed a man in open-necked shirt and baggy shorts, long hair blown by the wind. He sat in the prow of a boat, which, by the panorama of waterfront façades, and barley sugar mooring poles in the background, was recognisably Venice. The portraits of Roland Fredricks familiar to Jonathan were stagy, in the Angus McBean, front-of-house style: all dramatic lighting and self-consciously posed profile. This was unmistakably the same man: the George V beard, the bushy eyebrows, florid complexion and large, loose limbs, but in a completely different vein. He looked humorous, untidy and relaxed. His eyes twinkled among a mass of creases, and the broad smile showed chipped, uneven teeth. His sat in an easy slouch which afforded a glimpse of a distinct paunch; nothing like the romantic figure in white tie and tails promoted by the publicity shots. He looked like a rumpled, battle-scarred old lion.

Jonathan turned from this pleasing image of the young Anna's Roland, to the small disk. What and how much did it contain? For once he resented the unfathomable secrecy of computerised information. A typescript told you at once how much; you could flick through it, tasting the flavour of the language, gauging the pace and character of the construction. But electronic material was not only inscrutable but invisible, disk-only wise, until transliterated by a computer. My God, what a disaster it would be for future generations should they unearth the disks, but no longer have the machines that could decipher them!

He thought of asking the secretary to print it out, but was too impatient for even this delay. He switched on his own PC and loaded the disk. Words appeared on the screen.

*"At Millwater the sound of water was always in our ears; the sound of water and the sound of music..."* He had intended to scroll quickly down, making an estimate of what it covered; noting names, dates, events. As it turned out he became so mesmerised by the elegiac tone of Anna Cummins' prose that he continued to read without break. These were not jottings for a musical biography; these were intimate personal memoirs that revealed as much of the writer as of her subject.

The patch of sun moved across his desk and over the carpet, and still Jonathan stayed there. He didn't break off at the end of 90 minutes to seek refreshment, and the cigarettes remained untouched in his drawer.

Part 2 ends

ADIEU, SWEET AMARILLIS

Part 3 – "Here is for me no biding"

# CHAPTER 21

The midday sun beat down upon the steep, crumbling road. Glare reflected off broken white stone. The van came round the corner fast and slammed on its brakes in a flurry of dust and gravel. The back wheels slid sideways and dug into the high verge dragging it to a stop. The tawny puppy that had been playing in the road scuttled sideways and cowered shivering in the long grass beside the road.

"*Cazzo! Porco cane!*" A stream of imprecations poured out of the driver as he started up his stalled engine and pulled the little delivery van back onto the road. The puppy lay low until it was out of sight and the cloud of dust had settled.

She had been in pursuit of one of the noisy crickets that orchestrated the summer heat but which always fell silent or leaped astonishingly out of sight the minute she was about to put a paw upon them. The roadway was unfamiliar territory to her and the pursuit of interesting smells, sounds and objects had carried her quite a distance in half an hour. Now, as her heartbeat and respiration began to steady, she lifted a sensitive brown nose to see if she could detect any of the familiar smells of home. There was a cocktail of stimulating animal and vegetable aromas on the breeze, mixed with the lingering mineral scent of the van, but none of the smells that meant home: no kitchens, cooking or floor polish, no familiar animal or human sweat, no tapestry of odours that surrounded her at the palazzo every day.

The puppy whimpered, more in expression of her lost state than as a call for help. Then a large black and russet butterfly alighted on a stem close by, fanning its wings and commandeering her attention, and instantly she had forgotten home.

Back at the Palazzo ai Monti the puppy's absence was not discovered until evening when Alberto came to serve the evening feed. As he carried the three earthenware bowls of scraps into the rear lobby, he was not surprised to find only the cat and old Callas awaiting him. Habit ruled with domestic animals and the puppy was not yet old enough to know when and where food was to be expected. When the hour of the Principessa's dinner approached however, and the single bowl of food remained unclaimed, he thought it might be judicious to call the puppy. He went out into the garden and wandered the paths and terraces calling somewhat self-consciously "*Cucci, cucci, cucciola.*" The sun was low on the distant hills, slanting through the cypresses and etching the outline of the flowers that tumbled from stone urns bordering the terrace, but no small, barrel-shaped golden figure came trotting down the gravelled paths to meet him. Alberto even walked up to the gates: a high metal and mesh security construction set into the perimeter wall and operated automatically from the gate house, and asked old Gianfranco if he'd seen the little dog that day, or if the gate had been open and unattended at any time. Only the van that brought the groceries from the village at midday had been in and out he was told. No sign of the little dog, Gianfranco assured him, one eye never leaving the football game on television.

Alberto returned to the kitchens feeling distinctly cross with his small charge. The wretched creature was a pest in the house, but it was even more of a nuisance in its absence. At half past seven the nurse on duty took her leave, and he served the pre-dinner aperitif in the small sitting room between the Principessa's ground floor bedchamber, and the conservatory where she slept most of the afternoon. This was the hour when the puppy was expected to be in attendance to be petted, cuddled and later fed the scraps invariably left on the old lady's plate.

Carrying drinks, olives and the ice bucket on a silver tray, Alberto made his way to the conservatory overlooking the garden. The recorded music playing all the time in this part of the house was always deafening, and always, with slight variations, the same: Pignatelli's own greatest recordings. Pignatelli as Carmen, Dido, Lady Macbeth, Tosca. Alberto knew all the operas by heart by now; every nuance, every climax and every scratch; because some of them were very old. The great diva had ceased singing professionally before he joined her service.

The words he had been dreading came as his back was turned pouring the Principessa her sweet Martini. Where, demanded his mistress in steely tones, was the puppy? (*"Dov'è la cucciola?")*

Desperately Alberto attempted to assure his mistress that no stone had been left unturned in the search for the puppy. But his excuses fell on unsympathetic ears. His mistress divined that the precious beast had been lost, *"È perso?"*

*"È morto,"* replied the parrot in a passable imitation of his mistress as Tosca, having just stabbed Scarpia to death in Act ll.

*"Silenzio Gobbi!"* snapped the singer, indicating, with a lordly wave of a hand covered in rings, that Alberto should cover the bird.

Alberto endured a stern inquisition. Advancing years notwithstanding, his mistress could be a harsh employer. The tender years of the puppy were emphasised; the consequences of its exposure to foxes, birds of prey or kidnapping tradesmen; the sacred nature of his trust, and the precariousness of his continued employment. He was to institute a full search of the house and grounds. No avenue was to remain unexplored. Staff ran in all directions, lights blazed all over the palazzo and the local constabulary were informed. Throughout it all Pignatelli's voice could be heard issuing commands and calling down passionate imprecations on those responsible. With background music by Verdi, the occasion took on the character of grand opera. The diva hadn't enjoyed herself so much for years.

Alberto recognised his unenviable role in this drama;

"She's probably planning to have me executed at dawn – like Calvaradossi, at the end of *Tosca*," he thought dolefully.

* * *

The week after the burglary Anna's 'Special Other', Bill, equipped with unfolding toolkit, capacious overalls and friends in the trade, took over. The house in Holland Park resounded to the sound of power drills, saws and hammering. Metal frames, photoelectric beams, locks and bars were fitted to stable doors throughout. The atmosphere was not restful, and work in the studio, though restored to a semblance of order, was impossible.

"I shall go to Tottenham Court Road and buy a new PC on the strength of the insurance," said Anna to Ros "Will you come?"

Ros, who had been sleeping late and then mooning around looking miserable, shook her head.

"I've got to make plans; decide what I'm going to do in the vac. I let my job go, and I've no money; can't afford a holiday."

"Don't be such a wet blanket. You can entertain yourself at the British Museum or somewhere while I shop, then I'll buy you lunch in Covent Garden."

Ros grinned good-naturedly and said she'd come.

"Of course what you should really do is ring poor Jonathan and apologise for biting his head off on Monday."

"Apologise! I think that's something he owes me!"

"Pax, pax!" Anna held up her hands in surrender.

But Ros had not put Jonathan from her mind.

"You've sent Jonathan your memoirs; or at any rate, an edited version. Are you going to let me see them?" she asked in the minicab as they drove into town.

Anna smiled a secret smile, "Are you interested in a grandparent's past?"

"Of course I'm interested. Don't be self-deprecating; it doesn't suit you. I bet the gutter press would pay millions for your unexpurgated memoirs."

Anna's eyebrows rose in outraged innocence, "What can you think I've been writing?" But she couldn't help a smile tightening the corners of her mouth. "Actually, it might interest you a little. There are some curious parallels."

"Parallels?"

196

"Between my – er – liaison with Roland and yours with Jonathan. If you think you might learn by my experience I'll get a copy run off while I'm playing with computers."

Ros's face broke into a wide grin, "Promise? I can't wait to read it; especially any dirty bits."

When Anna arrived at their rendezvous in Covent Garden, Ros was not alone. It was a possibility that had occurred to Anna. Two young men, one fair and one coffee-coloured, were sitting knees to knees opposite Ros and talking ten to the dozen.

"Hi Granna! This is Kamau and this is George. George is one of my flat mates; my Gran, guys: Anna Cummins."

The two boys rose and pulled up a chair for Anna. A glass of wine was ordered. They were drinking vintage dry cider, apparently referred to as 'VD'.

"Tell her she's got to come with us Mrs Cummins," they urged.

"Oh 'Anna' please, 'Mrs' sounds so ancient,"

"Anna, tell her she's got to come camping with us. We've borrowed an old camper off some Aussies for a couple of weeks and we're going to take tents down to the south coast," said the boy called George, "It'll be great if the weather holds."

"Shitty if it doesn't," said Ros, nevertheless looking happier than Anna had seen her for days.

"Anyway, you only want me under the delusion I'll do some cooking."

The boys were vociferous in their rejection of any such ulterior motive.

"I always burn sausages," she continued.

"On this jaunt it's going to be nothing less than *haute* take-away," Kamau replied. They all laughed.

Anna made an attempt to excuse herself but, in the face of protest, stayed and insisted on buying all three lunch. Ros finally put her into a cab to return to Holland Park alone.

"Bill will keep an eye on you now, won't he? And I've left nothing at your place that I can't live without," said Ros leaning into the cab to give her a farewell kiss. "The guys will take me back to the flat to get my gear. I'll call the minute I get back."

"I suppose you won't be needing this in your camper?" said Anna, showing her a large manila envelope full of typescript.

"Your memoirs? You had it printed?" Ros's face lit up. "You bet I would. 'One should always have something sensational to read in campers,' isn't that what Gwendolyn says in *Importance of Being Earnest;* or something like that?"

"Jonathan has them, so why shouldn't you. You wouldn't like to tell him where you're going would you?" Anna asked tentatively.

The hackles came up instantly, "Like hell! He didn't tell me."

"And if he wants to contact you?"

Ros was adamant, "I'll be in touch; some time."

Jonathan was euphoric. Anna's memoirs were a revelation and he had covered several sheets with ancillary questions he wanted to ask her. The following day the registered package arrived: at last he could start piecing together Roland's elusive final years, and Anna, it appeared, was the quintessential element in them.

He went to Holland Park to thank her. The fact that he might also obtain news of Ros; possibly even see her, or ask Anna's advice on effecting a reconciliation, was an important secondary objective.

Anna's door was opened by a square, ruddy-faced man in white overalls. Jonathan peered at him over the armful of red roses and the off-licence bag of Glenfiddich he was carrying.

"Hallo sport. Where's the funeral?" inquired the man cheerily.

"Mrs Cummins at home?" said Jonathan feeling rather foolish.

"Sure thing. Come on in; make yourself at home. Who shall I say is here?

Jonathan told him his name and waited while he leapt the stairs two at a time and disappeared down a corridor. A few seconds later he reappeared on the landing.

"You're on mate," he called. Jonathan followed him and eventually found himself in Anna's attic studio.

She sat at a large table with a computer on it and swivelled round to face him as he arrived. Jonathan laid the armful of roses and the single malt in its gold box beside her.

"I bought all the roses they had," he said. She looked at him quizzically shaking her head. He continued, "What can I say? The annotated score of *Pippa Passes*; the experimental production notes, all the photographs, letters, music you had worked on together: each alone would have been enough. But your personal history," and he gestured towards the PC, "…it isn't really for me is it? Is it for Roland, for his memory? Or is it for you? Not surely for Simmonds and Sayle, academic publishers? Anna, you are one helluva great lady."

She gave a short, almost noiseless laugh.

"May I drink your health?" he concluded.

"What an excellent idea," she replied reaching for the Glenfiddich. She indicated some glasses on a cupboard behind him. "This is certainly the most charming rejection slip I've ever received from a publisher."

"It's not that, you know it. I'd like to use things from it: the insights into character, the anecdotes; but it's so much more than I need. It should *all* be published."

"Well, perhaps not quite all of it," she deprecated. "To be honest, I didn't send you absolutely everything that I wrote."

The level in the bottle of malt sank gradually as it grew dark, and still Jonathan and Anna talked. Bill shouted up that he was going for a take-away curry, and did they want some.

He had decided against discussing his encounter with Gudrun, hoping to hear her own version of Roland's death in good time, but he mentioned that he was determined to go to Italy and beard Pignatelli in her hilltop palazzo. She seemed cool and uncommunicative on the topic. Nor did she offer any solution to the mystery of the vanished Stradivarius. She was more helpful when he turned to questions about Roland's music.

"What I'd really like to do is go through scores page by page with you beside me. For example; the song cycle that Roland started in Italy fired by Ezra Pound's enthusiasm for fascism; did he finish it? And how does it square with *March from the North* dedicated to the British hunger marchers?"

199

"They're one and the same," answered Anna. "It was typical of Roland to switch allegiances with the tide of whoever was influencing him. When Ezra ranted about the Corporate State, Roland had visions of unity and strength under a strong leader. When Andrzej Kaminski raved about the hardships of the poor and unemployed, Roland switched to portraying noble workers marching for their rights. He had dynamism but so little sense of direction. He was a torrent shaped by the channels through which it flows."

The race at Millwater sprang to Jonathan's mind.

She came to the door to say goodnight when he left.

"I thought perhaps you would ask me about Ros?" she said, "She was with me when she telephoned you. She was tough on you."

"I suppose I deserved it. If she's right about Gudrun, only your forethought preserved all this valuable material. Do you really think that she could still be so bitter as to break into your house to steal what you are working on?"

"She did it before. And she didn't even try to hide it. She knows that I won't tell the police. I don't want anything to do with her."

"Is that because of what they did at Millwater, after Roland's death?"

"No." And her tone made it clear the subject was closed. "Don't give up with Ros will you? You know she cares for you?"

He shrugged. "I'm pretty hopeless with women I'm afraid. What should I do? I care about her too," he said, looking at her ruefully.

"Of course you do. So don't be defeatist. Keep trying. You're not hopeless; you're lazy and haven't discovered what's required of you. Keep researching. The truth will emerge."

He wondered if her words referred to more than just Ros as he climbed into the cab and she closed the door.

# CHAPTER 22

*I remember Paola in her prime: Paola in the gardens at Millwater under a parasol, swathed in exotic draperies that emphasised her fine shoulders and masked the solid flesh below. Paola at the wheel of the red Alfa 8C sports car, in a floppy sun hat, the miserable spaniel, Ferrier, at her side. Paola on stage: sexy as Carmen; noble as Norma; tragic as Dido. Paola as Ottima in* Pippa Passes: *blood-red velvet and a cascading Titian wig framing the famous shoulders. There was a touch of Lucrezia Borgia in her Ottima: a study for her Lady Macbeth: deadly, and devoured with sexual passion. No other singer ever played the role in London. Callas sang it once in Milan, or possibly Bologna – in Italian translation. The great American mezzos considered the part short on meat.*

*"The trouble with* Pippa Passes,*" the critic, Felix Aprahamian wrote, "Is that nobody dies in Act III."*

*Paola's opinion was that we had followed Browning too closely in the libretto.*

*"Would be better if Pippa killed in the end."*

*We had seen little of her in summer 1938. She had engagements at various festival. I was preoccupied with my first year exams and later went home to see my family. Roland had taken a house in Brittany with Helga, Gudrun and his mother. It was not, I learned through countless postcards, a great success.*

*Life wasn't much fun with my parents either. The doom and shame generated by the Munich fiasco hung over the household, augmented on my part by the misery of being separated from Roland, and having to hide it. My mother kept asking about Stefan whom she suspected of being connected with my alleged* 'study trip' in Venice, and I felt guilty about him, because he had noticed the coincidence of Roland's and my absence abroad, and was hostile and resentful whenever we met.

As soon as we could, Roland and I made excuses about needing to be in London, and this was when we established our base at Luke Gerard's. From that summer to the next, Pippa filled every corner of my life not occupied by my studies or political activity.

Roland was not easy to work with. Most composers write music mentally, hearing it in the inner ear. Roland resembled the cinema stereotype: hand pressed to fevered brow, inspirational chord on the piano and hastily scribbled notes on paper before it dies away. He carried only general concepts in his head, and needed to experiment and hear what he wrote.

This keyboard dependency did not prevent him receiving inspiration at the most inopportune moments, particularly in public. I would meet him at Pagnani's, a faraway expression in his eye, scribbling music on a paper napkin. He would jot down notes on newspapers, concert programmes or even his students' work. The muse struck on buses, during lessons, in his doctor's waiting room, at almost any time when he was bored and not the centre of attention. Once, during a dull dinner party at the Abrahams', he disappeared for an hour and came back bubbling with excitement having reworked the Act III silk-girls' chorus on lavatory paper.

He was also easily discouraged. Sometimes I returned to the studio to find him writing furiously, eager to play me the latest arrangement. But as often, he would be slumped in a chair, face flushed, whisky bottle at his elbow and a pile of torn up manuscript in the wastepaper basket. Once he reached this stage there was no resurrecting his faith in what he had destroyed. We could only start something new and hope that some new success would encourage him to revisit what had been rejected.

Things were still good between us that first autumn. His vigour and charm, and the breadth and depth of his musicianship still held me in thrall. He still played tutor to me in bed. We laughed a lot and wanted to know each other's thoughts. But thin patches had appeared where the garment of our love was strained and beginning to wear. As I gained confidence – in music, as in sex and life – he became more insecure. No longer always my mentor and guide, he made snide remarks about my new-found competence and those I shared it with, especially Stefan, whom he began to treat as a rival. But if he intended to retain me in a subordinate role, he failed. His criticism only alienated me and made me more determined to assert my independence and earn respect as an equal. In this Stefan was my lifeline, and I strove to keep the peace between them for my own sake.

And so the moment arrived when Pippa Passes was to be subjected to the scrutiny of others.

I had been dreading that this long gestation followed by this painful labour (Olga's childbirth imagery seemed to have attached itself to the idea of composition) would be abortive, or worse, deliver a monstrosity, or a mouse.

In the event, the new arrival was made welcome. John Abrahams was delighted at the new Fredricks offering. Ernest Grossman was lukewarm, but other friends and colleagues expressed approval. Even Helga said she was glad the composition stage was over, so that opera might now earn them honour and reward. The only critical fairy at the feast was Paola.

"Mamma mia, what sort of a language is this for opera? Who want to listen to anyone sing in English?" Somebody murmured 'Purcell, Delius?' But the diva did not deign to hear. "What the Prima Donna do in acts II and III, tell me? File her nails? What happen in this opera? The ragazza comes on and sing and go off, then what? No action; no drama; no great death climax!"

"Most opera plots sound a little thin when précised Paola," said John Abrahams apologetically, but Roland remained curiously undaunted.

"So you won't want the role of Ottima when we open in London next autumn then, Paola? Do you think Kathleen Ferrier would be interested, Ernest?"

"Maledizione!" said the singer with a flourish of her hand, "You do this opera without Pignatelli then you even more foolish than everyone think. Ferrier as an Italian noblewoman – a passionate woman who kills for love – bah! Give me the score. I make this opera work for you. I show you all."

But though she accepted the role of Ottima, she by no means accepted my role as composer's aide, still less as a performer. I had no inflated idea of my contribution in composing any more than performing. The skill and reputation were Roland's and I always assumed that Pippa *would be presented to the world as his.*

It was considered unfeasible that I should play Pippa on the London stage; the role required a soprano of established reputation. But Roland insisted that I sing the part in the experimental production, mounted without scenery, on the garden stage at Millwater. Paola was displeased.

"No voice; no stature; no presenza! You must have carne to produce sound." And she grasped the meagre flesh of my adolescent arm like one rejecting an underfed bird for the oven.

But Roland was adamant. "The undeveloped quality of Anna's voice is perfect for Pippa. It is innocent, otherworldly, angelic. The part needs a clear, high soprano, without vibrato. Its lack of volume won't matter in the garden."

I had noticed that as our relationship matured he gained confidence in handling Paola and his other women. He demonstrated less bravado and bad temper when they confronted him. He had a more 'take it or leave it' insouciance. And I think Paola recognised that her power over him had been diminished. With the production of the opera his confidence was more than psychological, it was practical. In the experimental production he had total artistic control; if Paola wanted the trial run, she had to accept it. In fairness she did so with good grace; converting her suppressed resentment towards me into an engulfing helpfulness.

"Is possible you become quite pleasant coloratura soprano – when you are bigger. Fill the lungs; expand the chest (if you call this a chest). Stand tall; your whole body makes the music risuona: ring like a bell."

Pignatelli's coaching involved a great deal of poking and prodding which, while not physically painful, made me painfully aware of my physical limitations. But these moments of instructional intimacy offered me insight into the rationale behind her resentment.

"You are not good for him; you know that? You think you make great man of him, but he does not want to be great. He wants to be a little man, looked after. Will you look after him? Not you. You will leave him and take other lovers. You

204

inspire him now, yes. He burns brighter, like a candle before it dies. You are like insulin: you burn him up with your ambition."

At the time I saw no truth in her words. I believed myself to be a liberating force in Roland's life, releasing the creative power within him. But later the simile of insulin, that releases energy by consuming the body's sugar reserves to the point of exhaustion, came back to me with fresh meaning.

For the course of the Millwater *Pippa Passes* there was a truce between us. Only when preparations for the London premiere in September 1939 were afoot, and relations between Roland and me became strained to breaking point, did her muscles ripple and her claws appear.

"Banned from the theatre!" Her voice rang out from the stage lit by cold rehearsal lighting. I remember she was wearing, incongruously considering it was summer, a Persian lamb Cossack hat; part of an ersatz Hussar ensemble, with frogging across the front of the jacket. Ernest Grossman, who was directing the piano rehearsal, turned to peer into the darkness of the auditorium where I had come to sit next to Roland in the stalls.

"I beg your pardon Paola? What's the problem?" he inquired courteously. In those days he was very smooth, every inch the opera maestro: hands long and eloquent, a proud head with its leonine mane of hair already emphasised with a broad streak of grey.

"Banned; not allowed here." The diva was resolute. Her be-ringed hand pointed implacably to where I sat. Ernest turned, saw me sitting next to Roland, and turned back, addressing his star with sweet reasonableness.

"We cannot ban the composer Paola."

"Not he. She: the girl. She banned. Is bad luck!"

"'Bad luck' my Aunt Fanny! Since when have you been superstitious Paola?" This was Roland rolling up his sleeves for a fight. "You're being childish and absurd. What possible objection can you have to…"

"She here; I, in my dressing room," hissed Paula with dramatic resonance, directing her fury at the director and ignoring the fuming composer in the stalls. And without another word she stalked from the stage. No amount of persuasion could prevail upon her to return until I left. I had visited the theatre little enough during rehearsals, and I was shocked by the vehemence of Paola's hostility, and by Roland's reluctance to support my presence openly as his collaborator.

I was excluded more hurtfully on the occasion of the special performance for the Duke and Duchess of Gloucester, who were Patrons of the Royal Academy, a few days before the opera was due to open. It had been organised by the Principal and Sir Henry Wood, who conducted the Academy orchestra, partly in honour of Roland, and also as an act of defiance in the face of mounting panic about war. What had been planned as a photo call became a full dress rehearsal for RAM guests and the cast's family and friends. As it turned out, war was declared the following weekend and London's theatres were closed and all productions cancelled. The city disappeared behind walls of sandbags as the population fled the capital in fear of Hitler's bombs.

After the performance there were to be formal presentations and a reception in the Circle Bar. Everyone behind the production was invited: designers, cast and orchestra, as well as relatives of the principal musicians, including me. Prince Spinola, with Paola's golden-haired little boy, joined the party in the Royal Box.

Roland met me on the landing at the top of the grand staircase. Behind him in the bar I could see the cast lining up to shake hands with the Duke and Duchess. He was almost speechless with rage, his cheeks flushed and his eyes blazing.

"There's nothing I can bloody do about it; the matter is out of my hands. It's childish and cruel, but I'm as impotent as a eunuch. Apparently there's been a personal request to the Duchess from Prince Spinola that you should not be present at the reception."

In the centre of the line-up I could see Paola, resplendent in her velvet costume and Titian wig, leaning upon the arm of her principal man. I could see the plump 40-year-old soprano who had sung Pippa (my part). I could see Helga in an elaborate tea gown and Gudrun dressed in German dirndl. I looked at Roland unbelievingly. The abruptness of the rebuff brought tears stinging to my eyes.

"But it can't possibly matter if I'm there? I won't steal anyone's thunder. My name doesn't even appear on the programme. Only you know my part in this."

He looked as though he were about to cry.

"I know; it's my fault. I could shoot myself. Your name should have been on the score. *If we'd given you a credit, this would have been impossible. But I thought there would be less jealousy if they didn't realise your contribution"*

*The flunkies came towards us to close the double door preparatory to the arrival of the royal party. Roland was torn between loyalty to me and his natural craving for his moment of glory. I looked at him, tall and striking in his evening dress, anguish written all over his weak, handsome face. He could have walked away. He could have put them behind him, with their petty jealousy and spite, come down the stairs with me and we could have gone across the road to a pub and toasted ourselves for what we had created, together; and damn the lot of them. Perhaps I should have asked him; encouraged him to stick by me?*

*But I was proud. It is not pleasant to have a door slammed in your face. It does nothing for confidence still green to feel the frost of envy and betrayal. My cheeks burned with shame, but I held back the tears and didn't ask for sympathy. I wouldn't give anyone the satisfaction of knowing that I cared. I looked at my wretched lover, drawn away to his place of honour. Then I turned on my heel and walked downstairs and out into the street.*

# CHAPTER 23

"You advertised for anyone who remembered Roland Fredricks. My friend Luke Gerard knew him well before the Second World War."

Jonathan had been uncertain whether the designer was still alive until contacted by this young man. He was painfully thin and nervous, chain-smoking long cigarettes throughout their meeting. He had suggested a rendezvous in a bar near Jonathan's office which featured a television screen tuned to afternoon racing, and his eyes moved restlessly to and fro from Jonathan, the screen, and the other people in the bar, as they talked.

"Would you pay for information? We're not well off these days, you know."

Jonathan was at a loss: it hadn't occurred to him anyone might want payment. "One doesn't usually pay. If there were letters there could be a reproduction fee. What exactly does Luke have?" he asked cautiously.

"I don't know the details. I mean… yes: there could be letters. I wasn't born then. But Luke's got boxes of stuff belonging to him; they lived together, you know." There was a hint of pride: celebrity by association in his inflection.

"Lived together?" This was news to Jonathan.

"Yes. During the blitz I think. Anyway, not long before he died."

The upshot was that Jonathan conceded the possibility of some payment, realising it was the only way he would be taken to Luke, but no sum was specified. He paid for the young man's lunch.

"Rikki? Is that you Rikki?" The querulous voice came from a room out of sight the moment they came through the front door. It was a large, ugly Victorian house close to the main road just outside Weybridge. It had belonged to Luke's mother, Jonathan was told.

"Who d'you think it is, you silly old faggot?" snapped Jonathan's companion irritably. "I've brought someone to see you, you old misery."

The young man walked ahead to a conservatory crammed with tropical plants, where an old man sat, framed in a Peacock basket chair. He offered Jonathan a bony white hand. He must have been in his 70s, but well cared for. The luxuriant white hair was well cut and the pale, translucent skin, subtly flattered by carefully applied make-up. He wore a silk shirt and cravat under a primrose cashmere cardigan. He looked elegant but unhappy.

"If I hadn't heard it from Anna Cummins, I wouldn't have believed you old enough to have known Roland Fredricks." Jonathan adjudged this to be an occasion when flattery would be well received, and he was rewarded by a gracious smile of acknowledgement. He heard Rikki snort behind him.

"Don't be vulgar *mon cher,*" said the old man, "Get us some drinkies like a good boy. What will you have Mr Simmonds? Or is it Mr Sayle?" Jonathan enlightened him. "Forgive my young friend, Mr Burroughs. These days it is a trifle hard to keep him in the manner to which he had become accustomed, and it has had a deleterious effect upon his manners."

"You and four million others," said Jonathan, accepting the dry white wine poured grudgingly for him by Rikki. "I hadn't realised you had a close relationship with Roland Fredricks."

The old man's hand flew defensively to his hair, then trailed back to the edge of his collar concealing his initial discomfiture.

"I was very young at the time …"

"Scarcely 20?" Jonathan flattered.

"Twenty two."

"But by 1939 you were sufficiently established to be asked to design the sets for the London production of *Pippa Passes?*"

"That's right. I went on to do a lot of stage work."

He had a way of screwing up his lips and sucking in his wine (it was extremely dry), making his lips a mass of little radiating wrinkles that reminded Jonathan of a cat's arse. And yet it was impossible not to recognise that he must once have been beautiful.

"Ballet Rambert, Bechart, ENO, Glyndebourne…"

"Rikki tells me you actually lived with Roland just before he died,"

Jonathan said cutting through this catalogue of past successes. (Gathering old people's personal reminiscences was making him a ruthless interviewer.) Luke Gerard's hesitation confirmed what he had suspected: that 'lived' might have been an exaggeration. He drew a breath between compressed lips, choosing his words carefully.

"I suppose really he lived with me… for a time. I think he started working at my place in Chelsea the autumn of 1938 – just after Munich. Things were a trifle fraught at Millwater after his little foray to *La Serenissima*. The Gorgons suspected it was serious this time. They gave him a hard time, those women. He got more loyalty from men in his life than women."

"Are you including Anna?" Jonathan inquired surprised.

The little creased mouth tightened and the fingers holding the glass cracked as he unfurled them, parrot-like;

"Including little Miss Williams indeed. She was supposed to be working on the score of *Pippa* with him. She was studying, so they used to meet at my place in the evenings. He liked her there when he was composing or orchestrating: to hear him play things, give praise and encouragement. But that autumn she often wasn't around. More likely off on some protest march with that crazy Polish boyfriend, protesting about what Hitler was doing to Polish Jews. So he used to play things to me; show me the scoring – not that I knew much about it. But I could see he needed looking after. I saw he had regular meals and tried to keep him off the booze."

"A regular little Miss Nightingale!" sneered Rikki, filling up everyone's glass because his own was empty.

With some prompting from Jonathan when the digressions became tangential, Luke recounted the progress of his friendship with Roland through the winter of 38/39 into spring 1939, when preparations for the Millwater production of *Pippa* were afoot, and he started work on the designs for the London production scheduled to open in September '39. "Roland took it badly when the opening was called off because of the war. He'd worked himself into such a state during rehearsals. And he was never very good at handling disappointment."

"Was he actually living with you then, or just working in Chelsea?" Jonathan asked. "And where was Anna then?"

Luke sucked in wine and paused, his pursed lips poised at the rim of his glass. Both hands were now raised, wrists bent back and knuckles clenched in a gesture of arch cautiousness. Jonathan sensed that he was engaged in some private attempt to make order out of confused memories, or possibly to construct them in the light most favourable to himself.

"The war changed things. There was the blackout: all the lights went out. It felt like the end of the world," Luke began, not answering Jonathan's question directly. It was clear that this was something important to him, but difficult for him to talk about. "Things were awful between Anna and Roland after the collapse of the London production. They'd cast an experienced singer for Pippa, you know. She was gutted; thought of it as 'her part' I think. And I believe she was quite the little star at the Academy. She stopped coming to Chelsea. (Something going on with the Polish boy I suspect.) But Roland stayed during the week and sometimes over the weekend. It must have been after Christmas that he did the insulin overdose."

There was no sound for a moment except a sharp intake of breath from Jonathan. Luke began again, his voice low and uncertain. "He and Anna had both been away from London at Christmas: Roland at Millwater – that always put him on edge – and Anna took the boyfriend to her parents I think. London was really jittery, I remember. It was weird: we were at war; there were sandbags everywhere, but there was only the occasional air raid; nothing to what we suffered later. The clubs: The Bag of Nails and Smoky Joe's were wilder and more crowded than ever, with a hysterical feeling: 'Eat, drink and be merry, for tomorrow we die.'

"Roland came back in the New Year looking really grim. You only had

211

to speak to him and he snapped your head off. He did hardly any work, just sat around exuding gloom – smoking and playing the gramophone, the Scotch always at his elbow. His eyes bloodshot, hair and beard straggly, teeth stained. His whole face sagged with depression. He'd lost weight and his clothes were in a terrible state. I tried to draw him out of himself, get him back to composing or playing, but nothing made any impression.

"She must have come when I was out. I saw it on the hall table as soon as I came in – Anna's key, with a note I didn't bother to read. Before I went to look for him, he came to the top of the stairs looking all *Death of Chatterton* in his shirtsleeves and said, 'I've done it this time Lucy,' (That's what he called me, you know.) 'I've cooked my proverbial goose. Crap Composer Makes Meaningless Gesture! And the pathetic thing is, I haven't the courage to go through with it. Help me Lucy.'

"I knew he was drunk of course. But he was often drunk, unless he was having a hangover. Then it dawned on me: she'd left him and he'd taken something. I was in a frightful panic. I wanted to call a doctor, but he wouldn't let me. He said he'd doubled up his insulin, but that if he ate enough sugar he could use it up. We called a taxi and got him to the nearest milk bar and he sat for an hour or more drinking orange squash and eating cake and jam doughnuts and singing vulgar songs until they threw us out.

"I brought him home and put him to bed. It was snowing and he was deathly cold. We only had the oil heater, but I made a hot water bottle and piled on blankets, but no matter what I did he still felt clammy and ice cold. Finally I climbed in next to him and tried to keep him warm in my arms."

Luke stopped, and Jonathan saw that the large watery eyes had filled with tears. His empty glass stuck out between his fingers and he rubbed obsessively at his knuckles with the fingers of his left hand. Jonathan looked round for a bottle to refill the glasses and found Rikki behind him already drawing another cork. His sarcasm cut across Luke's painful recollection like a knife.

"And when he woke up, he said you were a nauseating nancy, and keep your filthy fingers to yourself. Life's a bitch isn't it?"

Jonathan couldn't tell whether this was an invented jibe or a paraphrase of an earlier confidence. Luke's mouth tightened, but he neither confirmed nor denied the alleged rejection.

"Roland wasn't an easy man," he said defensively, "He was all ups and downs, and he could be very cruel; especially when hurt. He didn't mean half the things he said, but he wanted to be clever. And he hated himself afterwards. He despised himself. He needed others to make him feel talented and worthwhile. That's what made him so vulnerable – and so appealing."

He accepted the offer of a refill from Rikki. Jonathan covered his glass with his hand, glancing surreptitiously at his watch as he did so. Trying to move things on he said, "But he didn't die; not in 1940, did he? But was that what happened when he did die – later?"

Rikki also was getting impatient.

"How would he know? Kicked the old lush onto the streets after he rejected her, didn't she? Hell has no fury like a fairy spurned."

This time the old man did not ignore the yapping on the sidelines. With dignity he transferred his gaze to his friend.

"Rikki, *mon cher,* it must be frustrating for you that someone wishes to hear what I have to say, and unpleasant not to be the centre of attention, but your humourless sniping is becoming a bore. Put the bottle over here and go and fetch Roland's things that I put on one side. Then Mr Burroughs can tell us whether they are worth the money you are so desperately anxious to ask for them."

And slightly to Jonathan's surprise, the young man left the room without a squeak.

Reasserting his authority had restored Luke's composure and he resumed in a less elegiac tone. "He doesn't mean it, Mr Burroughs. Insecurity makes bitches of us all. But he's right. I wasn't with Roland at the end. We lost touch. But I saw him once more in strange circumstances. Some of us were organising a party later that year, during the Blitz. We went to Archer Street in Soho to hire musicians for the band. Among them, to my amazement, I saw Roland. He looked terrible: as though he had been sleeping under the arches, I spoke to him: told him he was welcome to come back to Chelsea to clean up and have a square meal, but he refused.

"He sounded crazy. I wrote down my phone number and told him to ring if he changed his mind. I got a call a few weeks later, in the New Year. He was in some ghastly hotel near Victoria, drunk and almost incoherent. He wanted me to contact Anna for some reason. Apparently she wouldn't talk to him after the suicide attempt. He said it was important because he had to 'put things right'. Don't ask me what he meant. Then he said, since Anna wouldn't see him, would I take a message to her, and his *violin!* That got to me; to send her his violin. That sounded so final. He was never parted from that Stradivarius. I thought at once he must be suicidal and planning to take another overdose.

"So when he rang off I tried Anna, without success. Then I rang Millwater, though heaven knows the last thing he would have wanted in that state was his wife. Helga told me to contact Paola Pignatelli who was in London. I finally got through to her some 30 minutes after I had spoken to Roland. I gave her the name of the hotel but, as I put the phone down, I began to think I'd made a mistake, handing Roland over to the women.

"I rushed out and tried to find a taxi. London was smothered in one of those claustrophobic 'Pea-soupers'. You're too young to remember, but you couldn't see a hand in front of your face, or hear anything further than a few yards. Cars loomed up like ghosts out of the darkness. And of course there were no lights anywhere. All lights had to be covered because of the bombing. Even when I found a cab we moved at little more than walking pace. It took me an age to cover the distance from Chelsea to Victoria, and then I had a problem finding the hotel Roland had named. When I found the right place they said that a lady had come and collected Mr Fredricks: a foreign lady. They said they thought Mr Fredricks had been unwell because the chauffeur had had to help him into the car.

"I asked if Roland had left anything for me; or maybe for Anna Williams: any message, envelope or package? And they said there was nothing. Some Irish kid had come to collect him for a musical engagement and had taken some stuff away with him. I went up to the room and there was just empty bottles and dog-ends; certainly no violin. I suppose everything went with Paola when she took him?"

Luke heaved a great sigh when he finished the narration and took a deep draught from his glass. He had talked for nearly and hour, and the sun had fallen behind the trees and the atmosphere in the conservatory had become less oppressive. Rikki returned with an ancient cloth-spined folder, its marbled covers tied with ribbon.

"There's a lot of music in handwriting here," he said. "It's got to be worth something surely?"

"It rather depends on what music, whose handwriting, and whether there are other copies," Jonathan said cautiously. The young man's eyes had taken on a distasteful gleam.

"When Helga died Roland's daughter Gudrun wrote, via her solicitors, asking me to return anything of her father's. I ignored it. I had little enough, and in his lifetime there had been no love lost between her and her father. I didn't see why she should have his mementos. But you're welcome to it if it helps. It has no sentimental value for me now."

Jonathan untied the folder and lifted up some of the sheets of manuscript music and notes it contained. He had seen Fredricks' script on several occasions, and this was not it. Fredricks' notation was cramped, sketchy and heavily corrected, as someone writes who has composed for many years but has a struggle to get things right; as Beethoven wrote. But some of these sheets were almost copybook in their clarity and precision: the open notes rounded, quaver tails carefully joined, every rest filled in, and they were written almost without correction: like Mozart's manuscript.

Jonathan flicked through the sheets. There were single staves of melody with words under them; some recognisably from *Pippa Passes*. But then there was other material, with words and notes he didn't recognise.

"There seems to be music from the first opera…" He hesitated. Whatever it was, it was not much use unless it could be authenticated. "I wonder; do you think this music could have been copied – perhaps, for performance?"

"Well, not those on top," said Luke confidently. "See the stain on that

215

corner; that's where Roland spilt whisky on it. There's a full annotated score for the Millwater production at the bottom somewhere, in a cellophane cover."

"If you don't want it perhaps this daughter of Fredricks will pay out," said Rikki tartly, reaching to collect up the spurned documents. Jonathan moved fast to secure his claim.

"It's difficult to say how valuable they are until I've shown them to the right people, but I'm confident enough to give you something on account if that's OK?" And before Rikki could whip the folder away, Jonathan produced his chequebook and pen.

"Have you any idea where Paola took him? Was it long before his death?" He asked as he tore out the cheque.

The old man's eyes had started to droop. The pale, tense hands lay limp in his lap and it was obvious that it cost him some effort to turn his mind back once more to that time. He raised his eyelids with some effort and spoke after a few moments thought.

"I met his publisher, John Abrahams, at Pagnani's not long after. You know, the restaurant in Great Portland Street where they embroidered the signatures of their celebrated guests onto the tablecloths? Not that I was among that elevated company at the time. And he said 'Have you heard? Roland's dead. Heart attack or something; suddenly, at home.' I think Paola must have taken him to Millwater. The women got him in the end.

"There was no notice of a funeral. A month later John and his friends got together and organised a memorial service at St Martin's-in-the-Fields. Helga and the daughter didn't put in an appearance, but Paola came, and brought her little boy: a divine, golden-haired cherub scarcely five years old; not a bit Italian looking."

Luke laid his head back against the chair and closed his eyes.

Jonathan prepared to take his leave. Luke opened his eyes and spoke simply.

"There have been a lot of lies told about him you know."

"I know," said Jonathan, picking up the folder.

"But he wasn't queer. That night he lay in my arms I was really close to him, but it wasn't as a lover. He needed comfort, that's all; undemanding love. And when he left it wasn't like Rikki said, though I may have twisted things to protect my pride. It was because he knew I loved him and was suffering because of it. 'I muck it up for those who love me Lucy,' he said."

Jonathan drove back to London, the prized folder on the seat beside him. He hadn't said anything at the time, and he had managed to hide his excitement at what he saw it contained. Quite clearly he had seen the name: 'Amarillis.' Did he have in his possession some of that lost work?

The tangled web was beginning to unravel and the person who could knit it together was still alive, living in Italy.

# CHAPTER 24

"What I need for this biography is a bloody theme!" said Jonathan, throwing his arms behind his head and tipping his chair back dangerously. "You know, the opening shots of Olivier's *Hamlet*; 'This…is the tragedy…of a man… who could not…make up…his mind.' Or 'One who loved not wisely but too well'; though that wouldn't do for Roland Fredricks: his loving had not been notably successful.

Old Rathbone peered at him owlishly over his spectacles;

"Where do you print the theme on a book?"

Jonathan let his front chair legs fall with a bang.

"Nowhere, I suppose. Themes are only visible to authors; or reviewers."

That morning he had blocked out the main sections of the biography and made a stab at the intro. "Work from the known to the new," he told himself. He would establish the social and artistic context, the material he had covered in his DPhil, emphasising the parallels between the 30s and the recession-blighted 90s – and relate it to Roland's early experiences and work and to the apogee of his achievement in the late 30s.

The last section would be the most important – musically – and the most difficult to write. Hopefully it would also be new and challenging: a Burrough's perspective.

He had made a list of key questions still to be answered: "One: when/ where/and why did he break with Anna and what was he writing at the time? When did Stefan rear his youthful head and became a serious rival? I hope

Anna is prepared to supply these answers," he thought. "Two: what's the significance of the strange manuscript hand? Three: what the fuck became of the Strad? Four (very important): exactly how did Roland die? And finally: where does Paula fit in; starting back in 36/37 up to his death? And for these latter answers I have to reach Paola herself."

He'd phoned Anna the morning after his meeting with Luke Gerard. She sounded tired.

"Poor little Lucy. I didn't know he was still alive. I haven't seen him for years. Did he tell you anything new?"

"He told me quite a bit about the final months; after your break-up with Roland." She was silent so he continued, "Naturally, I'd like to check things with you." Still, she said nothing. "He had some manuscript music Roland left at his place."

"Manuscript?" This time there was interest, not to say alarm, in her voice. "He's got music we – Roland left there?"

"Yes, would you have time to look at it?"

She hesitated, "I, I've been a bit tired. Is it one of Roland's scores? I thought Roland cleared everything out of Lucy's when he left."

"There's no hurry; I need to go through it myself first and, um, I think I shall be away for a few days. I've decided to go to Italy and secure an audience with La Pignatelli. So many questions come back to her. Did you know that she collected Roland from some dump in London and took him – back to Millwater I suppose? Just before he died?" He regretted mentioning it even as he spoke. Her silence was leaden and he continued, concerned, "Of course I really want to hear your version of that time?"

There was a pause before she replied, "Yes, yes, I must get it down on paper – soon. Perhaps you should let me see the manuscript music. It's probably nothing important."

Bill's voice could be heard nagging her to finish the call. Jonathan decided not to ask her about the disappearance of Roland's violin. This Anna, without edge, irony or attack ,was disconcerting. He remembered what Kate had said about her being ill. He didn't like to ask her directly; she would probably regard it as impertinence. He wished that Ros were around so that he could approach Anna tactfully, through her.

"Have you had any news of Ros?" he asked.

"She's gone camping with a couple of friends. I suggested she call you. I'm afraid I have to go. Good luck with Paola."

He rode Jeremy's bicycle to Helena's. She looked disarmingly scruffy, gardening in shorts and a pair of chunky green and yellow gloves. Hair hung in her eyes and her nose was sunburnt.

"Modelling for *Vogue* again are we?" he teased.

"Fat men who ride bicycles shouldn't throw brickbats," she retorted tartly, rubbing her nose with the back of a gloved hand and leaving a dusty smudge.

"I am *not* fat anymore," he said, hurt. "I just have a small spare tyre. I thought I should return the bike before Jeremy came home for the holidays."

"Dad, come and bowl, come and bowl!" Simon bounced up and down pressing a cricket ball into his hand. He had chalked stumps on the wall at the end of the garden and a strip of sorely-tried lawn acted as wicket.

"I have to be away for a few days." Jonathan spoke to Helena, who had returned to her borders, while pitching a slow toss to Simon who was whacking the turf in front of the stumps.

"Watch out sproglet! A ball through glass counts as a catch!"

"What about Jeremy's School Founder's Day? I suppose you've forgotten." she asked accusingly without looking at him.

"Oh Christ! When is it?"

"Boundary!" yelled his youngest leaping up and down in the crease as the ball skimmed past Jonathan's distracted hand and disappeared though the open kitchen door. The cat shot out as though jet-propelled and disappeared through the hedge. "You are spastic dad!" crowed Simon.

"Saturday week. When's your flight?" The interrupted conversation was resumed, *sotto voce*, once Jonathan had found the cricket ball. He was being put on the Neglectful Father spot again.

"I could probably delay things until then, if you like." He polished the ball on the back of his trousers with a professional flourish. Parental Brownie points were hard to come by.

"It's not a question of whether I like, it's a question of how much you care." She dug a trowel into the earth vigorously.

"I do care, Helena. I'm not going on holiday. It's work. The Fredricks trail leads to Italy; I have to try my luck at reaching Pignatelli. I shall telegraph that I am coming and then just camp on her doorstep. That's how the reporter from *The Late Show* got in."

"One has to suffer for one's work." Helena's voice had an acid note. The sun glinting on her tanned thighs reminded Jonathan that he had been celibate for more than a month. As if reading his thoughts she said, "And will The Lady of the Bicycles be going with you?" She was treading in plants in the border as she inquired, but Jonathan detected the irony in her voice.

"The Lady of the Bicycles is camping with her undergraduate cronies at the seaside. We are temporarily out of communication…"

"What a shame." Her voice traced a sympathetic inflection.

"…not unconnected with my absence in Cambridge the weekend she finished her exams." He continued pointedly.

"Howzat!" The ball hit the stumps, and although his son launched into a vociferous claim that the ball had been wide, the teams decided to break for tea.

Phone calls were made and Jonathan's schedule rearranged so that the Burroughs family could field a full team for Jeremy's Founder's Day. Helena would then drive Jonathan to Heathrow for an evening flight to Italy. Helena had a particular dislike of going to school occasions as a single parent and Jonathan now found himself attending marginally more of these boring, unlicensed functions, than when they were married. However the penance performed a dual salutary role: Helena was gratified and he was reminded of his unsuitability for public domesticity.

After the event, Helena drove him westward towards the airport, traumatised by an afternoon of mind-numbing boredom, smiling at people whose names he couldn't remember, commiserating with their off-spring's problems, eating a revolting tea in a stuffy tea tent and being subjected to the excruciating humiliation of playing cricket with the parents against the Junior X1.

Jonathan drained the final drops from the hip flask that had helped him survive until his flight.

"Why do we do it? What purpose is served, except to remind one that school days were certainly not the best of one's life?"

"Your problem is that you hate anything that requires effort. What schoolteachers call 'lazy'," she commented.

The rebuke reminded him of Anna's admonition; that his reaction to Ros's anger and subsequent departure was defeatist.

"Would you say I was lazy about women, Helena?"

Helena snorted, "Sexually or socially?"

"Either?"

"Both. I seem to recall your favourite position is flat on your back, and your favourite social activity is thinking up excuses for not doing whatever someone else proposes."

"That's not fair,"

"Ex-wives don't have to be fair."

They drove in silence for some minutes, Jonathan feeling disgruntled that she knew him so well that she gave him no incentive to improve. "I don't suppose Helena would believe the efforts I made to pursue Ros, not to mention my sleuthing on this biography. No wonder a chap feels fatalistic." Aloud he said ruefully, "I don't think I'm constitutionally lazy. I can be bloody determined when I'm motivated. I think I am discouraged by setbacks."

"Like I said, you do fine as long as it's easy; but you give up when the going gets tough."

He wasted no more time defending himself, but the conversation did prompt him to leave a contact number to reach him in Italy, not only with Helena but with Anna. If Ros changed her mind he wanted to be within reach.

Ros kicked the empty gas canister and swore. "What pillock left the stopcock on the camping gas open?" She yelled at the tiny figures of her companions leaping up and down in the distant sea. No one answered.

Above her in the wide blue sky, a silver-fish plane carved a silent trail of white vapour. Ros thought again of Jonathan, and wished she were with him. There was sand in her hair and her skin felt taught and salty. "God, I could do with a bath," she thought. The camper was a tip. Empty beer cans, take-away cartons and discarded clothes, all liberally doused in sand. "Fucked if I'm clearing up *again*." She hunted for her jeans and felt in the pockets: a fiver plus £2.57p. Not enough to get her back to London. Still, she could hitch from the main road.

Determinedly she began gathering together her belongings and stuffing them into a tote bag. She scribbled a note to her friends and set off up the cliff path. In the short term she would find a lift and go home. Later perhaps she would contact Jonathan; make peace overtures. "Perhaps Granna was right: I was hard on him. It was a nasty shock discovering that some bastard can hurt you; that you want the beast around."

The rep in the Ford Escort who picked her up was bypassing London to the west, so she got him to drop her at the junction of the M25 and the A3: the spot nearest her parents' house. Suddenly the thought of a swimming pool, clean sheets, luxurious bathrooms and nourishing meals seemed highly desirable. She found a functioning phone box and called home.

"Daaahling, lovely to hear from you." Carole's voice rewarded her with enthusiasm. "Where are you? Do you want to be collected?" Parents were at their best when unconditionally welcoming.

Her mother was, as usual, in the midst of the social whirl.

"Where have you been? You smell frightful. We hoped you'd come and stay part of the holidays. I'm up to my ears. It was the end-of-term do at Tom's school today. I've got a charity garden party tomorrow, Kate's birthday next week, and then it's Ascot."

A cartwheel straw hat that matched her mother's cyclamen suit had been on the seat when Ros got in. She could picture her mother tottering across the school turf in the outfit.

"I'm absolutely frantic with a party for the hospice; I could really do with some help. Your father's in New York and we haven't seen Steve since he started living with that French girl."

Ros lay back in the Rover's soft leather embrace and let her mother's chatter flow over her. There was something reassuring about the sameness of parents even when it had driven you away last time. One piece of information disturbed her however.

"You'll never guess who was at Founder's Day. That publisher – you know, Jonathan Burroughs, and *with his ex-wife!* Do you think they're back together again? I waved, but I don't think he recognised me."

Her mother knew nothing of Ros's involvement with Jonathan so she had no inkling of the shaft of pain this casual news inflicted. So Jonathan was with his wife again. She had known the separation from his children caused him anguish, but she had had no intimation that he was trying to get back with his wife. To take her mind from the conflicting emotions aroused by thoughts of Jonathan she changed the subject.

"Have you had any news of Granna?"

"No. That Bill seems to be in charge there since the burglary. I called once to ask how she was. He said he didn't want to disturb her." Carole harrumphed at the interference of outsiders. "I'm sure she's not well. If I wasn't worked off my feet I'd go up there and see for myself. I was worried sick about the burglary and her living on her own; or without any real family anyway. I can't think why we allow it. It would be better if she came to live with us; or why not Kate? I mean, it would be so much more suitable."

Ros avoided any direct comment or concession in response to her mother's conversational barrage, drank a huge glass of water and retired to soak in a long bath to the music of her personal stereo. Inside her was an unfathomed well of misery that she could neither chart nor ignore.

She was not given to emotional introspection. She experienced some uncertainty about her achievements and abilities normal for her age group, but it was not rooted in any deep-seated sense of inferiority or doubts as to her intrinsic value, such as fill the agony columns of women's magazines. When strong, disturbing feelings reared their heads they were not familiar gorgons. She needed new weapons to deal with the encounter.

Being with Jonathan was good. Being without, when she was studying hadn't worried her, so why the angst now he was away? Was it the thought of him somewhere else without her, and with someone else? Ros contemplated *another woman*. Jealousy was naff. "For Heaven's sake! She's the mother of his kids. Of course he sees her. We don't trespass on each other's territory. Unless she still wants to sleep with him, of course; or he with her?" Ros thought about sleeping with Jonathan, about his hands moving over her, and *in* her. "Though I wouldn't blame her if she did," she thought, smiling. "Fancying someone gives them power over you all right, but it's power for pleasure as well as pain. I'm hooked, landed. I want him."

She looked down at her body surfacing and sinking beneath the warm water and registered sexual longing like a physical hunger. Masturbation would be pointless because her body was both owned and disowned by Jonathan. Once or twice down at the coast she had been tempted to have a friendly screw with one of the guys, but when it came to it, she couldn't. She was locked onto Jonathan. "I want those teasing, come-to-bed eyes, those slow, sexy, confident hands. I want his big shoulders, the weight of his body on me. Shit! I want him inside me!"

Steam rose around her, and above the music of Vivaldi Ros howled like a dog for her lover.

# CHAPTER 25

Jonathan was in Italy less than 48 hours before he recalled Helena's taunt about giving up when the going got tough.

He had hired a Fiat Panda at the airport and driven through the mountains towards the small town near Pignatelli's palazzo where the travel company had booked him a room. The atmosphere was close and oppressive. Distant black clouds threatened a storm. He stared gloomily through the darkening windscreen at this foreign place.

He had assumed rashly that in Europe these days everyone spoke English, but had been rapidly and rudely disabused at the car hire desk at Pisa airport. Even when he managed (with the help of the pocket dictionary) to construct a hesitant question, he definitely couldn't understand the reply, and he was convinced they had added things to his hire contract that were excessive. He longed for Ros.

"I wish I could talk the lingo like her. Why isn't she with me? If only I weren't alone!" The last hit him most. He hated travelling, and working alone.

The medieval town, its stone walls and red tiled roofs clambering up the mountainside, was alive with suppressed excitement. Everywhere people were putting up stalls, hanging flags, cleaning and decorating shop windows.

"*Festa,*" they explained when he inquired the purpose of these preparations, *Festa de* what? He just about managed '*Santo* Someoneorother'. But who or what it meant in English no one thought it necessary to explain.

The hotel was old, with beamed ceilings and creaky staircases. It was on the edge of the walled town up against one of the arched gateways, and Jonathan's windows, fronted with wrought-iron balconies, looked uphill towards the monastery around whose skirts the town clung. In the light of the gathering storm it was a sombre brooding presence, emphasised by the toll of a single church bell.

Jonathan, lingering momentarily at the window, glass of relaxing duty-free Scotch in hand, gazed down into the narrow streets below. His attention was caught by a girl outside a bar 50 yards up the hill. She was standing on top of one of the little metal tables that furnished the terrace outside the bar to hang up a string of coloured flags. The precariousness of her perch, but more particularly the shapeliness of her brown legs, focused Jonathan's attention. The extended position of her arms had lifted her skirt until it barely covered her pleasantly rounded bottom. Briefly she lifted one foot from the table and Jonathan noticed a fine gold chain round her ankle. At that moment the table tipped slightly and Jonathan felt a cry of warning rise to his throat. But before he could vocalise his alarm, a man appeared from inside the bar and ran to put his arms round the girl's legs.

From the sound of his voice he was scolding her, but the girl seemed unconcerned. She finished attaching the flags, and, as he lifted her from the table, she threw back her head, covered in dark curls, and laughed as he lowered her to the ground.

She gave the man a gentle push in the chest, and turned to go back into the bar. The man followed still scolding and waving his hands.

From wallowing in his isolation, Jonathan felt a sociable urge to go out for a drink. He finished sorting his belongings, made his way downstairs and out of the hotel. Finding his way through the bendy little alleyways that led up the hill was harder than he had anticipated, and sadly, by the time he reached the bar on the hill, metal shutters indicated that it was closed.

The following day the weather had not improved. There had been rain during the night and the air was still and moist. Black clouds loomed behind the mountain promising worse to come. Jonathan went in search of a florist and arranged for 50 red roses to be delivered to the Pignatelli household a short drive away in the hills. At first there had been some confusion. He spoke of 'Signora Pignatelli' and the little florist, who was no more than 18 years old had looked blank. Then, when he had added Il Palazzo ai Monti, recognition dawned and she had said, "Oh, the Principessa! The old lady; yes, we know her." And Jonathan was reminded that Pignatelli had been married to Prince Spinola and no doubt retained the title after her husband's death. He followed up the telegram he had sent from England to forewarn of his arrival, with a phone call which met with the same polite brush-off that he had received the first time round. But this time he had prepared his counter ploy. With a deep breath he launched into carefully prepared, no doubt appallingly pronounced, Italian: "It displeases me much to not be able to see the Princess. I am come very far. It is a thing important and I am resolved not to leave without having spoken to her." He hoped the words contained the right mixture of courtesy, determination and urgency, to warn Pignatelli's minion that he was unlikely to leave without a long and tiring siege.

The response was a non-verbal noise of incomprehension and, with a sigh, the voice range off.

He called later that day with no greater success.

The following day he decided to reinforce his long distance communication with a personal visit to the Palazzo ai Monti. After lunch, armed with further bouquets and pre-prepared flowery Italian phrases (The *Istituto Italiano di Cultura* in London had been most obliging), he drove the Fiat out of town through the hills and towards a village in the next valley where he had been told he would find a road leading to the Palazzo ai Monti.

He had dressed with some care for the occasion just in case he were fortunate enough to gain entry to the diva, and now, as the sun broke momentarily through the clouds and set steam rising all around him, he began to feel hot and uncomfortable. Having, with difficulty, identified the turning – a rutted unmade road winding steeply uphill between trees – he stopped the car and got out in order to remove his cream linen jacket, which he was anxious should remain uncreased, and lay it on the seat beside him. As he stood beside the car a golden-haired puppy came dashing out of a farmyard, wriggled up to him and started jumping up his trousers. He repulsed it gently, unable to feel anger at something so appealing, and paused to scratch it behind its floppy ears and under the velvety chin. "Perhaps I'll take a break and have a jar in the village before my onslaught on the citadel," he thought.

Two hundred yards down the road a cluster of unremarkable buildings included the characteristic plastic-ribbon-hung doorway and battered tables and chairs that marked a bar. He walked towards it swinging the jacket over his shoulder. The puppy followed, cavorting happily at his heels.

"*Buon giorno Signora,*" he greeted the big-breasted woman presiding over a gleaming espresso machine and stainless steel bar.

He ordered a glass of white wine and seated himself at one of the tables by the roadside.

With the customary embarrassment of an Englishman attempting verbal communication in a foreign language, Jonathan fumbled clumsily with some Italian, "*È bello, il piccolo cane,*" he attempted indicating the puppy, as the woman put the glass on the table in front of him.

"*Ah, la cucciola,*" She bent, scooped up the animal and cradled it against her ample bosom. The puppy's rounded tummy was almost as smooth and pale as a baby's. Its tail beat back and forth with pleasure between its extended legs. The woman attempted to explain, in vibrant contralto, that the puppy was unknown to the bar personnel, probably lost (*persa*). But Jonathan's Italian was not up to understanding. He thought perhaps the puppy was called Percy, although he couldn't fail to notice that it was female. He stayed for another glass of the local wine, dispensed unrefrigerated from large carboys in slatted, yellow plastic baskets, and returned to the car, no cooler, but refreshed.

The road wound upwards, fringed now by staked vines, now by vivid green conifers, and finally by thick oak woodland. It was crudely surfaced with loose white stones and deeply rutted by the flow of surface water at each hairpin bend. He passed an occasional deserted shack or cottage, but no house of any size for several miles. When he had climbed 100 feet or more a high wire mesh fence topped with barbed wire began to run beside the road. There were signs indicating fiercely guarded private property: '*Vietato l'ingresso; Proprietà privata; Attenzione: cane feroce!*' Even Jonathan's Italian got the message.

"I gather strangers are unwelcome at the Pignatelli residence."

He came eventually to a broad tarmac driveway leading off the lane, which he turned into ignoring the screaming notices. After 200 yards the driveway opened out, the woodland fell back and he found himself in front of a gateway. It had once been fine and dignified with a wall and pillars of golden stone, crested with rampant heraldic beasts bearing shields, and supporting a pair of ornate wrought-iron gates some 12 feet high. But this, probably 18th century, defence of privacy had not been sufficient for the present day. Where the wire mesh fence joined the stone wall, broken glass had been added to the coping to discourage invaders, and behind the elegant wrought-iron, a pair of electrically operated security gates sealed the entrance emphatically.

Jonathan got out of the car and looked for a bell. Vehicles and persons presumably penetrated this fortress from time to time, if only to import further siege rations. On one of the side pillars he found the kind of voice box that operates entry phones in blocks of flats. Into this he spoke in beginners' Italian feeling foolish, like someone unaccustomed to the impersonal communication of an answering machine.

"I bear a message and flowers for the Princess."

After a few minutes a man dressed in a dirty sweatshirt appeared from a lodge visible just inside the gates. Jonathan could hear the sounds of massed cheering from inside and deduced that he had dragged the janitor from a ballgame on TV.

The man came up to the double gates without showing any inclination to open them and spoke unceremoniously with the Italian equivalent of "Whajewant?"

Jonathan explained, in prepared Italian, that he had come to lay the blooms currently filling the back of the hired Fiat at the feet of the great diva in homage.

The janitor was unimpressed. His Italian response conveyed something like, "Push off: no can do," and he turned to leave.

Jonathan took up armfuls of the rejected flowers and waving them at the man through the barrier. He had, he said, come to give flowers and give flower he would. He went to the entry microphone and began an unmusical rendition of the serenade from *Marriage of Figaro* as a demonstration of what he could do to spoil the ballgame. The man hissed an incomprehensible oath and then, from the pocket of his grubby trousers, produced incongruously the very latest in mobile phones. He banged a few buttons and spoke, waited, asked Jonathan for his name, and when Jonathan told him, repeated it approximately into the phone.

A pause; the man then indicated to Jonathan that, while Jonathan himself was not welcome, the flowers at least were acceptable.

The man took a remote control from another pocket and stepped back to allow both sets of gates to swing inward. Jonathan advanced holding the armful of flowers and the janitor took them. He had a glimpse of gravelled drive and well-tended lawns, of flowering shrubs and statues, and he thought he heard the sound of fountains and the distant screech of a peacock. There on the summit of the mountain was a secret garden, a hidden paradise, guarded by gates, like paradise. Jonathan wondered what would happen if he simply kept on walking now that Cerberus was temporarily encumbered. "No doubt I should be savaged by the *cane feroce,*" he thought, and dismissed the idea. Turning his back on the beautiful garden, he returned to his car as the gates swung into place behind him. He could hear Helena's words repeated in his head.

He drove slowly back down the hill. Clouds had again covered the sun and it was growing darker, even though it was only early evening.

He thought of the old lady walled up in her mountain eyrie with only servants and old recordings for company.

"Whatever became of the vibrant, sociable, woman we know from her recordings and the memoirs of contemporaries?" he wondered. "Why did she suddenly withdraw from life when her husband died? She can't have been 60. She was healthy, handsome – in her prime. She'd just made her film debut with Antonioni, and could have gone on to a whole new career as a teacher and patron of the arts." Yet here she was, apparently some cobwebbed Miss Haversham surrounded by old memories and the dust of the past. It just didn't fit.

Jonathan's route took him through the hills. It was not late, but the sky was overcast, and within half an hour, large drops of rain began to splatter his windscreen. After much groping and a comprehensive review of all the functions controlled from the dashboard, he finally located the headlights and wipers.

Minutes later the drops developed into a downpour, and visibility was so poor, Jonathan was struggling to discern the road ahead. It was therefore with disbelief that, rounding a corner, he passed a pedestrian. Not just any pedestrian, for example a peasant, suitably attired for these surrounding in gumboots and Macintosh, but a woman, with exposed legs and sandals, her head and shoulders meagrely protected by a short coat.

Careless of his communication problems, Jonathan stopped the car and looked back. She was picking her way carefully along the roadside, in no particular hurry. Her head was so shrouded in her coat she seemed not to have noticed that he'd stopped.

"What the fuck's the Italian for 'lift'?" thought Jonathan.

He reversed slowly and opened the passenger door.

"*Mi scusi, Signorina,* would you like a lift… a ride?" The urgency of the situation (rain was getting onto the passenger seat), led him to chicken out of his lousy Italian.

The woman bent to the open car door, and uttered a torrent of Italian, amplified with expressive gestures of her free hand. Jonathan recognised, "*Molto gentile…*", and the name of the town where he was going.

"*Lento, Signorina,*" he said, interrupting the flow, as the woman slid into the passenger seat, shaking rain from her hair and laying her wet coat, and a large bag of eggs, at her feet, *"Non parlo l'italiano.* I really don't speak much Italian. *"*

*"Ah, inglese,* you are English?" she said, turning a pair of lustrous brown eyes upon him. "Thank you for this courtesy."

Jonathan's heart beat appreciably faster. She had a mass of dark curls, a great pair of legs, and a fine gold chain around her ankle.

# CHAPTER 26

"*Mi chiamo Carlotta*," she told Jonathan as they drove back into town. Her husband's family ran the bar on the hill where he had seen her hanging out flags, and she had been visiting her parents in the hills, whence the eggs. Or that was the gist of what he gathered in a mixture of his bad Italian and her moderate English.

He told her he was in town 'on business' and, on the off chance, asked her if she knew anything of Pignatelli, the old opera singer who lived in the palazzo in the hills.

"Ah the Principessa, yes. My mother know a man who work in the garden at Palazzo ai Monti," volunteered Carlotta. "Is very old *la vecchia;* see no one now."

"Does she live all alone? Her son – *suo figlio* – he never visits her?" He asked. At the back of his mind Jonathan clung to the remote hope that somewhere there could be a Pignatelli/Fredricks offspring combining their musical talents.

Carlotta shrugged her shoulders and looked blank;

"No know a son. I ask my mother."

The rain had stopped when he dropped her off near the town gate. Like the storm clouds, the frustration of his day had lifted in the sunshine of her company and the additional possibility of new information on Pignatelli. Later that evening he walked up the hill to the family bar and spent a companionable evening surrounded by noisy locals, while watching the pleasant spectacle of Carlotta, tossing her black mane when she laughed, and swinging her generous hips as she moved in and out of the tables.

The following morning he woke disoriented, from a singularly unpleasant nightmare. He had been in bed unable to speak or move – dead in fact – surrounded by Roland's women. Hate emanated from them, and he was petrified with fear. They were dividing him up as their inheritance. One of them had a knife, and he knew they were going to cut off his penis. He'd been unable to cry out and voices, urgent and insistent, had been whispering in his ears. "It's hers, all hers. Tell them it's hers."

At the moment the knife was about to strike his groin, he had dragged himself back to consciousness, face down in bed.

For minutes he lay still, bathed in sweat, his heart pounding wildly, but gradually recollection returned bringing relief.

"I'm in Italy, in a hotel," he told himself. "Yesterday I failed to reach Pignatelli, picked up the voluptuous Carlotta, and visited the family bar. Did guilt prompt dreams of such dire retribution?" What did Helena say about him? "*Toujours faible devant les femmes.* Roughly translated: always a push-over with women."

He got out of bed and opened the shutters. The day was bright, the sky clear blue, and today the street was submerged in a tide of stalls. A market, decked in sunshades and coloured awnings, filled the streets and clustered against the town walls. Flags hung from house to house across the narrow streets. Balconies were crammed with flowers and draped with coloured rugs or banners. The town was dressed for *festa* in frilled petticoats, coloured ribbons and flowers in her hair.

The lively spectacle dispersed the anxiety that had fuelled Jonathan's dreams, and he hurried to shave and get dressed. "No reason to feel guilty. I only gave the girl a lift, even if she was excessively bedable," he thought, catching the expression on his face in the shaving mirror. "Perhaps I should call home; see if Anna has had any contact with Ros?"

He breakfasted on good Italian coffee and croissants.

"Call home JB; you know it's what you want to do," he thought. But call whom? Ros was away. Helena? Anna? First, he decided to call the palazzo again. The, by now familiar, voice responded in English.

"The Princess asks that you cease to call. She does not wish to speak to you."

"But *I* wish it. And I wish it enough for both of us. *Capisce?*"

"*Si Signore.*"

'I am, I hope, courteous and respectful; I am the Princess's sincere admirer. I will however continue to be a great nuisance to those who keep me from her: *da fastidio. Capisci?*"

He hoped he had the right phrase for 'be a nuisance'.

He had. The voice sighed deeply and rang off.

He dialled Anna's number. It rang a long time, but finally she answered. He told her about his abortive assault on the palazzo and about his strange dream. She was not sympathetic.

"You phone me, peak rate, from Italy, to tell me about a dream!" she expostulated.

"Can you think of anything I could offer Pignatelli that would induce her to see me? I've emptied all the local florists to no avail," he said, remembering that Helena had counselled bribery.

"Not really. You knew it wouldn't be easy. If you lift damp stones, undisturbed for half a century, a lot of creepy-crawlies start scuttling about. Take care; the Italians do things differently. As for your dreams: it's probably something you ate."

Rebuffed, he revealed his ulterior motive.

"You haven't heard from Ros have you?"

"No, though I'm seeing her at a family party this week."

"Tell her I miss her, will you? I work better when she's with me. You have my number here haven't you?"

Her voice had softened, "I'll tell her, I promise."

Anna returned to the word processor with Jonathan's words in her ears. "Men! Do women need men to 'work better'? Quite the reverse. It's easier to get on with it when they're not around."

Bill's voice reached her from downstairs, "Anna, pet; can I get you anything before I go?"

"Nothing, thank you."

The words on the screen beckoned.

*War was an anticlimax.*

*After the build up to the declaration in September 1939 we were left like the hosts at a party when nobody arrives.*

*The weather was balmy, and Hitler's dread bombers resolutely refused to appear.*

*I remember that autumn as one of unparalleled productivity. Released from the demands of working on the opera, I threw myself into my studies. My voice was filling out and I was offered the lead in an Academy production for next year. The Academy was adamant: war or no war, it was business as usual.*

*Stefan was regenerated. He was the star violinist of his year, jubilant that Great Britain had taken up arms against Hitler, and because of Poland. And he scented victory in the contest for me. I saw little of Roland, though I went over to the flat in Chelsea from time to time. Things came to a head just before Christmas. For all adulterous lovers, family occasions like Christmas and holidays, any public event which demands the relationship be denied, are crunch times. Even so for Roland and me. The evening started at Smokey Joe's, and a dozen of us adjourned to Stefan's rooms in Bloomsbury. Roland caught me alone on the stairs. He was drunk, which was nothing new, but he had a curiously wasted look about him. I realised later that his diabetes must have been out of control.*

*"I never see you at Lucy's these days; are you living with our young Polak?"*

*"Don't be silly Roland."*

*"It's all so matey and companionable."*

*"We're students together, for Heaven's sake!"*

*"Nothing more?"*

*"We help each other. We discover things together. He knows much more music history than I do, and I help him when it comes to harmony and composition."*

*"You can't tell me he doesn't want to get into your knickers."*

*"Roland shut up. Don't be vulgar. You're not my husband."*

*"Little miss hot-between-the-sheets…"*

*"You're disgusting."*

*"…no longer satisfied by her ageing, impotent lover."*

*I tried to get past him and he caught my arm. "Roland, this is pointless."*

*"Come back with me Anna; I need you. Let me show you what love means, let me…"*

*"Roland, I'm 20, unmarried, at the beginning of my life. What future can there be for us together?" The look of misery in his eyes affronted me. I had to be free. "Roland, I have to live my life for me." He still held onto my arm. "And if I want to sleep with Stefan I will!"*

*And that night I did.*

Jonathan left the phone booth feeling a bit of an idiot. He thought of the lovely Carlotta, and decided to go into town and find out what this *festa* was about; have a drink at her bar. After lunch, he might go back to the palazzo and try once more to gain access. However, to his disappointment, he found that Carlotta's bar was closed that day, as were several other places in town. It seemed odd if there was a celebration afoot.

He spent the morning wandering in and out of market stalls, jostled by housewives laden with baskets. He peered into shops selling exquisitely painted ceramics, aromatic local delicacies and fine lacework, and tried to translate prices in telephone number lire into real money. The narrow streets were choked with people and he dodged bicycles, carts, and groups of chattering townsfolk, some carrying children dressed in Sunday best, others wearing 15th century costume with masks or musical instruments. He couldn't see far among the high houses and narrow streets, and followed no particular direction, but the press of the crowd was upwards; up flights of shallow steps, steep alleyways, under damp arches overhung with flowers and greenery, until finally he found himself, hot and breathless, in the open. The heat of the noonday sun hit him like a blow, blinding him with its brilliance.

He was in a broad piazza filled with festive citizens. On three sides it was enclosed by fine Renaissance buildings in rose-coloured brick with painted friezes, delicately arched windows and pillared doorways. On the fourth side, a balustrade overlooked a precipitous drop to the streets below and a panoramic view of the valley beyond. There were stalls selling coloured sweets and ice-creams, tiny painted saints and balloons. There were jugglers, street musicians and a fire-eater belching flames and scattering the crowd with excited squeals. On a platform in front of the principal building, which Jonathan assumed to be some kind of town hall, stood a troupe of men in the parti-coloured dress of 15th century soldiers, carrying halberds, or pennanted trumpets. Jonathan found himself a sheltered vantage point in the doorway to a small bar.

Trumpets sounded, and on the platform men in coloured robes addressed one another, the massive doors of the palace swung open, and from the dark interior a procession carrying two massive objects loomed into the square

They were brightly painted and gleamed bright in the sunlight, towering above the heads of the crowd which parted before them. Their progress was unsteady and once or twice they appeared to stagger, like great giants emerging into daylight after sleeping years underground. The reason, Jonathan realised, pressing forward for a better view, was that they were so heavy each one had to be supported on the shoulders of several men, initially invisible amid the throng. Squeezing through the crush, (no one seemed to mind if you pushed in an Italian crowd), he saw two enormous totem poles with their top sections carved into something that resembled a face.

"*Santo* Someoneorother, I presume," thought Jonathan.

A priest carrying a ceramic pot started dousing the *Santi* with Holy water. The crowd fell silent with anticipation. Jonathan, looking directly into the sun, groped for his sunglasses and as he did so, glimpsed Carlotta among the crowd. She saw him and smiled in recognition.

There was a roar of excitement as the great objects were hauled gradually into an almost vertical position, spraying water as they rose. As they reared some 12 feet above the crowd, the priest scattered the remaining holy water on all around, then flung the empty vessel high over their heads to shatter on the stones.

People screamed and pushed in conflicting directions; some back, to avoid the falling vessel, then forward, in a desperate scramble for fragments to keep as souvenirs. Crushed by the crowd, Jonathan stumbled and found his hand held in firm fingers;

"*Attenzione!*" said Carlotta, steadying him. "People are often hurt at *festa*."

"Can you tell me what all this is about?"

"Is *Festa dei Santi Fratelli – Santi Giovanni e Paolo,*" she replied. (He had been right: it was *Santo* Someoneorother, *and* his brother; even Jonathan got the names.)

The crowed pressed in upon them. He could see nothing of the shapely legs and arse, and she was wearing dark glasses that hid her eyes, but as the cloud of hair brushed against his cheek, he caught the smell of apples. He glanced around surreptitiously to see if her husband was in attendance, and was about to ask her why they had closed the bar, when screams rose again from the crowd as they pressed back to allow the men carrying the *Santi* passage as they made a circuit of the piazza. Instinctively he extended an arm to protect his companion and his hand closed round her midriff. She lifted a hand to remove her glasses and looked up into his eyes.

"Where is your husband today?" he asked looking round cautiously, "I see you closed the bar. It's a bit rough in this crowd."

"She shrugged expressively and spread her hands, "*Male non fa* – it makes no harm. Mario and brothers run for San Paulo in the race today. Is why they close the bar."

As the teams carrying the *Santi* left the square and entered the narrow streets beyond, some of the crowd followed in their wake, while others pressed towards the balustrade in an attempt to follow their progress in the streets below.

Jonathan and Carlotta sat down at a marble-topped table outside the little bar and Jonathan ordered a beer, plus a glass of wine for Carlotta. From time to time the sounds of music and shouting rose from below, reminding them of the race in progress.

"You want I tell you about the race – the *Corsa dei Fratelli?*"asked Carlotta, setting her glass before her on the table, and resting her chin on her hand, "Is very historic, perhaps older than the *Cristianita?* The young men of the town show how much they are strong in race round the town with heavy trunk of trees? They make the *obelisci intagliati* – the obelisk carved with heads of Saints John and Paul – *Santi* – in the 15th century. Is possible they are *simbolo* – er – of the *virilità?* You understand? To spill the holy water… it has meaning, no?"

She had started to giggle, possibly at the difficulty of the English, but also, he thought, at the phallic allusion. Momentarily her eyelashes brushed against her cheeks, and the tip of her tongue hesitated against her front teeth. Jonathan felt a delicious tingling in his groin. To cover his arousal he took a deep draft of the fizzy *Nastro Azzuro.*

"An ancient fertility rite?" he asked, indicating that he appreciated her insight.

"Yes," and she moved on gratefully. "The young men make two teams: one for San Giovanni, one for San Paulo. It is great honour run for *Santi.* Mario's family is always for San Paulo. The morning they race round the town with the *Santi* on their shoulders. The people cheer the saint they support. The afternoon, when is very hot, they climb the hillside to the shrine of the saints above the town. Is a test of the strength."

"Seems a trifle dangerous; carrying massive objects through steep, narrow streets crowded with people," said Jonathan. "In our country everyone would be corralled behind barriers 50 yards from the action. We're obsessed with public safety in England."

She smiled, and the waiter laid plates carrying slim pieces of toast covered with slivers of savoury truffles before them.

"You like *tartufo?*" she asked, "Is speciality of our region."

Jonathan was unsettled. One part of him felt sheepish that a familiar vice was leading him astray when he knew the trouble it had got him into in the past. At the same time a persuasive voice murmured in his ear that he had neither the intention, nor the opportunity, of bedding the delectable Carlotta, and that anyway, her mother's acquaintance with Pignatelli's gardener might yet get him into the palazzo. *Male non fa,* after all.

The sun had moved and beat down directly on the hillside when they left the bar to climb towards the summit where the victor in the race would be decided. Way behind they could hear the sounds that marked the runners' progress. Looking back they caught occasional glimpses of them: the *Santi,* tall and ominous like the upright fins of sharks, cleaving through the waves of people thronging the narrow streets.

They climbed steps and paved alleys between the high stone walls of churches and palaces and eventually, through a gate in the walls, came out onto the open hillside. The heat was intense and Jonathan, the discomfort dulled with alcohol, took off his jacket and rolled back his cuffs. Carlotta was unruffled by their exertions. They passed groups of people resting from the long climb by the roadside, and behind they heard the runners coming closer. Then the path widened out and they were in front of a monastery. The crowd was building up again, hurrying up the steep path in order to have the best view of the finish. A cheer rose further down the hill as the first team came within sight.

"Is San Giovanni," said Carlotta, "Every year they win."

"Where are Mario and San Paulo's team?" asked Jonathan.

"I think they are far behind." She pulled a face, "They will be cross, I fear."

New arrivals crowded in upon those already gathered; the pressure of bodies in the small square in front of the monastery became intense. Boys climbed trees, or darted between adults' legs to get to the front; smaller children were lifted on shoulders for a better view. On impulse, Jonathan lifted Carlotta from the ground and stood her on a low wall that bordered the piazza so that she might have a better view. The cheering became frantic: "San Giovanni, San Giovanni, San Giovanni!" Swept along with the excitement, Jonathan joined in. Now the first team of runners had entered the square, their faces red and dripping with sweat. The *Santo* was lowered to a horizontal position, like a battering ram, and before it, the doors of the monastery swung open and the *Santo* of San Giovanni – the victor – was cheered noisily and received into the dark interior. The runners were engulfed in a mass of cheering supporters. The crowd was ecstatic. Hats, bags and cans flew into the air. Jonathan, battered by the hysteria on all sides, held tight to Carlotta, keeping her steady upon the wall. There was a brief lull, and, as the roar of the crowd in the square dropped, the cheers for the last team toiling up the hill could be heard. Carlotta above him said something Jonathan could not hear. He supported her as she bent to his ear.

"If they close the monastery doors, is very bad; dishonour for San Paulo," she said, concern in her voice.

A hush fell upon those packed in the square, then, like a wave breaking upon the shore, the cheer of San Paulo's supporters in the road below was taken up around them, and, as the *Santo* rose above the crest of the hill, a cheer swept across the square. The yellow neck kerchiefs that marked the San Paulo team moved in a phalanx as they carved a furrow through the congested space.

With a gasp, all eyes turned to the monastery doors which had started to swing slowly towards each other. The *Santo* of San Paulo, described a sickening arc and pointed at the closing doors, and around the accelerating troupe could be heard the screams and shouts of colliding bodies. With a dull thud the carved saint's head on the top of the *Santo* impacted with the closing doors.

There was a scuffle. Angry voices were raised. The doors yielded, and the lumbering *Santo* grazed through the opening and dishonour was averted.

The crowd went wild. Everyone was jumping up and down, shouting, singing, crying, clasping everyone else. As the pressure eased and people broke into groups, laughing and joking, slapping the bearers in their coloured kerchiefs on the back, Jonathan grasped Carlotta and lifted her down and whirled her round with excitement and relief. As his arms closed round her moist body and her bright face came close to his, he bent and kissed her.

There was a roar close by.

*"Svergognata! Puttana!"* shouted furious voices behind him.

Carlotta was wrenched from his arms, and he had a fleeting glimpse of red-faced, broad-shouldered men in yellow kerchiefs with bulging eyes and muscles. He staggered backwards before everything went blank.

# CHAPTER 27

"Oh Gawd," said Kate, "This whole bloody thing's going to be a disaster, I know it."

Anna sat in the passenger seat of her daughter's Golf Cabriolet, bowling down the A3 at 80mph. Bill was crunched uncomfortably in the back seat. Kate smoked incessantly and, since the roof of the convertible was emphatically lowered, a fair quantity of her ash landed in Bill's face or on his suit. Suits didn't actually suit Bill very well. They ended up tight where they should have been easy and baggy where they were meant to fit.

"Wear jeans, for Heaven's sake. Why disinter that ancient relic?" Anna had exclaimed, exasperated at the spectacle of her Special Other sheathed like a sausage in an oversized condom. "And anyway, what are you going to wear on your feet?"

Resolute upon the path of correct dressing, Bill had purchased a pair of black chainstore 'casuals'. Anna insisted he cut the tassels off.

"I can't think what possessed me to let Carole organise a party," Kate shouted into the wind. "It'll be gruesome. Who wants to celebrate the ghastly milestone of being 50 for God's sake? Only Carole, because I'm older than she is. Great tombstone more like!"

"Kate, pet," said Bill tentatively, "Do you think you could drive a little slower. Your mother's getting a bit battered."

Kate either didn't hear or took no notice.

In fact Anna was indifferent to the gale belting round her ears and lashing the hair against her face. It meant she didn't have to listen to anyone; Kate or Bill. These days on those rare occasions when she was unable to avoid going out in public – or having to meet her family, which counted as 'public' in her book – her main objective was to insulate herself from intrusion, particularly intrusion of the emotional kind. Cold, wind, noise, other people's anger and irritation: most of which threatened to be in abundance at this family festival, were best excluded by a few stiff Scotches and her ever increasing preoccupation with her own thoughts.

Right now she was in 1942, standing beside Stefan, tall and handsome in his RAF uniform, at the stone font of a bomb-damaged Catholic church, clutching Kate wrapped in a scrap of lace curtain. She had protested lustily even then, right up to the moment when the service had been interrupted by the air raid siren and they had all bolted to the shelters. Twenty four, Willow Road: just a couple of rooms, but enough for her, the children, and Stefan on the rare occasions he was home on leave. That summer she had been able to walk Hugo's pushchair on the heath, doze on the grass and feel the baby moving inside her, impatient to be born. At night there had been the fiery glow of the incendiary bombs lighting up the City. Strange how wartime remembered seemed no more terrible than peace. It was your personal, rather than the political, climate of the times that coloured the past. For her, marriage and war had been calm compared with the last years of peace.

As their wheels scrunched on the gravel a small band struck up tunelessly somewhere out of sight in the garden.

"Happy Birthday to yoooo, Happy birthday to yoooooo …"

Kate sat in the driving seat, her arms rigid on the steering wheel.

"Why don't I turn round and go back home right now? It could save so much unpleasantness," she said between clenched teeth.

"Come on old girl. It's your day. Make the most of it," said Bill, slapping her on the back as he clambered over the side of the car in blessed relief at still being in one piece.

"Take me to your Champagne," said Anna, aside.

"It's the Birthday girl." Carole came round the side of the house in a sarong skirt, split to the thigh, in vivid oriental silk. "Yoo-hoo! We're all here." The smile that widened her scarlet mouth froze at the sight of Bill bearing down on her, broad palm extended.

"Hello there Carole, ye look a right picture," he said, putting an arm familiarly round her shoulders and planting a loud kiss on her cheek. Anna had gone on ahead, homing in like a missile on the bar. Kate came slowly, submitting passively to a barrage of enthusiastic greeting like a virgin led to sacrifice. Tall flutes of sparkling wine were offered – "Kate's friends wouldn't care about real Champagne," Carole had decided – and the Birthday girl's arrival was made as conspicuous as possible.

The sun shone on Carole's efforts. The garden, thanks to old Dobson, was barbered to perfection, and she had imported a few pot plants and hanging baskets for extra colour. Her gamble in not hiring a marquee had paid off, and it *had* allowed her to employ a barman so that Hugo could be free to circulate. The caterers had done well on their budget and Steve had spent all morning vacuuming the pool, although it was a pity about his girlfriend's skirt: or lack of it. All in all, the occasion did her credit, considering... considering that Kate was not the most appreciative of relatives.

"*Matka*," Hugo handed his mother a glass of sparkling wine. "It's lovely to see you. You are so elusive these days. What are you up to in that eyrie in the sky?"

"I'm writing my memoirs. I should inform you that they are both libellous and pornographic, but that if you are very attentive and buy me lunch at The Savoy Grill, I may delay publication until after my death."

Hugo spoke solemnly to a scandalised guest in earshot at his side.

"In all possibility it's perfectly true. We have learned never to underestimate my mother. I shall have to pay up with good grace."

"God, what is this stuff: nail varnish remover?" said Kate glaring over the edge of her glass at the dumb-struck barman. "Could you find me a beer, please?"

"Well, how does it feel to have reached the big Five O?" said Bill, delivering a hearty antipodean slap to Kate's back. "Think you've grown up at last?"

"What makes colonials think they can commit assault and battery upon any casual acquaintance in the name of camaraderie?" said Kate in her most cutting manner, and moved off leaving him uncertain as to the exact nature of the insult.

Ros stayed upstairs for as long as she could inconspicuously get away with. She had helped the caterers set up their equipment, programmed the CD player with innocuous background music; put clean towels in the loos, given her mother an early double gin and then retired 'to get changed'. Periodically she heard the sound of a car in the drive, squeals of greeting, gusts of laughter and her mother's own distinctive whinny. After about an hour there was also live, rather inexpert, music – a responsibility that had required all her ingenuity to escape – and a particularly prolonged bout of noisy cheering, and she gathered her Aunt Kate had arrived. She heaved herself off the bed, combed her hair, put on a clean shirt and steeled herself for the fray.

She knew about half the company distributed between the sitting room and garden. Apart from immediate family there were a few old family friends, a girl Kate had known at college, her assistant in the department and some boring men in jeans who Ros suspected were also colleagues. She was relieved that there appeared to be no Zak. The average age, she calculated, must be about 101 – she and her brothers excepted. The guests were helping themselves to a variety of cold dishes on a long buffet and carrying them to small tables set on the terrace by the swimming pool. Ros found a can of beer and went to sit beside her grandmother who reclined under a parasol with her feet up.

"You couldn't get out of this one then Granna?" she whispered as she kissed her.

Anna pulled a face. "Perhaps someone will throw someone into the swimming pool and give us a laugh. How was Cuckmere or wherever it was you went camping with your friends?"

"Boring." Ros pulled back the ring pull on the beer, "I started pining for the beastly book-wallah."

"Your book-wallah was pining for you – in spades."

"You said I was hard on him. Will I look a fool if I relent?"

"He's rather out of reach at the moment. He's in Italy."

The dull ache inside Ros caused by separation from Jonathan stabbed like a corn that had been trodden upon. She had tried to forestall her obsessive thoughts of him by promising herself she would see him as soon as she got back to London. If he was away again; away without having seen her once, plans were pointless. She realised she had sought out her grandmother in the hope of talking about Jonathan; a poor substitute for talking *to* him, but now, as she looked sideways, she saw that Anna's face had a faraway look that didn't encourage intimate discussion.

A few feet away Kate's voice could be heard raised in heated discussion with a big bald-headed man in a blazer.

"The whole campaign was a tissue of lies and innuendo."

"Oh come on; it wasn't just electioneering that made Kinnock look ineffectual."

"What could be more ineffectual than Major and Lamont's pathetic performance, but they're still in power?"

The man put a good-natured hand on Kate's shoulder.

"You were always the firebrand of the family Kate."

Kate's snorting riposte was drowned by Carole descending to lead the old buffer away, out of reach of Kate's vituperation.

"No Zak I see," said Ros to Anna, noting the extra venom in her aunt's invective. Kate's boyfriends were an ill-assorted bunch, but at least Zak appeared to have drawn the fire of the big guns. Anna looked startled, as though she had been asleep, then said, "I think it's better not to mention Zak. She had been on the beach in Brittany, soon after the war. Kate, her intense face streaming with tears, was being forcibly separated from a stray dog. It had been one of the few holidays they had taken as a family, all together. She must have been with the BBC at least two years by then to have been able to afford it. Stefan hadn't earned much after his crash, although he'd had his RAF pension. How old had Kate been: five, at most six? Such a skinny thing with matchstick limbs and a rebellious mouth, always quarrelling with Hugo and usually getting the worst of it. There had been a row over the puppy: a scruffy underfed mongrel that had run after them on the sand. They'd given it what was left of their sandwiches and it had attached itself to them. Every day it had waited, greeting them with wild delight, dashing back and forth and leaping in the air, and Kate had responded with fierce devotion. The animal had had fleas and probably worse, but she had hugged it and lavished affection upon it with a physical passion six-year-olds sometimes show for a battle-scarred teddy. Each night the separation was grief-ridden. When the day of their departure came they couldn't make her understand why she couldn't take the puppy home. She'd hidden among the rocks on the beach for hours while they hunted, then clung screaming to it as they endeavoured to prize them apart.

On the ferry Stefan had cradled her in his arms as she sucked her thumb, still weeping. He had promised her a puppy in England. Of course it hadn't been practical with Anna out at work all day.

"Lame dogs. Always lame dogs."

"What was that Granna?" said Ros. Her grandmother had been silent for a long time. She had wondered if she were asleep. Then she had spoken inaudibly. Anna looked at her as though she hadn't realised Ros was beside her.

"Kate always attached herself to lame dogs. Perhaps that's why she took up social work; lost causes and lame dogs."

Kate was standing by the side of the swimming pool. Hugo was talking to her.

"…She organised all this for you. You didn't have to be so cruel. She's very generous and kind-hearted you know."

"She's got a hide like an ox. She didn't even notice."

"Yes she did; you really hurt her feelings. Whatever you feel about her choice of wine, or guests, you don't have to express it so brutally. You don't care whose toes you tread on do you?"

His voice was low, but the intensity of what he was saying attracted attention. Ros and Anna listened anxiously.

"Do you really believe she does it out of the goodness of her heart? You must be joking. She plays lady bountiful just to show how superior she is to all the rest of us: poor, single working women. It is not our good fortune to be kept by a rich man."

"Kate!" He had taken hold of her wrist now and guests standing near Anna and Ros had noticed that something was amiss. "Stop this at once; it's destructive."

Kate was on the verge of tears. They had been here before; the argument was not virgin territory for brother and sister. The more he remained calm and in control, the more unbridled became her savage attacks, with the goal of provoking him into equally naked retaliation: a goal she rarely attained. Now she reacted violently to his hold on her wrist.

"Don't you strong arm me, big brother!"

Her arm came up sharply to break his grasp and although Hugo made no attempt to hold on to her, her clenched fist passed within centimetres of his nose and he leaned back to avoid it, lost his balance and fell sideways into the pool.

Everyone moved at once. Ros rushed to the edge of the pool, Anna was on her feet, and Carole swooped across the lawn in alarm.

"What happened? Goodness me, who fell in? Thank goodness it's a fine day."

Ros leaned over the side of the pool and lent her father a hand to pull him out. He spoke amiably.

"Don't panic; apart from the host's Gucci loafers, there's no harm done."

"Do again Dad. We didn't catch it on camera," called Steve, who was operating the camcorder.

Hugo stood dripping by the pool emptying the water out of his shoes. He looked quite unruffled while Carole fluffed round him.

251

"Come inside and get changed. Take your trousers off, and your shirt, or there will be water all over the carpet."

Hugo's good-nature allowed the onlookers to relax. The focus shifted from the pool side. Kate herself, stifled a smile and lit up a cigarette. She still looked tense as she spoke to Anna beside her.

"He always does it," she was half laughing, half crying. "He always makes me look a fool or small-minded. He can't see that other people have ways of putting the boot in. That some people smother with cotton wool, or stab with rubber gloves on?"

Anna looked at her daughter helplessly, and shook her head.

"But Hugo isn't like that. Perhaps you'd prefer it if he did try to hurt you; if you could get under his skin? Perhaps what riles you is his God-like indifference."

She reached a hand tentatively towards her dejected daughter. But her words had refuelled Kate's anger. Without seeing the hand, she turned upon her mother.

"'God-like'? Yes, that's how he seems to you, isn't it? Your golden boy: talented, handsome, happy and successful. The sun shines out of his bloody arse as far as you're concerned."

Anna turned away from this tirade. This also was a familiar territory. But Kate would not let things rest.

"Go on then, walk away! It's what you always do."

Anna stopped as the jibe hit her. She turned with infinite weariness, and steadied herself on a chair.

"Kate, dear, what more can I say? We've said it all before."

"You could show that you care; that you accept some responsibility. You've always retreated when people were hurt. Back to your beloved music, your precious work; hiding yourself in your ivory tower."

"Don't go on Kate. Even if it's true, you know it's not the whole truth."

But reason didn't heal bruised feelings. Nothing could head Kate off now. Alcohol and old wounds propelled her. "The fact is that you've walked out on everybody: on Fredricks, and he killed himself; on our father when his career was in ruins after his plane crash; on us, your children. I've seen you chuck a whole series of men throughout your life – whenever they made demands. No wonder they called you Amarillis. 'Here is for me no biding' could be your motto couldn't it? Adieu, bloody Amarillis. Farewell, fuck off, adieu!"

# CHAPTER 28

The shadows lengthened across the grass and still Anna slept. About five o'clock Ros put a cup of tea at her elbow in case she should wake, but an hour later Hugo took it away, cold and untouched. The summer evening was mild, but he decided to cover her knees with a light rug, notwithstanding. He frowned. She had never cultivated a suntan, but now her skin had an almost papery transparency, noticeable when the make-up wore off. "It's not like her to be so tired, keeping her feet up and dropping off like this. Wish we knew what that urologist had said." He said.

"You'd think she'd have told us if it was something minor, surely?" said Ros.

"Not necessarily. But if it were minor there would have been treatment. We'd have known about that."

The guests had not stayed late. The dramatic departure of the guest of honour immediately after lunch had not encouraged relaxed lingering. Bill took some persuading, but finally agreed to a lift back to London with Steve and his girlfriend. The caterers had tidied and gone, Ros and Hugo had swum and dozed by the pool. Carole 'went for a lie down' and wasn't seen for some hours.

It was a mixture of sleep, dreams and daydreams. From time to time Anna surfaced but felt no inclination to re-engage with the outside world. If she raised her eyelids imperceptibly she saw a haze of green, dappled with patterns of fractured light beyond the pool; nearer, the tips of her pink sandals and her bony feet. She had rested her legs so that she could see her ankles. Despite keeping them high she knew from the way the skin had become smooth across the arch that they were swollen. If she closed her eyes she could imagine her ankles and legs as they had been 10, 20, 30 years ago. She remembered a pair of pearlescent-pink sandals that had done memorable things for her legs. She had bought them for Hugo and Carole's wedding, and worn them until, clambering over rocks at Lindos, a heel had snapped and she had walked home barefoot. These sick, swollen limbs that felt so alien were theoretically the same legs that had carried her over rocks, climbed trees and attracted wolf-whistles as they flashed under The New Look, miniskirts and hotpants, or wrapped themselves round men's backs...

Sex with Stefan had been a revelation; the energy, the passion, the erection that wouldn't go down. Making love with Roland had been all tenderness and slow burn; subtle arousal, but uncertain consummation. Twenty-year-old fucking made up in frequency and fervour what it lacked in finesse. Stefan never worried about being tired, drunk or depressed. Whatever his condition, he had only to look at her to be ready for love. And he had loved her with such simple, single-minded, devotion it had been like warming herself at the fire of youth after the chilly draughts of middle age.

Once she had overcome the guilt about Roland they'd done it everywhere at every opportunity. The Christmas after war broke out that they spent with her parents, they had done did it in the lavatory of the train, in the bathroom, in the car and in the snow. She didn't remember being the least bit cold, embarrassed or uncomfortable; the urgency of their coupling had discounted all obstruction. His lean muscular body was like an extension of his penis. He had thrust into her with his whole body, his whole soul.

She stirred, aroused by the contraction of the muscles at the base of her stomach that still responded to the memory of good sex. She could hear Ros and Hugo's voices quite near. His voice had the same timbre as Stefan's – children who inherited facial dimensions from a parent often had similar voices – but his intonation was 100 percent British: British public school.

She hadn't wanted him to go. He'd been so young, so attached to her. But she'd had to work, even before Stefan's death, and his grandfather, Andrzej had stumped up for the fees. Like so many expatriates, he wanted the family to be more English than the English. Stefan thought changing the family name was foolish enough, and he'd fought the idea of boarding school for Hugo with all that was left of his old spirit. There had been so little of that left at the end. So much had been destroyed in the flames: hands that could hardly play, the face a distorted mask of its former beauty. No wonder the spirit had crumpled too.

Her bladder woke her in the end. As she came into the hall, she could hear them in the kitchen.

"Is that you *Matka?* You OK?"

"Granna? You've slept for hours!"

"I'm going to the loo." And she disappeared and stayed there some time.

"She's in a funny mood."

"She never enjoys family parties."

"There was a time when she enjoyed them in her own way a little too much," said Ros. She and her parents looked at each other, united in concern.

"What did Kate say to her? Did you hear?" Carole asked Ros.

"I heard. It was quite a mouthful." Ros didn't volunteer the details though she knew her mother was agog with curiosity. Finally they heard the lavatory flush. Anna had tidied her hair and freshened her make-up. She appeared rested and alert, but she walked with slight stiffness. All three looked at her in silence as she came into the room, aware that she intended to say something.

"Right. I've taken my pills, put back the mask. I can face the world, or my family at any rate. I have been unfair to you. You deserve to know that I am ill. If I recall aright, I have something called glomerulonephritis. Basically the filters in my kidneys are packing up, which accounts for why my legs appear to have elephantiasis, why I keep rushing off to the loo, and why I'm more tired than is my wont."

Carole's gasp was audible. The other two just looked at her, eyes wide. Carole rushed to Anna's side to urge her to sit down, but Anna continued without acknowledging the response.

"You hardly need me to tell you I don't want any fuss. The fact that I may drop dead any minute puts no extra responsibilities upon any of you. But I realise you have a right to know: to prepare yourselves. And before you ask, it could be any day now, or as much as a year."

"But there must be some treatment," protested Hugo. "I mean, otherwise you seem so fit. You're not really old."

"Well, there are pills for the blood pressure. They wanted me to have regular kidney dialysis. But it wasn't for me. I wouldn't wish it on my worst enemy. There's nothing else that can be done about it; at least nothing I intend to do."

Carole made inarticulate noises and collapsed into a chair in metaphoric sympathy. Hugo's mouth was open, but he said no more.

"This information does, however, betoken certain imperatives for me. No one can change the course of their lives when the end is in sight, but they have, *I* have…" She hesitated for a moment searching for the right phrase, "I want to put the record straight. I really have been writing my memoirs Hugo, as Ros knows. Some of it may go into this biography of Roland that your friend," She said, addressing Carole, not Ros, "Jonathan Burroughs is writing.

"There is something more." She looked round and Hugo sensed that she now wanted to sit down, and pulled a chair towards her. She sank into it. Her speech was no longer as fluent. When she had something important or difficult to say she usually prepared her words in advance. Ros and Hugo, who knew Anna well, guessed that she was now about to say something extempore. "Kate's words to me just now focused it for me. I am…experiencing regret. I know it doesn't change what has been done, saying 'sorry' is such a cop-out: like you Catholics at confession, seeking absolution knowing full well you will do it all again."

Hugo spoke again. He was no longer a practising Catholic, but the faith of his father and grandfather had coloured his thinking.

"There's nothing hollow in having regrets, or needing forgiveness. If we never experienced regret it would imply we never learned from our mistakes."

She met his eye questioningly and held his gaze. "So little self-doubt…" It was half question, half plea. "I never entertained alternatives." Watching them, Ros felt that some unspoken communication took place between mother and son. It was as if mentally he took her hand and gave her strength, because from faltering on the threshold of breaking down with repressed emotion, Anna became calmer, her words no longer hesitant.

"Damn it; I did things that were wrong: to Kate, to you, to your father, perhaps others, but above all, to Roland. I denied the responsibility of love. As you say: one must learn from one's mistakes."

Hugo came and put his arms round her as she sat. She clung to him in silence, her knuckles white. Tears ran down his cheeks. He cried with a frankness that belied his British upbringing. He cried like a Pole. It was infectious. Ros felt the tears rising to her own throat, saw those on her mother's cheeks. This was about to become an extremely wet occasion. But Anna pulled away before the emotion snowballed. Gently she broke from her son's embrace.

"And now, could you call me a car to drive me home?"

Everyone protested at once.

"Mother, stay with us; tonight at least. I've made up the Blue Room for you," said Carole.

"Stay with us *Matka*. Let me drive you home."

"Granna, don't go. I need to talk to you."

"It's a lovely offer Hugo, but I'd rather have one of my regular drivers. I'd like to talk to Ros as we drive back to London. You will have time to get ready before he arrives. I need to talk to you, alone," Anna added, addressing Ros.

They sat in the back of the minicab, turned to each other and said 'Jonathan' in unison. Ros laughed with surprise.

"Is that what you wanted to talk about? Oh Granna, what shall I do?"

"What do you want to do?"

"I want to kiss and make up."

Anna paused for a moment, then said, "Why don't you phone him in Italy and say you'd like to join him? He wanted you so much he left his number

258

for you. Actually he phoned twice. I gather his initial assault on Pignatelli's palazzo was a failure. He says he can work better with you beside him. It's not uncommon," she added with a smile.

Ros gave a sort of howl. "And I want to be with him. I want to help. I want him to unravel Roland's secrets, and reveal the fascinating, sad, funny Roland who shines out of your memoirs. I want him to write a best-selling biography and to be in demand as an author, and give up the frustrating business of working for Simmonds and Sayle, and…"

"Whoa, whoa, slow down," said Anna. "One thing at a time. First you must get to Italy. You have, I imagine, no money?" Ros looked sheepish and hung her head. "I thought not. I expect something can be arranged.

We'll ring him as soon as practical tomorrow. It's a bit late tonight."

Ros rang Jonathan's hotel early next morning. Her happy urgency instantly became panic.

"He's not there. He had some kind of accident. He's in hospital!"

Ros's eyes dilated until the white showed round her pupils. "I've got to go. At once. Can you lend me the money?"

"Of course. We'll book you on the first flight available. I'll come with you in the car to the airport and get you some travellers' cheques. For two pins I'd come with you myself."

Tiredness and self-doubt were left behind. Anna was elated with the adrenaline of action as she set about organising the Jonathan rescue mission. At the back of her mind were her words to Hugo about learning from one's mistakes. Not everyone had the chance to correct them the second time round.

She paused in the process of leafing through the international flight directory. "Did you see what I meant about the parallels between your love affair and mine with Roland? You've been a catalyst in Jonathan's life as I was in Roland's. It's a bit of a responsibility."

"Yes, but it's also great fun," said Ros.

Anna looked at her and thought, "What can she be expected to know about responsibility at her age?"

* * *

Ros flew into Rome without a formalised plan of campaign.

"I'm coming to the aid of my man," she thought, humming *The Ride of the Valkyries* as background music. "Here comes the cavalry."

Ros knew that survival 'abroad' was greatly facilitated by knowledge of the language, lots of money and an independent means of transport. She scored well on the first two, with good Italian, and Anna's travellers' cheques, but was from the start, incapacitated by lack of the third. The town where Jonathan was staying was some distance from Pisa, not on the railway, and she was too young to hire a car. So she took the train as far as she could, on the principle that it's easier to go further, when you are as close as you can get

On the journey, she sought the advice of her fellow passengers and, by the time she reached her station, they had not only shared their lunch with her, but also promised to organise a relative to transport her to her ultimate destination. She waited on a stone bench outside the station with walls covered in roses, clutching her rucksack and licking an ice cream. In due course the relative rolled up, in a ramshackle truck carrying a large pig in the back, and Ros climbed in.

On arrival at Jonathan's hotel she used her Italian to discover from the staff what had happened. It appeared that Jonathan had apparently been carried there the previous afternoon, bleeding and semi-conscious, and been transferred for appropriate medical attention, in an ambulance. They spoke of '*festa*' with an Italianate shrug, as though that explained everything. Ros assured them that she would take charge, and organise everything, "*Mi occuperò di tutto.*"

Directions for finding the infirmary were complex, so a car was called to drive her there.

Jonathan slept a sedated, dreamless sleep for 15 hours and woke to find a nun in white bending over him. For a moment he thought he was receiving the last rites, then, the sight of a thermometer plus a sharp pain in his head, informed him that he was hospitalised. Recollection flooded back: Carlotta, the race of the *Santi Fratelli*, Carlotta's enraged menfolk...

"Oh, Burroughs," he groaned into his pillow, "So soon after all your good resolutions. And this time it's really got you into hot water."

260

The nun administered hot soup, smoothed his pillow, and he slept again. He woke convinced he was hallucinating;

"Ros? Ros; I don't believe it!"

But it was. She stood there in scruffy shorts and a T-shirt, so unbelievably blond, brown and beautiful that his love hurt him as much as his bandaged head. She squeezed her lips together as though trying not to cry, or laugh, or both.

"You stupid, bloody fart, what have you done?" And she threw herself into his arms.

The nuns declared that it was totally impossible he be discharged for at least another 24 hours. He had had concussion and they were awaiting X-rays of his right hand. Ros did not probe too deeply into the cause of his trauma, accepting his story of excitable crowds at the *festa*.

Jonathan told her of his ignominious rebuff at the gates of the palazzo. He brought her up to date with his latest discoveries.

"You see why Pignatelli is so crucial. Quite apart from any material she holds, the pictures that Gudrun mentioned, the Stradivarius, I need to know the truth about Paola's relationship with Roland, and her child's. But above all, I want to know more about his final hours and his death."

Ros returned to the hotel with Jonathan's keys and sifted through the notes and documents she found on the desk in his hotel room. Everything was surprisingly methodical. She had expected him to be as disorganised and untidy in his work as his flat. But here she found lists, maps, contact names and addresses, and notes, all carefully co-ordinated.

The only thing she needed that was not supplied was a bus timetable.

# CHAPTER 29

The bus to the village nearest Pignatelli's palazzo took over an hour. There Ros got off, bought a coffee at the Bar della Vittoria, and enquired, as best she could without sounding too nosey, about the Palazzo ai Monti, its owners, the staff and who came and went. She was told that the butcher, the baker, the grocer, the fishmonger, the doctor and of course, the *veterinario* – the Principessa was as concerned for her dogs' health as she was for her own – made regular visits to the palazzo, but visitors were unheard of.

The only way to the palazzo was in a motor vehicle, or on foot.

Ros bought a bottle of mineral water and set off. The sun was high but there was a light breeze. When she reached the spot where the dirt track started to climb steeply out of the valley she scanned the white road ahead and felt a tingle of apprehension. No sign indicated the palazzo and it was invisible from the road. The map Jonathan had acquired showed the track doubling back and forth to the summit at 450 metres before the driveway to the house was marked; five, perhaps six kilometres and uphill all the way. Considered as an afternoon's hike it didn't look too terrible. But when she reached the impregnable fortress: then what?

"Oh well," thought Ros, "domestic dwellings are not normally impregnable when examined in detail." (The lavatory window at Holland Park came to mind.) "In all likelihood only the drive gateway is dauntingly defended to discourage intruders. And if the vet, the gardeners and the chief-bottle-washers go in and out... so can I." And she set off at a brisk pace.

Once, in Crete, Ros and her brother Steve had gone to visit the Minoan ruins at Knossos and found them closed because of a public holiday. They had searched the fencing for a suitable tree overhanging the site, and simply climbed in. It had been fun having the historic site all to themselves.

She had reached the first bend in the road, and looked back over her shoulder at the sound of scrabbling in the stones behind her. A plump golden Labrador puppy was running after her, its stubby tail waving like a flag of greeting.

"Hi there!" she said, crouching down as the puppy came up and stood on its rear legs to reach her face with its rough warm tongue. "Fancy a walk, do you? I'm not sure your short legs are up to where I'm going."

She petted it gently for a few minutes, then turned her back in the hope that it would make its way home again.

But the puppy was not so easily discouraged. Sometimes it ran ahead, occasionally fell behind, so that Ros thought it had given up until it raced to catch her up again. Sometimes it charged off into the long grass verge beside the track, nothing visible but a vigorously signalling stub of tail, to investigate the myriad scents and sounds that tempt a puppy's nose in the countryside. As she left the vineyards and small fields of maize behind her and entered the woodland, the puppy still trotted unflaggingly in her wake.

She paused to drink from her bottle and, seeing the puppy's eyes upon her, its tongue hanging wet from its mouth, tipped water into her scooped hands and it lapped greedily.

"If I walk six kilometres to the top of this hill, you will have done 18," she said, scratching behind its floppy ears and feeling the moist heat of its skin.

Here, between the trees, it was cooler as shade stretched intermittently across the road. The crickets were less deafening. Instead there was the occasional rustle and crack of twigs as some small, invisible animal took fright at their approach. Once the coarse croak of a pheasant sounded close at hand and the lumbering bird broke cover and bolted across the road with the puppy in hot pursuit. Looking back through a gap in the trees, Ros could see the road far below her; the occasional car, tiny as a toy.

To keep her spirits up she started to sing. Often when she had a long walk or bike ride she entertained herself with trying to remember the soprano part from some choral work that she had sung. Singing helped regulate your breathing during exercise, and rhythmic exercise was equally good at fixing words and notes in your memory. For some reason she found herself singing the Fredricks setting of *Pippa's Song* from the opera, with its final lines – "God's in his Heaven – /All's right with the world!"

Unusually, she found herself thinking about the words, perhaps because they were in English. The choral works they sang were mostly in Latin and difficult to remember.

" 'All's right with the world!' Things are most definitely not all right, right now," she thought, "Granna ill, Jonathan in hospital and Pignatelli immured, incommunicado in her palazzo refusing to spill the beans."

But when you came to think about it, things were rarely all right in the wider world, if you cared about what happened outside your own backyard. It was good news that Maggie Thatcher had got her marching orders, that the Iron Curtain was coming down and that Mandela was now free and president of South Africa, but there were still wars in the Middle East and massacres in Africa. Pippa's vision of all being right was probably considered charming 130 years ago when Browning wrote the poem, and when the lower orders – and women – were supposed to know their place, but it certainly wouldn't have been considered acceptable today.

Then suddenly she noticed the puppy.

It was standing in the middle of the road, erect and still, with an intent look on its face. It was 'pointing' like a true gundog.

Looking back, she saw that for some distance a tall wire fence had started to run along the side of the road. Upon the fence were notices announcing that this was private property and that everyone should keep out, on pain of dire consequences. She was approaching the Pignatelli residence. This fence was the outer redoubt.

Ros returned her gaze to the puppy.

Its position hadn't changed but it was making little whimpering noises and moving its head as though waving its nose in the wind and searching for something: a scent perhaps?

Suddenly it was off, running with its nose close to the ground towards the fence.

Ros watched with fascination as it approached the barrier. The grass was shorter here and she was able to keep the puppy in view as it crossed the space that separated the fence from the road and began to run along the perimeter.

"It's smelled a rabbit," thought Ros. "Any minute now it will start to dig furiously."

But the puppy didn't dig.

It put its feet up against the fence and whined. Then dropped to the ground and let out little yapping barks; not the focused bark of a dog with an objective, like a cat up a tree, but the short "Hey, it's me!" barks they make when trying to attract attention.

And then, in a flash, it dawned on Ros why the puppy was so excited.

It lived here. It was Pignatelli's dog – or one of them – probably a bitch, and named after some famous singer, if the tradition was still observed.

Pignatelli's puppy! And if Pignatelli's puppy had got out....

Even as her mind made the connection, the puppy started to run further along the edge of the fence, its nose close to the ground.

Ros followed it, her breath short in her throat, stumbling on the rough ground, catching her arms on brambles, her hair in overhanging branches, but never letting it out of her sight.

The puppy, now oblivious of Ros, ran fast and purposefully along the fence for about 200 yards, then stopped, wriggled and scrabbled for a bit as Ros drew closer. Then, just as she was catching up with it, it disappeared from view.

For a moment Ros could have wept.

"No, I can't lose you now!" she said, teeth clenched. "You're my key to the locked citadel, and I'm so close to the keyhole!"

The fence skirted a steep slope at this point so that she was looking up at it from several feet below. The ground was broken here and earth had fallen away.

Then she saw the place.

Several sorts of animal, none very large, must have scrambled under the fence at this point. The wire was bent back and free from the ground for about a yard; the earth hollowed away underneath with the scratch of many claws. But the opening was shallow, and she would have to climb almost vertically up the slope to reach it.

Ros could feel the pulse throbbing in her neck and hear the singing of excitement in her ears.

She was about to do something foolhardy, possibly dangerous. She was about to break into a fortress bristling with dire warnings to intruders, inhabited by a powerful woman who, according to all sources, defended her privacy fiercely.

"I'm mad, I'm mad, I'm clean off my bloody trolley," she said to herself, half scared by her own daring and half proud that, not for a moment, did it occur to her not to go on. "If you can't enter legitimately by the front door, the only way in is illegitimately." And she concentrated her mind to how to overcome the next obstacle in her path.

She broke a branch from a nearby tree and dug at the earth of the slope, which was soft and moist, to make footholds. With the assistance of these she managed to grasp the wire above the hole where the puppy had squeezed through. From here she hauled herself up on her hands, kicking frantically with her heels. The jagged edges of the wire scratched her arms and chest, tearing her T-shirt.

"Shit," she swore, steeling herself to ignore the pain.

She reached up with her right arm and found an exposed root for better leverage and eventually, tired, scratched, sweating and covered with mud, she lay on the grass inside the perimeter fence. Only now did she allow tears of relief to spring to her eyes.

"Christ, I've done it, I've done it! I'm inside the grounds of Pignatelli's flaming palazzo."

266

She was surrounded by saplings so close together she could see little in any direction. Once she had regained her breath, she continued to climb steeply uphill, treading carefully lest a snapping twig or rustling leaves attract the attention of Pignatelli's minions or the *cane feroce* the notices warned of.

The crest of a hill was thickly planted with firs and cypresses. There were sweet-smelling needles underfoot, and Ros glimpsed clear sky between the tree tops. She was immediately behind a small ornamental building: some kind of summerhouse in the classic style, furnished with pillared urns and a rustic stone seat. Reassuring herself that there was no one in sight, she crept cautiously round to the front of the building. The view beyond unfurled before her like a Persian carpet.

She was so enraptured apprehension left her and she spoke softly, but aloud.

"It's paradise: a fabulous, fairytale garden!"

On either side sweeping lawns clothed the arc of a natural amphitheatre. From the summerhouse, a gravelled path curved between borders filled with flowers and hedged with neatly cropped box that competed with the scents of rose and pine. Lichened statues and stone urns punctuated the sea of flowers at intervals, and in the heart of the basin the red tiles and stone walls of a large house could be glimpsed above dark, clipped yew. Beyond the hedges the plumes of fountains tossed themselves in the sunlight and she heard the splash of water and the call of an unseen peacock.

Ros squatted on her haunches in the lee of a large tree and abandoned herself to the enchantment of the view. It was with some difficulty that she pulled her mind back to her precarious position. "So: I'm through the first line of defence. How now do I penetrate ranks of ferocious guard dogs, locked doors, burglar alarms, and, for all I know, armed retainers, to reach the inner sanctum of the old Principessa herself?"

Clearly what she was going to need was a cover story. And, as she thought of it, kind fate reminded her that she had come ready equipped all along.

Up the gravel path came a familiar figure, but not alone.

The Labrador puppy, manifestly at home, came lolloping up the path taunting a stout old spaniel in a game of "Catch me if you can, fatty!" It gambolled a few steps ahead, then turned and faced its pursuer, crouched over extended forepaws. As the panting spaniel pulled level, the puppy was off again, always out of reach, turning to bait the older dog lumbering heavily in its wake.

"But of course," said Ros, "I came to return the puppy. Now the only problem is to secure said puppy's co-operation." And, adopting an unthreatening posture, she endeavoured to attract the attention of her recent companion with soft calls.

The puppy stopped in its traces and turned to see the source of the noise, cautious for an instant, then recognising her, it bounded up and started licking Ros's face like a long lost friend. The spaniel, less certain, plonked its rear heavily upon the gravel eyeing the new development with dripping tongue and head on one side.

Ros cast around for some means to secure her cover story.

"If you're going to be my passport to Pignatelli, we have to go together," she said, excusing herself to the puppy for attaching the belt from her jeans to its neck like a collar. Fortunately the puppy found it a great new game, and immediately started chewing its leash and tugging good-naturedly against the anchor on the end.

The gravel path looked very exposed.

"Shit; I wonder if they can see me from the house?" she thought as she stood up and took a couple of steps into the open, bathed in full sun. Her feet made a deafening crunch on the gravel. "Stand proud *Signorina*. Your best defence against being taken for a burglar is to boldly go as though you hadn't a care in the world."

She gained the shelter of the yew hedges after what seemed an age of exposure, although the puppy's natural momentum had forced her to cover the ground at a healthy lick. The spaniel sniffed at Ros as they came level, then turned to pad downhill in their wake. Surveying the two dogs, Ros wondered where the *cane feroce* might be. "Could the whole battery of threats be an elaborate façade?" she wondered. It seemed too good to be likely.

Beyond the yew hedge another breathtaking panorama came into view. A pattern of pools and interconnecting waterfalls stretched before a grey house bordered by a paved terrace. Fountains rose and fell shattering the reflection of tall windows and blossom-clad walls. Urns of flowers cascaded over the edge of the terrace and flights of steps descended graciously to the water.

And now a new element added to the spell. The sound of music floated over the water to Ros's ears, and, delight of delights, it was music she knew: soprano and mezzo singing in thirds: the *Flower Duet* from *Lakmé*. The music came from a conservatory at the far end the house, with French windows currently open onto the terrace. "Opportune and yet more opportune," thought Ros, feeling a little like Alice in the fantastic garden of the playing cards. "Not only do I have my passport, but the drawbridge is down. And who is most likely to be listening to opera in this palazzo?" The rhetorical question needed no answer.

Puppy dancing ahead and old dog behind, screened from the house by the yew hedge, Ros walked the length of the water garden and crossed to the conservatory by way of a rose-covered pergola, which appeared to have been designed expressly to offer a shaded walk around the fountains.

It brought her to within 20 feet of the house.

As she approached the steps leading up to the conservatory both dogs took off. Or rather the old spaniel ran ahead and the puppy strained at Ros's makeshift leash, making the leather cut into her hand. With difficulty she prevented it from dragging her headlong through the doorway, which was shielded by a dangling bead curtain that made her unable to see into the room. The windows were covered for most of their length with slatted blinds.

"Take it easy. It's home for you, but for me it's the beast's lair," she said softly, grateful that, close to the house, the music drowned both her footsteps and her words. Its slightly boxy quality indicated that it was an old recording, probably, if legend was accurate, one of Pignatelli's own.

She crossed the paved terrace bent double, holding the puppy's mock bridle close to its neck. She hardly dared breathe as they approached the bead curtain, which jangled softly after the passage of the spaniel.

No sound save the music.

Ros picked up the puppy and held it close to her chest, then with her free hand, gently parted the bead curtain and looked in.

The conservatory was tiled in black-and-white and filled to the high roof with exotic plants. But on this occasion Ros had no eye for the decor.

Beneath a whirring fan, an old lady slept in a chair, a fringed Spanish shawl across her knees.

# CHAPTER 30

In the conservatory the voices soared to a climax as the record came to an end. In the silence that followed Ros could hear the whirring of the fan and the panting of the old spaniel flopped at the feet of her mistress.

The sleeping woman was recognisably the great post-war diva, though considerably aged. The face, shaded by a straw hat and dark glasses, was a mass of fine wrinkles, but someone had taken the trouble to apply spots of rouge to the sagging cheeks. The fleshy liver-spotted hands in her lap wore expensive rings and were professionally manicured. A fine cameo fastened the high neck of her blouse.

Ros stood before her short-term goal uncertain what to do. "Do I wake her? Will she be frightened and sound the alarm? If I wait someone may come. My chance to speak to her will have gone."

The puppy was unhampered by such equivocation. It was home: back with the treat-giver-in-chief. In a frenzy of joy and recognition it wriggled from Ros's arms, crossed the floor and jumped onto the old lady's lap and began licking any part of her that it could reach.

Pignatelli surfaced from sleep slowly. Her hands came up round the puppy, then mounted to its head and, holding it away from her with one hand, she removed the dark glasses.

"*Cucciola; piccola cara! Sei tornata. Oh gioia!*" And she began to shower the excited puppy with kisses.

Ros decide to pitch in with her Italian, to explain her role in returning the puppy while joy still reigned supreme.

"*Mi scusi la Sua Altezza…*" Ros began, with careful respect. Then, swiftly claiming her brownie points, and praying that the Princess's gratitude for the puppy's return would override any affront at her unorthodox intrusion, she explained that she had found the puppy in the village and had decided to return it in person.

Paola Pignatelli transferred her attention to this new interruption. One hand remained occupied holding the squirming puppy; the other groped on a side table for a pair of spectacles which she conveyed shakily to her eyes.

"Thank God she appears to be surveying me with interest rather than antagonism," thought Ros, metaphorical fingers crossed.

"*L'ha trovata nel villaggio, Lei?*" asked the old lady after a pause.

"*Sì.*"

With half her attention on the wriggling puppy the diva registered this new, unfamiliar arrival. In Italian, she asked Ros who she was. She didn't recognise her. Was she one of the staff?

It was tempting to let Pignatelli think she worked at the palazzo, but her appearance, and her Italian, would surely betray her in the end. Ros decided to speak in English.

"No Your Highness, I am a humble English tourist who found your puppy, and wished to return it to you." And perceiving the flaws in her story even as she spoke, she thought, silently, 'Let's hope she doesn't want to know how I knew it was hers, or – ahem – how we breached the battlements to get in?"

But Pignatelli did not appear curious, let alone suspicious. It occurred to Ros she might be unaware of the defence cordon surrounding her. She decided to behave as though popping in to see princesses in palaces was an everyday occurrence for her. She approached the old lady and knelt down to pet the puppy.

"What do you call her? Is she named after a famous singer, as all your dogs have been?"

Pignatelli obviously understood, because her face brightened at this signal of her fame, but she formed the English words in her reply with some care, as if out of practice.

"I – we not – call puppy name. Is only *cucciola*. Old dog is Callas," and she indicated the spaniel thumping a tail on the floor at her side. "They please you – the dogs?"

"Very much," Ros replied enthusiastically, giving the spaniel a share of her attention. "And music, great singing… and you're one of the greatest, diva. I admire your recordings, though I'm afraid I never heard you sing. "Don't lose your momentum girl," she told herself, "You're in there, just hold on to the initiative."

Another record had started up: Mozart's *The Marriage of Figaro*. Ros plunged on, sensing that the old lady was flattered and receptive. "You were a wonderful Countess in Figaro. Is this the recording you made at Salzburg?"

The old lady listened, then, with a shrug and dismissive gesture said, *"Non lo so*. I make so many recordings. How to say what is which?"

There was a discreet cough in the background. A small round woman in a neat blue-and-white nurse's uniform stood at the door to the house behind them.

"*La Principessa vuole qualcosa?*" She asked if he Princess wanted anything.

"She probably wants to know what the fuck I'm doing here, but doesn't dare ask," thought Ros. "That's good. The old bird is not considered so senile that they don't respect her authority. Stick with the *Pincipessa vecchia, Signorina*, and you'll be OK."

Pignatelli, who had her back to the nurse, grasped Ros's hand the better to turn and inspect the woman in the doorway.

"Is my servant," she said to Ros; and addressing the woman in Italian she commanded, "Signora Brunelli, order English tea, with milk and also with cake." Pignatelli turned again to Ros. "You like cake?"

"Diva, I like everything about your enchanted palace. I think I'm in a fairy tale."

The word spread like wildfire: the Principessa, who never saw anyone, had a visitor! And not just any visitor, but a scruffy young English girl who seemed to have materialised out of thin air.

The nurse told the housemaid and the housemaid told the cook – making special mention of the tea, *with milk and cake* – and the cook told Alberto, who hurried to the small sitting room dusting the lapels of his jacket and craned his neck to try and glimpse the strange phenomenon through the door to the conservatory.

Meanwhile the shadows that had been pools beneath the trees when Ros arrived moved round and stretched themselves across the lawn and terrace. And Ros and the old singer drank anaemic tea made without boiling water, ate cream cakes, served from a silver cake dish, with tiny pastry forks; wiped their fingers on linen napkins, and took a turn in the garden. Pignatelli, who scarcely came to Ros's shoulder, leaned heavily upon her arm, employing an ebony-tipped Malacca cane to point out features of the grounds too far away for them to reach.

"I must have grass: lawn, as in England. You know we have no word for 'lawn' in Italian? *Prato all'Inglese; tappeto erboso* – hah! Well I have my carpet of grass as at Glyndebourne; and my temples and water as at Stourhead and Hampton Court. I send the designer to England to see real gardens. These gardens are my life for 30 years."

Ros had placed the cushion she was required to carry on a stone seat and held the parasol shading the old lady's head as they sat gazing out over the water garden. They had spoken of music: of opera and of Ros's singing in oratorio, (though not Ros's musical grandmother); of dogs past and present; of favourite food and of gardens, but they had touched on nothing intimate. Ros cast about in her mind as to how to return to the purpose of her visit.

"Why did you give up singing diva? You were in your prime when you retired. You could have had a great future giving recitals, teaching, making films?"

Pignatelli gave a deep sigh. "Was not my decision," she said quietly, almost to herself. Ros did not press her. Pignatelli gazed across the garden, her thoughts elsewhere, then spoke, choosing her words carefully, "When my husband is dead and my son become Prince: *capo della famiglia*, he feel it better I lead a quiet life; that I have no more the long hours to travel, rehearse and to perform. Was his wish, and l am – er – of accord. He suffered much, my son."

Ros would have liked to learn more about the son. Was he still living? Was he musically talented? Above all, who was his father? But Pignatelli brought her reflections to an end briskly, as though fearing to say too much, and put her hand on Ros's arm indicating that it was time to go in.

"And now, I wish hear you sing. Come, we go in. We shall order the Champagne."

Word spread through the startled household like wildfire;

"The old lady has ordered Champagne!"

"She's ordered Champagne! Never."

"Yes, idiot; she's ordered Champagne."

"But we don't have any chilled. What shall we do?"

The household was in a hubbub of disorder. There was no Champagne in the fridge and Alberto couldn't find the key to the cellar. The ice bucket hadn't been polished. It was all most irregular.

And while they were still reeling from the initial disruption to their unvarying routine, Pignatelli ordered the non-stop background music to be silenced and the dumbfounded staff heard a young, uncertain voice singing a Cherubino aria from the *Marriage of Figaro* to a shaky accompaniment on an out-of-tune piano.

When Alberto carried in the ice bucket containing the hastily dusted and cooled Champagne, he witnessed the singular spectacle of his mistress seated at the piano, prodding the ribs of a tall, fair-haired young woman wearing the T-shirt, jeans and sports shoes favoured by the young the world over, and none too clean at that.

"You have *presenza, cara mia,* but is need of *carne* – meat, beef – to make the big sound. Sing on the expanded chest. Fill the lungs. You have a fine mezzo in you, bring the voice to the front of the mouth." And the old lady reached to lift the girl's chin forward, cupping the young cheeks in her old hand.

"What are you staring at?" said Pignatelli sharply, catching her majordomo gaping in amazement, "Where are our glasses? Bring them here and leave. *Presto!*"

Rebuked, Alberto hastened to dispense the Champagne, and beat a retreat.

"… and Alberto," Pignatelli hadn't finished; in tones to strike terror in negligent servants she commanded Alberto to take the puppy and feed it, and to ensure it was never lost again.

The story of the puppy's role in the day's unusual events had already been related below stairs. Maintaining his mask of deference with difficulty, Alberto took the detested animal firmly round the stomach and left the room. Behind him he heard the chink of glasses and the two women continued talking in English.

"Diva, you have been so kind. May I speak to you of something difficult and personal?"

"Hah! I thought there was a special reason you are here. I am not stupid, even if old, *mia cara*. Drink; then you tell me all."

An hour passed. The puppy, the spaniel Callas and the old cat had been fed and the bowls cleared away and preparations for dinner were under way. The sun was sinking behind the cypress trees along the ridge and it was the time for closing windows and doors throughout the house. The hour of the aperatif having been advanced, Alberto was at a loss as to where to take up his routine. The singing had stopped. No one had requested that the recorded music be resumed. The household waited in suspended animation.

When the bell came it was accompanied by a fortissimo bellow. The cook dropped a pan on the floor and Alberto and the housemaid, running at once, got jammed in the kitchen door.

"The old lady is ill; she's collapsed; call the doctor!" he called as he ran panting across the intervening rooms. Doubtless the unaccustomed excitement, not to mention the Champagne, was the cause. He would be blamed. Servants always took the rap when disaster struck.

But when he opened the door to the small sitting room, his mistress was neither prostrate nor unconscious. She stood erect, head high, eyes burning, one arm extended in a dramatic gesture; a pose that reminded Alberto of the picture of her as Lady Macbeth hanging in the salon. Her voice rang out as he hadn't heard it since the brouhaha on the night the puppy had disappeared.

"Call for the car Alberto: the Rolls."

The majordomo was flabbergasted. His mistress never left the palazzo. The palazzo limousine, a 50-year-old Rolls Royce, was used exclusively as a courtesy car to collect visiting medical specialists. Pignatelli turned to Ros.

"Say again, where is this infirmary where is your friend?"

Ros explained carefully how to find Jonathan's place of convalescence, and the diva relayed it in Italian to her servant. Then she added, still more incomprehensibly,

"And Alberto, this evening we will be three at dinner: three – *Capisci?*"

He couldn't believe his ears: guests at the palazzo! It was unheard of. His mistress continued, in an afterthought, "And more Champagne, Alberto; *subito!*"

Alberto left, running in all directions.


"Don't fight this thing; it's bigger than both of us," thought Jonathan, lying back on the cracked leather seat and flicking idly at the walnut veneered drinks compartment, which turned out to be empty. Beyond the glass window, the chauffeur's head and shoulders were four square and uncommunicative. Jonathan occupied himself in trying to compose questions in Italian.

"*Dove andiamo?*" had been the logical choice, and he'd tried it back at the infirmary when the Rolls Royce had pulled into the courtyard, and the nuns fluttered about like doves when a fox invades the dovecot. To Jonathan, who had been demanding either his clothes or a telephone unsuccessfully for several hours, the speed of his release had been welcome, not to say miraculous.

"*La Principessa ordina,*" had been the reply to his question. "The Princess commands it."

There was only one Principessa, and Jonathan was not about to gainsay her. When the "*Principessa ordina*" things clearly happened. Incredible though it seemed, Ros's mission had born fruit.

Ros. The thought of his lissom, long-limbed lover warmed him all over. She was so direct, so dynamic, so confident. He had vacillated over how to re-establish relations for a fortnight; she had simply made up her mind, caught a plane and arrived. And now, amazingly, she seemed to have gained access to the impregnable palazzo.

The car moved silently between hills. After a time it began to sway and bounce as the road became rougher and the bends steeper. A familiar crested gateway reared up and opened smoothly before them, hardly halting their progress.

As if my magic, Jonathan found himself within the fiercely guarded portals of the paradise garden.

"Jono, allow me to present the great, the incomparable Paola Pignatelli, Principessa Spinola. She's going to tell you what you want to know about Roland Fredricks."

Jonathan's eyes moved from Ros, her eyes and cheeks blazing, in her grubby jeans and T-shirt, to the incongruous contrast of the little old lady, attired in a long Burgundy-red gown, offering him a hand clad in long lace mittens.

"Principessa," he murmured, bending to kiss the hand, since this seemed to be expected.

"Signor Burroughs, if it does not displease you, we will take dinner at once. We have waited until you arrive," said Pignatelli.

She stood, surprisingly upright for her years (over 90), chin high, every inch the prima donna, and indicated that she would take Jonathan's arm. They took their seats at table, their glasses were filled, and dishes placed before them. For Jonathan, looking across at Ros, her face glowing in candlelight, the occasion had a surreal quality. To be dining with the great Pignatelli and with the woman he loved and had so recently been reunited with, was uncomfortably like a wish-fulfilment dream. But the Champagne was excellent, and the soup tasted good, and as far as he could recall he never experienced tasting so distinctly in dreams.

It was only after the main course had been cleared away and fruit and pastries put before them, that their conversation turned to important matters. It was as if all before had been overture or recitative and now Pignatelli prepared herself for her aria.

"*Ragazzi* – my children. Today, daylight has come into my life after a long night. I had thought to go silent on these matters to my grave, but this afternoon Rosamunda crossed my threshold and spoke again of the past, and she has persuaded me. The light of truth must enter these dark rooms. Pain, error and guilt, must be swept away."

Part 3 ends

# ADIEU, SWEET AMARILLIS,

## Part 4 "Sweet Adieu"

# CHAPTER 31

They sat in the back of the Rolls, Jonathan's arms round Ros, gliding sedately back to their hotel. It was late, but the excitement of the evening had made the idea of sleep impossible. After all the frustrations, the pieces of the jigsaw puzzle finally seemed to be falling into place. Beside them, on the capacious back seat was a box full of letters, photographs and drawings that Pignatelli had given them.

"So, the mystery surrounding Roland's death is finally explained. Or maybe, not totally," said Jonathan. "But the secret of his late-flowering genius as a composer is deeper than ever. Do you believe her story?"

Ros did not reply. Her mouth was against Jonathan's throat and her hand had insinuated itself between his waist-band and his stomach. For a moment the near silence of the Rolls became the background to the softest of noises: little moans, the intake of breath, and the swish of hands in clothing and against skin. They had been separate from one another for several weeks. Desire began to reassert itself.

"Have you ever bonked in the back of a Rolls?" said Ros in a muffled voice, her mouth travelling across Jonathan's chest and nibbling at his nipples. After some gasps and groans he replied,

"You're torturing me, Ros. Spare me, for Christ's sake!"

"Do you think we would frighten the chauffeur?" she giggled, and threw herself back on the seat with a sigh.

Undistracted, Jonathan's mind reverted to the previous topic. "I think it cost her more to talk of her son, than of Roland's death, don't you? I suppose it's not surprising. What a cruel disappointment for Prince Spinola: a son is born after they had almost given up hope, and then for him to discover that the boy was not his, but Roland's. I suppose he must have had suspicions when he discovered that Roland also was diabetic, like the child? And then the boy grew to be tall and red haired…no wonder the Prince wanted nothing to do with him. I wonder if he'd have had Roland's talent, if he had lived?"

"There is a message for you, Miss Cummins," said the hotel receptionist, with a note of added deference probably related to their return in the Spinola Rolls. Ros took the slip of paper and was immediately concerned.

"My father called. Jeez! What's happened? I didn't tell him where I was. How did he find out?"

She dialled the number as soon as they got up to Jonathan's room. She held the receiver to her ear as various clicks and whirrings indicated that she was being connected with distant lands. With her other hand she reached into the bathroom to throw on the taps. She then removed the filthy T-shirt she had worn all day. Leaves twigs and pine-needles scattered on the floor around her.

"Is that you, Dad? Yeah look, I'm sorry. Yeah, I know it's late. But I thought for you to call it must be urgent."

Jonathan strained to hear what was being said at the other end. Sitting on the edge of the bath, Ros kicked off first one shoe, then the other, and began to peel off her socks, while concentrating on her conversation.

"It's a bit complicated…. Yeah, I know all that…no. It was really important, honestly…Well yes, there is: but it's not what you think… Well actually, you do know him. It's a bit difficult to explain… It's about a book…No; a book he's writing. No, not Granna; though Granna's memoirs have got something to do with it … Look I will explain everything once we get back." By this stage she had unzipped her jeans and was pushing them down with one hand.

Jonathan lay on the bed, watching and listening, trying to fill in the gaps in the dialogue.

"Anyway; what's all this about Granna Dad?"

By now her jeans had followed the shoes and socks in a heap on the floor, and Ros stood at the telephone in her juvenile Marks and Spencer underwear rubbing unselfconsciously at her body where the marks left by twigs, and various cuts and bruises bore witness to the adventures of the day.

"When did you speak to her last?… Yesterday evening? Well, she was in London when I took my flight. She's probably out somewhere. Have you spoken to Bill? Doesn't he know where she is?… Oh, he's not. Well, she's independent like that. She'd hate to think you were checking up on her…Yes I know it's worrying, but she did say we were to treat her exactly the same. She'll turn up. She could be back now and refusing to answer the phone; you know what she's like when she goes up to the studio…"

Jonathan could see that she was getting restless with the conversation. She ran her hand back and forth through her hair making it stand up in little spikes, and one long leg bent, stork-like, to scratch the back of the other with her toes. Her back was very brown, except for a thin white line where her bikini strap had been. Jonathan found watching her exceedingly arousing.

"Look, we're flying home tomorrow, or as soon as we can get a flight. We'll go round to Granna's the moment we get back. I'm sure it's nothing serious. If she were ill, someone would have got in touch with you, surely?" She yawned and stretched one arm above her head before wrapping it round the back of her neck. She was so slim and flexible that, with her spiky fair hair, she looked like some slender-stemmed flower – a daffodil, or a narcissus – thought Jonathan, and the veins in his penis were beginning to throb. He got up from the bed and went over to where she was standing by the bath. He put a hand on her shoulder and slid it down to where she was holding the phone.

"This call is costing us a fortune Dad. I'd better ring off. Talk to you when I get home… Yes, and I love you too."

Jonathan took the receiver from her hand and returned it to the cradle. He lowered his head to the nape of her neck. She smelled warm, and slightly musty; of sunburned skin and sweat. Her skin tasted salty.

"He's in a tizzy about Granna because she's been out of touch all day," she said, without turning round. "It's nothing new. But just before I came away she'd told us she had some ghastly illness and might die any minute. It's difficult not to worry in the circumstances."

On another occasion the news would have prompted Jonathan to further inquiry, but at that moment he had other things on his mind. He reached across the bath and turned off the taps. The water in the bath was tepid. He pulled out the plug.

"I think you should come to bed and bath in the morning," he said. "You're obviously dead beat. Besides, I think there are things we should... discuss."

Still behind her, his hands moved round her ribs, then down into the silly, little-girl knickers. Ros leaned back against him and let out a sigh. Her restless hands fell to her sides and her back rippled in pleasure. Gently but insistently his hands caressed her, one in front, the other behind. Holding her between her thighs, he almost lifted her to the bed and bent her forward over it. Ros's head burrowed into the pillows smothering the gasps that broke from her lips. He lifted her pelvis and spread her thighs, never relaxing the gentle activity of his fingers. Arms spread wide, she groped for a hold, and grasped the bars of the brass bed-head. After a few seconds her head began to be thrust forcefully and rhythmically into the pillows. Her stifled cries rose in volume as she was driven into the bed. Then, with a convulsive arch of the spine, she raised her head momentarily and cried out, "Jonathan, oh God, God, Jonathan!" before collapsing sideways away from him, curled up on her side, shivering with pleasure.

He waited a minute, his breath thick in his throat, then firmly opened her out, turned her on her back and re-entered her. The tension had flowed out of her and she could only moan helplessly as he continued to pound into her for the remaining seconds, until he too climaxed and fell panting on top of her.

They lay there, scarcely moving, for some time. But before he fell asleep, Jonathan roused himself sufficiently to drag the bedclothes over them. Ros slept, her lips parted, limbs spread-eagled, wide and loose across the bed. To his own disbelief desire stirred inside him once again. "Down boy," he said to himself, gathering her to him as he wrapped the covers round her shoulders.

Relaxed and spent though he was, sleep did not come. His mind ran back over the strange events of the day; the dinner and the momentous story they had been told. He wished he could have recorded the diva's words. He had taken notes, but her words still rang in his head.

"It was cold, and the fog was thick. They gave me the name of a hotel somewhere, near a railway station where I found him. He was drunk and incoherent when I collected him.

"We all knew he was ill; that his heart was weak. He would not have lived long, not the way things were. He was an empty husk; burned up with self-disgust. Without Anna he had nothing to live for. And he had betrayed her. The wonderful melodies in his last works – in *Pippa Passes* – were hers alone, and he had let the world believe it was all his.

"At first, when I collected him and drove him down to Millwater, I didn't realise that he had taken his insulin, but eaten nothing. What should I have done? I tried to get him to drink fruit juice and I prepared a syringe of glucose, but he was thrashing about in his delirium and dashed the syringe out of my hand.

"So I walked away, and shut the door.

"It was best that way; an end to self-destruction and despair. When he became unconscious I called the hospital. He was dead when they arrived. I told only Helga of the overdose, though not my part in it. I did not kill him. I let him die."

"Jesus," thought Jonathan, shortly before falling asleep, "How much of this can I possibly include in the book?" A nagging little thought of something that remained unanswered, occurred to him, "I wonder what happened to the Strad. Pignatelli didn't mention it. According to Lucy, Roland had wanted it to go to Anna and Stefan. I wonder where it went?"

Anna saw the man first when she arrived at the hospital and her driver took her to the Casualty entrance by mistake. He had blood pouring down one side of his face and he staggered as the orderlies helped him from the ambulance. He seemed unwilling to accompany them. "It'll be all right I tell ye. 'Tis nothing, a mere scratch. I can't stay, really I can't. I've left my Judy you see."

It was the nose that was most arresting: large, hooked and strawberry-coloured. Even the blood did not disguise it. He might have been concussed, but he could equally well have been drunk. His arms flayed wildly as they pulled him towards the swing doors.

"Will you leave go of me now. 'Tis a mistake I tell ye. I must get back to her," he shouted, his speech slurred and indistinct. Anna remarked the soft, Irish brogue, and then her driver came back saying they had to go round to the Private Wing entrance.

The man disappeared, protesting, beyond the doors as her cab pulled away. Was it just that distinctive nose, and the accent? He reminded her of someone.

Her mind was wandering again. Almost before she realised, the background music faded up. The old memory tape was running again, and she was hearing Irish voices, singing, speaking: *Down by the Salley Gardens*; and Yates: 'When you are old and grey, and full of sleep…', and someone singing to the accompaniment of a fiddle…

"Do you want me to wait Mrs C?"

The cab driver held the passenger door open.

"No. I don't know how long they'll keep me." She pushed a note into his hand as she stared up at the red-brick building in front of her. Why were hospitals so like prisons? Was it because, like all institutions, they were uncompromising, without seduction or invitation, or because you entered them unwillingly and were detained there against your will?

The Private Wing was painted soft pastel colours. There were armchairs, flower arrangements, rugs on the floor and unremarkable reproductions on the walls, but the institutional bony structure showed through the make-up: "Abandon hope all ye who enter here."

On this occasion she obtained her release after several hours. They performed a battery of tests; wheeling her from one department to another on a trolley, like a corpse.

The memory tape kept playing in her head. These days it had taken over from reading or listening to music, entertaining her whenever she was unable or unwilling to be more purposeful.

This time it was playing war-time London: sand-bagged door-ways, windows crisscrossed with gummed tape against the bomb blast; the wail of the air-raid siren and the whoop of the All-clear; skies bright with anti-aircraft flack, or dark with smoke and looming barrage balloons; streets littered with fallen masonry and broken glass; bomb craters choked with willowherb between shored up buildings. Roland's voice again, always Roland's voice.

"I want to marry you."

"Don't be stupid; you're already married."

"I'll get a divorce. We'll live together, write together. The next opera will be Fredricks/Williams. No: Williams/Fredricks."

"Roland, it won't work. You don't really want to leave Millwater and your Monstrous Regiment of Women. And I'm too young and we're too far apart. With Stefan I have a future: marriage, babies, a lifetime together. You and I aren't the stuff marriages are made of. It was wonderful, illuminating, memorable, but it's over."

They had been in a taxi going back to Chelsea. They could hear the dull thud of gun-fire and the drone of aircraft above the engine and at one point the blast was so close the vehicle was momentarily lifted into the air. Instinctively they clung to each other and she felt his body racked with tears. There was still love. She would always care for him, but her body now belonged to Stefan and the joyous, frantic, coupling that consumed them. If Roland had allowed it, they could have continued in friendship and musical collaboration, but she could no longer bear the burden of his constant self-destruction, and his need.

Back at Chelsea he had wanted to make love. He'd smothered her with passionate kisses, carried her to the bed and buried his head in her bosom.

289

She lay passive in his arms feeling no desire and unable to pretend. As his sobs became more convulsive she gently stroked his hair. His words were inaudible but she had said, "We have to stop this Roland. I have to get on with the rest of my life."

She had left him without looking back, leaving her key and her farewells to Luke upon the hall table and going straight from Chelsea to her new love. She'd walked away. "Adieu, sweet Amarillis."

As the mini-cab that collected her from the hospital drove south towards the river, she saw the old man with the huge nose going in the same direction. Someone had bandaged up his head, but his gait was still shambling and erratic. As they passed him, he appeared to be talking to himself.

"Seamus O'Reilly," She spoke suddenly, sitting bolt upright in the back seat. Seamus O'Reilly: the fiddler who'd introduced Roland to the Archer Street market; who'd taken him to play at hops, weddings and bar mitzvahs and who'd put him up on his sofa when he was too drunk to go home. Seamus O'Reilly who'd brought her Roland's Stradivarius the night after he died. Could it really be the same?

"Stop!"

"What's that Mrs C?" The cab driver hadn't heard her.

"Stop! I want to go back to that man."

"Can't go back here, Mrs. We're in a one-way street."

"Well, pull in, and go and get him."

The cab driver clearly thought she had taken leave of her senses. He pulled to the side of the road across the blaring horns and flashing lights of the affronted traffic, and waited while the old man drew level with them. Anna wound down the window.

"Seamus O'Reilly, what did you do with the Stradivarius?"

The cab driver and the old man with the big nose stared at her as though she were mad. But the past was so close to her these days, it did not occur to Anna that, were he still alive, Seamus O'Reilly would be 100 years old.

The old man stared at her with blood-shot eyes. He really did have the most amazing nose. He bent down to the window of the car and a whiff of alcohol and dirt swept over her. There was a tide-mark where the skin round his bandage had been cleaned. She addressed him again.

"I should have kept the violin you brought me Seamus: Roland Fredricks' Stradivarius."

A light came into the man's blood-shot eyes.

"Ah, but isn't it my father that you're taking me for Ma'am? My father, that played the fiddle and who knew all the fine musicians on Archer Street. Now I'm O'Reilly, but Dominic Seamus of that name. And as it just happens that I know what happened to the Fredricks violin."

# CHAPTER 32

*I refused the violin and sent the man with the big nose away. I didn't trust myself*
*even to open it, lying in its scuffed old leather case with the broken straps he'd*
*always intended to get repaired.*

*"Who is it?" Stefan shouted from the bedroom as I stood shivering in the hall*
*wrapped only in the kimono I had thrown on to answer the bell.*

*"No one. I won't be a minute," I shouted back, propelling the Irishman*
*through the open door.*

*"You keep it. You're a fiddle player too, aren't you? I can't accept it. It's much*
*too valuable. And anyway, my fiancé wouldn't allow it."*

*I felt a coward and a fool even as I said it. It was true. Stefan was pathologically*
*jealous as only a Pole could be, especially about anything connected with myself*
*and Roland, but I should have taken the violin. I should have seen its presence*
*there, in the arms of this musician from Archer Street, as a gift, a message, a*
*final salutation, "Hail and farewell!"*

*Roland was never parted from his Stradivarius. He had other violins of course:*
*reserve instruments and 'kipper-boxes', as he called them, kept for his pupils at*
*Millwater or the Academy, upon which he would occasionally demonstrate that*
*his touch could conjure magic, just to encourage them. But the Strad was his*
*darling and his joy. His second cock, he called it.*

*"Perform a damn sight better on this instrument than on my other one," he*
*would say.*

*His mother had given it him when he was first appointed a professor at the*

292

*Academy and it had been at his side ever since. And now it was at my door, speaking to me more eloquently than words of his despair.*

*"Sure lady, I can't possibly take it. 'Tis much too fine a thing for the likes of my jigs and reels," said the Irishman. "He wants you to have it; he insisted I bring it."*

*"Anna, what's going on?" Stefan's voice came again and I drove the fiddler with his funny-ugly Mr Punch nose, over the threshold and closed the door behind him.*

*In rejecting his precious violin as a gift to me, Stefan and to the child I was carrying in my womb, what did I do, but confirm how totally I rejected him?*

*Roland was the dominant force in my life for two significant years: from raw, country schoolgirl, to woman-of-the-world. Under his tutelage I earned my musical, sentimental and sexual spurs. Without him I would have been neither the musician who, later that year, landed a job with the BBC, nor the woman who embraced love, marriage and a family with Stefan. And yet… I buried him. I walked on by.*

*I saw him last at Luke's as I took my leave after our last disastrous meeting. I only learned later that he had overdosed on insulin, and that Luke had helped him recover. I had heard his voice on the phone occasionally, but, once he realised that Stefan was there, he stopped calling. Letters came, but I forced myself not to open them – until after his death. The violin had been his last word. After that, only the shocked whispers at the Academy; the bald paragraphs in* The Times. *"Suddenly, at home… in poor health for some time… a player and composer of distinction."*

*The man I loved was dead.*

It took her longer than she had anticipated to set things in order. The profound tiredness, breathlessness and her painfully swollen legs, now beginning to ooze fluid, made it all the more difficult. Most of it, of necessity, had to be done in the studio at the top of the house, and when the sorting and cataloguing finally became impossible, she collapsed onto the chair in front of the VDU and simply left instructions, messages and lists.

"One of the blessings of being literate," she thought, "Is that one can continue to write when all other physical systems fail."

She entered her Memoirs file last, did some editing, labelled it – she wouldn't have time to print it out – and finally, included a few paragraphs about Roland sending her his violin.

She had written little recently; nothing since she noted the first unmistakable signs of an infection. The weirdest was not peeing. For months the diuretics had sent her to the lavatory every two hours, then suddenly, nothing. And she knew she had a fever because she kept falling asleep, even without alcohol. They'd warned her it could happen.

The GP had directed her instantly to the hospital. It had been a battle persuading them to release her, even pumped full of antibiotics. "They should realise that when you're really ill a hospital is the last place you want to be? Besides, when one has a last, pressing engagement, there are things to organise."

She fell asleep on the chaise some time before dawn but was awake again before Dominic. He and the little dog had slept downstairs on the kitchen floor on a pile of old coats and newspapers she had found them.

"So long since we've been in a bed we wouldn't be able to get to sleep in one," he explained.

Still, he'd seemed happy enough to avail himself of the bath, food and drink she had put at his disposal.

That morning, as soon as the office at the Royal Academy was open she must phone and find out what she could about Roland's Stradivarius which, Dominic told her, he had given them when his father died.

"He played it but once, and then returned it to its case. 'Such a fine an instrument,' he kept saying. 'Sure it makes me nervous just to touch it.' And so, when I started my studies there, I suggested we give it to the Academy. He agreed, but still kept it by him for a while. He liked to take it from its case and polish it now and again."

"We have to find out whether they still have the violin," said Anna. "They probably regard it as theirs after all this time. But at the very least they'll let you see it, since you gave it to them.

"Look in the pocket in the lid of the case, where he kept the silk handkerchief he used to cover the chin-grip. There's a hole in the velvet lining, inside the pocket: he kept a packet of condoms there, as a joke. He showed me once. If, as you say, there was no letter with the violin, there may be one addressed to me there. It's possible he put it where only I would think to look. Don't ask me why I believe it, I may be wrong; but look will you?

"Tell the Academy we don't want to reclaim the violin if it's being put to good use, even if Roland intended it for me, but I would like his last letter, if there is one. And I want them to know the violin was his."

She sat beside the telephone and called the Academy while Dominic washed and shaved and cooked himself breakfast. She had found him a few pieces of clothing belonging to Bill who was away, thankfully.

"You'll pass muster," she said, smiling at the transformation. "I don't think the commissionaire is going to throw you onto the street before you explain your mission. Would it be a help to stay here while you find your feet, organise work, benefits, or something?"

He looked at her uncertainly. "You're tempting me with the bluebird, hope, now."

"Well, think about it. It's your choice," she said not wishing to seem patronising.

She saw him into the cab, then slowly climbed once more to the studio and fell into a doze. The dreams came again, confused and disturbing: she was being driven along twisting mountain roads by Ros, and the car was about to plummet into a ravine. She was being wheeled on the hospital trolley, except that above her was the vaulted ceiling of a church and she was lying on a bier. Masked faces peered down at her, discussing her condition in hushed whispers. Kate was among them pointing an accusatory finger. "You run out on everyone. You're a quitter." And she was helpless, unable to reply or move, as though she were already dead.

Jonathan and Ros travelled in the private capsule reserved for those in love. Their eyes kept returning to each other, their hands touching, as though by magnetism. Arousal acted on the body fluids, Jonathan noted: he had to suck saliva from the corners of his mouth and take deep breaths to stop himself bursting into tears. Ros was smiling like an idiot and her eyes were wet too. Silly things made her break into an uncontrollable grin and bubble with laughter. No matter what went on around them, their unspoken, personal communication took precedence.

Touchdown at Heathrow, brought them back to earth.

"I must call Granna," said Ros.

"And I'd like to check out with my family," said Jonathan.

They dived into neighbouring phone booths and reappeared with worried expressions.

"She's back home, but she sounds very peculiar," said Ros. "I told her I would be over straight away."

"I've come back to a bit of a crisis too. Helena has to fly to Geneva for some meeting and was about to dump Simon on friends. Once he heard my voice he insisted I come and stay. So I said I'd go over and hold the fort. Helena's coming straight here to pick us up."

He sounded anxious; not just about their sudden change of plans, but about Ros's reaction. "I couldn't let the little sprog down once he knew I was home, could I?"

"Of course not. You're a dad. Your kids come first," she said, nonetheless disappointed that their enchanted bubble had been shattered by the outside world. "I'll take a cab."

"Nonsense; Helena will take us both. I'd like you to meet them," he countered, putting his arms round her.

As the car pulled up, Simon shot out like a bullet and buried his head in his father's body. Helena climbed out more slowly. She looked cool and professional in a linen suit and high heels. Ros, crumpled from their journey, felt a scruff.

"Ros, this is Helena; and this tornado belabouring my person is Simon. Guys, meet Ros – my Lady of the Bicycles."

He made the introductions, feeling a little uncomfortable. Did Ros sit in the front, next to Helena, or should he? Ros settled the matter by clambering into the back seat after Simon.

"Hi there. Do you want a chocolate, Simon," she said easily. "Or do they call you 'Si'?" And she produced the mint that had been on her meal-tray on the aircraft. Jonathan caught Helena's eye, her eyebrows raised quizzically, as he put their bags in the boot and climbed into the passenger seat.

Helena spoke to Ros via the rear mirror.

"I'm sorry if I've upset your plans. It's an important meeting for me, but Simon could have gone to Gaynor's."

"No sweat," said Ros gruffly. "So, Simon, you don't mind putting up with your dad's cooking then?"

"It's the drug-scare I told you about ..." Helena filled Jonathan in about the medical meeting she had to attend, then ran over the domestic arrangements in her absence. "The daily comes in tomorrow morning; Gaynor will collect Simon from school and give him tea..."

Listening to them talking, Ros felt marginalised. They were organising life in the front. She was in the back with the children. The age-gap that had seemed trivial when she and Jonathan were alone together, yawned when she saw him with his family. It wasn't age that separated them. It was life experience.

Helena put her down outside Anna's house.

"When shall I see you? I want to know how she is," said Jonathan, standing beside her on the pavement.

"I'll ring," she said feeling deserted despite of herself.

Helena came round the car and gave Ros a card.

"Take this; it has the number and address. Promise you will come over while he's there. You mustn't abandon him. He's found a new lease of life since he met you."

Ros looked down at Helena. "She's trying not to be threatening," she thought. "So why do I feel such a child? There are creases at the corners of her eyes, and grey-streaks in her hair, but she's really attractive. Why did she and Jonathan break up? They seem such a couple."

"You must both come and have dinner with me when I get back." said Helena, putting her hand on Ros's arm. And then she got back into the car and left Jonathan to kiss Ros goodbye, alone.

Ros had had her own key to Anna's house since the burglary, nevertheless she rang the bell to announce her arrival, and was rewarded by the sound of a dog barking.

As she opened the door she could not believe her eyes. A little black and white dog with a parti-coloured face ran to greet her and started dancing ecstatically on her hind legs.

"Judy? Surely it can't be?" said Ros. She called her grandmother's name and received the usual no reply. She walked through the house, and the dog ran into the kitchen and mounted guard over a pile of newspapers and old clothes. "Curiouser and curiouser," thought Ros, continuing up the stairs towards the studio, where the whir of the word processor beckoned.

Her grandmother lay asleep on the chaise.

The VDU blinked at her from the desk.

Drawing closer, she saw it displayed a master-list of files; Letters: Hugo, Kate, Jonathan, Ros. Memoirs: March 1938 – February 1941. Personal Finance: 1992. Scores: Fredricks/Williams 1938 – 39. Scores and tapes: Williams 1940 – 85...

Ros gasped. The scores listed under Fredricks/Williams were three: *Pippa Passes*, and *The March to the North* and *Adieu, Sweet Amarillis*. Those listed under Williams were so many they disappeared off the bottom of the screen.

# CHAPTER 33

Ros sat beside her grandmother and waited patiently for her to wake up.

Anne looked ill: her skin was puffy and grey and her breath smelt strange. At one point she stirred and a pained expression crossed her brow. Ros thought she was about to wake and reached to touch the pale hand. A fine silvery dust came off on her fingers.

"Is that you Ros?" Anna spoke without opening her eyes.

"Yes." She confirmed with a touch.

"Where's Jonathan? How did your trip go?"

Anna sat up stiffly and put on a pair of tinted glasses, but she smiled, and her voice sounded more normal than on the phone. Ros's anxiety eased a little.

"He's at home – with his son. We had a wonderful trip. We met Paola, and she was very helpful in the end. I'll tell you about it later. What about you. Shouldn't you be in bed?"

Her grandmother's voice took on its old cutting edge.

"We have much to discuss, but my health is not part of it. I'd started to write to you all, but became too tired. It's good to be able to hand things over to you Ros. Run off the master-list and bring it here."

Ros walked to the computer and told it to print.

"All this stuff you composed over 40 years," she said, "Song cycles, choral works, chamber music, quite apart from the completed score of *Adieu, Sweet Amarillis*; why did you never publish? Were you protecting Roland's name? And why are you coming clean now?"

She brought the list to Anna on the chaise. Her grandmother registered her question with a brief smile; illness had made her no more inclined to answer difficult questions.

"Have you any idea what prejudice there was towards women composers in those days?" She asked. "I did think about it. But you should have heard what Abrahams the publisher had to say; that he couldn't take anything except 'Little songs' from a woman. It wasn't exactly encouraging. Making and commissioning programmes was more rewarding. And I must confess, there is a little Williams in some of the incidental music I used – unaccredited. Who knows, maybe there will be some interest now?"

"Are you going to tell us how much of *Pippa* was you?" Ros persisted. "The score Luke gave Jonathan is not in Roland's hand. Is it yours?"

"Let's say we collaborated. It's listed under Fredricks/Williams in my catalogue. That's all I'm prepared to say. Roland was my teacher. Without him I would have composed nothing. I don't want his reputation destroyed," she said briskly, not looking at Ros.

She took the list. "These are the things in my safety deposit box. You appreciate that I didn't keep much in the house after the burglary. This is the address of my solicitors. They have my will." She looked at Ros directly. "I have – er – left you my intellectual property. That means my music and writing, if you didn't realise. I debated leaving it to you and to Jonathan, but I knew you would make everything available to him, and if there should be any financial benefit I'd rather it was yours. I've left the bricks and mortar and material possessions to your father and Kate, as it should be, but…" She reached for Ros's hand, smiling a little self-consciously. "You are my musical heir, aren't you?

"And now we come to something that makes the bequest more significant." She put a transparent folder into Ros's hand. It enclosed a letter in Roland Fredricks' long, sloping hand, with frequent corrections and crossings out, written on brittle, yellowed paper, powdered to breaking point with age.

"This is Roland's last letter to me. It's a long story. Spare me the effort of explaining. He had sent it to me hidden in his violin 51 years ago and, unknowingly, I turned it away. This afternoon it was returned to me. I'll tell you what he writes because Roland's handwriting is illegible.

"He gives me the name of the solicitors who hold his will, and says he leaves me all rights to his published and unpublished work. I was his 'musical heir' you see. He left with them a letter acknowledging our collaboration on the works we composed. The Stradivarius, he says, is mine, and Stefan's, our children's and…" She paused, "He says he hopes we will make wonderful music –'unto the third generation'."

Ros felt the tears pricking her eyes at the intimation of being addressed personally from the grave.

"So you see, I am leaving you not only my music, but Roland's. Gudrun has no power to halt publication on anything. I've asked Hugo and Kate to give the Strad officially to the Royal Academy. It came too late for the violinist in our family."

She lay back and closed her eyes. Ros sensed that the story had taken a lot out of her. Her hand was still in Anna's.

"Now will you go to bed?"

"Later, later." She smiled, eyes still closed. "Tell me about Italy. How was the incomparable Pignatelli at 90? And what about you and Jonathan? Are things going better?"

Ros told her of their adventures, and what Paola had told them of Roland's death. She recounted her meeting with Jonathan's ex-wife and child.

"Do you think he will go back to them?" Ros asked.

Anna chuckled, "Only fools think they can go backwards. And Jonathan's no fool. But being a parent is for life. You wouldn't want him to walk away from his children, would you?"

"No, of course not."

"Love affairs can be rewarding and educational, even if they don't last forever, you know. And if you're clever, and turn them into friendships, they may even do that. Were you thinking of spending the rest of your life with your sexy older man?"

Ros squeezed her grandmother's hand. She seemed too fragile to embrace.

"What a wise old bird you are, Granna."

A few moments later she saw that Anna was asleep.

She telephoned Jonathan first, at Helena's, then her father.

"She's pretty ill, Dad. Apparently the hospital wanted to keep her in, but she insisted on coming home to arrange her affairs. I'm going back to drop my stuff at the flat, but coming straight back. Can you get away? I thought you'd want to see her."

Anna woke again after half an hour, alone. She went downstairs, took her antibiotics, and called a car.

Buildings, cars, and greenery flew past the car windows in a blur: meaningless strands in the pattern of stimuli, brushing her senses almost unnoticed, like the sun that came and went with the changing direction of the vehicle, the light breeze from the open window and the steady drumming of the engine.

They hadn't wanted to take her.

"You're looking a bit rough Mrs C. Should you be going out? It's quite a drive. Sure you're up to it?"

She had made it clear that if they didn't want to drive her someone else would, and the driver had helped her into a 'feet-up' position on the back seat and driven off with a shrug.

She had dressed to cover herself up as much as possible and wore dark glasses. Silver crystals had begun to appear on her skin, like frost, and she hadn't the energy to keep dusting it off.

She dozed, dipping in and out of dreams.

To her relief she found that in this area of her fragile existence she had some control. With only slight effort she conjured up happy times: the children playing on the Heath when they were small; Hugo with a kite that soared in the sky, mocking the barrage balloons with its frivolity; holidays with friends in France; Kate learning to cycle on a wide space of sand; the bodies of men she had loved: looming above her, enclosing her in their arms, fucking.

"You OK back there, Mrs C?" The driver was still anxious.

She didn't reply at first, resenting this interruption of her day-dreaming. But then he craned round to see behind him and the car swerved, so she replied to put his mind at ease.

"I'm not so great this morning, Jeff, but don't worry. Let me rest and I'll make it to our journey's end."

Roland came unbidden.

First he was a memory. He was playing the Strad; bent over the instrument, squeezing out a melody: probably some sugary Viennese bonbon by Fritz Kreisler. She smiled quietly to herself.

'Café music' he called it. "I should have been wandering in and out of the tables in some Austrian restaurant, making love to the courting couples with my musical cock. All this serious music crap is out of my league."

"Perhaps he was right?" she thought to herself. "Perhaps that was the attraction of Archer Street and he really would have been happier making that sort of music all the time. But what hope had he of such modest goals? Poor little pot-hunter, driven by Flora's fierce ambition. He had had to strive for the summit to satisfy her. And scaling the heights he had no head for, he had missed his footing and fallen to earth."

"If you're big, they expect you to achieve great things, Anna. You don't know how lucky you are being small," he said.

"Not necessarily," she answered. "Perhaps I would have done greater things if people had expected more of me?"

"Don't denigrate yourself. It's not you. You brought up two fine children. You had a successful career. You wrote good music."

"Oh I wish you had known it, Roland, I wish you knew."

"I know, darling, I know."

"You'll have to check the turning soon Mrs C," said the driver. "We've left the motorway and we are coming into the village. I'll let you know when I see the pub called The Plough."

"We used to walk down to The Plough, Sunday lunchtimes, do you remember Roland, and play darts with the locals? You were hopeless."

"I had no eye for targets. I was all ears," he replied.

"Heavens; just look at those tacky little houses! It doesn't look like your village anymore."

Where there had been open fields and woodland, there was a parade of shops and a brash petrol station. Neat, detached houses, with privet hedges and flower borders, either side of the road which boasted made-up pavements, a Zebra-crossing and street-signs in place of a ragged grass verge. Anna stared out of the car window trying to pick out something familiar and recognised a stone horse trough, now planted with geraniums. 'Ye Olde Plough Inne' had been extended; painted wagon-wheels; manger baskets crammed with flowers on its walls. A gravel car-park and lawns covered with tables and sun-shades surrounded it.

"Turn here, Jeff," she said to the cab driver; almost missing the road, it seemed so alien.

They turned down a lane once overgrown with trees. A sign behind white chain-link posts proclaimed 'Millwater Golf Course'. Anna glimpsed the sun glinting off ranks of Mercs, Porsches and BMWs in the car-park.

"Oh God," she thought silently. "It's been gentrified."

A No Thoroughfare symbol marked the drive to the house. The rough track leading to the disused mill, scruffy farm cottages and an old barn with tractors, was now black tarmacadam with quaint, converted street lamps set in the grass verge. The barn had huge picture windows, and the cottages announced 1 and 2 Mill Cottages on flowered china plaques. Millwater itself was almost invisible behind high brick walls and wrought-iron gates.

The cab driver pulled up where a barrier blocked the road. He turned off the engine and looked over his shoulder. "What now Mrs C?"

"Shush," she said, sitting upright and winding down the window. "Listen."

The sound of the water was the same.

"When did she go?"

"Apparently the call came more than an hour ago? Not sure what time the driver picked her up." The cab company didn't have a precise address.

Anna had given them just the name of the village and the house they were aiming for. The driver had been worried about the physical condition of his passenger, but her mind had been clear so he had set off. "She's not senile, Dad. She can do what she wants," said Ros.

"It's a helluva responsibility for the cab driver. Supposing she collapses – or dies in his cab," said Hugo. "Let's follow her to Millwater, just in case. She's made no secret of where she's going."

The retired couple who had acquired Millwater six years ago were not accustomed to receiving visits from strangers. They came to the door, a fat, blond Labrador at their heels, to find a strange little old lady in dark glasses leaning on the arm of a young man.

"I should like to sit in the garden for a while," the old lady said, as though it were the most natural request in the world.

"Mrs Cummins knew the house before the war," explained the young man who appeared to sense the eccentricity of the request. "We've driven a long way so that she could see it once more."

The couple were nonplussed. After gaping at the strangers for some seconds, the woman's social graces came to her rescue. She noticed the old lady's breathing was laboured and the knuckles of the hand that held the young man's arm were white with strain.

"Won't you come in a sit down?" she said with solicitude. I could make a cup of tea?"

"I'd rather have a Scotch," replied the old lady firmly, coming through the door and sitting on the first chair she came to.

"Will you be all right then Mrs Cummins?" the cab driver said, hovering in the doorway. "I'll wait for you in the car. That OK?"

"We'll call you when I'm ready to go Jeff," the old lady answered.

"Are you sure you're all right dear?" asked the woman anxiously "I'll put the kettle on."

The old lady was staring at the gilt consul table opposite where she sat. It was tastefully arranged with artificial flowers.

"Oak. It should be oak; flowers reflected in the polished surface," she said softly, as though to herself.

"Oh, you like the flowers do you?" said the woman brightly. "I'll show you round if you like. We spent a fortune you know."

As the woman sailed into her fine fitted kitchen, her husband grunted, and padded off in the opposite direction, the dog at his heels. He returned after a few moments with a tumbler containing a little Scotch.

"Sure you should?" he asked gruffly as he put the glass into the old lady's hand, "Water? Ice?"

"I probably shouldn't. But it's always worked before," she replied and sipped the whisky gingerly. "I'm sorry to put you to this trouble. It's important to me. As you see; I'm not well."

The woman returned with a tray laid with bone-china tea-cups and polished silver.

"You're very kind," the old lady said, "But could I just sit in the garden and listen to the water? I don't want to disturb you."

"Never mind the tea Mother," said the man kindly. "I'll take Mrs Cummins down the garden." And he offered her his arm.

The garden had changed less than the approach to Millwater. It was tidier and more disciplined than in Helga and Roland's time. There was the obligatory conservatory and patio. Trees had grown bigger; some had been cut down. There was no longer a lavender hedge, but the paved path still led to the stone steps. The statue of Daphne and Apollo had been replaced by an urn of flowers, and the terrace and landing stage had been rebuilt. There was a little summerhouse where the man found cushions and made Anna comfortable on a covered hammock overlooking the millpond.

"Did you know the musicians who lived here then?" he asked.

"Yes, very well," Anna replied. "It was an important place: the crucible of much talent; many happy, fruitful lives."

"That's nice," the man said and tactfully he left her.

The millrace ran gently. There had been little rain that summer, and the sound crept soothingly into Anna's ears. The Scotch had been reliably

306

anaesthetic and discomfort of her sick body seemed less now. She lay back against the cushions and closed her eyes. There had been the sound of a nightingale and instruments playing; voices singing.

In the last act of *Pippa*, the old priest, hearing Pippa's song, weeps because he recognises her as his daughter. Much of Pippa's singing takes place off stage, its effects being marked only in those who hear it. Anna had stood out of view of the audience for the Millwater production, but within sight of Roland conducting. As she sang she had seen the tears in his eyes.

"You had a voice like a nightingale," he said. "Clear, high, and heart-breaking."

The hammock rocked gently as he sat beside her. She didn't open her eyes but she recognised the smell of the Balkan Sobranie tobacco. After a few minute he started stroking her swollen legs and all the pain went out of them.

"You must not reproach yourself, you silly old thing," he said. It was funny to hear him call her 'old'. "We all have to be true to our own nature. Yours was a free spirit. It couldn't be tied, not by a crapped-out alcoholic, or by any of us. You cut your own swathe; there is nothing to regret in that."

"And Roland, what about you; what was your nature?"

She heard him laugh gently, his great frame shaking as he considered the conundrum.

"I am, what you want me to have been. No more, no less. Life is a comedy and we're mostly bit-part players. If you wanted a hero, I gave it a try. You wanted a libertine or a villain; I made a stab at it. Occasionally I played the lover, as I truly did with you, my dear. But I was best in the role of the clown."

His voice was low and tender as a caress.

Anna remembered how safe she had felt as he held her in his arms on this spot, lifting her naked feet to keep them from the wet grass, and she sighed.

Ros and Hugo found the mini-cab driver asleep in his parked car. Anna had been in the house a couple of hours, he said. They went up to the door and knocked. The man who answered it looked surprised when they said they had come for Mrs Cummins.

307

"Quite honestly, I thought someone came to collect her more than hour ago. I could have sworn I heard voices down there by the pond. Must have been my imagination."

They went together down the path to the millpond. The hammock was still swinging gently, but Anna had been dead some time. There was a smile on her face.

The end

# Acknowledgements

I owe massive thanks to eagle-eyed Peter Williams and Martin Tucker for copy-editing the final text of this book, and to Alan Maryon-Davis for his advice on the treatment of glomerulonephritis and to Lorena Tonarelli for improving the Italian. My thanks also go to the team at Design Deluxe who created the cover, to Eri Griffin who drew the cover illustration, to Wayne Strudwick for assembling the image of John Wilbye's madrigal, Adieu, sweet Amarillis and to Georgina Aldridge from Clays for guidance through the maze of self-publishing.

# About the author

Philippa Pigache trained for the stage but has spent most of her working life as a journalist, latterly specialising in medical science. Her plays have been broadcast and her short stories and books on health published, but Adieu, sweet Amarillis is her first novel. She was brought up in a house surrounded by amateur and professional musicians, writers and actors, but otherwise this story is not autobiographical. www.philippapigache.co.uk